BORDERS CROSSING

A novel by Archie Borders

Copyright © 2013 by Archie Borders
All rights reserved

No part of this publication may be reproduced, distributed or transmitted in any form or by any means, or stored in a database or retrieval system without the prior written consent of the publisher, except for brief quotations in an acknowledged review.

Blue Juice Publishing   220 Bell Ave. Findlay, Ohio 45840
bluejuice@woh.rr.com. or phone 419-721-1551.

For more information on the author and updates on current projects, please visit www.archieborders.com.

First Edition: September 2013

The characters and events in this book are fictitious. Any similarity to real persons, living or dead, is coincidental and not intended by the author.

The publisher and author are not responsible for websites, or their contents, that are not owned by the publisher or author.

Editing by Kelli Borders

Cover design and concept by Archie Borders

Cover art by Marbee Printing and Graphic Art, 2703 N. Main St. Findlay, Ohio 45840   419-422-9441

Library of Congress Control Number   2013910811

ISBN   978-0-9895700-7-7

Printed in the United States by Morris Publishing®
3212 East Highway 30
Kearney, NE 68847
1-800-650-7888

Table of contents

Prologue

Part I
Rude Awakening
Page 11

Part II
Hotel Hell
Page 153

Part III
Deal With the Devil
Page 393

Afterword
Page 421

This book is dedicated to Kelli.
I don't know how I got so lucky.

Prologue

The skis on the bottom of the bush plane sliced into the softening pack ice like the proverbial hot knife through butter. The heart stopping sound of the scraping, squalling skis as they cut into the weakening ice was horrifically loud. It was late spring and the drifting ice sheets had begun to crumble due to the advancing mild weather and increased sunlight. As little as a week ago this landing might have proven uneventful. But that was a week ago.

A thunderous, cracking report came from beneath the craft, as loud as a shot from a high powered rifle. The plane dipped sharply downward and to the left as the ski on that side disintegrated amid the large, jagged chunks of ice. The five point harness of the pilot's seat was the only thing that kept me from being thrown forward against the plane's windshield like a child's rag doll.

As the crippled craft started to skid along on the sharp, serrated ice, the wing on that side snapped off like it was nothing more than a small, dry twig. The cockpit window on the left side of the cabin turned into a shattered, patchwork looking pattern and then flew inward, landing with a thud directly behind my shoulder. The intense grating of the fuselage against the pulverizing ice chunks below grew so loud that it sounded like a giant set of teeth were chomping on the metal for lunch. Unable to withstand this extreme level of punishment, the thin aluminum shell of the plane started to shred and come apart.

Massive openings began to appear in the battered fuselage and a steady torrent of ice sprang through to assault my body. Some of the pieces were no larger than a fair sized rain drop and proved inconsequential. Some were the size of an ice cube and their impact left bee sting-like sensations everywhere they struck me. Surviving those would have been no problem, it was the ones that were the size of softballs and basketballs that finally did me in.

One particularly large piece struck my left shoulder and my entire arm immediately went numb. Then my head was violently thrown forward as the crippled craft snagged it's nose on a protruding ice ridge and ungracefully somersaulted completely onto it's other side. Landing with a mighty crash, the lone remaining wing of the airplane disappeared in a showery explosion of metal fragments. The window on that side of the cabin imploded and came rushing at me.

Forcefully thrown the opposite way, my body's extremities were left powerless to counteract the extreme inertia. My arms flew up and out, toward the now jagged edge of the sliding craft. The fingers on my right hand extended through the opening that, until a few seconds ago, used to contain the plane's side window. Although the speed of the wingless missile was mercifully slowing, it was still going plenty fast enough to cause some serious damage. Forced back against the edge of the vacated window frame, my fingers were bent backward and quickly snapped by the overwhelming force. Unable to pull my arm back because of the oppressive weight pinning my fingers beneath the craft, I watched helplessly as the hard, grating surface of the ice obliterated my flesh and bone.

Through the crumpled hole that used to contain a windshield, I could see the end of the floating ice island quickly approaching and the beginning of the dark, open water beyond that. Having just enough momentum to carry it's bulk over the edge of the ice sheet and into the water, the tattered tube that a minute ago was a state-of-the-art airplane, slid into the cold liquid with but a slight splash.

Near freezing water rushed into the cabin through the craft's decimated body and it's chilling effects were instantaneous. The feeling of a billion tiny, icy needles penetrating my body drove the air from my lungs in a tortured scream of horror and pain. The frigid water caused my muscles to contract so strongly that I found myself virtually paralyzed.

Fighting the encroaching grip of the rising arctic water, I managed to draw in a small, precious breath of fresh air. My greedy lungs were desperate to try for more, but the unsympathetic cascade of icy water simply wouldn't permit it.

I tried to release the catch on my harness but my left arm was numb and completely unresponsive. I didn't know if my shoulder had been separated or my arm had been broken, but repeated attempts to move it proved futile. One glance at my mutilated right hand told me that it would be of no use, either. As the ever-increasing depth of the ocean obscured the weakening light from above, I knew that my fate had been sealed.

While the frigid liquid quickly covered my head and filled the remaining spaces inside the sinking airplane, my eyes frantically searched the undersea realm around the descending capsule through the crystal clear arctic water. The light from the bright blue sky above was fading away and losing it's effectiveness as my depth steadily increased. I wondered how long I could hold my breath and how deep this bit of water was. Looking down, I saw an approaching blackness, so deep and all-encompassing, that it looked like it could quite possibly go on forever.

The ever increasing pressure finally collapsed my aching lungs and forced the last of the air from them. I turned my eyes skyward and watched the trail of exhaust bubbles busily race each other toward the distant surface. The darkness of the depths enveloped me like a waiting tomb as the fuselage slowly spiraled downward, toward it's final resting place on the waiting sea floor below.

Part I

Rude Awakening

1

I awoke in a panic. Snapping into a sitting position, I looked about frightfully. Realizing that I wasn't really drowning, I drew in a deep, sweet breath of fresh air.

"Just a dream," I whispered to myself. I could feel beads of perspiration running down my chest and my entire body was bathed in sweat.

Wondering if my sudden start had disturbed anyone else, I looked around apprehensively. Off to my left, both of the boys appeared to be undisturbed and were sleeping soundly. To my right, Kelli was still breathing in the slow, steady rhythm of a deep, peaceful sleep. I was relieved to see that I hadn't bothered anyone, getting a good night's sleep was a rare thing these days.

The only family member that had noticed my alarmed lurch was Walter. The family dog was lying close to the boys, his large head gently resting on top of his front paws while he stared at me intently.

The moisture blanketing my body started to evaporate rapidly and the cold air inside our little shelter became a glaring reality. I could see my breath in the still night air, not much of it, but nonetheless, it was still there. One of Mother Nature's many thermometers, I supposed.

Knowing that I wouldn't be able to go back to sleep anyway, I decided to get up and rekindle the fire. Reaching over to my side, I grabbed my sweatshirt and pulled the cold, crispy garment down over my head. The fabric felt icy cold against my wet skin but I knew that within a couple of minutes it would feel perfectly fine. Just one of the innumerable things that we had learned since the old world went away.

Grabbing my long john bottoms, I slowly eased out of our warm sleeping bag. My bare feet seconded what my breath had told me a minute ago, it was most definitely cold. Quickly slipping into my long johns, I noticed, much to my dismay, that there was frost on the inside of the door to our little hideaway. The temperature outside must have really plummeted overnight to make it's presence felt in here like that, I thought.

The shelter that we were in was very small, but definitely better than some of the others we had to use.

Alertly watching all of my movements, Walter stood up and thoroughly stretched his legs and massive chest. He was a big German Shepherd. At just over one hundred pounds in weight and four years old, he was in the prime of his life. He was also very tired. We all were.

Jeans followed the long johns. After that came thick, wool socks and high, thickly soled leather boots. We had been lucky enough to find some good outdoor clothing in our wanderings. They seemed to make our daily struggle a bit more tolerable. The physical part of it, anyway. In the era of no electricity, dressing warm was a necessity.

Stepping toward our improvised firebox, I searched it closely for the tell-tale signs of glowing coals. Not seeing any, I thought to myself, "Shit, now I'll have to start from scratch again." Hoping to get lucky, I picked up the stick that I had used as a poker the previous night and eagerly stirred the gray ashes. Discovering a handful of red embers buried deeply within the powdery ash was great news. Having to start a fire from scratch would mean having to use our last lighter again, and we had no idea how much butane was left.

I found some small slivers of kindling and laid them over the glowing coals. Quickly sorting through the small pile of wood that the boys had gathered the preceding evening, I grabbed the smallest sticks that I could find and stood them over the smoking kindling like a little teepee. It only took a few soft puffs of breath to ignite the little, smoldering pieces.

Rubbing my hands briskly over the rapidly growing fire felt good. Too bad I had to trudge outside in the snow to relieve myself.

Two large handfuls of thick, sturdy sticks momentarily deadened the sprouting fire, but not for long. The resilient yellow-orange flames began to lick at the new fuel, eager to conquer and consume.

As the hungry arms of the fire enveloped the waiting sticks, I turned and rubbed Walter on his big, melon-sized head.

"Good morning, boy," I whispered. I wasn't overly thrilled about going outside to use the bathroom, but these days you did what you had to do. Oh well, I thought to myself, at least it will give me a chance to look around a bit more.

In this new version of what passed for the world, it was impossible to be too safe.

2

    We had stumbled upon our little shelter with about an hour of light left the day before. Not that anyone really cared about time anymore; it was an old-fashioned, outdated memory. The only times that mattered these days were sunrise and sunset. It had been a wonderful surprise to find the old truck sitting next to our path. Entangled in a mass of thorny briars and tall, burr filled weeds, the vehicle sat right beneath the low hanging branches of an ancient, snarly apple tree. Among the wide open terrain dominating that area, finding such a secluded shelter was a real coup.

    Nearby, in a large pile of trash, we found what appeared to be an old gas tank that had been cut in half. Freeing it from the small mountain of debris that it was buried in, we put it to use as our firebox. The boys had harvested some dry wood from a few of the dead trees that stood just across the little gravel road from where we were.

    Dinner hadn't been much. Two cans of chili, a sleeve of crackers and four slices of cheese. Certainly no gourmet meal, but better than some we had recently ate.

    With food in our bellies and our little shelter warming up

nicely we had taken the time to attend to a few luxuries. Finally being able to take off our heavy boots and massage the aching blobs that used to be our feet was pure delight.

It felt really good to find a place where we could hole up for a few days and rest. We were still alive, but our bodies had paid a heavy toll.

The countryside of southeastern Michigan was a constant blur of farm fields, woods and small ponds. None of us had any idea exactly where we were. Our best guess was somewhere between Dundee and Milan. Not that we spent a lot of time worrying about it. Just to survive everyday took up all of the time and energy that we could muster.

3

    Before the world went to hell our family had lived in a mid-sized town in northwestern Ohio. Everything happened so suddenly that I'm not sure if anyone really knew what all transpired. All I can say for sure is that in the last few days leading up to the end of the old world, the news was inundated with reports of terroristic threats.

    Authorities hinted at plots designed to totally annihilate thirteen major cities, including Washington D.C.. The intelligence agencies said that the number was chosen on purpose by the terrorists because of some ironic, twisted logic about the original thirteen colonies.

    One evening while Kelli and I were watching CNN, the station abruptly went off the air. At first we thought that it was a momentary glitch or that the station was experiencing some sort of technical difficulty. After a few static-filled seconds, I impatiently switched over to Headline News. Being greeted with the same fuzzy gray screen, I pushed the button on the remote, yet again. And again. And again. My efforts proved futile, though, because no matter what channel I tried, all we got was static. Then the T.V. screen went completely black. The digital clock went out and I could hear the ceiling fan begin to decelerate in the sudden silence.

If not for all the ominous news reports about terrorists, we would have thought nothing of it. After all, cable and power outages were a common enough occurrence where we lived. Feeling mildly alarmed, I got the brilliant idea of digging out our battery powered radio to try and ease our troubled minds. Unfortunately, the inability to find anything on the little emergency radio, other than the same crackly static, had the exact opposite effect on us. Mild panic began to set in.

Kelli and I looked at each other and a troubled ambience filled the room. Fearful of the implications, we were unable to come up with the words to properly describe what we felt.

Almost in desperation, I reached out and slowly began to twist the dial on the radio. After searching nearly the full length of the lighted display panel, I finally happened upon a human voice. Sounding very nervous and speaking in rapid bursts, the unknown announcer tried to accurately convey what little information was available. We listened with increasing horror as the details of the destruction became known.

Constantly updating the trickle of news from around the country, the unfamiliar disc jockey never played a single song. Telling his listeners that the radio station was only able to operate because of a back-up generator and radio that they had kept in a special protective housing called a Faraday cage, he promised to continue to broadcast any incoming news for as long as possible.

The first information that came through was sketchy and incomplete, but it certainly seemed as though the terrorists had made good on their threats. Reports said that the eastern seaboard was hit particularly hard. Boston, New York City, Philadelphia, Washington D.C., and Norfolk, Virginia were largely decimated. In a lavishly planned, well financed surprise strike, the blood-thirsty terrorists had unleashed all holy hell upon the United States.

The initial wave of attack had featured hi-tech weapons called Electro Magnetic Pulse bombs, or EMPs for short. These specialized weapons exploded while still in the air, high above their intended targets. The powerful electronic discharge from these airborne explosives would instantly fry anything within their range that contained wiring or circuitry. All automobiles, telephones, computers, light bulbs and anything and everything else that used electricity would fail catastrophically.

Airborne wires and metal objects would act as giant lightning rods.

These powerful electronic pulses happened far too fast for ordinary lightning protection to be of any use. In a society so blindly dependent upon computers, cell phones and automated everything, we didn't stand a chance.

Things went on pretty much as normal for the first few days. Sure, people felt uptight and had no idea about what to do, but life went on.

Due to the modern supply method, known in the industry as "just in time" shipping, stores only stocked about three days worth of perishable goods. Things like milk, bread, fruit and vegetables were the first to disappear from the store shelves. Other kinds of food lasted a little longer, but as soon as people began to realize that no more shipments were coming they frantically snatched up any and every morsel that they could get their hands on. Although the stores only operated during daylight hours, the long lines of desperate, hungry shoppers grew dangerously unruly.

Threatening was a common occurrence, with assault not far behind. The police were so busy with protecting all of the so-called "high value" targets that soon the retailer's parking lots turned into nothing more than staging grounds for repeated muggings and thievery. After two people were robbed and shot dead one evening, all of the stores in the area closed their doors for good.

But that wasn't the worst of it. The lines at the few gas stations that were still operating during those first couple of days were an even more intense spectacle. Vehicles of all shapes and sizes were lined up for miles down the street, every one of them hoping that the gas wouldn't run out before they could fill their own tanks.

These long gas lines turned into hotbeds of gossip and information as the waiting drivers tried to pass their time. Mostly small talk at first. Then some really bad news began to trickle down the lines and that's when the shit really hit the fan.

Word was that the terrorists had destroyed all of the control facilities at every refinery in the country and now controlled their grounds. There was still plenty of oil, just no way that it could be refined for use. It wasn't long, a matter of mere hours, before the gas lines deteriorated in the same way that the grocery lines had. With thousands of cars still waiting in line, the gas pumps finally ran dry. Utter chaos ensued as the ramifications of this news sank in. There would be no more deliveries of any kind of fuel. Whatever was now on hand, was it.

Still clinging to the old way of driving as a means of transportation, people began to steal gas. From their neighbor's car or truck. From down the street. From anywhere. People wanted gas. No, people *needed* gas and did whatever they could to get it. Anyone who looked as if they might have fuel was targeted for theft.

The situation continued to worsen. Rampant looting targeted every business and storefront in the area. Soon every scrap of food was either hoarded or consumed. With no food available and no fuel to be had, the city quickly succumbed to murder and mayhem. Then, to make matters worse, what was remaining of our tattered local government decided to pull the plug, so to speak, and a lawless community was left to their own devices.

All around the country, the situation turned dire. Millions upon millions of half crazed, starving people now turned on each other. Armed gangs began roaming through every city from coast to coast. Going from house to house, they would kick in the doors. If no one was there, they would greedily help themselves to whatever food or supplies were available. If someone did still live in a house that they targeted, there was no mercy.

If the inhabitants were of no use to the marauders, they were immediately killed. If they happened upon someone they deemed interesting, mostly younger females, they would savagely amuse themselves with their new human toys for a while. Once the party was over, however, they were unmercifully dispatched, as well. After all, they were of no real value, just another mouth to feed.

4

Our little neighborhood fared well for about the first week after electricity, or A.E., as we began to refer to it. A lot of our neighbors were middle aged folks who usually kept to themselves.

Our false serenity was finally shattered on a sunny, fall afternoon. Kelli and I were cutting and splitting firewood in the backyard, while the boys did the stacking. We were lucky because we had a wood burner and our property was filled with large trees. Trying to think ahead about the coming winter, we meant to stockpile plenty of wood for heating and cooking.

A familiar figure had ridden up to my neighbor Roy's house on a bright red bicycle. Rodney was a friend of Roy's and a regular visitor next door. We were acquaintances and had spoken with each other numerous times over the years.

After spending a short while inside Roy's house, Rodney came across the yard in our direction. He appeared to be somewhat shaken as he addressed us and we soon found out why. During his eight block bicycle ride to our location, he had passed by two different groups that were looting from house to house. Being shot at by one of the groups, he was lucky enough to be turning a corner at the time and was able to ride out of harm's way. The other gang he saw had been far enough down a side street that they hadn't spotted him as he pedaled by.

Since he was a bachelor and lived alone, the neighbors had invited him to stay overnight, out of concern for his safety.

Already nervous and sleeping with a gun in our headboard, Kelli and I decided to start sleeping in shifts. Little did we know how old that arrangement would become.

5

    About ten o'clock the next morning we heard gunshots. With no other source of noise to deaden our ears anymore, they sounded particularly loud. After exchanging wide eyed looks of alarm, I headed for our bedroom at a sprint. For some reason, I couldn't feel my feet touch the floor. I knew that they had to be but I felt like I was running on an invisible cushion of air.
    I grabbed the Ruger 9mm pistol that we kept in our waterbed's headboard and quickly headed back toward the living room. My mind was swirling around in circles and my hearing seemed to be acutely better. I kept imagining footfalls on our porch and a big foot crashing through the front door.
    My family had gathered around the large living room window on the west side of our house to look out towards Roy's property next door. We could clearly hear loud, shouting voices and the sound of things being smashed and broken. A blood curdling, high-pitched, female scream preceded two quickly paced, booming reports.
    We all looked at each other in disbelief. Surely this couldn't actually be happening. But, it was. The bad dream that all of us were living had just turned into one hell of a bad

nightmare.

I looked down at the pistol clenched in my right hand and the realization dawned on me that I might be seriously outgunned. After all, we had no idea how many hoodlums were ransacking our neighbor's house or how well they were armed. All I knew was that I couldn't afford to take any chances.

Without a word, I turned and hightailed it back to the bedroom. Snatching my ring of keys from the dresser's top, I located the one that fit the gun safe and quickly jammed it home.

Having always loved the outdoors and being a hunter and an avid gun buff, I had built up a decent supply of weaponry over the years.

Even before the steel door swung open, I knew that I only had two real choices. One was a Ruger Mini 14. A nice piece. I had customized the rifle with a folding stock, flash suppressor and high capacity, forty round magazines. The other was an old, Russian SKS. It was also outfitted with all the necessary goodies. Fortunately, my choice was made for me. As the heavy door swung outward, I saw two fully loaded clips for my SKS lying on the top shelf of the safe.

I hastily shoved one of the magazines into the hip pocket of my pants with one hand and simultaneously lifted the rifle with the other. Thrusting the remaining clip into the bottom of the weapon, I turned and rushed back toward the living room. I pulled back on the bolt and chambered a round as I made my way. The sound of the slide solidly slamming home brought with it an eerily comforting feeling. If not for my fortunate choice of a hobby, we would have been left as helpless as most other people were.

By the time I had reached the middle of the living room, the sound of gunfire erupted again. This time sounding much louder than before.

I could hear yelling from outside and joined my family at the window just in time to see Rodney fall, face first, in Roy's backyard. Apparently, he had tried to make a break for it out the back door. He didn't get very far. His unmoving body lay at a distance of about six or seven strides from the back steps.

The two thugs that had just cut him down looked around the immediate area to see if anyone had witnessed their latest execution. One of them turned toward our house and we all quickly recoiled from the window. The very pane of glass that had been our front row seat to cold blooded murder now threatened to expose us to the same danger. Satisfied that no one seemed to object to their latest barbaric outburst, the goons turned and headed back inside Roy's house.

We all looked around at each other, obvious relief etched on our faces.

Wanting to live is a strong stimulant and my senses seemed to be in overdrive. My mind just couldn't seem to wrap itself around the idea that these armed thugs might try to invade our home next. Needing a moment to think, I asked the boys to go to their rooms and dress warmly in case we had to leave in a hurry.

After they had gone I told my wife that we needed to be prepared to protect ourselves. If necessary, I warned her, we may have to kill to keep from being killed. I had never seen her exhibit the depth of concern that was on her face and it made my heart sink. Left speechless for a few seconds, all I could do was stare into her brown eyes and lose myself in my own boiling emotions. In that brief, soul searching moment, I knew one thing, for sure. There was no way that I could allow that pack of murderous marauders to invade the sanctity of our home. If I wanted to save my family, I had to act now.

Looking out the window towards Roy's house, I could see no movement at all. Deciding that we would have a much better chance if we all stuck together, I latched onto my wife's hand and we quickly scurried towards the boys' bedrooms.

Jacob's room was in the front of the house. It overlooked the front yard from one of it's windows and the front porch from the other. It also happened to look out on my next door neighbor's house and property, so that's where we went. There was a good thirty yards of open space between our two homes and I resolved myself to not letting anyone cross that gap. If that band of hooligans started this way, they were in for one hell of a fight.

Unlocking Jacob's window, I slid the bottom sash up into the top of the opening. The cool air that flooded into the room was a pleasant surprise. With all of the running around that we had done, I had heated up a pinch.

The crime scene that used to be our neighbor's house sat ominously silent. No more sounds of items being smashed and broken, and no more tortured screaming. By resting the front end of my rifle on top of the window sill, I had a perfect sight picture of no man's land.

Kaleb joined the rest of us just as two of the hoods next door sauntered outside. I remembered one of them as the punk that had chased Rodney out the back door and then pumped four slugs into him for his troubles.

Slowly easing the safety off, I placed my finger on the rifle's trigger. The duo turned our way and started walking toward our house. A thousand thoughts raced through my mind in what seemed like just a couple of seconds.

Were these two degenerates the only ones? What if I opened fire on this pair and there were still more of them lingering around inside Roy's house? Which one of them should I take out first? But luckily, I wasn't forced to make any of those decisions, just yet. The pair of creeps turned left at the driveway and headed out back, towards Roy's unattached garage.

At least they're thorough, I thought to myself, as they walked up the concrete driveway to the little outbuilding. A couple of seconds after they had disappeared around the far side of the garage, we plainly heard two loud, thumping noises. They had kicked open the entry door of the garage, and before long, more sounds of deliberate destruction could be heard coming from inside the structure.

Please, I silently pleaded, let them find enough to satisfy their selfish needs over there so that they won't want to come this way. Let them fill their arms with so much plunder that they have no other choice but to take their stuff back to wherever it is that they feel safe and leave us alone. I knew what a selfish thought that was and I felt really bad about it. After all, I had known Roy and his wife for a long time and had even become friendly with many of their family members. But no matter how embarrassed I felt at my apparent lack of empathy, my family came first.

As I was busy thinking about all of this, the marauders must have grown bored with ransacking our neighbor's house because two more of them came out of Roy's front door. Closely followed by two more.

One of the murderous clods was grinning maniacally between big gulps of whatever liquid he had pilfered. The group was steadily moving toward our house with fiendish looks on their faces, as if lost in some evil, hypnotic spell.

They paused at the head of Roy's driveway to loudly inquire of their accomplices as to what, if anything, they had found inside the garage.

I found myself desperately wishing that they would disappear. Just vanish and fade away, like ghostly apparitions are supposed to do when someone opens their eyes. But, it wasn't to be.

The two intrepid explorers of the garage came traipsing back up the driveway, the bigger of the two toting a small, plastic gasoline container in one hand.

Then I noticed something that had the potential to tilt the game in our favor. One of the mongrels in the pack appeared to be in charge and giving orders to the others. He was dressed in a long, black trench coat and wearing shiny, black leather gloves. If not for the matching knitted cap situated on top of his head, he would have reminded me of a stereotypical investment banker out for an afternoon stroll down Wall Street. The others were standing around him in a semi-circle looking like a bunch of lost puppies. They patiently waited while their leader opened his coat and retrieved a pack of cigarettes from an inside pocket. One of his devoted cronies reached out with a disposable lighter and compliantly lit the cigarette with a practiced hand. After drawing in deeply on his fresh cancer stick, the head honcho exhaled a large volume of bluish gray smoke. Due to the windless conditions, it neatly hung above his head like a low altitude storm cloud.

When he turned to face in our direction, I could see him clearly enough to watch his eyes hungrily sweep over our house. Time seemed to slow down to a crawl and all I could hear my heart noisily thumping away inside my chest. Then I watched in horror as he picked up his right arm and pointed a finger in our direction.

"This one's next," he said.

6

    The four hellions that were grouped together now readied to step off of Roy's driveway and onto our lawn, but the other two hoods weren't yet halfway up the driveway on their return trip from the garage.

    If I opened fire right then, I knew that I couldn't get them all, but I also didn't want to let them get any closer. Determined not to let us become their next victims, I decided to shoot first and worry about things later.

    I picked out the leader and put my sights in the middle of his chest. From past military experience I had learned that if possible, you should always take out the person in charge first. The tactic is designed to create confusion, hesitation and uncertainty among the enemy. Maybe, I thought, if I could surprise them and freeze them in their tracks for a second or two, I would have a much better chance at getting them all.

    I slowly squeezed the rifle's trigger. The sound of the large caliber weapon going off inside of the enclosed space was well beyond loud. It was deafening.

I saw the group's leader go down. His body fell backwards and he limply sat down like he was plopping into his favorite easy chair. Except, I knew that I didn't have an easy chair out on my front lawn.

I really didn't have much time to pay attention to that, though. I already had my sights centered on the next body. The one who looked as though he was carrying a rifle similar to the one that I was using.

By then the goons had figured out where the first shot had come from and were looking straight at me when I fired the second time. There was another deafening roar. I detected a slight look of surprise on the brute's face as my shot found it's mark.

After that everything happened so fast that it was just a blur. I don't know exactly how many times I fired. I just kept finding targets and pulling the trigger.

The remaining thieves were moving now. Moving fast. They weren't about to stand still and be shot at any longer.

I think I killed three of them. I say *think*, because I never did go out there to check. All I know for sure was that there were three bodies lying on my front lawn and my ears were ringing loudly in a never ending high-pitched whine. I'm sure that I hit a fourth, but he didn't go down. He ran up onto Roy's front porch and out of my sight. Maybe he ended up dying later from his wounds, I don't know for sure. I can only hope.

The two thugs that had been coming back from the garage got away clean. I never had a good shot at either one of them but I pumped a few rounds their way for good measure. They escaped around the back of Roy's house and I never saw either one of them again.

7

    In all of the shooting that I did, I had only heard a few pops of return fire. They had sounded very insignificant compared to the cannon's roar of the weapon in my hands.
    I felt numb, both physically and emotionally. I had just killed three, possibly four, human beings. I certainly felt justified in doing so and I don't think that any jury in the world would have convicted me of murder for killing them. For some reason, though, I still felt remorse. I don't really know why. After all, they were only common thieves and cold blooded killers who would have ruthlessly destroyed our family if given the chance. But, nonetheless, I still did.
    I remembered my family and whirled around to check on them. They were huddled tightly together in the room's far corner, their eyes wide with terror. Both boys still had their hands tightly clamped over their ears trying to ward off the thunderous booms from my rifle. Kelli was trying her best to shelter them both with her outstretched arms in the manner of a mother bird trying to cover her newborn hatchlings.
    I turned back to the window, afraid of what I might see. But, there was nothing. No movement, at all. I spent the next

few minutes looking back and forth between the window and my shell shocked family.

My mind churned as I tried to figure out what to do next. At first, I tried hard to convince myself that it would be better for us if we stayed there. But in my heart, I knew that we would have to leave. The safety of our family far outweighed any selfish need to be comfortable. We couldn't take the chance of staying in our house and becoming sitting ducks. I felt certain that the marauders wouldn't forgive and forget. Since we had fought them, and appeared to be willing to die fighting in order to protect our home, they would think that whatever we were protecting would be well worth having.

They would be back. The questions was, in how long and with how many more people? What if they came back with a whole horde of invaders? They could rush the house all at once like a big swarm of bees and easily overpower us. Or, they could simply sneak back and set our house on fire, then shoot us as we tried to flee the burning structure. Revenge always was a tough pill to swallow.

The only remaining question was, go where? If every city and every town across the whole country was like this, where could we go? Should we try to survive off the land and hide out in the woods, far away from everybody else? Should we take what camping and survival gear we own and head out into the countryside and try to live there? According to the calendar, winter was only two weeks away. Would we be able to survive the freezing cold elements and find enough food for us to live on outside, in the barren winter landscape?

No matter how much I hated even the thought of the idea, I could see no other solution. Perhaps, if we were lucky, we might stumble upon a place where we could feel safe again. Eventually.

I guess it didn't really matter, anyhow. Just like everyone else, we had no electricity. We had no jobs and there were no more groceries to be bought. Even if you had enough money to buy the store's entire stock, nobody would have taken it because money was of no use anymore. Rich or poor, the world had gone to hell.

People were busy killing and dying all around us. The helpless and the innocent didn't stand a chance against the tidal wave of murder and looting that was sweeping the land. The only real chance of surviving the nightmarish catastrophe would come from separation. Even though it would be uncomfortable for all of us, seclusion was the only viable answer. I was unsure of the probability of finding sufficient food and shelter during an upper mid-western winter, but I knew that we had no chance at all if we stayed there.

What a pain in the ass, I thought to myself. At forty-six, I felt far too old for that kind of crap. I had become accustomed to hot meals and sleeping in a warm, comfy waterbed. Oh well, I lamented, there isn't any time to whine about that. Every minute that we stay here our danger factor increases.

So, having decided at least that much, the sixty-four thousand dollar question was, go where? In what direction? Since we lived in northwest Ohio, I immediately thought of Canada. Perhaps our neighbors to the north hadn't been decimated like the States had. We could make our way to the border stealthily and return to the relative safety of civilization once we crossed over. It was definitely a better choice than heading south and finding nothing but endless ruin and devastation everywhere that we went. Plus, if there had been any nuclear detonations during the attack, the chance of running into radioactive fallout would be greatly reduced.

As far as I could tell, if there had been nuclear weapons employed, we hadn't received any of the fallout yet. Of course, I didn't own a Geiger counter, but nothing appeared to be out of the ordinary. However long that would last was anybody's guess.

Kelli and I took turns watching from the open window while the boys were busy helping whoever wasn't on watch. Scurrying around like a colony of ants, we grabbed all of the provisions that we thought we might need and placed them in a huge pile in the middle of Jacob's bedroom floor.

By the time we had picked out this, packed that, forgot this and organized that, a full hour and a half had passed. Finally done, we all grabbed our massive assortment of bags, boxes and backpacks and, with heavy hearts, headed for the back door. Quietly exiting the house without incident, Jacob unhooked Walter from the end of his long log chain and we left.

I was tempted, every step of the way, to take a glance back. To take one last look at our house and property as it slowly disappeared from sight, but I never did.

Our escape from the town that we lived in was made easier because we lived right on the outside edge of the incorporated area. Behind our house was nothing but open country, full of farm fields and small patches of thickly wooded areas. We knew the area pretty well because we had taken Walter out there and let him run free on numerous occasions.

In less than ten minutes we were on the far side of a dense hedgerow and completely out of sight. We were heading north.

8

I was nudged out of my memory by a cold nose rubbing against my hand. It was Walter. The poor dog probably had to go pee as bad as I did. I noticed, with some disgust, that the small fire that I had started to get going so well had almost died out again.

"Shit," I mumbled.

I grabbed some more sticks from the pile and hastily built another small teepee. There were still plenty of glowing coals laying there, though, and the wood ignited easily. Throwing another big handful on the growing blaze to make sure that it would continue to burn while we stepped outside, I patted Walter on top of his head.

"Come on, boy," I whispered. "Let's go."

I grabbed my rifle and opened the door of our shelter a crack. It had snowed a little overnight. Not much from the looks of it, maybe an inch or two, but I was very glad to see it. The fresh coating would help to obscure the tracks that we had left yesterday.

I scanned the area carefully as the door slowly swept open. It was eerily silent out there. There was absolutely no sound, whatsoever. I could see no hint of movement, either. There were no signs of any animal, even so much as a bird. Perhaps there had been some radioactive fallout in this part of the country and that's why I didn't see any animals, or maybe it was just a coincidence. Either way, my aching bladder superseded everything else for the moment, so I slowly walked outside with Walter at my heels.

I carefully looked over everything around our shelter for any sign of danger. Walter, though, didn't seem to be as concerned as I was about our safety. Rushing past me at a gallop, he found the closest tree and hiked his back leg without haste. After taking one more quick look around, I leaned my rifle against the side of our shelter and answered nature's call, myself. After successfully completing my business, I waited patiently for Walter to finish his.

Trying to make good use of the time, I further examined our unfamiliar surroundings. It seemed like that was all any of us did anymore. Constantly looking around had almost become second nature to us, but it was better to be safe and nervous, than to be careless and dead.

A small plume of steam rose from Walter's leavings as he bolted back in my direction. I couldn't help but smile at his playful antics. Walter had always loved snow. Something about the white, fluffy substance always brought extreme joy to the big dog. With a quick burst of acceleration, he rapidly crossed the distance of the small clearing that we were in. Exuberantly extending his front paws in an exaggerated manner as he ran, he threw powdery sprays of snow skyward in explosive, wide spreading arcs. Zig-zagging to the left and to the right, Walter made like a running back faking moves to juke a determined defender.

His showy display was a pleasant distraction from our near constant misery. Smiling widely, I started for our shelter's door and motioned for Walter to follow. Snatching up a large mouthful of fresh, white snow, he swallowed it down in one big gulp and eagerly bounded my way. Gently easing the small door open, we climbed back inside the safety of our darkened shelter.

9

We had been very lucky to find the little hideaway before it got dark. I had already resigned myself to the fact that we would probably have to endure another cold night of sleeping outdoors on the ground.

Our new shelter was an old delivery truck. The hood of the vehicle stood wide open, as if trying to yell out in protest at having been left out there to slowly rust away. The engine was missing, someone had undoubtedly salvaged that years ago. The sheet metal box that sat on the back of the truck was about twelve feet long and eight feet wide.

Whoever had owned the vehicle had certainly gotten their money's worth out of it. From the look of it, the truck had been in a few accidents in it's day, but nothing too major. Most of the damage was confined to the cab. The only visible damage to the box was a hole in the top, right hand corner at the front.

That happened to work out just fine for us, though. We used the opening as our chimney.

The back of the box was one of those roll up doors. The kind that used to be so common on the sides of beer trucks. On the opposite side of the path that the old truck sat next to, the box also had a little access door. That's what we had used to gain entry.

10

As Walter and I re-entered our temporary abode, I could already feel a difference in the temperature. Our shelter was beginning to warm up nicely. I threw a couple of larger sticks on the glowing fire and heard a rustle of movement behind me. Evidently Walter had decided that if he wasn't sleeping anymore, Jacob didn't need to be, either.

Lately, Walter had developed a habit of sticking his big, cold nose in Jacob's slumbering face. Jacob groaned and raised his startled, sleep-filled head just in time to receive a wet, slobbery lick in the face from the wide eyed, big, brown dog.

Agitated, Jacob pushed him back. "Get away, Walter, I'm trying to sleep," he said in a gravelly sounding voice.

I whispered at Walter to get his attention and motioned for him to come over beside me and the ever-growing fire. I knew that Jacob would go back to sleep. Even though we were in the middle of an unprecedented national disaster, he would have no problem. A sure sign of being a normal teenager, if there ever was one. As soon as Jacob woke up all would be forgiven, anyway, and the two would be the best of buddies again. Jacob had been ten years old when Walter joined our family and there had been an instant connection between the two. Jacob and Walter had grown so close that Kelli and I had taken to referring to the duo as brothers.

My stomach was growling, but then again, it almost always was. Our food supply was running dangerously low because we hadn't been able to find anything worthwhile to scavenge in almost a week.

Our last opportunity had been at an old farmhouse that sat next to a wide, rushing river. We had spent hours staking the place out from the trees that lined the water's edge. After darkness had taken over the landscape and we still hadn't seen any light or movement, we decided to chance a closer look.

Moving slowly and cautiously, I crept up to the house while Kelli held onto Walter's leash. I circled around the entire house, carefully looking inside all of the windows. Unable to see or hear anything, I went to the front door and tried to turn the handle. I heard a small, muffled click and the door moved inward a bit.

If there had been any response at all I was prepared to let go of the doorknob and run as fast as I could for cover. There was none, though.

I stood on the porch of the dark farmhouse pointing my rifle at the middle of the door with one hand and holding onto the doorknob with the other. It felt like I stood there in that position for hours. But in reality, I'm certain that it was only for a couple of minutes.

Feeling certain that it was safe, I pushed the door in, ever so slowly, with the barrel of my gun. Without moving my feet on the porch one inch, I pushed the door all the way back against the wall behind it. I concentrated hard on trying to detect any sign of danger, no matter how small it may be. After what seemed like another eternity, I decided that it was alright to move forward.

Patiently waiting for my eyes to adjust to the darkness of the room, I began to cautiously search my surroundings. I tried to step as lightly as I could while I eased forward. With my rifle pointed ahead of me and my heart in my throat, I nervously made my way through the dark, spooky residence.

I had gotten nearly halfway through the old farmhouse before I came upon a grisly scene. A vision so ghastly, that it will forever be imprinted upon my mind. When I first saw the body from the hallway, I almost jumped out of my skin. I'm actually surprised that I didn't pump a bunch of errant rounds all over the house in my shock.

It's hard to see anything with certainty in the darkness and sometimes you see things that simply aren't there. Your eyes tend to play tricks on you. But, not this time.

I recoiled in horror as what I was seeing sunk in. In what was obviously a bedroom, sat a human form with it's back propped up against the headboard of an ornate, wooden bed. At first, I thought that the shape above the corpse's head was a large, decorative hand fan. You know, the paper kind that proper ladies use to casually unfold and wave back and forth on stifling hot summer days. There was also what appeared to be maybe a rifle or a stick leaning against one of the form's shoulders, with the other end cradled between it's outstretched legs.

The odor coming from the room was absolutely gut wrenching in it's putridness. I slowly inched my way forward, moving as quietly as I could. With every small step that I took the gruesome picture became clearer. The object that was propped against the figure's shoulder was a shotgun but I didn't feel worried at all, because right about the same time I also noticed that the shape above the fancy headboard wasn't a large, decorative hand fan, either. It was certainly a good impression of one, though. Almost an exact copy. It looked like the unfortunate soul had stuck the shotgun in his mouth and then pulled the trigger.

It took me a few moments to slowly pull myself back together. In the end, though, I think that it was my strong desire to get out of that creepy room that finally got me moving again.

I searched the rest of the house but never saw anyone else. Satisfied that I was alone, I automatically turned my attention to what it was almost always focused on those days: food.

I went back to the farmhouse's kitchen to scrounge around. I didn't bother to look in the fridge. Nobody wasted time looking in anyone's refrigerator anymore. Thoroughly searching the cupboards and the little pantry, I found a small amount of usable provisions. Mostly canned goods, with a few boxes of macaroni and cheese thrown in for good measure. There were also some other items lying around that we could use, but I could only carry so much without carelessly dropping it along the way.

I went back to the tree line by the river and dropped off my load of salvaged booty. I told my family that I hadn't found anything unusual in the house, but that there was still more food. Donning backpacks to ensure that we could grab everything left of use in just one trip, Jacob and I returned to forage around in the darkness of the secluded farmhouse.

Later that evening, after we all laid down to bed for the night, I told my wife what I had seen when I looked into that bedroom. Her response was thoughtful and to the point, as it almost always was.

With a calm, steady look in her eyes, she had softly whispered, "I can almost understand why he did it. Being all alone in a world like this would be more of a misery than anyone could reasonably bear. Nowadays," she added as an afterthought , "it's hard enough to make it at all, even with the love and support of a family."

I certainly couldn't argue with that.

11

The fire was burning very well and it wouldn't be long before we would have another bed of brightly glowing coals.

I retrieved our last chunk of rabbit from one of the outside compartments of my backpack. There wasn't a lot of it, but it was the only meat that we had. Unwrapping it from the piece of plastic that I had stored it in, I used my survival knife to slice the meat into thin strips to make jerky with. I took a few short sticks out of our woodpile and laid them across one corner of the firebox. Stretching the pieces of rabbit across the top of the sticks, I left it to slowly dry next to the growing fire.

Hearing a soft rustling sound behind me, I turned to discover that Kelli was awake. Still sitting in her sleeping bag, she stretched her arms mightily toward the delivery truck's roof. Walter noticed her movement and cheerfully rushed to greet his "mommy" good morning.

After everyone else was awake, we ate our humble breakfast. It wasn't much, a few peppermint candy canes, some shelled peanuts and an old loaf of nut-filled fruitcake. No one voiced any complaints, though, and no fruitcake was left when we were done. Walter ate the last of the instant mashed potato flakes and the remaining bones from the rabbit.

We needed food badly. If we couldn't find something substantive to eat soon, our situation would become very serious.

The morning's conversation turned to how much we liked the little shelter that we were staying in. In fact, we almost felt safe there. The beaten dirt path that the truck sat next to was far from any paved road. There were no towns close by and all of the houses around were thinly scattered. If we could locate some food nearby, we would be able to rest our weary bones here for a few days before resuming our northward trek.

We discussed this idea amongst ourselves and were very excited at the prospect. Hiking for hours every day, laden with all of our burdens and worldly possessions, had worn each of us down to near exhaustion. The lack of proper nutrition was undoubtedly the main reason for our lack of energy, but I also suspected that the daily drudgery of our plight had begun to adversely affect our morale. If we were somehow able to stay put for a few days, I was certain that the rest would do us wonders.

12

    Walter stayed behind with Kelli and Kaleb while Jacob and I left to scout out the area.
    Jacob was starting to become quite an avid outdoorsman. It was he who was responsible for the rabbit drying next to our shelter's fire. He shot it with an old, Winchester .22 caliber rifle that he now carried about continually. The little, semi-automatic rifle had been in my collection for many years. An accurate and dependable weapon, it had become the family favorite for recreational target practice. Jacob had become relatively familiar with the gun over the years and handled the weapon enough to become a fair shot with it. But since the untimely eruption of this man-made catastrophe, his skill had grown considerably and he had become very good with the little rifle.
    We started to re-trace our trail in from the day before. I wanted to make sure that we hadn't been spotted and followed to our hideout. If anyone else became aware that we were in the area, it would be far too dangerous for us to remain there. We followed our path for about a mile before veering off. Neither one of us noticed anything out of the ordinary along

the route and that was great news, but we didn't exactly have time for a celebration. We were hungry and becoming weaker by the day. We needed to find some food and we needed to do it fast.

    The countryside was beautiful in that area. I couldn't help but think that it must have been a great place to live before all of this crap happened. We roamed over gently sloping hills and through some nice, thick stands of timber.

    About an hour into our exploratory trek we happened upon a medium sized creek. The crystal clear water was flowing swiftly, creating nearly transparent ripples and miniature white-capped waves as it worked it's way through the massive rocks that tried unsuccessfully to hold the current back. Stopping long enough to take a short break next to the water's edge, we listened to the soothing sound of the dancing water as it flowed by.

    As we were carefully crossing one of the few paved roads in the area, we saw a large billboard. Walking a little closer to the gargantuan piece of advertising, the words finally came into view. "Pierson Farms" the sign proclaimed. "The largest sod farm in Michigan." Below that, in smaller letters, was what must have been the company's witty slogan: "We've got ya covered".

    The folks who had commissioned the sign weren't kidding, either. The farm was breathtakingly huge, and from where we stood on top of a little ridge, we could see enough sod around there to cover the entire city that we used to live in. Huge, open spaces flanked by tree lines and hedgerows, as far as the eye could see. There were numerous outbuildings positioned across the property, at regular intervals. We could see a backhoe sticking halfway out of one. Tractors and other large, odd looking machinery idly sat about, all over the expansive property.

    Jacob and I searched the area thoroughly, hopeful of finding something that we could make good use of. Every door, on every barn and outbuilding stood wide open. All of the tractors, backhoes and other assorted machinery looked like they had been siphoned of their fuel. Each one of their gas caps had been removed and left to dangle.

    Really not too much of a surprise, I thought to myself. I was certain that everyone in the area knew of the place. After all, a fair number of folks had obviously worked there.

A raccoon had taken up residence in one of the smaller sheds. I was very tempted to have Jacob shoot it because we were in bad need of nutrition, especially fresh meat. The only reason that I decided against it was for fear of someone else hearing the shot. We did make a mental note of exactly where it was located, though, so that if need be we could return.

Jacob and I had also found the owner's house. A two story, red brick structure that sat back a long, snaking driveway, far away from the main road. There were numerous broken windows visible as we approached the dwelling. Debris was carelessly strewn about on the lawn and the front door stood wide open. No human tracks were evident in the snow surrounding the house, so I felt no real apprehension in entering.

The front door had been nearly ripped completely off it's hinges. The only thing holding the slab of wood to the house was one lone screw in the bottom hinge. The door was leaning awkwardly back against the brick outer wall, the bottom, right hand corner resting heavily on the painted surface of the porch.

Upon entering the residence it became abundantly clear that an intensely violent struggle had taken place within. Overturned furniture and scattered belongings littered the thickly carpeted floor. Every item in the room looked as though it had been thoroughly searched for any hidden valuables. I took a closer look at the thick, brown carpeting and saw a trail of even darker spots that led further on into the clutter bathed house.

Up until this point, I had felt relatively comfortable in there. Now, all of a sudden, I didn't feel so at ease. I had no idea where that trail of ominous looking spots ended or what might be waiting there, but I was certain that it wouldn't be pretty. Hoping to shield Jacob from whatever horror awaited, I asked him to wait where he was for me and keep an eye on the front door.

The mysterious trail ended in the kitchen. As soon as I entered the room I was glad that I had asked Jacob to hold back. The spotty drops that I had been following turned into a large, dark colored pool beneath one of the straight backed, kitchen chairs. There were three of them placed back to back, forming a crude triangle in the middle of the kitchen floor. The table was leaning against the far wall, resting on one of it's thin edges. Someone had wanted room to work.

Three unfortunate souls were tied to the triangle of

chairs, and from the looks of it, they had taken an awful lot of abuse. A middle-aged man and woman occupied two of the kitchen chairs. The third contained a human form that had been so badly disfigured, that I could not properly determine it's age. From the manner in which it was dressed I deduced the figure to be male, but that was as much as I could tell. I couldn't help but think that this guy must have really pissed someone off. There were so many holes in his flannel shirt that his chest looked like a bloody chunk of Swiss cheese.

    There was no food left in the house except for a few pint sized jars of some kind of jelly or preserve. I didn't take the time to check them out, I just grabbed them all and stuffed them into my coat pockets.

    Jacob and I left the house and began our long trek back to the little shelter. We had been gone a long time and I was sure that Kelli would be getting worried. Besides, we were both starting to get pretty tired.

    I was glad that I had asked Jacob to wait for me in the living room back at the farmhouse. Both boys had been traumatized enough already without having to witness that sort of senseless brutality.

    We saw no sign of human activity, whatsoever, on our return trip and that didn't hurt my feelings at all. In fact, that was just the way I liked it.

13

  Kelli, Kaleb and Walter were all very happy to see us when we finally got back to our secluded hideaway.
  The first thing that I noticed as we entered our shelter was a gargantuan stack of newly gathered firewood. A beaming Kaleb excitedly showed off his fuel gathering prowess to me and Jacob with a long, sweeping motion of his right arm. The pile of wood was indeed impressive, covering nearly the entire length of the truck's box.
  "I've been collecting firewood since you guys left this morning," he said with pride.   "I even put a bunch in the cab, up front."
  "That's great, Kaleb," I told him.   "You did a really good job.   Your brother owes you one.   Don't you, Jacob?" I said, while glancing in his direction.
  After seeing the look in my eyes, Jacob reluctantly grunted his agreement.
  Producing the three small Mason jars from my pockets, I asked Kelli to open them and find out what we had.   The first jar turned out to be blackberry jam, one of her personal favorites. The next one was apricot jam, not a particular favorite of anyone's, but tasty, nonetheless.   We couldn't quite figure out

what the third one was. Even though we all braved up and tasted it, we still didn't have a clue. We ended up giving that one to Walter for lunch while we ate the other two jars and the rabbit jerky that had been drying next to the fire all day.

While we ate, I told Kelli about all of the deer tracks that Jacob and I had seen while on our way back. A highway's worth of fresh deer tracks that went right by a perfect spot for an ambush. I could see a flash of hope in her eyes, she knew how desperate our situation was.

We all badly wanted to stay there for a while and recuperate, but if I couldn't take a deer it would be impossible. We needed food.

"How can we cook a deer?" Kaleb asked, a puzzled expression adorning his face.

All eyes turned toward me and I felt immense pressure to ensure that our fragile morale remained high. Scrambling to come up with a feasible plan on the fly, I started to think out loud.

"Well," I started, "since we have a shelter, we could keep the fire going twenty-four hours a day without anyone else being able to see it. We would work in shifts, around the clock, cutting and drying the meat. In a few days we would be loaded down with all of the fresh jerky that we could carry."

I saw Kaleb's eyes light up at that sentence and could have sworn that his mouth actually began to salivate. Although somewhat small for his age, Kaleb had a huge appetite. I outweighed the boy by fifty pounds and he could still easily out eat me. Kelli and I always liked to joke about how he must have been born with hollow legs.

A video gamer at heart, Kaleb had always preferred being indoors, instead of out. Although more frail than most of his classmates, Kaleb never saw his physical limitations as a hindrance. In the way that a blind person's sense of touch and hearing became more acute, Kaleb's pleasant disposition and genuine sensitivity more than made up for any lack of sheer brawn. Making friends always came easy for him because he was unusually generous and possessed a heart of pure gold.

14

    After lunch we excitedly discussed our hunting strategy while Kelli washed our extra socks. She was insistent that, if nothing else, we could at least put on clean socks every day. The way things were, though, even something as simple as that wasn't very easy.
    She had been melting snow because no water was available. Having found an old, beat up, aluminum pan in the same rubbish pile as the firebox, Kelli kept it next to the fire for just that purpose.

15

    Jacob and I started out for what we hoped would be our lucky hunting spot. This was our first real opportunity to hunt something substantial like a deer. Up until that time we had only been using the .22 caliber rifle and hunting small game, like rabbits and squirrels. We preferred the small bore weapon because it wasn't very loud and we had no desire to attract attention.
    I was carrying my SKS, like always, while Jacob had the Mini 14. I bet he felt like he was on top of the world. I remembered feeling the same way the first time I carried a high powered rifle, so many years ago. Jacob had never even shot the gun before, but I was sure that he could handle it. Kelli usually carried that rifle, but today we needed it.
    Arriving back at our chosen spot with about an hour and a half of daylight left, we decided that our best chance for success would be for one of us to be on each side of the hedgerow. A tangled line of trees, underbrush and thorn bushes, the thick cover came to an abrupt end right next to the bank of a creek about twenty yards down. Finding a suitable place for Jacob to hide on one the dense barrier, I went back to the other side and did the same. Now that we were in position, all we had to do was wait and watch. There was no way that a

deer could get past us without being seen.

It was decided between us that we would only take one shot. Another one of those things that I had learned from my days in the military. If someone fires only once, it's difficult to pinpoint exactly where the report had come from, but if they shoot more than once, it became much easier to locate the source. That's why Jake was carrying the Mini-14. If he happened to get a good shot before I did, he would take it. We couldn't afford to pass up any chance we had to obtain proper nutrition. Especially fresh meat.

After waiting motionlessly for a while, the minutes started to turn into hours. The wind had changed direction since our arrival and was currently blowing straight into my face. I was glad that Jacob was on the other side of the hedgerow, at least he would get a break from the wind over there.

Being half afraid to move in fear of making a noise and spooking our quarry, my sedentary extremities began to feel the effects of the chilling winter breeze. At first, it was my nose. Openly exposed to the freezing elements, I could feel it growing steadily colder with each passing minute. Not long after my nose finally gave up and went numb, my fingers and toes began to get in on the act. I started to wonder if my freezing fingers would work well enough to pull the trigger when the time came or if I would be relegated to watching our badly needed nutrition walked on by, unmolested? Only time would tell, I guessed.

About a half an hour before it got dark, I spotted a squirrel moving through one of the many trees that dotted the long, tangled hedgerow that we were in. If only Jacob had been carrying his .22 rifle, I thought, we would be dining on some fresh squirrel later on. I was half tempted to shoot it anyway, but I knew that if I did, any chance we had of bagging a deer tonight would be gone. Unless it was a deaf deer.

I wondered how things were going back at our shelter. They had to be feeling as anxious and nervous as we were. We had all been running on nothing but fumes lately and desperately needed something solid to eat. Thus far, this was the first time that we had found ourselves completely out of food. Well, not completely out. I had stashed six little, tin foil wrapped, chocolate Santas in the bottom of my backpack. They had been in a small plastic bowl on the coffee table on the day that we had to leave our house.

The bowl was decorated with all of the traditional images of Christmas. Gingerbread men, snowmen, red stockings and candy canes. I had looked at that bowl hundreds of times over numerous holiday seasons and never thought twice about it. Now, though, for some reason, the image that I couldn't shake from my mind was how lonely that Christmas tree in the bottom of the bowl looked after I took the last pieces of candy out of it. Funny what we remember.

We were all so happy back then. Christmas was on the way and Kelli and I had nearly finished all of our shopping. It would have been a great Christmas, too. We had a good year financially and everyone had gotten everything that they wanted, and more. Ipods and video games. CD players and fancy new shoes. All of it worthless now, nothing more than expensive rubbish.

I heard something move a little way down the hedgerow and turned to see Jacob standing up, looking my way. With a look of slight discomfort on his face, he breathily whispered, "I can't hold it anymore. I have to go, right now!"

A smile broke across my frozen face. Jacob had a way of being hilariously funny, even when he wasn't exactly trying to be. I nodded my head and waved my hand in a quick, "go ahead" gesture. The wind was working in our favor anyway, so the scent shouldn't pose any problem. It would just blow harmlessly out across the open fields.

Just as I heard Jacob getting back into his hiding spot and sitting down, I caught a slight movement out of the corner of my eye. I leaned forward and turned my head to the right so that I could get both eyes on the object. About two hundred yards down the hedgerow I could make out two shapes that looked like deer. I couldn't tell for sure because of the encroaching darkness and the lengthy distance, but I wasn't about to take a chance. I turned my head and whispered at Jacob to be quiet because something was coming.

As the dark shapes closed the gap to less than a hundred yards I started to become downright giddy with excitement. It was indeed two deer. They were moving steadily toward the creek, their noses raised and testing the air with every tentative step. Their heads seemed to be moving as if on swivels, kind of like one of those stupid things that sat in the back windows of people's cars; heads bobbing up and down and all around in an endlessly annoying, mindless manner.

They appeared to be extra cautious for some reason. I couldn't blame them. I guess I would be, too, if I were a deer. It's a sure bet that all of the cows and pigs had been killed and eaten long ago. Probably even the horses. Deer were the only substantial source of meat left, so they had undoubtedly been heavily pressured as of late.

They nervously made their way down the hedgerow, the power of thirst driving them to the water. As long as we remained quiet, everything would be fine. If I could, I'd wait until they were directly in front of me to fire. I knew that the deer couldn't smell us, even though I could surely smell myself, because the wind was still blowing straight into my face at a good clip.

I slowly raised my rifle and aimed it straight out in front of me, into the oncoming frigid wind. If I could manage to sit still long enough, the deer should walk right in front of me. I wasn't concerned about being spotted by the animals any longer, the curtain of darkness had finally dropped and the last of the twilight was quickly disappearing.

Moving nothing but my eyes, I watched the deer as they moved closer. Little puffs of white steam came from their noses as they advanced and I could hear the sound of their approaching footfalls.

If I can hold this pose for a few more seconds, I thought to myself, we'll be eating like kings tonight.

As they grew near our position, their gait seemed to quicken. Perhaps in their haste to quench their insatiable thirst they had suddenly forgotten about being so vigilant.

I'm sure that the animals didn't know we were there. I picked out the closest one and put my sights right behind it's bulging shoulder blade. Concentrating on making my frozen finger squeeze the trigger slowly, I hoped, for all of our sakes, that I didn't miss.

The SKS roared out it's presence to the still winter night. My frozen eardrums crackled like they were on the verge of exploding and my head was filled with a continually whining, high-pitched ring. It's true that it had been a while since I had fired a large caliber weapon and my ears had certainly gotten used to a quieter world, but I honestly couldn't remember that rifle ever sounding so loud.

16

    The deer bolted for the creek like runaway freight trains. Even though the ringing in my ears was exceedingly loud, I could still hear the sound of large splashes in the nearby water. "Did I miss?" I asked myself. "I couldn't have," I answered just as quickly. "That deer was way too close and I had taken my time. I had to have hit it."

    I stood up and called for Jacob to follow me. I didn't wait for him, though, I was far too anxious for that. Stepping out from the cover of the hedgerow, I started to quickly walk in the direction of the water. I had made it all the way down to the bottom of the steeply sloping creek bank when I heard Jacob call out behind me.

    "Where you at?" he asked the darkness.

    I whirled around and called back, "Down here, by the creek."

    The slope was very pronounced down there next to the water. When I looked back, I could make out the upper half of Jacob's body silhouetted against the newly emerging evening stars. Turning my attention back to the deer, I looked toward the creek, hoping hard to see some sign of our prey.

It was extremely dark next to the water's edge. Aided by the soft moonlight, I could see faint reflections on the rippling water as it flowed by. As the ringing in my ears slowly subsided, my eyes also began to adjust to the near total darkness. Peering through the pitch black shadows of the deeply cut creek bank, I spotted a large, stationary patch of white protruding out into the streaming black water.

My heart leapt boldly in my chest when I saw it because I knew what it had to be. Blood began to race through my veins and my breathing grew quick and short. I wanted to jump up and down and shout out loud in glorious joy, but I forced myself to stay quiet and move a little closer, needing to know for sure.

The buck was lying on his left side, tail outstretched from his body. The upper two thirds of the animal lay within the flow of the cold water. Part of his impressive rack broke through the water's surface like the branch of a small tree.

As Jacob reached the bottom of the slope, I turned and gave him a huge, celebratory bear hug. I'm certain that he must have thought I had lost my mind. A massive, silly looking grin adorning my face, I danced around in circles like the happy idiot that I was. I felt absolutely euphoric and, at first, the emotions of our success completely overwhelmed me. The meat that we harvested from that deer could mean the difference between life and death for our family and I'm not ashamed to say that it took a few moments for me to gain control of myself.

It felt like a ton of bricks had just fallen from atop my shoulders. I just couldn't wait to see the look on Kelli and Kaleb's faces. They would be so happy, too. By taking a series of deep breaths and thinking about all of the work that now needed to be done, I was finally able to calm myself down enough to properly function.

Jacob helped me drag the buck out of the water. We gutted it right next to the creek and threw everything of waste into the flowing water. If we wanted to stay in the area safely, it was best if we didn't leave any evidence of our presence.

When Jacob and I had finished field dressing the animal we were both a bloody mess up to our elbows. Kneeling at the edge of the water, we took the time to wash ourselves off now that the worst of it was over. By the time that we were done washing, our hands had gotten so cold in the near freezing water that they became nothing more than useless, unfeeling blobs. After sticking them inside the top of our pants and in our armpits for a couple of minutes, we started to get some of the feeling back in our frozen fingertips.

I wasn't worried about skinning the deer right then, we could take care of that later. Jacob and I cut it's head off, right at the top of the neck, and threw it into the middle of the rippling creek. Then, in order to be able to carry it, we began to cut the buck into quarters. Without the entrails and head, I guessed that we had about a hundred and twenty pounds of deer to carry back. Jacob and I could take half of the animal back right away and make a return trip later to get the rest.

At first, the thought of making two trips in the dark, carrying a heavy load of bloody, dripping deer meat didn't sound overly appealing. Then the vision of a joyously smiling Kelli burst to the forefront of my mind and I grabbed a skywardly protruding deer leg and happily hoisted the chunk of venison up onto my waiting shoulder. I heard Jacob groan as he followed suit and, together, we started out for our little shelter.

Even though the load was heavy and our shelter stood a good distance away, I couldn't help but smile.

17

When Jacob and I got back to the shelter, we stashed his deer quarter in a big snow drift about fifteen yards from our door. Hopefully, the snow bank would conceal the meat and keep it from spoiling until we could get back to it.

Kelli was so happy to see the large chunk of meat that she actually shed a few tears of joy. She worried herself endlessly about what would happen to us. It seemed like worrying had become her full time occupation.

Walter couldn't take his big, brown eyes off the massive piece of fresh venison. It must have smelled like heaven to the big dog in his half-starved condition. I rubbed the top of his furry head and promised him a full belly for supper that night.

Now that the elation of a successful hunt was beginning to wear off, I felt tired. The adrenaline that had boldly coursed through my veins a short while ago was dissipating and the heat inside our little shelter was feeling incredibly comfortable.

Kaleb, who had been dozing when we got back, sat up in his sleeping bag and surveyed the proceedings with red, sleep filled eyes. When he focused on the large chunk of fresh venison, a grin spread across his sleepy face and his eyes grew as large as silver dollars. Seeing him smile made me smile. The boy with the hummingbird's metabolism had went from being slit-eyed and groggy to fully alert in the blink of an eye. He looked almost as mesmerized by the food as Walter did. My heart felt a sudden pang of sorrow as I took in Kaleb's reaction. He had always been such a pleasant child and it hurt me to see him caught up in such a shitty mess.

I wanted badly to stay in that luxurious heat. I wanted to watch Kelli cook my steak, eat it and then go to sleep. But I knew that there was still more work to be done.

Kaleb volunteered to go back with me and retrieve the rest of the dead deer but I feared that he lacked the physical stamina to efficiently carry out the task. I thought that we could get it back to our shelter quicker if he stayed there with Kelli and Walter again. The look on Kaleb's face when I shared my thoughts with him made me feel really bad. I knew that he had been growing continually frustrated at having to take a back seat to his younger brother, but this was no time to let my emotions be overtaken by my sensibilities. We needed to get the rest of that deer back there, and as soon as possible.

"Don't worry, Kaleb," I told him, trying to soothe his bruised ego. "Tomorrow morning you'll have all the work that you can handle." From the look on his face I could tell that didn't help any, so I made a mental note to try and make it up to him later.

Kelli promised that she would have some big, juicy steaks ready for us when we returned with the rest of the deer. As Jacob and I left the warmth of our shelter and entered the chill of the dark winter's night, I honestly couldn't remember a time in my life when I had looked forward to a meal as much.

18

    The total opposite of his older brother, Jacob was bigger than most of his classmates. He loved being outdoors and used to play for hours by himself out in our little woods. Not nearly as outgoing as Kaleb, Jacob was far more introverted and shy; sometimes to the point of detriment. Unusually quiet around strangers, Jacob would often times go out of his way to ensure that he had no contact with them, whatsoever.
    Artistic and imaginative, he liked to draw and loved to listen to music. He enjoyed watching movies, especially comedies, and could bring an entire room full of people to laughter with one of his memorized, cinematic zingers. When he wanted to be, Jacob could be as hilarious as any person on the face of the planet. At least, to us.
    Kelli and I were certainly lucky to be raising such fine children, there was no doubt about that. Maybe that's why our heartache was so severe as we watched them toil and suffer through every day, just to stay alive.

19

Jacob and I made it back with the rest of the deer without incident. We stashed the remainder of the venison in the same snowdrift that we had put the other meat in earlier and wearily headed toward our shelter for some much needed rest.

Snow had begun to come down at a pretty good rate. The flakes were large and fluffy and floated down to the ground like little frozen parachutes. An unfamiliar feeling stole over me and it took me a moment to identify exactly what it was. When I finally did, I smiled in amazement. I felt content.

For the first time since this man made catastrophe had erupted it seemed like things were going our way. We had plenty of food, a decent shelter, and now the falling snow was erasing all traces of our presence. Perhaps I would be able to sleep a little more soundly, for a change. Wouldn't that be nice?

The old, rusty delivery truck probably didn't look like much to most people, but to Jacob and me, it sure was a beautiful sight. Jacob pulled open the shelter's door and we gleefully entered the luxurious warmth of our temporary abode.

The smell of grilling venison immediately excited my olfactory senses. My mouth watered as I took in the enticing aroma of the sizzling steaks. None of us had seen this much fresh meat in a long, long time and the thick, juicy steaks had understandably become the center of attention.

Not that anyone could blame us. We had eaten rabbits, skunks, squirrels and even cats, (although no one else knew what they were. I had skinned them while alone and told my family that they were baby fox,) but nothing of this size or quality. Our timing couldn't have been better.

Beaming a radiant smile, an obviously happy Kelli looked our way and said the words that Jacob and I had longed of hearing since we left the shelter, earlier.

"The steaks are done!"

She had cooked the thick slabs of meat perfectly and we all ate like madmen. Having been hungry for so long, we gorged ourselves on the tasty venison until we were dangerously bloated.

While Walter lay next to the firebox lazily chewing on his dessert - a big, marrow filled piece of deer bone, I dug into the bottom of my backpack and retrieved four of those little, tin foil wrapped, chocolate Santas. I felt like our recent success at finding a suitable shelter and harvesting a deer was cause enough for celebration.

When the boys saw the chocolate Santas they couldn't help but laugh out loud. All of us took our time eating them, savoring every little nibble of the velvety, chocolate goodness, except for Jacob. He unwrapped his and stuffed the whole thing into his mouth, all at once, with a devilish, little grin on his face.

The explosion of the candy's flavor in my mouth was almost indescribable. I couldn't believe that we used to take chocolate for granted. Used to take everything for granted, as far as that goes. My how times had changed.

We all got ready for bed and threw the biggest chunks of wood that we had on the fire. It felt so good knowing that we could finally relax and rest our aching bodies for a few days. Our bellies stuffed full of warm deer meat and smiles on our faces, one by one we slowly drifted off to dreamland.

20

Over the next four days we operated our own little jerky factory inside that old delivery truck. We sat up an assembly line to help speed up the drying process and operated it at full capacity until the job was finished. One of us would go outside to the snowdrift, dig out a piece of deer and bring it inside to thaw out. Once the meat was ready to go, it would be sliced into thin strips and placed on an improvised drying rack that we had made out of a couple of tree branches and some salvaged wire. The time went by fast and we made the best of it. We all got plenty of rest and endlessly stuffed ourselves full of venison jerky and thick, juicy steaks.

The only difficulty that arose during our blissful reprieve from the madness was trying to figure out how to store all of the jerky that we were making. We had a few Ziploc storage bags with us, but they didn't last very long. Even after looking through all of our belongings for anything that we might possibly be able to use, we still came up empty. With the jerky piling up quickly, we had no choice but to find some suitable way to store all of it.

On the third day of 'round the clock jerky production,

Kaleb and I made a daylight excursion back to Pierson's Sod Farm to look there. I wasn't overly thrilled about going back into their house, especially knowing that there were three rotting, dead bodies in there. But there was no other place around.

The first time that we were there I didn't get a chance to search through the upstairs; it was dark and I was in a hurry. As desperate as we were to find useful supplies, though, I knew that we couldn't pass up the opportunity.

I asked Kaleb to wait for me just inside the open entry door and cautiously climbed the wooden stairs to have a look around. Unable to locate anything that we could put to use on the second floor, I came back down the stairs to re-join Kaleb.

When I first saw him, he was standing off to the right at the foot of the stairs with a look of absolute horror on his face. Either unwilling or unable to speak, he could only point repeatedly toward the kitchen with large, staring eyes.

He had gotten curious while I had been foraging around upstairs and ended up finding the deceased residents.

Grabbing him by the shoulders, I turned his body around and herded him back toward the front of the house.

Once again positioning Kaleb next to the door, I now felt confident that I could go around the corner to look through the kitchen for plastic bags without him moving again.

The three mutilated bodies were still bound to their wooden platforms, and in the light of the bright, winter's day, the grizzly scene inside the room proved to be even more grotesque than before. The ghastly display of human carnage was beyond description. The bodies had begun to bloat and were bulging outward in discolored bands between their restraining ropes.

Something had begun to eat on the guy who's chest looked like a piece of Swiss cheese. Perhaps a dog or, even a coyote. The predator had dug a big hole into the swollen abdomen of the badly mangled, rotting corpse. The remains of the body's half eaten intestines limply dangled from the opening, surrounded by a cascade of nasty looking, pus-filled fluid.

Forcing myself to look away from the horrifying scene, I tried to concentrate on the reason that we went back there. In the end, I found a few re-sealable, gallon sized storage bags and a whole bunch of those thin, disposable shopping bags with handles. Happy with the success of our forage, we gladly left that horror filled house and never went back.

    Those little, plastic shopping bags turned out to be just the ticket. By the time that we were done cranking out our jerky, we had used all but a handful of the things. The rest of them were stuffed into our backpacks for later use. It didn't pay to throw away anything.

21

On our last evening inside the shelter of the delivery truck, we sat about feeling almost bored. After being as busy as a beehive for the last few days it seemed that we didn't quite know how to deal with our inactivity.

I think that we had mixed feelings about our situation. The shelter that we were staying in was the best one that we'd found since the whole damn ordeal had begun.

That first night we left our house had been a total nightmare. We were all scared half to death, thinking that the remaining thugs would track us down and kill us. Between the four of us, I don't think that we totaled eight hours of sleep.

The boys were absolutely miserable. They grumbled about everything and sulked about in a bad mood. Walter, on the other hand, thought that what we were doing must be some type of fantastic new game and was thoroughly enjoying himself.

Back then we had two big, blue tarps and a medium sized dome tent. The tent was long gone, having given in to the constant stress of the wild outdoors.

That first night out we were too afraid to set it up because we knew that it's bright, green color could be easily spotted in the bland winter landscape. Rolling ourselves up in crinkly, ice cold tarps, we spent the first night away from our home freezing and in a stuporous state of shock.

Like the rest of the human population, we were totally unprepared to survive out in the wild like this. But yet, we were still alive. I wasn't all too sure if you could call that being lucky or not, at that point. We had been through a lot and had no earthly idea what lay ahead. Even though we really liked our little, out of the way shelter, we knew that we couldn't stay in it forever. If we ever wanted to live a halfway normal life again, we had to move on. None of us were looking forward to trudging across the countryside through the mud, snow and ice again, but we had come too far to quit now.

I took out the maps that I had torn from our road atlas on the day we fled from our home. Three pages of colorful, folded paper that I hoped would lead us out of this dismal nightmare. I had taken page ninety-two, showing all of northern Ohio. Page fifty-seven, which showed the southern half of Michigan's mitten and page one hundred thirty-six, the map of what I hoped would be our final destination. Western Ontario, Canada.

I laid the pages down and put them together like a jigsaw puzzle on the truck's metal floor. Everyone carefully studied the three outstretched maps for quite a while before a single word was spoken. Then, over the next half hour or so, we discussed what we thought would be the best route to take.

Crossing over to Canada in the Detroit area was out of the question, who knew how many desperate, starving survivors would be in that heavily populated area? We felt that to try and cross there would be far too dangerous. Instead, we decided to circle around the western outskirts of the Detroit area and aim for the St .Clair River, just south of Port Huron.

Laying down to go to sleep that night, I lost myself in thoughts of the trail yet to come. I knew that the hardships ahead would be long and many. But I was also sure that no matter what future obstacles we may face, as long as we stuck together, we would be able to overcome just about anything.

22

The first day away from the truck's shelter we didn't make very much progress. The area that we were traveling in was full of a lot of open farm fields and it was difficult to move around without breaking cover. In country like that a person could be visible for miles under the right circumstances. If someone happened to spot us, we could be ambushed as easily as a bunch of sitting ducks.

Late in the day, with the sun sinking low, we found a decent place to hide near a sharp "S" bend in a lightly flowing creek. A large oak tree had fallen across the width of the creek's banks and it's enormous canopy filled the entire middle bend of the "S" shape. The upstream side of the tree's swathe of branches had been covered with a virtual wall of cornstalks, sticks and other assorted debris from repeated deluges of high water.

It didn't take us long to cover the other side of the tangled canopy with one of our big, blue tarps and close out most of the cold winter air. The boys gathered a large stack of dry firewood and we spent the evening talking quietly around the warm glow of a small fire.

Before the whole mess began we had lived on the northern edge of Findlay, Ohio. When we were forced to flee our home, we traveled pretty much straight north, keeping Interstate 75 about a quarter of a mile off to our right. Once we got around the Toledo metropolitan area, we used route 23 north as our guide. Knowing that the delivery truck we stayed in was located just a few miles north of Milan, our next big obstacle would undoubtedly be Detroit.

I brought up an idea that I had been thinking about. At first everyone looked at me like I was crazy, but after a thorough discussion of it's merits and drawbacks, we decided that it was indeed the best way for us to safely reach our goal.

We would travel only at night. Starting at dusk, we would hike throughout the night and find a suitable place to hide away during the daylight hours. It would be a pain in the ass, for sure, but we were together and we were alive, and as long as we stuck to the plan, we might just stay that way. We had plenty of food, so we wouldn't have to hunt for that, and besides, moving only at night wouldn't slow our progress any. In that part of the country, at this time of year, there is an almost exact, even split between daylight and darkness. Twelve hours each.

It didn't take long for us to adjust to our new nocturnal lifestyles. Our night vision rapidly grew more acute and we began to actually feel more comfortable moving around under the cover of darkness. If something happened to pop up along our path that looked safe, we scavenged what we could, but we stayed well clear of all towns and villages.

23

    Staying on our northerly course, we continued to move through nothing but rural territory, with very few houses and widely spaced, small towns. It stayed like that until we got closer to Detroit. About thirty miles outside of the city, the area started to become more densely populated and we frequently saw other people. It started to become hard to move around unnoticed and we all began to get kind of nervous. The sooner that we could get away from the place, the better off we'd be. One could only imagine the barbaric horrors taking place inside a city of that size, and my imagination was plenty close enough for me.

    On the night we neared the outskirts of the metropolis it was cloudy and dark. Jacob was the first one of us to spot the fires. Pointing ahead and slightly off to the right, he directed our eyes toward the yellowish, orange blob glowing low on the horizon. The closer that we got to the southwestern edge of Detroit, the more apparent the severity of the situation became.

    The sky was lit up for miles around and black, acrid smoke endlessly billowed up into the dark night. It looked like the whole city was on fire. Speechless, we watched in awe for a while as the wall of flames consumed everything standing in it's path.

It was a frightening and surreal experience witnessing a city burn. Never in my wildest dreams did I ever think that I would see such a thing, and I was deeply sorry that Kaleb and Jacob had witnessed it.

We tried hard not to look back as we moved on, but it was nearly impossible. Every time that we stopped for a short breather our eyes would automatically turn in that direction.

24

    Now that we were so close to Detroit, our progress became much slower. Not only did we see more and more people, we began to hear them as well. Mostly loud shouting and angry yelling, with the occasional banging and pounding to accompany someone's overly destructive tirade.
    When we got to the northwestern outskirts of Detroit, we were hard pressed to find our way without running into residential neighborhoods. Up until then we had always tried to avoid populated areas, but every acre of land around there was so highly developed that it was difficult for us to even find a vacant lot.
    At about midnight we ran into a situation where we had no choice but to go through a residential area.
    Although it was windy, it was relatively warm for a winter's night in Michigan. My internal thermometer told me that it was about forty degrees. Kaleb was wearing his favorite Cleveland Indians baseball cap. He usually wore his stocking cap but, due to the relatively mild temperature, he had decided to wear his baseball cap instead.
    We were walking through a large apartment complex trying to use whatever cover we could to help conceal our presence. Moving between two of the multi-storied buildings, a gust of unruly wind snatched Kaleb's cap from his head and sent it skittering across the asphalt parking lot in a semi-graceful, end

over end, rolling motion.

Kaleb looked mortified over the loss and could only watch helplessly as the wind drove his only prized possession away at break neck speed. He looked so exasperated and tired that I instantly felt sorry for him. I think we all did. Each of us had brought along an item that had special meaning to us. I had brought my guns. Kelli had brought along family pictures and other small momentos. Jacob had brought his Game Boy. Even though the batteries had run out long ago, he still refused to ditch the item, saying that sooner or later, he would find some batteries and be able to play his games once again. Kaleb's item had been his Indians' cap.

Jacob generously volunteered to go and retrieve it but I didn't like the idea of any of us being alone, even long enough to chase down a baseball cap. Since we hadn't stopped to take a break for a while, I thought we could kill two birds with one stone.

"Why don't we all go get it?" I proposed. I pointed toward a little storage shed about fifty feet from where the hat's progress was stopped by a chain link fence. "We'll pick up the hat and then take a rest in that little building over there for a few minutes."

No one voiced any objections, so we headed that way. As we neared the small, metal structure, Jacob veered off slightly to go and pick up Kaleb's cap.

The doors of the shed were open and trashed littered the plywood floor. The riding lawn mower that used to occupy the space was parked out front, no doubt emptied of it's gas. Gardening tools lined the inside of the walls. They reminded me of how much Kelli used to like to work in her garden, back home.

It felt really nice to be out of the gusty wind. I released the straps on my backpack and sat the bulk down next one of the metal walls. Jacob entered the shed with Kaleb's hat in one hand and held it out in front of his older brother.

"Thank you, Jacob," Kaleb softly mumbled.

Jacob nodded in response and turned to set his pack down next to ours. Before he had a chance to sit down, himself, I asked, "Jacob, will you slide the door closed a little bit to help keep out the wind, please?" Without a word, Jacob reached back and slid the shed's doors closed most of the way.

As Jacob sat down on the floor next to Kelli I noticed some sort of movement out in the apartment complex's parking lot. After doing a long double take, I finally figured out what it was. It had taken a moment for me to register what I was looking at because I had never seen anything quite like it before. It was a large gang of scruffy looking hellions, armed to the teeth and riding bicycles.

Everyone else must have noticed the look on my face because they followed my gaze and turned to take in the bizarre sight for themselves. We all stared mutely, totally awestruck by what we were seeing. A genuine, honest to goodness, leather jacket wearing, machine gun toting bicycle gang.

There looked to be between twelve and fifteen of them and they appeared to be in no real hurry as they casually pedaled by. Even in the dark of night the group looked exceedingly shabby. To me, it looked like they had just pedaled their bicycles through the middle of a bad grunge storm.

If I had been in a better mood I might have even laughed out loud at the absurdity of the sight; but I'm glad that I wasn't. The bicycle riding bullies did look a little bored and the last thing that we needed to do was draw their attention toward us.

They cruised by in total silence, eyeing the area like a pack of hungry wolves on the prowl. After they had passed out of sight we looked around at each other in wide eyed disbelief. Did we *really* just see that?

Kaleb lifted his face to Kelli and with wide eyes whispered, "It's a good thing that we weren't still out there walking."

A good thing, indeed! As the realization dawned on us that we had just barely dodged a catastrophic disaster, we all breathed a big, collective sigh of relief. Coming out of the darkness and in those numbers, they could have easily taken us all out. From that day forward, we started calling Kaleb's baseball hat our family's lucky charm.

Seeing that band of two wheeled whackos really gave us a jolt. We ended up staying inside that metal storage shed for the rest of that night and all of the next day, until dusk. If we weren't busy sleeping, we huddled together in our sleeping bags and chewed on deer jerky. Actually, I guess it wasn't all that bad. We did get to sleep out of the biting wind for a change and if it snowed, we had a roof over our heads.

25

    Once that we got away from the worst part of Detroit, our spirits improved and we started to make decent time again. It was so nice to be back out in the open where we could talk and laugh again without constantly being afraid that someone might hear us. The further away from the city that we got, the better we all slept. Being able to relax and let down our guard a little bit seemed to help our frayed nerves a lot.

    For miles on end outside the big city we passed by a multitude of dark factories, office buildings and convenience stores. Every mile that we walked, it seemed as though we saw something different. Automobile dealerships, strip malls and big box stores lined every crossroad that we passed.

    We tried to steer clear of most of them but sometimes our curiosity would get the best of us. If one of us had a particular need for a certain item and we passed by a place that looked as though it might supply it, we checked it out. In a clothing store at one of the strip malls we found a nice down jacket and two pairs of pants that fit Kaleb. At a TSC store we found a pair of wool socks that we badly needed and a large box of dog biscuits. Walter's favorite, too. Beef flavored.

Without a doubt, the best thing that we found was toilet paper. Six glorious rolls of the fluffy stuff. Having to go to the bathroom without toilet paper was one of the worst aspects of the whole mess. Whoever made up that old saying about never knowing what you had until it was gone must have been talking about toilet paper. When Kelli saw it her eyes lit up like she had just hit the jackpot in Las Vegas. She had such a beautiful smile and, although it was a rare occurrence at the time, it was nice to see. It always made me feel so good when she was happy.

We were eating well again, thanks to the plethora of canned goods that we found stashed in an old barn. There were beans of every kind. Green beans, lima beans, kidney beans. You name it, it was probably there. There were sliced carrots, diced potatoes and even a few cans of soup. Also included in the stash were two boxes of saltine crackers and four boxes of instant mashed potatoes. None of it could be confused with gourmet fare, but it was better than eating nothing but jerky.

We were really happy about finding all the food, but not so happy about having to tote all the extra weight. I tried to carry as much of the burden as I could because I was the one who insisted on bringing every last item. As time went by I was certain that there would be less and less food available, so I was very reluctant to leave anything behind. Our backpacks bulging with canned goods and jerky, we marched northward and away from the Detroit Metro area. Once we crossed over Route 75, we set our sights on skirting the north side of Pontiac and then heading due east, toward the St. Clair River.

Our spirits were high and some of the spring had returned to our step. The last leg of our long and arduous journey lay ahead. Loaded down with food and feeling better than we had at any other point during our trek, we were confident that the rest of the trip would be a piece of cake.

26

Numerous lakes dotted the area and whenever possible we would stop and shelter for the day near one of them. The only fishing pole that we had with us was one of those tiny, hand held, survival-style, spool reels. We also had a few extra bobbers and some hooks in a miniature plastic tackle box; the bobbers no bigger around than a nickel.

Fishing provided us with the first real enjoyment that we'd had since the whole mess began, and enjoy it we did. It always seemed to help relieve some of our pent up frustrations and made us feel a lot better. Every chance that we got to drop a line in the water we took full advantage of. For a short period of time we ate plenty of canned goods and all the fresh fish that we could catch.

We all liked the sport so much that it was only natural for us to compete with each other for bragging rights. Jacob started it all. One day he caught a couple of bluegill near the bank and immediately let everyone else know that we were now having a fishing tournament and he was in the lead. "And it's going to stay that way," he triumphantly announced, for good measure. Unfortunately for Jacob, though, it didn't stay that way for very long, at all.

Kaleb hooked into a nice bass that was nearly a foot

long, late that afternoon. He pulled the fish onto the shore of the lake with a mighty tug and proudly hoisted it above his head in triumph. I knew that he wanted so badly to scream out in delight. He energetically danced about on the shoreline with his prized trophy held high for all the world to see.

Kelli and I watched Kaleb's animated celebration from the nearby tree line, smiling from ear to ear with both pride and pleasure. Alerted by Kaleb's burst of sudden activity, Walter ran over to see what all of the excitement was about.

The wet fish began to flop around wildly when Kaleb reached into it's mouth to remove the deeply imbedded fish hook. He managed to successfully free the hook from the wriggling animal's mouth, but as soon as he did, the fish slipped from his slime impaired grasp and quickly dropped downward.

It hit the ground and began to thrash about wildly in an attempt to make it's way back to the safety of it's watery realm. Kaleb, determined to not let that happen, dropped down on his knees in a desperate bid to close off the fish's apparent escape route.

Jacob had made his way to the scene of action by then and grabbed onto Walter's collar to help try and keep the rapidly deteriorating situation under control.

In a series of moves that would have made Barry Sanders envious, the fish began to flap his tail in a frenzied flourish and expertly evaded Kaleb's clawing fingers. It started to rapidly bound back down the bank toward the waiting water and that's when Walter made his move.

Unable to contain himself any longer, he bulldozed forward and broke free of Jacob's grip. In an instant the big dog was down at the lake's edge with the violently shaking fish hanging from one side of his muzzle. Eager to show off his lively catch, Walter pranced back up the gradually sloped bank with his thick, bushy tail raised at high mast.

Kaleb spent the next five minutes furiously chasing Walter around the lake trying to get his fish back. The rest of us were too busy laughing our heads off to be of much help.

In the end, we decided to score the catch for Kaleb and credit Walter with the assist. Laughter is often said to be the best medicine of all, and that day there was no doubt in my mind that it went a long way toward easing the deep seated pain that lurked just below the surface within all of us.

27

It didn't take us very long to become experts at cooking over a fire during the daylight hours without making very much smoke. Using nothing but dead, standing timber for our fires, we took the time to patiently shave a stick down into pieces of kindling barely bigger than a wooden match to get the fire going. Careful not to smother the fire by putting pieces of wood on that were too big, too soon, we took our time and built it up very slowly. As long as we fed the fire dry wood and left plenty of space between the sticks for air to pass, we could cook all day long virtually smoke free.

On the day that we left home, we had one full book of waterproof matches and a lighter in our possession. I took great pride in being able to start a fire with a single flick of the lighter, in most cases. If I could continue my streak of good luck, even if the lighter did finally run out, we should still have more than enough matches to last until we crossed the border.

28

    A few nights after we rounded Pontiac we ran into what was easily the worst weather of the trip, thus far. The wind began to howl ferociously and showed absolutely no sign of slowing down. Easily topping forty miles an hour, with gusts much higher, the wind was blowing almost straight out of the west, helping push us along to our destination.
    In an attempt to combat the biting wind, we decided to shelter for the day in a large grove of thick pine trees. We found two big spruce trees that were close enough to shake hands in the middle of our little Christmas tree world and pitched our sleeping bags underneath. Even with an evergreen forest completely encircling us, the wind was still able to snake it's way through.
    The boys crawled into their sleeping bags and went to sleep talking about Canada and all of the things that they would do once they got there. Kelli and I lay there listening to their wishful chatter and watching the pine boughs dance back and forth in the stiff breeze.
    Looking at all of the evergreen trees around us, my thoughts turned in the direction of Christmases past. Lost in those wonderful memories and smiles of long gone holiday seasons, I slowly nodded off into a deep and blissful sleep.

29

My first hint that something was wrong came when I woke up at about noon and the whole bottom of my sleeping bag was completely soaked. Not only had the high winds brought a severe weather front and heavy downpours, it had also stripped away both of the tarps that served as our only shelter from the harsh elements. I had no idea how long they had been missing, but from the way my legs felt, it had definitely been for a while. Looking in the direction that the wind was blowing, I could see no trace of them, whatsoever.

Kelli and the boys were still sleeping soundly, in spite of the drenching rain. Jacob was curled into a ball at the top of his sleeping bag. It looked like he had decided that, water or no water, he was still going to get his sleep.

After about fifteen or twenty long minutes, the rain finally slackened a little. I woke Kelli and told her what had happened.

"I'm going to put on our raincoat and go look for them," I told her. A look of concern immediately came over her groggy face.

"Do you have to?" she asked.

"Unfortunately, yes," I answered. "If I don't, we won't have any way to keep the rain and snow off of us." Reluctantly, she nodded her agreement in my direction.

"Be careful," she ordered.

I dug through Kaleb's backpack for our one and only raincoat and slipped it on.

Pulling the hood up over my head, I started walking downwind to look for our wayward tarps.

The wind was blowing fiercely and it felt like the temperature had started to fall. I followed the likely path of our lost tarps for about three or four minutes before I found one of them. Actually, the remnants of one. The ragged remains were wrapped around a tree looking so tattered and torn that Freddy Krueger would have had trouble matching the level of destruction, on a good day.

Saddened by the sight, I moved on to try and locate the other one. I walked on downwind for at least five more minutes, and maybe more, without seeing any sign of it.

Those tarps were so important to our survival. They were the only barrier that we had to keep the wind and the water off of us during inclimate weather. "How could you have been so careless?" I scolded myself. I should have taken the time to properly anchor them down instead of just stuffing them under the edges of our sleeping bags.

"Please," I pleaded to the whistling wind and pounding rain. "Please, just give me a glimpse of it."

But no matter where I looked or how hard I tried, I could find nothing. I wanted to keep on looking so badly because I didn't want to go back empty handed. Being without a tarp in that cold, driving rain would spell serious trouble for our family. I looked about desperately, hoping to spot anything that might offer a clue.

But, try as I might, I could spot nothing. In wind like this, I thought to myself, I wouldn't be surprised if that tarp was a hundred miles away by now. Hesitantly, I turned around and walked back toward the middle of the pine grove with my head hung low.

The wind seemed to be blowing harder now that I was on my way back. The gusts were incredibly strong and they were blowing straight into my face. Worse yet, I could feel the air growing colder by the minute. The sky was a tangled mass of black and gray clouds that appeared to be continually jostling with each other for position. Without any sort of shelter, except for the already wet clothes that we now wore, it wasn't exactly what I was hoping to see.

30

When I got back to Kelli and the boys I didn't have to say a word. My empty hands told the whole story. The forlorn look in my family's eyes echoed what I was feeling inside.

I removed our rain jacket and handed it to Kaleb. He had less mass than the rest of us and was more susceptible to chills. We were getting hopelessly drenched by the freezing cold rain and the temperature was dropping fast. Having had enough of Murphy's Law for one day, I wasn't about to ask what else could go wrong.

We sat Indian style underneath the pine trees, keeping as close as possible to the trunks. Holding our sleeping bags up over our heads like a makeshift tent helped to keep the worst of the weather off of us, at least for a while. Before long, though, it didn't seem to matter. The wind was driving the rain so hard that it flew in nearly horizontal sheets. Regardless of the pine trees and the sleeping bags draped over our heads, we got hopelessly drenched. We felt so miserable sitting there that our morale started to plummet to a dangerously low level and we fell into a semi-conscience state of stupor.

Meanwhile, the temperature continued to steadily fall.

None of us noticed until it had grown to about an eighth of an inch thick, but a layer of ice had begun to form on the ground and trees. Jolted back to reality by the sobering sight, the seriousness of our predicament hit me like a ton of bricks. If we didn't find a way to get warm soon, our situation would take a very grave turn.

I thought about trying to build a fire, but as soon as it entered my mind I dismissed it. With all of the rain that had come down earlier, now underneath a building layer of ice, we didn't stand a chance of finding any dry wood. Our only hope of staving off hypothermia was to find a good shelter and, hopefully, something to burn for heat.

As we began to walk the wind blew freezing rain on us with what felt like the force of a hand held, do it yourself car wash wand. We became so waterlogged that it felt like we had just jumped into a swimming pool, fully clothed. Our coats, hats, boots, gloves and everything else became totally saturated with the frosty cold water. The ice was slowly beginning to grow thicker and every time that we took a step it sounded like we were walking on top of a bed of broken light bulb shards.

I hoped like hell that no one else was in the area. Without a second of time to spare we crossed over open fields and down the middle of the roads, instead of sticking to cover, like normal. At that point we didn't have the luxury of worrying about our safety. If we didn't find some shelter and dry off soon, we were all going to die of hypothermia, anyway.

I was starting to lose the feeling in my fingertips and toes, I'm sure that we all were. Being soaked in freezing cold ice water and continually assaulted by the outrageously strong gusts of wind was causing our body temperatures to drop fast.

A row of buildings that looked like businesses appeared through the driving sheets of freezing rain. They stood in line like soldiers just beyond the upcoming crossroad. I guessed that they were about a quarter of a mile away from us across the open field that we were traversing.

I truly hoped that we would make it that far. I had terrible thoughts going through my mind about my legs freezing solid and leaving me unable to walk. If something like that happened it could easily spell our doom. I don't think that I had the strength to help someone else up if they fell down. I doubt any of us did. The shaking in our muscles grew to be so severe that they became useless from the cold and fatigue. It got to be so bad that I had to consciously think about lifting each foot and bending my knees in order to make any forward progress.

Walter's fur became so saturated with shiny ice crystals that he looked like a giant, walking ice cube with feet. He must have been carrying around an extra twenty pounds in frozen water.

Our lower jaws convulsed so badly that we were unable to speak clearly. Every time that we tried to talk it came out as nothing but jumbled garble, and half the time we would end up biting our tongues.

We had closed to within a hundred yards of the buildings by then, but it might as well have been a mile. I began to have serious doubts that we would be able to make it that far.

My eyelids had nearly frozen shut and it was almost impossible for me to see clearly. I had never even been close to being that cold before. Funny, I used to think that I got cold when I went out early in the morning to start my freezing truck and scrape the frost off the windows. What a joke!

Squinting through my ice encrusted eyelids, I checked out the building that was directly ahead of us. I could barely make out the letters on the big, red sign that sat out front through all of the windblown, freezing rain.

Foster's Furniture, it read. I kept my eyes peeled on the place as we edged closer, searching for the closest entrance. I didn't care if anyone else was inside or not, we were going in.

With my first shuffling step onto the store's asphalt parking lot, I found the footing to be insanely unsure. After walking across nothing but open fields and on grassy surfaces to get there, I had developed a certain false sense of security. I put my left foot down on the edge of the icy blacktop and picked up my right to step forward. When I did, my left foot started to move forward and out from under me. Still lagging behind me, my right leg never did get the chance to find a suitable footing.

I started to slide forward on my left foot like a figure skater competing in the winter Olympics. My right foot tried desperately but could find nothing but a toe hold. Not nearly enough of a foundation to counteract the powerful forces of gravity. I started to feel my body fall backward, and for some reason, all I could picture in my mind was Fred Sanford. Fred, standing there with a hand on his heart and a dramatically pained look on his face, saying, "This is it. I'm comin' to join ya 'Lizbeth, in that great big skatin' rink in the sky."

    I thought that I would fall, right there in the parking lot of a potentially life saving shelter, and lay there unable to muster the necessary strength to right myself. Except, I never did fall. My right knee came down with a solid crack on the slick, icy surface. I slid forward for about another ten feet before I came to a complete stop. Even though my body was stiff and frozen, I could still feel white hot pain explode through the knee that I had landed on.

    I heard a bevy of barely audible, mumbled words behind me. If I turned my head as far as I could and looked from the corner of my eye, I could see my family. In spite of their faces being so frozen that they could barely move them, I still saw concern. They had all stopped short of the parking lot after witnessing my ungainly acrobatic display.

    I wanted to raise an arm and signal that I was okay but neither one of them wanted to work. They felt solidly frozen to my sides. My right leg felt like it had broken completely in two at the kneecap. I couldn't exactly decide which was worse, having numb, frozen legs or legs that screamed out in pain.

    I looked back at the furniture store. The big display window to the right of the door had been broken out. At first glance the front door looked fine, but as my eyes focused a little better I could see that the glass in it had also been busted out.

    I heard a mumbling behind me again, this time a lot closer. Turning to look, I could see Kelli cautiously inching her way toward me.

    Walter didn't have a clue what all the fuss was about. He had little trouble negotiating on the slippery sheet of ice. He walked over to me and planted a big, sloppy lick on my frozen right cheek.

    Kaleb and Jacob looked reluctant to step out on the ice covered blacktop. At least their *brains* aren't frozen, I thought to myself.

    Walter licked me again. I turned my head away and tried to say "good dog, good dog," but it came out sounding like someone trying to start up a weed whacker.

    Kelli had almost made it to me by then. The boys had even ventured out onto the ice coated parking lot, but it didn't look like they were in too big of a hurry. The combined efforts of Kelli lifting up and me pushing down on the top of Walter's back, allowed me to gain my feet again.

Walking side by side with linked arms, Kelli and I made our way forward in a much more stable manner, while Walter casually trotted back toward the boys with no apparent effort. I suppose if I had four legs and wore a pair of baseball cleats around the clock, I wouldn't be having any problems, either.

As our tandem shuffled away toward the entrance, I looked back and saw that Kaleb and Jacob had mimicked us and were also edging forward, arm in arm.

We finally made it to the store's doorway only to be confronted with another obstacle. The glass in the doorway was missing alright, but the metal bar that needed to be pushed in order to exit was still in place, effectively splitting the opening in half. Way too cold to move unless I had to, I just looked at Kelli and rolled my eyes.

I tried to lower myself slowly but no longer had control over my frozen legs. Crashing down into a kneeling position, a fresh bout of pain tore through my body. It felt as though my right knee had just landed on top of a red hot poker. With no time to worry about it at the moment, I dropped forward on my hands and began to crawl through the bottom half of the store's front door.

31

    As soon as I got through the doorway and could no longer feel the biting wind, the temperature felt as if it instantly rose twenty degrees. I had entered the main showroom of Foster's Furniture store. Brushing past me, Walter trotted into the display room and began to busily sniff about.
    It looked as if the looting inside the store had been very minimal. After all, you couldn't eat furniture, and these days there was a much larger supply than demand. If you had survived the recent, man-made catastrophe and desired a new couch, you didn't go shopping for one, you just picked out one that you liked from your own block. Aside from minor vandalism and the few broken windows, the place appeared to be unscathed.
    I looked behind me as Kelli came in through the doorway. She must have held back for a minute to make sure that the boys were going to be alright.
    Turning to face the showroom again, I started to crawl toward a nearby chair that had been knocked onto it's side. Positioning my hands on top of the chair's armrest, I used the piece of furniture to help me stand up.

Checking on everyone else to gauge their progress, I saw that Kelli had nearly made it to the chair lying next to me and Jacob was now crawling in through the bottom of the door's opening. Kaleb stood on the other side of the doorway patiently waiting his turn to enter. Focusing my attention on the inside of the store, I could see that it was filled with a large assortment of furniture. Tables, dressers, couches and chairs stretched the entire length and width of the huge showroom. The shipping and receiving area was located against the far, back wall. On the left side of the big building were clearly marked his and hers bathrooms and a little office.

I forced my frozen body in the direction of the bathrooms, glancing back once more to check on everyone. Kaleb was now completely inside the building and catching up to Jacob fast. As elated as I was to know that we were all finally out of the nasty, life threatening weather, we would still almost certainly die if we couldn't get warm.

Because it was the closer of the two, I pushed open the gray, steel door of the women's bathroom and peered inside. The floor was covered in solid, white ceramic tiles. Looking up, I saw that the ceiling was a grid work of white, acoustical tiles. Perfect for what I had in mind.

Using the business end of my rifle barrel, I poked up on one of the ceiling tiles and pushed it aside. A large, black rectangle appeared in the middle of the white bathroom ceiling, just right for allowing smoke and noxious fumes to escape.

Using my teeth, I pulled off my gloves and tossed them aside. Lifting the release catch located on the shoulder strap of my backpack took so long that by the time I had accomplished the task, Kelli and Jacob had already entered the room and Kaleb was pushing his way in through the heavy, metal door.

I slung my pack against the tile wall near the baby changing station and tried to get my frozen fingers to open the compartment containing our matches. The buckle was packed so full of ice that I couldn't get the nylon catch to release. A steady torrent of obscenities rushed from my frozen face. I became so angry that I could no longer control my emotions. We had just battled our way through an epic ice storm and barely made it to a place of shelter. Every step of the way was pure hell. To think that we had done all of that only to end up dying, anyway, totally infuriated me.

Being stubborn is certainly not one of my better traits, but in this situation it served me quite well. I absolutely refused to give in. I resolved myself to getting that buckle open, one way or another.

Grabbing my rifle, I began banging the butt of it up against the ice clogged pack buckle. After about three or four good wallops I heard a gasp behind me. I looked that way involuntarily, without stopping my assault on the frozen buckle.

Kaleb and Jacob were looking at me as if I'd lost my marbles. Their eyes seemed to say, "Oh great, the old man's gone bonkers. We're toast for sure, now."

Looking back at my pack I noticed that most of the ice around the buckle had disappeared. I pushed my frozen fingers against the sides of the buckle and it reluctantly clicked open. Trying to calm myself down, I took in a deep breath and slowly exhaled. The lid of the compartment lifted easily.

I stuck my cold, stiff fingers inside and pulled out the small, plastic container that held our matches. Holding it up to my mouth, I used my teeth to pop the lid open. Dumping the book of matches out into the palm of my hand, I stared at the little square of cardboard like it was as breathtaking and fascinating as the Hope Diamond, itself. What a lifesaver, I thought to myself. Only this time it was more than just a cute little quip. It was for real.

I gave the plastic container to Kelli and she laid it on top of the large, double sink attached to the bathroom wall. The matches had made it through the storm without getting wet but they were still useless without something to burn.

Everyone else had dropped their packs by then and were looking at me, expectantly.

"Kaleb and Jacob," I said, through jittering teeth. "You guys go find the lightest pieces of wood that you can and bring them in here, on the double." The boys started for the door and I turned my gaze to Kelli. "You come with me," I told her.

Kaleb and Jacob split off and headed toward the showroom floor while Kelli and I made a beeline for the store's office. The glass window had been broken out and the door to the room stood wide open. The desk had been ransacked and reams of paper from the filing cabinets were scattered everywhere. What a beautiful sight.

Stepping over next to the open filing cabinets, I started to to stack as many files that I could possibly carry into my arms. Kelli followed my lead and began to dig into the metal cabinet standing next to mine.

Toting the heavy armload of paper back to the women's bathroom, I dropped the files on top of the big, white sink. Kelli pushed her way in through the door and Kaleb was right behind her. He was carrying two dresser drawers, one dangling from the end of each arm.

I motioned for him to put them on the tile floor and grabbed a large handful of paper from the sink. I stood both drawers on end and placed them side by side in the middle of the bathroom floor. I began to clumsily crumble sheets of paper and pile them in and around the standing drawers.

Jacob burst in carrying a rocking chair and dropped it with a bang, just inside the door.

Looking up, I said to the boys, "Get more. Lot's more."

Kelli knelt next to me and began to madly crush the sheets of paper between her palms until they became loosely packed paper balls. Working together, it didn't take long for us to bury the bottom of the drawers in a small mountain of crushed paper kindling.

Kaleb returned with two more dresser drawers and Jacob wrestled an end table through the metal door.

I opened the matchbook cover and attempted to tear out a match but my fingers were shaking badly from the constant quivering of my frozen muscles. Finally, I managed to get a good enough grip on one of them to yank it free. I looked at the match that I held between my half frozen thumb and forefinger. What a strange world we live in, I thought, when such a tiny thing like this could hold the key to our family's future existence. This skinny little strip of paper that had been soaked in a few chemicals and dipped in sulpher would decide whether we lived or died. Half sitting and half falling, I parked myself on the white tile floor next to the standing dresser drawers. I pressed the tip of the match to the friction strip and pushed. A small, snapping sound came from the end of the match, immediately followed by a puff of smoke and a small, sputtering flame.

32

  My heart jumped at the sight. I carefully lowered the trembling match next to the small pile of crumpled kindling.
  The flame eagerly took to the dry filing paper and began to quickly spread. The light colored wood of the dresser drawer began to darken, almost immediately. A yellow flame appeared a few seconds later and began to dance it's way up the newly charred wooden surface. I couldn't help but notice that all of our eyes were locked on the rapidly growing fire.
  When I laid another drawer on top of the two standing ones, I broke the growing flame's mesmerizing spell. Having gained everyone's attention, once again, I told them all to undress. Looking back at me with alarm in their eyes, the trio's expressions seemed to ask, "Did I just hear you correctly?"
  Kelli voiced what they were all thinking. "Undress?" she asked. "Are you crazy? We're already freezing and it's cold in here."
  I repeated myself and tried to explain that the only way we would stay alive was by undressing and warming ourselves next to the fire.
  The flames climbing up the dresser drawers were getting

bigger by the second and I could feel heat beginning to emanate from them. I removed my waterlogged coat and flung it against the bathroom's wall to show my family that I was serious. "Come on," I yelled. "Get undressed." After exchanging a series of doubtful, questioning looks again, they reluctantly began to remove their own heavy, wet, outer clothing.

I headed toward the door and told Kelli, "I'll be right back."

As I swung the door inward, Walter squeezed his way into the bathroom. Brushing past me, the massive dog headed over to sniff the boys and check out the ever growing fire.

I went back to the showroom looking for something that was heavy and would burn for a long time.

Starting for the middle of the huge showroom, I began to carefully scan it's contents. Couches and chairs were of no use. The foam stuffing would emit a ton of toxic smoke and fumes, and the last thing that we needed to do was compound our problems.

I spotted five desks sitting in a row halfway between me and the broken out picture window at the front of the store. Drawing closer, I could tell that these weren't the new lightweight computer desks made out of pressed board or plywood. These were the old style, secretary desks, made out of solid hardwood. The only difference between the five of them was the shade of the wood's finish and the color, and style of the hardware.

I thumped on one of them with the knuckles of my right hand. It certainly sounded solid. Lifting up on a corner of one of the desks a little confirmed that it was, indeed, a well constructed piece of furniture. "Bingo," I said. I would need some help to move the heavy desks, but the heavier they were, the longer they would put off life-saving heat.

My step was a bit lighter on the way back to the ladies room.

As I opened the door a blast of warm, dry air hit me in the face. I can't even begin to describe how heavenly it felt. All three of the dresser drawers were now fully engulfed in flames and the temperature difference inside of the room was already dramatic.

Kelli was the farthest along of the bunch and was in the process of removing her red long johns. Kaleb was busily tugging on his wet pants and Jacob was standing close to the fire unlacing his boots. Walter looked like he was melting. The big dog's ice covered coat was thawing at a brisk pace and, except for a few scattered clumps clinging here and there, was almost gone.

Joining my family by the fire, I began to disrobe as fast as I possibly could. I was the last one of us to make it all the way down to my underwear. By that time the fire had begun to die down a pinch so I grabbed the last remaining drawer and threw it onto the burning pile.

Without any sort of barrier to get in the way, the heat from the flames was particularly intense. We rotated a little bit at a time trying to soak in the warmth from every angle. When the last dresser drawer had passed it's peak, I grabbed the rocking chair by it's armrests and placed it in the fire.

The glare of the heat felt so exquisite. Our shivering and shaking finally stopped and we were all starting to warm up nicely. A mixture of pure adrenaline and primal fear had been the only thing that had saved us. But, now that we felt relatively safe and gloriously warm, all of our remaining energy started to promptly vanish. Big, open mouth yawning, red eyes and drooping eyelids replaced the rubbing of hands over the fire. We were getting tired. I jolted everyone back to reality.

"Before anybody nods off," I said. "I'm going to need some help dragging a few desks in here."

Kaleb raised his eyes in a hopeful manner. "All of us?" he asked.

"Yes," I replied. "It's going to take all of us."

To ensure that the fire didn't go out while we were busy hauling the desks, I added the end table to the blaze.

Our first trip out to the showroom was the worst, by far. After beginning to feel toasty warm again, having to walk out of the bathroom and back into the cold showroom, dressed only in our underwear, was tantamount to pure torture.

Working in pairs, we grabbed two of the heavy desks and, through a combination of pushing and pulling, managed to finally get both of them into the ladies room. We scooted one of them over the fire right away and used the other one to hang our wet clothes over to dry.

It took quite a while for the first desk to be consumed by the ravenous flames. By the time that it was we had enough dry clothing to hold the worst of the chill at bay on our next trip out to the showroom. Two more heavy desks reluctantly found their way into the women's bathroom.

Now that we had a moment to relax and catch our breath, the growling in my stomach became much more noticeable. For the next hour, or so, we ate deer jerky and silently watched the dancing flames chew away at the large desk.

Kaleb was asleep by then. He had crawled into the first dry sleeping bag and was out like a light. Jacob and I made a run for the last desk while Kelli shuffled our drying items about. We parked the remaining desk right outside the bathroom's door and then went looking for more good wood. Locating two more heavy end tables and a long, low chest of drawers, we also placed them within easy reach, right outside the bathroom door.

Jacob's sleeping bag had dried by then, so he laid down to get some sleep. Kelli and I kept ourselves busy the rest of the night by drying out our remaining belongings and keeping the fire going.

33

We ended up staying in the furniture store for two days and nights. Taking turns in our four person rotation, we split our time between sleeping, busting up furniture and standing watch. Whoever wasn't on watch would either be breaking up furniture to burn or trying to get some sleep. After two days of rest and recovery, we were itching to move on again.

According to my best calculations and page fifty seven from our atlas, Canada was only about forty miles away. The colorful map page showed nothing but open land dotted with small towns between our present location and the St. Clair River.

Since we had made it that far, I was confident that we would be able to complete the remaining part of the trip, as well. The real problem, I thought, would come in trying to cross the river and get into Canada. But that was a problem for another day.

We said goodbye to the furniture store and headed on our way, the closeness of our target making us more determined than ever before to complete the journey.

34

Since we had been in somewhat of a hurry when we came in, we hadn't had time to notice what other buildings were in the area. We decided to walk down the road a little bit and have a look around before heading cross country again.

About two hundred yards down the road, on the right hand side, stood an Army/Navy Surplus Store. My eyes lit up at the sight.

"Wow," I exclaimed. "I wonder what we can find in there."

As we drew closer my expectations diminished greatly. The parking lot was littered with the store's merchandise and almost every window that I could see had been broken out. The place looked like it had been doing a brisk business. After all, what better place to go after a disaster than your friendly neighborhood surplus store?

I almost decided not to go in but just couldn't seem to help myself. Every time that I went in one of those places I was like a kid in a candy store. I always seemed to find something that I couldn't do without.

"Maybe we could find some more tarps," I thought, out

loud.

"That would be great, if we could," replied Kelli, her eyebrows lifted in a hopeful manner.

In front of the store we split into two groups. Kelli and Jacob would wait outside the front of the store while Kaleb and I went in. Taking off our backpacks, we sat them on the ground near where Kelli and Jacob were standing and walked to the front door.

Upon first entering the store, I noticed that it was very dark inside. A maze of high shelving covered the walls and clogged the floor space. Most of their contents were on the floor, though, and Kaleb and I had been walking on piles of merchandise from the moment we entered.

The further that we went into the surplus store, the more difficult it became to walk. Every imaginable kind of outdoor gear lay in tangled masses throughout the narrow walkways. Except, of course, for tarps. Feeling discouraged but knowing how important they were to us, Kaleb and I decided to look around a bit more before giving up. After all, I figured, they had to be somewhere.

As we searched through the heavily cluttered building trying to find the tarps, we happened upon a little clear spot on the messy floor. Since we were only about twenty feet from the back wall of the store and I could plainly hear Kaleb's labored breathing, I suggested that he wait for me there while I finished having a look around.

Climbing over endless piles of jumbled surplus articles, I finally reached the rear of the store. It was really dark all the way in the back and I could hardly see the stuff well enough to know what I was looking at. My eyes began to carefully scan the items that covered the floor and lined the shelves. Mosquito netting, insecticide and Boonie caps. Canteens, duffel bags and old, heavy combat boots.

Looking behind me to check on Kaleb, I noticed that my eyes had adjusted to the depth of darkness in this area so much that Kaleb almost looked as if he were standing outside under a full moon.

I smiled and then thoughts returned to finding a couple of tarps to replace the ones that had blown away. Stooping down made it a little easier to see, but it was still hard trying to figure out what was what.

While I was looking through a mass of tangled items on the store's floor I heard a rustling noise behind me. It sounded like Kaleb might have grown tired of waiting on me and fell down on his way to come and help me search. I glanced in that direction to see if he was alright and what I saw filled me with unspeakable horror. Someone had grabbed Kaleb from behind and was dragging him backwards with a hand clamped over his mouth.

35

    I raised my rifle but couldn't see the sights well enough to be sure of where the bullet would be going. Unwilling to take a chance on hitting Kaleb, I watched helplessly as he disappeared into the darkness.
    I stood up and began leaping over mounds of loose merchandise in a panicked rush. When I made it back to the small clearing where Kaleb had stood in wait, I turned left and followed their trail.
    Just when I was about to catch up to them my left foot got snagged on something and I fell forward and landed in a twisted heap. Luckily for me, though, my face broke the fall. If that part of the floor hadn't been littered with surplus military sleeping bags, Kelli may never have been able to recognize me again. My tumble was quick and hard but the old, moldy sleeping bags were soft, so I landed with a sudden, padded thud.
    Immediately after I raised my head I heard the unmistakable sound of a heavy door closing. It sounded like it had come from straight in front of me. Catapulting myself up, I

quickly rejoined the chase. Being more careful as I ran through the tangled masses meant taking more time, but I just couldn't see very well.

As I neared the outer wall of the building, the shadowy image of a doorway appeared off to my left. I briefly wondered how I should go through the door. Open the doorknob slowly and try to sneak my way in? Or throw caution to the wind and go through the opening full bore?

By the time I reached the entryway, I decided that discretion was the better part of valor. This wasn't a scene in a "shoot em' up" action movie. There was no doubt in my mind that someone like Clint Eastwood would have kicked the door in and entered with both guns blazing. But I knew that the best chance for both of us to survive was to go in nice and easy, so that's what I did.

While gently turning the handle, I listened intently with my ear pressed firmly against the door. When the knob ceased to turn I pulled on it slightly to see if it was locked. It started to move toward me a little and I could tell that it wasn't.

With the door cracked about an inch, I peered inside. There was some sort of a flickering light reflecting off the sliver of wall that was visible. After watching the soft reflections dance and bob for a couple of seconds, I recognized the light to be from a fire. Then I heard Kaleb let out a scream and my blood ran cold.

When you have a child you can always tell how bad something actually is from the severity and tone of their screams. I heard both of those things reach a level that I had never heard before and every other thought perished from my mind. I hastily yanked the door open and went through, gun barrel first.

There was a man standing next to a fifty-five gallon drum in which a fire had been built. He was roasting something over the fire on a long, skinny stick. His attention was focused on something off to his left and he had no clue that I was even there. Keeping the heel of my boot up against the surface of the door, I let it ease together until it quietly closed.

Only after I had taken a couple of shuffling steps forward did I discover what had been holding his attention so well. Kaleb was being held down on his stomach by two large, grimy looking goons. His hands had been tied behind his back and they were in the process of tying his feet. I quickly scanned the room but saw no one else.

Raising my rifle, I took careful aim at the one tying Kaleb's feet. His head exploded and littered the wall behind him with a chunky spray of pinkish-red liquid.

The ruffian that had been holding Kaleb down jumped upright in surprise. He looked at me with wide eyes and started to move but he didn't get very far. My SKS roared and a big, blackish-red hole appeared in the middle of his chest. I saw him start to drop as I swung my aim to the right.

"Mr. Cook" had dropped his meal and had his hand on a shotgun that was leaning against the wall. He managed to get as far as picking it up before I fired. I shot him twice and watched his limp body fall to the floor.

As I moved forward to untie Kaleb, I accidentally kicked whatever the man by the fire had been cooking and it rolled out into the middle of the floor. Now that it had moved away from the side of the big, steel drum, the light from the fire fully illuminated the object.

At first my mind didn't register what I was looking at, but for some strange reason I couldn't turn away. Slowly it dawned on me what it was. In the middle of taking a step, I stopped cold. Although it was blackened and deeply charred, the shape was unmistakable. There, lying on the floor in front of me, was a human forearm and hand. A meat skewer was sticking from the thick forearm and the fingers had been chewed off halfway to the palm.

It took a moment for me to soak all of it in. Those guys were using humans as food and were going to kill Kaleb so that they could eat him. With every other source of nutrition depleted, the remaining inhabitants of the community had resorted to cannibalism.

Kaleb rolled over on his side and looked my way. Our eyes met and it snapped me out of my fog. In two big, lurching strides I was at his side. My survival knife made quick work of the yellow nylon rope that bound his hands and feet together. Putting a hand underneath Kaleb's arm, I helped him to his feet. We embraced each other tightly for a few moments. I hugged him so hard that the poor kid probably thought I was going to kill him by squeezing him to death, now that I had rescued him.

I told Kaleb that I loved him and would never let anything

happen to him and we started to exit the room. We were almost to the door when he suddenly stopped and turned to me.

"Wait," he said, loudly. "Hold on."

"What's wrong?" I asked.

"They took my gun," Kaleb said. "When they drug me in here, I felt one of them take it."

"His" gun, as he called it, was my old Ruger .22 caliber target pistol. The gun fit his hand perfectly and he didn't mind it's light recoil. He had become very fond of that little pistol. Not willing to leave without it, Kaleb turned and began to look around the room. His eyes settled on the two dead bullies that had been in the process of tying him up and he started that way.

We began looking around in the corner where Kaleb had been held down.

Not wanting to stay there long, I told him, "Let's do this fast, we need to get out of here."

"Alright," he replied. "No problem. I just want to find my gun."

After looking the room over and not seeing the pistol, I had a sneaking suspicion that I knew where it was.

Turning over the goon that had been tying Kaleb's feet, we searched through his pockets. All that we found was a small pocket knife, a filthy pair of women's underwear and half a box of nine millimeter bullets. I kept the bullets and stuffed them into my left coat pocket.

As Kaleb and I began moving toward the next cannibal, a quick movement caught my attention. From the corner of my eye I saw Kaleb kick the guy that we had just searched. There was an audible thump when his foot came in contact with the corpse lying on the floor.

I faltered and almost came to a stop but decided against it. I had far more important things to worry about at the moment. Besides, I thought to myself, the guy had it coming.

While searching the next kidnapper we found Kaleb's gun. We also found a Bic lighter, five 12 gauge shotgun shells and a slew of rings, watches and necklaces. My guess was that there were at least forty different pieces of jewelry.

I was reminded of a movie that Kelli and I had watched back when the airwaves still crackled with life. The film had been about the extermination of the Jews in German concentration camps. The Nazis took away every item that their doomed prisoners possessed. Their shoes. Their clothes. Of course, their valuables. The cold hearted bastards even inspected each prisoner's mouth to see if they had any gold or silver fillings. If one happened to be found, the sadistic Nazis guards would latch onto it and with a pair of pliers and brutally yank the precious metal free.

I wondered how many people these monsters had preyed upon in order to accumulate that much jewelry. After a momentary pause I came to the conclusion that it really didn't matter anymore, they wouldn't be able to hurt anyone else.

The booty filled both front pockets of my jeans and the weight of the stuff was incredible. Although I felt bad about possessing all of that ill-gotten plunder, it was certainly of no use to those guys. Besides, gold and silver might be the only things of value, anymore. American currency could be totally worthless, not even worth the paper it was printed on. The eighteen hundred dollars hidden in the bottom of my backpack might not be good for anything. Except, perhaps for starting a fire.

On our way out of the corpse-riddled room, I used my foot to tip the fifty-five gallon drum over onto it's side. A shower of sparks and half burnt lumber cascaded out of the can and all over the floor.

We turned and rushed in the direction of the door. As we neared the opening terrible thoughts started to race through my head. What if there were more of these guys? What if their partners had heard the shots and were waiting for us, right outside the door? Maybe they were holding Kelli and Jacob hostage and licking their chops in hunger. Those unsettling thoughts temporarily ceased when I opened the door and went through, though, because there was no one on the other side.

Moving as quickly as possible through the clutter, Kaleb and I made our way back to the front of the store. Being able to see the outside drawing closer was comforting, but I still couldn't get my mind off of Kelli and Jacob.

Kaleb and I could see much better on the way out. On our way in, our bodies had been filling the narrow walkways and blocking out all of the available light. Both of us were breathing heavily when we finally made it back outside. I felt like I had just ran some sort of bizarre, sight-impaired obstacle course.

As we hit the parking lot, though, sucking air became the

least of my concerns.

Kelli and Jacob were gone. They had both been standing near the corner of the building serving as lookouts and babysitting our packs when Kaleb and I went in. Now there wasn't anything there but an empty parking lot. No Kelli. No Jacob. No packs.

36

I swallowed hard as mild panic began to set in. Racing over to the corner where they had been standing, I looked down along that side of the building. Nothing. I shook my head in frustration and turned around to run toward the other front corner of the building.

Kaleb must have been able to read my mind because he beat me over there. He poked his head around the corner and looked off into the night. I stopped and watched him while I listened to my rushing breath whistle in and out of my mouth. After a few tense moments he returned his worried gaze my way. Shrugging his shoulders, he raised his arms with the palms turned upwards in an "I have no clue" gesture. Our eyes locked across the distance and I could clearly see the fear registered in his eyes.

Then we heard a whistle. Unable to tell exactly where it had come from, I began to look around frantically. Then came another.

My eyes were drawn to the road in front of the store, and there, standing on the other side of the pavement and looking our way, was Kelli and Jacob.

My heart leapt in my chest at the sight. It was such a relief to see that they were both safe. I readied myself to yell over at Kaleb but when I looked that way, I noticed that he had already spotted them. Without a word being spoken, we both dashed across the parking lot in their direction. Hurdling the little downward slope on the other side of the road, I landed directly in front of them.

We all drew together in a tight, little circle and hugged one another.

"What happened in there?" Kelli wanted to know.

Kaleb and I gave a Reader's Digest version of our backroom skirmish and our grisly discovery.

"I would really like to get out of here," I told everyone. "They might have friends."

We all looked toward the surplus store once more and then back at each other.

"Let's go, then," Kelli said.

Nobody argued.

37

      While walking across a frozen field, I looked to my right at Kelli. She seemed to be lost in thought as she steadily trudged along. Reaching out, I gently took her gloved hand in mine. Slightly startled, she jerked her head in my direction. I studied her face without saying a word. She looked so beautiful that I had to smile.

      Her expression changed suddenly and tilting her head a little, she asked, "What? What's so funny?"

      "Nothing," I said softly. "Nothing, at all." I looked forward again but the smile didn't leave my face.

      What a horror my life would become if something bad had happened to her. As terrible as things already were, a tragedy like that would have driven me to an entirely new low. She had been my life for so long that I wasn't sure if I could function properly without her.

      She was the perfect yin to fit my yang. We complimented each other in nearly every imaginable way. Where I was weak, she was strong and vice versa. I was more confrontational and she was usually passive. She was outgoing and gregarious, while I was more introverted and shy. No matter what situation we found ourselves in, as two halves, Kelli and I combined to make the ideal whole.

Every couple has their problems and we were certainly no different. We had been through our share of ups and downs over the years. But, instead of driving a wedge between us and forcing us continually apart, each bit of adversity that we steadfastly endured seemed to strengthen our bond and deepen our respect and love for one another.

Born in a small town near where we used to live, Kelli loves all kinds of music and has a great singing voice. She sings at every available opportunity. Her father has been crowned the State Fiddle Champion of Kentucky several times and had clearly passed on his fervent passion for music.

She is unusually pleasant and easygoing, a pure joy to be near. Always happiest around friends and family, she loves to talk and laugh for hours on end. A wonderful mother and a great friend, without her my life would have no direction.

She is my true love and my inspiration. I couldn't have made a better choice of someone to share my life with.

38

  Most of the night was spent thinking about what we had seen in that surplus store. As we plodded along I wondered how many other places across the country were like that. Our hike was unusually quiet that evening, so I know that my thoughts weren't alone.
  After about an hour of walking it began to snow heavily so we took a short breather in the shelter of a dilapidated, old barn.
  When we got ready to move on a small, orangish blob became visible on the horizon. It came from the direction of the surplus store. We all took in the sight with distant, dreamy eyes, totally lost in our own world of thought.
  According to our map, the river that divided the two nations was less than four nights of travel away, if our luck held out. Using that as our target, we headed due east toward Canada.
  It snowed heavily well into the early morning hours. When we stopped hiking for the day close to three inches were covering the ground.   If we only had our tarps, I lamented.
  We searched for at least an hour before we finally found

a halfway decent place to sleep. Crawling underneath the western end of a small, concrete bridge was the best that we could do. Not exactly four star accommodations, but at least it kept us out of the snow and most of the wind.

Being exhausted certainly has it's advantages when it comes to sleeping. It wasn't long before we all dozed off, dreaming of the St. Clair River and what lay beyond.

In the morning we ate a light breakfast. Partly because we were all so hyped over our close proximity to Canada and partly because our rations were getting low. We had been eating much better lately, but it had taken a heavy toll on our food supply. Five mouths to feed, at three meals a day, adds up fast when food is scarce.

Unfolding our map of Michigan, once again, I tried to visually chart the best route for us to take. If we continued to go straight east we would end up near the southern end of the dividing waterway. From there we could work our way north until we found a way to cross over.

Sometimes all of it seemed like a bad dream. Every once in a while I would catch myself thinking about our house back in Ohio and wondering if it still existed. Wondering if the day would ever come when we could return home and live peacefully. Pushing those unpleasant thoughts from the forefront of my mind, I donned my backpack and watched as everyone else did the same. Heading due east, we left the cover of the bridge with Walter eagerly leading the way.

39

    The hike that night turned out to be largely uneventful, which was just the way we liked it. Snow fell in sporadic bursts all night long and added to the mounting total already on the ground.
    The only excitement of the evening turned out to be Walter's little skirmish with a careless raccoon. He had apparently surprised the animal by silently sneaking up on it in the snow. From the looks of their intertwined tracks, the two had gotten into a slight tussle. Little raccoon footprints spun around in a couple of tight circles and then ran straight for the nearest tree.
    When Jacob and I arrived a few minutes later Walter was still rotating around the base of the large oak tree with his nose stuck high in the air.
    Half of the night was spent attempting to explain cannibalism to the boys. Now that both of them had ample time to think things over they were full of questions. Kelli and I tried our best to answer them. I could only hope that our spotty knowledge on the subject was adequate.
    As we came around the end of a thick hedgerow, a

gravel road appeared in front of us. To the south lay the main road that we had been paralleling all night. To the north stood a couple of isolated houses with some small outbuildings near them. Needing a decent place to stay for the day, we went north.

After a short walk down the lonely, snow covered road, a small house appeared off to our right. Thinking that it might provide a suitable place to hide for the day, we left the roadway and checked it out.

Making ourselves at home in the storage area above the garage, we climbed into our sleeping bags and spent the day either quietly talking to each other or snoozing.

40

    Well rested and in good spirits, everyone was anxious to get underway. Starting a little early, we thoroughly enjoyed the first sunset that we had witnessed for a while. Being so close to our destination was beginning to make all of us downright giddy. We took turns telling funny stories from our old lives and laughing a lot. Perhaps it was just the best way to relieve the tension that we had been drowning in for so long, I can't say for sure. All I know is that we really enjoyed each other's company for a while and it was nice.

    I was reminded of how things used to be back home and how badly I missed it. Once again, I could feel the rage within me begin to rise. Why did this have to happen? I asked myself for what seemed like the millionth time. Sure, the country was troubled and far from perfect, but it was better than this.

    I was so angry at all of those greedy bastards that ran the big oil companies and the money grubbing special interest groups. The politicians and their back door deals. The bribes and the inept representation of the people. The Wall Street rip-offs and the hordes of evil lobbyists. They totally destroyed the fabric of our nation and sold us all down the river for their own personal gain. I wondered how much they thought of their large bank accounts and their lavishly priced possessions now?

If there was any real justice left in the world, those worthless bastards would be suffering the most.

A short while before the sun showed it's face Kaleb spotted a big treehouse in a massive, many branched maple tree. Either some industrious kids or a group of local hunters had went to a lot of trouble to haul lumber back there and build the thing.

Elevated about fifteen feet off the ground, the structure offered little in the way of shelter. The entire back wall was missing and it didn't have any windows. The front and side walls had holes in them where windows used to be, but there was no glass. There was only one thing that the place *did* have going for it and that was a roof.

The wind had quit blowing and the snow was floating straight down. As long as it didn't kick up again, at least the cover would collect most of the snow that fell. The only problem was, how in the heck were we supposed to get Walter up there?

Although we all thought it over, we couldn't come up with any safe ideas. At over a hundred pounds, none of us could carry him up. He was a relatively intelligent dog, but certainly not aware enough to climb the crude steps that ascended to the treehouse.

In the end, Walter and I slept on the ground all day while Kelli and the boys slept up in the shelter. I chopped about a half dozen armloads of evergreen boughs and made a cozy, little mattress for us to lay on. Leaving my hat, coat and gloves on, I covered both of us with my unzipped sleeping bag. My sleep could be described as spotty, at best. Every time that Walter moved, his claws would catch in the fabric of the sleeping bag and pull it around. There were lots of cold drafts and more than a few cuss words uttered throughout the day. The only thing that made it halfway bearable was knowing that sometime later that night, we should finally make it to the long-awaited St. Clair River.

41

As we sat around the last bit of our fire for the day, we filled up on jerky. It was easy to see why the Indians and pioneers had made the stuff a major part of their diets. It was easy to carry, delicious and almost pure protein. Plus, no cooking was necessary and you could eat it while on the move.

Our conversation turned to Canada again. All of us desperately wanted to find a place where we could stop running and feel safe again. A place where we didn't have to fear someone sneaking up on us as we slept and murdering our whole family. We had been running for long enough and we were tired. I didn't know what we would find when we got to Canada, but it couldn't be any worse than where we were. All we needed to do was figure out how to get across the river.

The map indicated that we would hit the river right around Marine City. It looked like there was a bridge there but we couldn't chance crossing that. Once you got out in the middle, you were nothing more than a sitting duck from either side. No, we would have to find another way.

What we needed was a boat big enough for all five of us. A rowboat about ten feet long would be just about right. I wondered to myself how many other people had thought the same thing. Maybe we wouldn't be able to find so much as an inner tube left, anywhere along the river. But we wouldn't know for sure until we got there.

      It seemed like we walked a little faster than normal that night. Being so close to the river, it was certainly understandable.

42

Around 2:00 a.m. we crossed over Route 29 and saw the lights. The bright, beautiful glare of electric lights, warmly glowing on the other side of the river. Looking at the sight left us speechless. As our faces kept alternating between them and each other, the emotions were plain to see. After exchanging celebratory hugs and shedding a few tears of joy, we headed down the long, gently sloping bank to the St. Clair River.

Elated doesn't even begin to describe how we were feeling. After all the crap that we had went through along the way, to be standing within sight of Canada felt so fantastic that we could barely stand it. Looking at electric lights illuminate the river's coastline was a dream come true. We had taken a huge gamble and, thus far, it had paid off.

A sense of pride briefly swept over me, the satisfaction of a job well done. Getting my family to the doorstep of our destination safely brought with it a feeling that topped all others. Now all I had to do was figure out a way to get them across the river.

Jacob spotted a fire burning down by the water, about a quarter mile south of us. We moved behind a large, tangled pile of driftwood for cover. Sweeping the area with my binoculars, I spotted about ten or fifteen people milling about the flames. Almost every one of them appeared to be sick or injured in some way.

I saw splinted arms and bandaged heads. Some of them were missing limbs and using crudely made, primitive crutches in order to walk. They looked haggard and desperate. There were a few rifles or shotguns visible among the crowd and a couple of the band carried sidearms. None of them so much as looked our way, and that was a relief. The last thing that we needed to do was skirmish with this M*A*S*H unit when we were finally on the doorstep to Canada.

Looking to the north, I could make out a few houses upriver. More importantly I didn't see any fires in that direction, so we headed that way.

As we drew near the first house I could see a storage shed in the back yard near the water's edge. Using the structure for cover, we took a break and caught our breath.

Farther to the north some sort of factory was nestled up against the river. In the darkness it was impossible to tell exactly what the plant had produced. All that we could make out from where we sat were big trucks and stacks of pallets. A light bulb went off in my head.

"Maybe we could hide out there during the day and then figure out our next move," I suggested to my family.

Wanting to be certain that there were no surprises in store, I looked the factory over closely with the binoculars. Seeing nothing that looked suspicious, we moved that way. When we arrived I figured out why I had only seen trucks and pallets: it was a pallet factory, and the place was huge. From the signs posted everywhere, we gathered that the name of the business had been Marine City Pallets.

Stack after tall stack of the wooden skids covered acres of riverside property.

"I bet there are a lot of places to hide in here," Jacob commented.

After cautiously making our way through the first few outer rows of pallets, a small opening appeared in the enormous wooden maze. Perhaps an oversight by a forklift driver who didn't use all of the available space, but it worked out just fine for our purposes. We unslung our packs and rested our weary bones for a while. As we downed our meager meal I was totally preoccupied. All that I could think about was how to get across the river.

Deciding to go on a little recon mission, Jacob and I stripped ourselves of everything that was non-essential and left our little cubby hole. We searched for something tall to climb on in order to get a good view of the surrounding area. The only thing that we could find like that was a truck with it's bed loaded impossibly high with pallets. With no other option immediately available, we decided to give it a shot.

I slowly inched my way up the side of one of the tall wooden stacks until I reached the level surface at the top. Lying prone atop the piled pallets, I lifted the binoculars to my face and looked north. The river curved to the right a short distance ahead and on the left bank stood a small city.

"That has to be Marine City," I mumbled to myself.

Rising from the frigid water and stretching from bank to bank was a massive, steel bridge. I tried to pick out some useful details about the bridge but it was just too far away. Fighting a combination of distance and darkness, all I could tell for sure was that it was about two miles away.

I swung the glasses to the right. The river was a mile wide but with the help of those beautiful, electric light bulbs, I could see fairly well. Unfortunately, though, I didn't like what I was seeing. The waterfront was totally closed off with a ten or twelve foot high chain link fence, topped with razor wire. Watchtowers were scattered up and down the shoreline at about four hundred yard intervals and searchlights continuously crisscrossed the rippling surface of the dark, fast flowing river. The roads were patrolled by armed guards, both in military looking, camouflaged jeeps and on foot.

I became utterly immobilized by the heart breaking sight. A queasy, nauseating feeling filled the pit of my stomach. Had we come all this way for nothing? I wondered. It was obvious that the Canadian government was trying to keep everyone out. There must have been one hell of a big wave of refugees trying to get across the river after the attack, I thought, and from the look of things, they sure weren't taking the task any less seriously, now. The only explanation had to be that there were still people trying to cross. The question was, had they tested and hardened the Canadian defenses to the point that we had no shot at all of finding a weak point? I sure as hell hoped not.

Damn, I thought. How are we going to get through all of that? Kelli wasn't going to like this one bit. She would be devastated. How was I going to tell my family that even if we did find a boat we couldn't just float across the river to freedom? How were they going to react when they knew the hopelessness of our situation?

So many questions filled my head that they fell on my brain like heavy raindrops from a torrential thunderstorm. All of the What ifs? and What nows? clouded my mind to the point that I could no longer think clearly. I felt numb, as if under the influence of some powerful narcotic. My head felt huge and as light as a balloon.

I thought that perhaps lying my head down and relaxing for a moment might be a good idea. The top pallet had a light coating of snow and it felt nice and cool against my exposed cheek. It reminded me of a New Year's Eve party that I had attended many years ago. Having had too much to drink, I stumbled my way into the bathroom and clumsily closed the door behind me. After my stomach had emptied it's contents and ceased it's violent eruptions, I slumped onto the floor in a twisted heap and felt the blissfully cold ceramic tile against my pickled face.

As I began to gingerly climb back down the tall stack of pallets, doubt and self pity began to rear it's ugly head. Why was this happening to us? Why couldn't we just cross the river and casually stroll right on into Canada? Why? Why? Why? Perhaps I wasn't as big of an asset to my family as I liked to think I was. I had been so damned sure of myself and the only thing that I had accomplished was getting us nowhere. Maybe I would be the reason that we would all end up dead.

By the time that my feet touched solid ground I felt like a defeated man. All of those disparaging thoughts vanished in the blink of an eye, though, when I turned and saw Jacob. Eagerness and expectation emanated from his smiling face.

"What did you see?" he asked. "Anything good?"

Trying to smile didn't feel right at the moment so, turning my head, I pointed north and told him about the bridge that I had seen.

Jacob's smile widened and he asked, "Can we get across it, to Canada?"

"No," I reluctantly told him. "I'm afraid not. The Canadian military has it blocked off."

A questioned look appeared on Jacob's face. "But, why would they keep us out?"

"The only thing I can guess," I told him, "is that so many crazed, half-starved people started flooding over the border after the disaster that they became overwhelmed with refugees and decided to close it down."

Jacob looked at me expectantly. "Well, what do we do now?" he asked.

I had no answer for that. All I could do was shrug my shoulders.

43

Arriving back at our little opening among the pallets, Kelli knew immediately from the look in our eyes that the news was not good.

As I started our fire for the day I relayed the details of what we had seen to her and Kaleb. Our hearts broken, we sat around silently sulking for a while. Nobody offered any comforting words. None would have sufficed, anyway.

I wish that I had known what to say, but I didn't. No matter how it was phrased, everything that I thought of would have sounded hollow and fake. There were no answers. The whole trek north had been predicated on us being able to cross over into Canada. Now what? That certainly wasn't the only place in all of Canada to be sealed off. The whole damn border probably was. I felt so hopeless.

After expending so much energy and pushing ourselves to the point of exhaustion to merely *get* there, we now sat around the fire like zombies. Devoid of emotion and feeling, we felt no urgency to do anything at all.

My body actually felt like it was collapsing in upon itself from the weight of the situation. What were we going to do now? Where would we go? How would we survive? Those and at least a thousand other questions swirled around inside my head. After silently brooding for a little while, I gradually returned to my senses. I knew that no matter what happened, we had to try and make the best of it. Sitting there moping wouldn't get us any closer to a solution.

Raising my head, I spoke.

"We'll find a way to get to Canada. There has to be some way. All we have to do is find it."

I tried to say it with as much conviction that I could muster. Our spirits needed a major boost and I was hoping that my reassurances would help to temper the severe disappointment that all of us were feeling.

"Let's go take a walk and look for some better shelter," I said to Kaleb. " We can't be out in the open like this if it rains or snows."

Kaleb looked at me like I had just told him to go jump in the freezing river, head first. His eyes gradually cleared as what I actually said sunk in.

"Huh?" he uttered. "Yeah, okay." So, with heavy hearts, we left our little nook among the sea of pallets to try and find a suitable shelter.

Walking actually felt nice, for a change. There was no way that I could have sat still, anyway. I needed to do something to help keep myself occupied. If not, I would end up dwelling on our problem way too much and that could be dangerous.

Since we had lost our tarps, finding a way to get out of the precipitation was a must. Being exposed to the cold while being wet could lead to hypothermia, and the last thing that we needed to deal with at the moment was another problem.

Kaleb and I headed west, toward the back of the factory's expansive property. There were far too many other people around for me to feel safe enough to use the main building, itself. Hoping to find a storage shed or perhaps enough material to make a small structure with, we meandered through the maze of stacked pallets.

The wind was picking up speed. It was blowing noticeably harder than it had been when we started walking.

Kaleb and I strolled past more pallets on that expansive lot than I had seen in my entire life, up to that point.   It was unbelievable how many there were.

The place must have done a good business back in the day. Being located at a major intersection on one of the busiest shipping routes in the world obviously didn't hurt any.

Plenty of wood to burn, though, I thought to myself. At least we'll have enough heat. The trick would be finding a place to shelter where no one else could see our fire burning at night.

When we got to the back of the lot a line of gargantuan shipping crates came into view. The large boxes contained what looked like millions of wooden slats and runners used to construct pallets.

Kaleb's face broke into a huge grin and his eyes grew as wide as hard boiled eggs. "Look at all of this wood," he wondrously exclaimed. Since the task of gathering and stacking firewood fell largely on Kaleb's shoulders, I'm sure that he felt like he was seeing an illusion. "I won't have to look for wood, now," he gasped. "All I have to do is come over here and grab it."

Seeing his joy gave me a lift. I couldn't help but get a chuckle out of it. Here we were, caught in the middle of a life and death situation, and he's overjoyed about not having to search everywhere to scrounge firewood. I guess everything really is relative.

Patting him on the back, I told him, "That's right, it looks like you'll have it easy for the next few days, or at least until we figure out where to go next."

Moving on past the big crates full of wood, we headed for a location near the western edge of the lot, directly across from the main building. There appeared to be an area worth checking out over there.

When we arrived at that spot, a myriad of welded tubing and flat iron covered the ground. Everything from old, steel racks and shelving, to strange, bizarre metal shapes that one could only guess at their purpose and use. All I knew right then was that we needed shelter, and in a hurry. Daylight wasn't going to wait for us and the longer that Kaleb and I walked, the stronger the wind became.

"Maybe we can use some of this stuff to build a shelter with," I told Kaleb. "Make sure you look around real good."

Studying all of the various shapes and sizes scattered about I tried to fit them together in my mind. Perhaps if I would put this piece next to that one and then add that one at the end. No, that wouldn't work. It would leak like a sieve. What we needed was a roof.

Then I saw something from the corner of my eye. Sitting clear in the back by the property's fence was a big, boxy looking hulk of a thing. When I turned and got a better look at the bulky object, I couldn't believe my eyes. Now it was my turn to feel like I was looking at an illusion.

Covered over by an old, knotted mesh of thick vines and partially hidden behind large pieces of discarded metal debris, sat an antique railroad caboose.

44

If not for the little, square windows on it's side and the short chimney on top, I would have never recognized it for what it was.

Kaleb noticed my astonished gaze and asked, "What are you looking at?"

"That," I said, pointing at the big, dark shape.

He looked totally lost. "What's *that*?" he asked.

Starting towards the old caboose, I answered. "Maybe our shelter."

Weaving my way through the clutter of what must surely have been that company's junkyard, one thought kept going through my mind: Please let the roof be good. I was pleasantly surprised to see that the windows had remained intact after all of those years. Hoping that the rest of the boxcar was in similar shape, I climbed the stairs to the back deck.

As I neared the entrance door I noticed that the passageway appeared to be in good shape. Pushing down on the old, lever style handle caused the rusted mechanism inside to produce a high pitched squeaking sound, but it still worked. The door proceeded to swing inward easily enough, although accompanied by protesting groans from the old, cast iron hinges.

What a surprisingly beautiful sight it was to see the inside of that caboose. Everything looked perfectly preserved and intact, almost like an eighty year old time capsule. The floor was without holes and uncluttered. There was a light coat of dust on all of the exposed surfaces, but that wouldn't pose a problem for us. A small, Ben Franklin style wood stove stood way down at the front end. It's exhaust pipe snaked up and out of the caboose's western wall. I looked the roof over thoroughly and could see no obvious holes. Wow, I thought. This place would be perfect. Out of the way and untouched for years, I felt that our family would be safe there.

By the time I remembered Kaleb he was sitting on one of the bench seats cooling his heels. The boy never missed an opportunity to take a break.

With my arms outstretched, I whirled around in a circle taking it all in.

"What do you think, Kaleb?" I asked him.

Crinkling his brow and grinning slightly, he replied, "I think it'll work just fine."

Patting the top of his shoulder, I said. "Let's go get your mother, then."

When we arrived back at our little opening among the pallets this time, smiles decorated our faces. Kelli looked back and forth between me and Kaleb with that "have-you-lost-your-mind?" look.

"What are you two so happy about?" she asked, half agitated, half curious.

Unable to wait any longer, I spit it out. "We found a shelter!"

Her eyes opened wide. Suddenly not looking so peeved, she asked, "Where?"

Kaleb enthusiastically spilled the beans about us finding the old caboose and I tried to fill in all of the blank spots.

The relief was clearly evident on her face. Kelli was always busy worrying about us. She was the emotional glue that held our family together.

We merrily donned our backpacks and started out for the antique caboose.

The wind was blowing harder than ever, by then. In the

near light of early morning I could see a line of dark, turbulent clouds growing closer, and at the rate that it was moving, we didn't have a lot of time left before they would hit us. Quickening my step, I pulled up next to Kaleb and Jacob.

"That storm front is going to be here pretty soon," I told them. "As soon as we get to the caboose, let's drop our packs inside and gather some firewood. Jacob and I can carry it over and Kaleb, you can stack it up along the wall. We'll have to get plenty, though, because we don't know how bad this storm will be."

Jacob and I carried pieces of wood from the giant crates of pallet parts until Kaleb had enough to build a stack about ten feet long and almost three feet high. Starting in the corner, immediately to the left as we came in, Kaleb had stacked it high enough to start covering the window on that side before Kelli had finally stopped us. "Enough," she ordered.

Mama didn't raise any fools, though. Learning from past bouts with bad weather, we didn't want to have to dig through the snow for firewood, if we didn't have to.

The wind outside continued to pick up speed. It started to howl fiercely at about the same time that the small flame inside our little stove began to grow into a real fire.

"It shouldn't take too long to heat up in here," I told everybody. "Then we can relax and get some sleep."

A look out of the eastern facing window showed that the sky had almost entirely blackened and bits of trash and debris were being hustled about by the ever increasing gusts of wind.

"We really got lucky to find this place," I announced to everyone. "It looks like this storm is going to be a real doozy."

Kelli joined me at the window. Looking deeply into my eyes, she whispered, "You did good, but, then again, you always do."

Smiling from the compliment, I winked at her. "Thank you, dear," I said and planted a small kiss on her upturned lips.

Jacob noticed our little peck and groaned out loud. "Okay, okay, that's enough of that," he said. "I don't want to barf."

"Awwww, Jacob," Kelli said in a taunting, high-pitched, baby voice. "Come here and let mommy give you a kiss."

"No thanks, I'm fine," he answered back, with an exaggerated look of alarm on his face.

We all laughed loudly. A deep, hearty, belly laugh. It felt really good.

The boys each claimed one of the two bench seats that lined the eastern wall of the caboose and Kelli and I spread our sleeping bags out on the floor. It wasn't long before it felt like we were in a small hotel room. We were finally able to take off our coats and boots and be comfortable again. It felt so exquisite to be indoors, especially with a storm brewing.

For me, the only problem with being warm and comfortable was that memories of the past seemed to come along with it. Visions of our home in Ohio and all the good times that we had there came flooding back to the forefront of my mind. How much we had enjoyed the holidays and the change of seasons. My heart desperately yearned to return to those days. I badly wished that I could just snap my fingers and make the whole mess disappear. If I had my way, we would all be at home sitting on our huge, curved couch, watching a movie and laughing out loud. Stuffing ourselves on popcorn and pizza until we were ready to burst.

Unfortunately, it wasn't good for me to think about that at the moment. I had to keep my head in the game. I knew that we were all feeling down but somehow, some way, we *would* make it to Canada. I was extremely determined to get my family out of the mess we were in and make sure that they were safe and happy, once again. I might die trying to accomplish it, but that was the only way I would ever give up.

Jacob took the first watch, as usual, and everyone else laid down to sleep. Outside the train car, the wind was still gusting mightily. As I closed my eyes and slowly drifted off to sleep I heard the sound of a hard, steady sleet falling, playing a percussive symphony on the train's metal roof. It made for marvelous sleeping.

45

    By the time that Kelli woke me up for my turn at watch in the early afternoon hours, there was about three or four inches of fresh, fluffy snow on the ground. The wind was still blowing hard and the sky showed no sign of a let up.
    Putting on my coat, I kissed Kelli goodnight and motioned for Walter to follow me. When I opened the door of the caboose a gust of wind blew a cloud of loosely scattered snowflakes into the warmth of the train car. As they made their way in the door they seemed to rise with the heat and hang suspended in mid-air. Turning into small, mist-like droplets of water after a couple of seconds, they fell to the floor as soft as morning dew.
    Stepping outside into the blowing snow, it was clear that the temperature had dropped significantly since I had went to sleep. Bitterly cold gusts of arctic air, at least forty miles an hour, swept across the snow covered ground.
    Walter and I made our way behind the railcar so that we could relieve ourselves. As I turned the corner of the caboose I got a good view of the picturesque, snow covered landscape on the other side of the pallet company's fence. A Christmas card

couldn't have sported a prettier picture. Too bad the world wasn't in much of a festive mood, I thought. Once our business behind the caboose was finished, Melonhead and I decided to have a quick look around before the intense cold got the better of us.

As W.C. Fields used to say, "It's wasn't a fit day out for man, nor beast." Anyone caught outside in that kind of weather without some sort of shelter to find refuge in would almost certainly perish. Blasts of cold air found their way through my clothing and assaulted me like I was walking around virtually naked. It invaded every crevice on my body and evicted any trace of warmth that it found.

Taking an abbreviated stroll around our immediate area, I saw no signs of any activity. Not very surprising, I thought. One would have to be either hopelessly crazy or dangerously desperate to brave this weather.

I felt so fortunate that I didn't have to face this crazy new version of the world by myself. The way that things were it would be so easy to just give up, if there was no one else around to help shoulder the burden. Lucky for me, though, I had the best company that a man could ever ask for.

Opening the boxcar door and entering our humble abode, I felt as though I were walking into a tropical paradise. The heat felt so incredibly inviting that I felt like putting on a grass skirt and grabbing a Mai-tai. Instead, I grabbed some venison jerky and took a drink of the fresh water that Kelli had been melting to refill our canteens.

While chewing on a big mouthful of jerky, I glanced over at the boys. Both of them were snoozing with their sleeping bags flung wide open, arms thrown out wildly. Knowing how comfortable they were in that glorious warmth made me happy and a smile spread across my rapidly thawing face. Kelli and I wanted the boys to be happy in life, to do better than we did. But we worried that, without even having the opportunity to give it a try, this screwed up disaster had taken away any chance that the boys would have of living a normal life. My smile faded at that thought, so I turned my head away from Kelli and faced the pile of wood that we had so carefully stacked inside our shelter.

Needing to do something to keep myself busy, I cleaned the glass in the old dusty windows. We had a full 360 degree view of our surroundings through the caboose's four little square windows. If anyone was ignorant enough to be out and about in that stuff, they would have to be dressed from head to toe in stark, white camouflage to go unnoticed.

The snow continued to come down in huge, fluffy, windblown flakes and the landscape encircling our rail car looked totally different than it had that morning. The snow had obscured almost every detail of our surroundings in a thick, smothering, white blanket.

I felt a little disappointed by the severity of the storm. My plan had been to wait until it got dark and then hike the couple of miles north to Marine City. We were getting tired of eating nothing but jerky and I wanted to scrounge around up there and see what I could find. Oh well, I thought, it's probably better to postpone it and be safe.

For the remainder of my sentinel duty I fed the fire and watched the snow pile up outside. By the time that I woke Kaleb up for his turn, it was easily over six inches in depth. The sound of the whistling wind had ceased and the snow was falling, rather than flying. For some reason the weather made me feel tired. I didn't know whether it was because I felt safe inside that snow covered caboose in the middle of a winter storm, or if it was my body telling me to get some rest while I had the chance.

I put a couple more pieces of wood into the fire to give Kaleb time to finish tying his boots. My eyelids drooping heavily, I hugged him goodnight and plopped down on top of my sleeping bag. In less than a minute, my boots were standing guard next to each other on the old, wooden floor and I was fully stretched out. Listening to the crackling fire serenade me, I slipped off to dreamland.

46

Darkness had completely re-conquered the day when my eyes opened again. Shadows were dancing on the walls and ceiling from the constantly flickering flames of the fire. Looking toward the little, tabled booth, I noticed that Kelli and Kaleb were looking straight at me. Wondering what in the world was going on, my eyes focused on Kelli.

"You slept a long time," she said in response to the "what the hell?" look on my sleep lined face. "We tried to be as quiet as we could, so that we wouldn't wake you."

"How long has it been dark?" I groggily asked.

"For a couple of hours," Kaleb piped in. "It stopped snowing, too" he added with a delighted look on his face.

No wonder he looked happy, I thought. The boy had hated snow since the day he was born.

Jacob was sitting on the wooden bench seat staring out the window into the night. One of his favorite pastimes was thinking. Back home he would take long, meandering walks through our little woods and just think.

Many times I had asked him, "Jacob, what do you think about as you walk?"

His answer was short and to the point, as it almost always was. "Everything," he'd reply. "I just think."

Without a trail to walk on, it looked like Jacob was now doing his thinking while sitting and staring out of the caboose's window.

Righting myself, I glanced outside and saw that the snow had indeed stopped falling. Under the cloud broken moonlight, the crusty surface looked like it had been blown as smooth as glass. Gently rolling hills of fresh snow turned everything within sight into a mesmerizingly serene spectacle.

Stepping outside of the caboose to answer nature's call, I was immediately struck by the frigidness of the air. The snow may have stopped falling but the temperature hadn't. An arctic air mass had invaded the region and now held it captive in it's icy grip. Never in my life had I been so happy to finish relieving myself. Hanging your bare rear end out at that temperature was close to torture. My privates shrank so much that it felt like they were trying to burrow their way back up into my abdomen. Oh, how I missed indoor plumbing! Stuffing my frozen appendages back into my drawers, I made a hasty retreat for the warmth of our lair.

"Woooweee!" I said, barreling through the door. "The temperature must have dropped at least twenty degrees." Turning my frozen posterior toward the warmth of the flames, I defrosted my dignity.

Since Mother Nature had decided that we weren't making a trip to Marine City that evening, we split the rest of the night between talking and sleeping. Reliving old stories between refreshing naps, we passed the time quite pleasantly. In fact, if not for the knowledge of the apocalyptic catastrophe all around us, our stay in the caboose would have been a very enjoyable experience. It was almost like a combination of camping in a secluded mountain cabin and being in summer camp.

At about noon the boys began to replenish our wood supply. Instead of making continuous trips as they had done yesterday, every trip to the woodpile and back now was followed by ample warm up time in front of the fire.

Two hours later, the stack of firewood inside the boxcar was bigger than ever. Determined not to have to haul wood again for as long as possible, Kaleb and Jacob had went all out in their endeavor.

After declaring our wood supply sufficiently recharged, they both collapsed heavily onto the old, wooden bench seats. Even though their bodies were weary from the repeated exertion, a smile adorned both of their faces. Proud of their Herculean task, they basked in the glow of a job well done.

Reaching down to unlace his snow dusted boots, Jacob announced, "I'm gonna sleep until tomorrow night."

Stuffing his legs into his sleeping bag, he appeared to be set on doing just that. Kaleb had his boots off by that time. Flopping his socked feet up on the end of the bench seat, he revealed his plans to everyone.

"I'm not," he said, informatively. "I'm going to sit here and relax with my feet up by the fire."

When it came to the art of relaxing, Kaleb was a bonafide expert. "If somebody else could breathe for him," Kelli had once remarked, "he would sure let them."

As dusk approached I bundled up in extra layers for a sight-seeing tour around our area. With the thick blanket of fresh snow on the ground, I would easily be able to tell if there was anything moving about. I had spent a lot of time outdoors during the winter, when I was a boy. I found that tracking animals in the fresh snow was easy to do and quite an enjoyable way to pass time. With a new layer of the white, fluffy stuff that deep, it would be impossible for anything to stir without leaving a trail that I would be able to see.

47

    After rubbing Walter's melon sized head and kissing Kelli, I stepped out into the enormous icebox called Michigan. Taking in the first breath of polar air was a real eye opener. From the burning sensation in the back of my mouth and throat, I could tell that the temperature had fallen even more. My best guess was that it was now less ten degrees.

    A frozen crust had begun to develop on top of the snow and every step that I took produced a muffled crunching sound. It reminded me of the noise that someone made when they were eating a well done piece of toast. Funny how everything seemed to remind me of food all the time. The human psyche is a complicated and mysterious thing, there's no doubt about that. The subconscious mind is a very powerful force and has the ability to override the conscious mind, at times. After eating nothing but venison jerky for the last week, my brain had once again become helplessly preoccupied with food.

    Heading south, I walked through an endless number of tall snowdrifts, having to lift my knees high with every struggling step. Walking had become second nature to us over the previous several weeks. Our bodies had become accustomed to the task of traveling long distances on foot. Walking in snow of this depth, however, was a whole new ball game. Much more effort is required to wade through thigh high snow drifts than to walk on unobstructed ground. After only a quarter of a mile, I wasn't cold anymore. My breathing had become heavy and I felt perspiration begin to well up under my arms. Working up a sweat at such a low temperature is highly unadvisable. Once you ceased activity the moisture would freeze against your skin and could cause the onset of hypothermia.

Stopping for a second, I un-zipped the down jacket that I was wearing to help regulate my body's temperature. Almost immediately, the super cooled air found it's way to the damp surfaces under my clothing. In less than thirty seconds I went from feeling extremely overheated to being chilly, once again.

When I resumed my southward trek, I proceeded at a deliberately slow and steady pace. To prevent myself from heating up again I knew that I would have to walk a lot slower. Turning left at a short line of fruit trees, I began moving east, toward the river. I realized that the trip was going to take a lot longer than I had anticipated, due to the depth of the snow. Damn, I thought. Kelli and the boys will start worrying about me before I had even completed half of my planned route.

As I neared the fast flowing St. Clair, some deer tracks crossed my path. They looked to be no more than a few hours old from how sharp and fresh they were. Three deer were moving south together, paralleling the water's flow. They didn't appear to be having as much trouble as I was in getting through the tall drifts.

With the rocky shoreline of the river in sight, I turned north. It was an odd experience to be walking along on one side of the water in almost primitive conditions and seeing electric lights burning on the other. A scene from one of my favorite movies came to mind.

Charleton Heston was riding along on a horse in the ocean's roaring tidal surge with a movie rent-a-babe on the back. Spotting something up ahead on the beach, he brings his trusty steed to a halt and climbs down without taking his eyes from whatever he's looking at. A close up of his face shows that he is obviously devastated by what he sees. Limply collapsing to his knees, he begins to pound his fists into the wet sand repeatedly while screaming out, "Why? Why?" over and over again, at the top of his lungs. The camera angle shifts and the view from behind Charlton reveals what has driven him to react in such an exaggerated manner. Standing in front of him on the sandy shore, with waves continually frolicking to and fro, was the very upper portion of the Statue of Liberty. Leaning drunkenly like the Tower of Pisa, she stood facing Mr. Heston with her torch still held defiantly high.

"Damn you! Damn you all to hell," he bellows in horror and disgusted disbelief. "You blew it up! You blew it up! Damn you all to hell." Sobbing madly, he lets his body fall forward into the turbulent wash of the ocean. Film credits begin to roll down the screen and a helicopter mounted camera flies over. After getting a good shot of Charlton kneeling next to what was left of the Statue, the chopper continues to film as it soars down a secluded portion of some remote, northeastern shoreline.

I had always felt a touch of sorrow for that unfortunate character. Now, though, after the series of events that had transpired, my understanding of what the director had been trying to convey to the audience had risen to a whole new level. For anyone caught in a survival situation, the feelings of isolation and loneliness could be just as painful as the physical struggle and the never ending, gnawing hunger.

Continuing northward to a point that I believed to be sufficient, my path began arcing back to the west. Clear, unobstructed moonlight lit up the snow covered landscape with an eerie, reflective glow. Shadows accompanied the few objects were tall enough to escape the crusted white depths. Looking down from the top of a small rise that I had crested, the pallet yard dominated my view. The lofty platform enabled me to see the true expanse of the company's grounds. Absolutely gargantuan in size, it must have taken up at least sixty acres.

Looking at the western edge of the giant manufacturing plant, I tried to locate our old, forgotten caboose. I was glad to see that even though I had the advantage of both the bright moonlight and an elevated perch, it was still indiscernible among the many piles of tangled objects.

Wanting to complete my task and get back inside the warmth and safety of our caboose as quickly as possible, I didn't waste a moment of time. Starting down the western side of the hill, I began to slowly high step my way through the last leg of the journey. When I had gotten nearly halfway down the long, gentle slope, I was startled to a sudden halt. About a hundred yards in front of me I saw a wide, dark line in the snow. Crossing my path on a southwest to northeast line, it kept going for as far as I could see.

      The hair on the back of my neck stood up and a tingle ran from the top of my head to the tip of my toes. They looked too big to be anything other than human. I wondered if they were heading toward or away from the pallet yard? I knew that none of us had been over in that area. We hadn't left the yard, at all, since our arrival. I got the sudden urge to run, to sprint right up to where that wide, shadowed swath cut through the rolling snow drifts. I needed to find out for sure which direction the makers of that trail were headed, and I hoped like hell that it was away from us.

48

     My mind began to debate itself over the best course of action to take. If I did attempt to run in the deep snow, exhaustion would set in before I even got close to the line of tracks. The only thing I would accomplish like that would be freezing to death. Even if the trail did head toward the pallet yard, I would be of no use to anyone arriving hypothermic.

     Quickening my pace and taking longer strides, I began to feel adrenaline surge through my body. Trying to let as much body heat escape that I possibly could, I slid my stocking cap off and pushed it into the left front pocket of my down jacket. That was followed by removing my gloves and stuffing them in my right front pocket. Then I grabbed the tongue of my coat's zipper and pulled it downward to let the two sides of the garment fall apart. With my jacket open and flopping about in the breeze, the frigidly cold air was free to move in and take care of all that trouble making heat that my body was generating.

     Having seen thousands of examples in the past, I knew for sure that they were human prints when I was still thirty feet away. My heart sank a bit more. Please let them be heading northeast, I silently pleaded. By the time I had gotten to within ten feet of the tracks, though, my eyes saw the telltale signs in the snow that meant danger. The dragging marks on the heel side of the footprints showed that two people were walking southwest, directly toward the pallet yard. Following their trail with my rifle at the ready, I broke into a fast walk. Trying to look ahead for off-shooting tracks, I peered along the length of the trail but couldn't see any deviation from my vantage point.

Worries of unspeakable tragedy flooded my thoughts as a whole procession of gruesome horrors went through my mind. Why are we humans preconditioned to always think about the worst possible outcome? I wondered. "Run, run", half of my brain screamed out. "Your family is in trouble!" The other half, though, somehow still operating under the control of rational reasoning, countered. "Don't overreact," it said. "Relax and take deep breaths. Keep your eyes peeled and everything will turn out fine."

My fingers started to go numb from holding the rifle out in front of me without gloves on. I was finally covering the open ground in a hurry and making much better time than I had been. Examining every object within sight for any sign of danger, my head swiveled back and forth like a pendulum on a grandfather clock. Drawing close to the outside edge of the enormous factory, I could see where their trail entered among the tall stacks of pallets.

I stuck the butt of my SKS under my left armpit and let the forend rest in the crook of my arm. Both of my freezing hands were now free to put on the gloves that I had removed a short while ago. My fingers needed to be able to work properly in order to fire a weapon.

Hoping that I wasn't walking into an ambush, my pace slowed to a crawl. To try and make less noise I lightened my steps. Not wanting to miss any potential danger, every detail in the surrounding area was double checked. A feeling of impending doom surrounded me as I went between the first of the seemingly endless stacks of pallets. Emerging on the inside of the first few outer rows, the tracks turned right on one of the numerous forklift paths that ran throughout the place like a maze. Sneaking a glance around the corner and down the alley sized lane, my eyes followed the trail until it disappeared after making a left turn. The tracks were heading in the direction of the main building.

From that point on I knew that I would have to be very careful. Anyone could be hiding anywhere in that wooden house of horrors. No matter how much I looked around, one set of eyes couldn't cover everything.

Creeping along on the snow covered path, my crunching footfalls echoed lightly off the eight foot high stacks of pallets that enclosed my present, wintery world. It was then that I caught a whiff of smoke on the breeze. Someone close by was burning a fire, no doubt trying to ward off the effects of the bitterly cold weather. For a moment I wondered if Mother Nature was playing a joke on me. When the temperature is extremely low air tends to sink and hover just above ground level. Perhaps what I was actually smelling was the exhaust fumes from our own fire. After all, the caboose was located somewhere in that general direction.

I almost jumped out of my boots when a loud, hoarse sounding cough exploded nearby. It sounded like someone was either a heavy smoker or had one hell of a nasty cold. Freezing in place, I tried to figure out exactly where it had come from. Looking toward the main building, I thought I saw a small tendril of gray smoke rise up and dissipate into the cold winter night. When they coughed again the phlegmy hacking sounded more intense and lasted a lot longer. It definitely sounded like the noise was coming from the same direction that the smoke was.

Starting to get cold again, I took the time to re-zip my coat and put my stocking cap back on. My frozen ears were very thankful. An enormous chill shot through my body like a bolt of lightning, jolting me with abrupt, jerky muscle spasms. After I had ceased shaking like a wet dog, I started to ease forward again.

The big, main building was certainly an imposing structure. It probably had the largest footprint of any single building in the whole area. With it's bright, red brick facade and shiny metal roofing, blending into the surroundings must not have been high on the architects list of priorities. On the southeast corner of the structure the walls formed an inverted "L" shape.

Peeping around the stacks of pallets sitting closest to the

building's outer wall, I saw what looked like part of a snow covered concrete patio and the end of a picnic table. A shadow appeared on the surface of the brick wall and wavered back and forth in time with the flickering of a small fire. Wanting to get a better look, I moved forward and filled the space between the tall pallet stack and the building. I was right. A poured concrete pad measuring about twenty feet by twenty feet filled the inside corner of the big, inverted "L". Four picnic tables sat in the little area. Undoubtedly the company's effort at a combined outside lunch and smoking area. Against the wall, straight in front of me, sat two people warming their hands over a smoldering fire. They were trying to use the wet, snow covered wood to burn for heat. Not responding very well, the damp lumber looked like it was smoking just as much as it was burning. In such bitterly cold weather, though, I guessed it really didn't matter if it was burning with peak efficiency, or not. A fire was a fire.

49

    Huddled together for warmth between the brick wall and struggling fire were a middle-aged man and woman. They both looked gaunt and pale as if malnourishment had taken a heavy toll on their bodies. The male had a large, dark stain on the left side of his head and face. That's blood, I thought to myself. Sometime recently, he had either injured himself or someone else had done a real number on his skull.

    No wonder they were trying to burn that wet wood. They looked far too weak to do anything else. Both had on winter clothing, but nowhere near adequate for these temperatures. Desolate, blank stares on their faces, they rotated their hands slowly over the weak, sputtering fire.

    I looked them over for weapons but didn't see any. My breathing had slowed and my heart rate was beginning to drop, in turn. The feeling of danger that had driven me forward in a panicked rush was beginning to subside. These folks didn't look like much of a danger, at all. They just looked hurt and hungry. Exposed to the frigid conditions without proper food, clothing and shelter, like they were, they weren't going to last long.

    I felt sorry for them, any decent human being would

have, but I wasn't about to risk losing my family to save two total strangers. I wanted so badly to turn around and leave. To just wash my hands of the whole situation. Except my feet refused to cooperate. Standing there hidden behind tons of pallets and looking at those two poor souls, my conscience kept telling me that I had to do something.

I remembered the small amount of jerky that Kelli had stuffed into the inside pocket of my jacket. "For a snack if you get hungry," she had said. Should I give that jerky to them? I wondered to myself. Even if I did, what good would that do? It would merely prolong the inevitable. Not only that, but maybe they would try to follow my tracks back to the caboose looking for more. Hunger is an extremely effective motivator. People behave very much like animals when they are desperate and hungry. They will fight, and if necessary kill, to get the nourishment they need to survive. Could I take a chance on that? My family was the most important thing in the world to me. My only goal at the moment was to get them somewhere that was safe. Deep down in my heart, though, I knew that these people also had family. Somebody, someplace, cared what happened to these folks as much as I cared about what happened to mine.

How much easier it would have been if they had looked like beastly thugs out on the warpath and up to no good. There would have been no hesitation in me - I would have killed them both, in an instant. With them being so close to us, it would have only been a matter of time before we were discovered and that was something I wouldn't have allowed. How much easier, indeed.

Whatever my decision was going to be, I had better make it fast. My nostrils had quit their burning and were now starting to go numb. If I didn't get warm soon my nose would freeze solid.

Boldly stepping forward with my rifle barrel leading the way, I exited the relative safety of the dark shadows. Neither one of the strangers noticed my presence until I had taken five or six steps in their direction. Staring into the fire, lost in their world of misery, they were completely surprised by my sudden appearance. Looking up from the smoky fire, their wide eyes stared first at me and then my weapon.

Closing to about ten feet, I stopped with my rifle at the

ready. We stared back and forth at each other without saying a word. It probably only lasted for about five seconds but it seemed like a lot longer than that. Now that I was so close to them, all of my earlier fears left me. Too weak to even protest, they just stared at me with sunken, tortured eyes. These two were in really bad shape. The look in their eyes said that they fully expected me to shoot them. In fact, they even seemed resigned to the fact. Maybe they had had enough of this new world and decided that they would rather move on.

Then the man with the bloody head feebly spoke. "We don't have anything of value," he said. "No food, no jewelry. We were robbed yesterday." I must have looked like I didn't believe what he was saying so he offered up more details. "We were in a city just a couple of miles north of here," he went on. "These guys told us that they could help us get across the river to Canada. As soon as they got the chance, though, someone hit me in the head and knocked me out. My wife said they took everything that we had. Even took her wedding ring." His voice quivered at that and his eyes dropped back down to the fire.

All wedding rings are special to their owners but, for some reason, this one must have held a very special place in his heart. Perhaps it was a family heirloom that had been passed down from generation to generation. Maybe it was just the emotional attachment that they felt to a symbol that showed everyone how special their love was for one another. Whatever the reason, that band had certainly meant a great deal to them.

Standing less than ten feet away from their fire, I could feel a little of it's warmth and It felt good. For a moment I had forgotten how brutally cold it was.

Fighting to move my half frozen lips and cheeks, I asked, "Where are you folks from?"

Raising his face back up to meet mine, he looked puzzled. His expression seemed to say, "Where are we from? Why does it matter where we're from if you're just going to shoot us, anyway?"

The woman spoke up this time. In a hopeful, half whispered voice, she said, "We're from Ohio." My mind went blank. For a few seconds all that I could manage to do was look back and forth between the two of them and the fire.

When my brain fart had passed, I asked the couple, "Can

you walk?"

Exchanging a curious glance with his wife and then looking back to me, the man asked a question of his own. "To where?" The concern in his eyes was clearly evident. Only being a day removed from their last mugging, who could have blamed them?

My frozen mouth uttered, "Not far." Then, for good measure, I added, "We have food and a warm shelter."

Once more they closely surveyed each other's face. I'm certain that they wanted to ask more questions, but really, what was the use. They knew that they only had two options. Either stay where they were and slowly freeze to death or take the risk that I was really telling them the truth. And after all, at this point, what difference would it really make. Death would come quick enough, either way. So, willing to let their fate be controlled by destiny, the man with the bloody head turned back to me and quietly said, "OK."

It was then that I noticed that the barrel of my rifle was still pointed toward them. Looking down at the blued steel weapon and then back up into their waiting eyes, I lowered the rifle slowly. "Follow me," I sheepishly told them. "It's not far." I watched as they grasped each other's hands and struggled to gain their feet.

Watching the weary duo rise, I became concerned as to whether or not they had the stamina to make it to the caboose through all of the deep snow drifts. Our little derailed shelter was only about three hundred yards away from where we were but, with no energy left to burn, it might as well have been ten miles. Hoping that the fellow Ohioans could make it there before they broke down or froze to death, our little caravan began to cut a route for our snowbound shelter.

50

Arriving at our destination after about fifteen minutes of hard travel, I wondered what Kelli and the boys would think of our party crashers. Not that I had any real doubts about it, at least once the initial shock of it had worn off. Kelli's main concern would be the safety of the boys. If she felt okay about that, then things would be fine. She was a very gracious host and would extend herself to ensure that our guests felt welcome.

If, for some reason, she didn't take a shine to the weary travelers, we would let them rest and re-group for a couple of days before strongly suggesting that they leave. Over the years I had come to trust my instincts about people fairly well and my intuitive feeling about this pair was positive. Hopefully I wasn't wrong.

In order to climb the steps on the rear of the caboose the two emaciated travelers required my assistance. With no get up and go left and frozen blocks for feet, they had reached the limits of their endurance. Grasping onto the antique, wrought iron handle on the train's back door, I lifted it and entered the sanctity of our boxy shelter.

51

Warmth exploded all around me as I stepped inside. The heat felt so intense after my prolonged jaunt out in the deep freeze that, with my eyes closed, I might have mistakenly thought that I had stumbled into a sauna.

Standing in front of me, with her rifle pointed at the door, was Kelli. Kaleb and Jacob were standing at attention behind her, one on each side. Their faces were locked on the two stumbling, half dead zombies following me in through the open doorway.

Turning to our guests, I motioned with my hand and said, "Move on up by the fire and get warm."

With uncertainty clearly evident in their eyes, the two began to hesitantly move forward as I closed the door behind them.

Heavy tension hung in the air inside our shelter.

Hoping to break the ice, I introduced my family. "This is my wife Kelli and our boys, Kaleb and Jacob," I announced to the two frozen refugees.

As the strangers drew near the fire Kelli could see the severity of their condition and finally lowered her rifle. The flickering glow of the firelight seemed to make every line on their frozen faces more pronounced than before.

"They're from Ohio, like us," I added, in an attempt to spur some conversation.

Softly speaking through jittering teeth, the man told us, "My name is Butch and this is my wife, Vickie."

After a moment of awkward silence Kelli haltingly uttered, "H-hello."

Stepping up next to the fire, our guests began the long process of warming up their weather-ravaged extremities.

Over the next couple of hours Butch and Vickie slowly shed and dried their outer clothing. Taking off gloves, hats and coats, they hung them on the edge of the woodpile to dry out in the warm air. Especially relieved when they removed their footwear, the weary travelers rubbed their stiff, frozen feet with a look of pure ecstasy on their faces.

Venison jerky was passed out and consumed in mass quantities until it had swollen to fill their famine shrunken stomachs.

I asked Butch, "What part of Ohio are you two from?"

"Just north of a little town called Melmore," he answered.

The puzzled glances exchanged between my family and I made it obvious that we had no idea on earth where Melmore was.

"It's on the southern edge of Seneca County," he added, in an attempt to clarify the location for us.

"I know where Seneca County is," I said. "It's right next door to us. We're from Hancock County."

A look of familiar recognition came across Butch's face. "We go to Findlay all the time," he said.

Kelli smiled. "We're *from* Findlay. Well, at least that's where we lived before...." she paused momentarily trying to think of exactly how to characterize what happened. Seeming not to be able to come up with a satisfactory term, she turned her palms upward in an "I don't know pose" and then simply said, "before all of this."

With the close proximity of our starting origins established, conversation began to flow freely. These were our first friendly interactions with other human beings since before the incident at my neighbor, Roy's house. Everyone in the group thoroughly enjoyed our comradery and in short time we started to build a real rapport. After about two hours, though, our guests were fighting to keep their eyelids open. Aided by stuffed, swelling bellies and the luxurious heat, their exhaustion had finally overwhelmed them.

"Why don't you two lay down for a while and get some sleep?" I suggested. "You can use our bed," I offered, while pointing to Kelli's and my unzipped, open sleeping bag lying on the caboose's floor.

Maybe they had wanted to say "No, we couldn't do that. It would be too much of an imposition on you and your family." But they had no say in the matter at all. Their bodies could simply take no more. Within two minutes of laying their heads down on our makeshift pillows, our guests were lost in the world of sleep.

As they slumbered like newborn babies we had a short family meeting. Pulling everyone close, I quietly told them, "Whoever is on watch, make sure you keep a close eye on those two. We don't know enough about them yet to let our guards down."

Part II

Hotel Hell

52

    For the next three days Butch and Vickie did little except eat, sleep and go to the bathroom. Between naps, Kelli and I would try to pry as much information out of them that we could without appearing to be interrogators. Trying to look for any signs of deception, we paid extra attention to their faces and body language. The most interesting conversation that took place was about their visit to Marine City.
    I had asked them, "What made you two come to the pallet yard in this kind of weather?"
    Vickie's answer was short and simple. Raising her eyebrows and tilting her head slightly, she said, "Because we didn't want to die."
    Wanting to clarify what his wife meant, Butch quickly added, "Along the river, up there, we met another couple from Toledo, Ohio. They told us about a man who could help us get across the river and into Canada, for a price. So, we went to talk to this fella about it. He has a bunch of big guys around that protect him. Some really *nasty* looking characters, too." He said the word "nasty" with great emphasis. Continuing on, he told us, "So, three of these guys lead us to a hotel. It's up

there on the main road, the same one that the bridge is on." Taking a deep breath, he looked down at the floor before continuing his story.

"They took us to a room on the first floor. Two of the guys stayed there in the room, I guess to watch us. The other guy went somewhere else. We don't know exactly where. When he came back, he had another man with him. At first this new guy acted really nice, like he was concerned about our situation."

"Yeah," Vickie added, jumping into the conversation. "They acted like they were really going to help us."

Butch's mouth thinned into a straight line and his head nodded in agreement. "They sure fooled us," he admitted. Picking up from that point, a clearly agitated Vickie went on.

"Then they asked us how we were going to pay them for getting us across the river." She paused and gulped hard before going on. "We had $600.00 in cash, a gold necklace and two rings. One was my wedding ring." Her voice trailed off and it looked as though she might cry again. Kelli extended her arm and gently placed a hand on top of Vickie's and the tears began to flow freely.

"I'm sorry," sighed Vickie. "I don't know why I'm crying. Everything that's going on in the world and here I am acting like the few things that I lost are so important."

Placing his arm around his wife's shoulder, Butch soldiered on. "I asked them how much per person it was to go across. The guy in charge laughed at that like he had just heard a really funny joke." Clenching his jaw muscles tightly, he continued. "Then the fellas that were in there with him started laughing, too." Dropping his eyes, he told us, "That's when I knew we were in for trouble."

Vickie had her sobbing under control by then and spoke up. "The guy in charge told us that the money we had wasn't worth the paper it was printed on, anymore."

Butch broke back in. "He wanted to know if we had anything else of value that we could use as a trade. I was afraid to ask what he was talking about at first, but then, by the time I had worked up the nerve, I didn't have to."

Watching Jacob poke around in the fire, he continued to recount their recent scrape.

"The guy told us that they only took gold, silver, platinum

or precious jewels. So, just out of curiosity, I asked him how much gold it would take for us two to get across."

Looking straight at me, Butch said, "I should have just kept my mouth shut. When I said that, the guy in charge seemed to get real interested."

Vickie had restrained her tongue for long enough. Unable to hold back the hostility any longer, it came out in her words. "They thought that we had a lot of gold, or something, because of the way Butch asked." She went on, her voice continuing to rise in pitch. "They started asking all kinds of questions. How much gold did we have? Where was it at?"

Indignation in his voice, Butch spat out, "We tried to tell them that we didn't have any gold or jewels, but they didn't believe us."

Vickie chimed in again. "They started to get really mad at us when we didn't give them the answers that they wanted to hear. After a few minutes of yelling at us and getting in our faces," she paused and gulped, "they hit Butch in the head with a rifle butt." Starting to cry again as she relived the moment, Vickie slowly continued. "He was bleeding really bad and those animals wouldn't let me help him," she said through a downfall of tears. "They just stood there laughing and watching him bleed."

"It knocked me silly," Butch said. "By the time that I knew what the hell was going on again my head felt too heavy to lift off the floor." Lowering his voice to little above a whisper, he said with the shame clearly evident in his voice, "I had to lay there and watch them smack my wife around." A couple of stray tears found their way down his grief stricken face. "I tried to move towards her to help but one of those assholes kicked me in the ribs really hard and knocked the wind out of me."

In a quiet, reflective voice, Vickie said, "I thought that they were going to kill us, right there in that room. They took everything we had, even the $600.00 after they said it wasn't worth anything. I wish we would have had a gun," she hissed. "I would have shot them all as sure as I'm sitting here."

"No, Ma." Butch said, comfortingly. "They just would have shot us, right away. We still would have lost everything we had, but we'd be dead right now, too."

Eyes locking, the two entwined arms and embraced. Watching them squeeze each other tightly and exchange "I love yous," almost made Kelli start to cry, herself.

Kaleb appeared to be unfazed by all the emotions involved, he just wanted to know what happened next in this real life action movie.

"So how did you guys get away from them and end up here?" the wide eyed boy asked.

In a move that couldn't have been choreographed any better, everyone in the train car simultaneously turned and looked at him.

Seeming somewhat alarmed, Kaleb looked around at all of the staring faces and sheepishly asked, "What? Why is everyone looking at me?"

Kelli started first, but it wasn't long before everyone else joined in. Warm, rich, hearty laughter filled the little boxcar. It was a really nice moment for all of us and it helped to relieve some of our built up tension.

When Vickie could stop laughing long enough to talk, she said, "Well honey, something happened at the hotel. We heard a bunch of gunshots, but we couldn't tell if they were coming from inside or outside the building."

Butch cut in long enough to add, "But there sure were a lot of them."

Vickie took over again. Looking at Kaleb, she said, "Those goons looked at each other all wild-eyed when the shooting started, like they didn't quite know what to do. Then one of them asked the guy in charge what they should do with us." Giving a quick glance around at everyone else before returning her gaze to Kaleb, she told the rest of the story. "The lead man told the other two guys to lock us inside the room and they would deal with us later. 'We'll be right back, anyway.' he said. 'It shouldn't take very long.'"

"So," she went on, "after they left we tried to figure out what to do. The doors were too thick and solid to try and break down. Besides," she says, raising her eyebrows, "it would have been far too noisy. They would have heard us long before we could have gotten through."

"The only other option was the window," she said, looking over at Butch. "But with him being hurt like that, I didn't know if he could get up and out of it without hurting himself even more." Scrunching her face in a show of displeasure, Vickie then asked us. "Do you know those stupid hotel windows don't slide open?"

Butch jumped back into the conversation. "They're the kind that you push straight out, and they only go so far," he said, while holding up his hands about a foot apart to visually demonstrate the distance. Adding, "Vickie had to help me pick myself up off the floor and then slide out."

With a thin, playful smile on her lips, Vickie lightened the mood. "Good thing we were on the first floor," she joked. We all laughed out loud.

Butch told Kaleb, "We took off out of the city and headed back this way. About a week ago," he says, turning to me, "we came right through here. Never even saw this caboose sitting here."

"No," Vickie agreed, "we sure didn't. If we had, we would have come back here instead of being out there in the cold where you found us."

We all smiled brightly again. Vickie, we were finding out, still had a sharp sense of humor. Not an easy thing to maintain while surrounded by such misery.

Head tilted down, Butch looked at me from the top of his eyeballs. A somber look on his face, he said dryly, "We thought you were one of his guys when you walked up on us. Thought you had tracked us back here to kill us."

Instead of the earlier laughter, silence now filled the boxcar. Thick, deep silence. With no external noise sources, like in the old days, the silence truly was deafening. No airplanes. No trucks. No cars. No trains. No nothing that made any mechanical noises, whatsoever. The only sound, at all, was the intermittent popping of the wood burning in the fire.

Kelli always seemed to know just what to say at times like that. Putting a big smile on her pretty face, she said, "A few more days of being stuck in this caboose with us and you may start wishing he had been."

Smiles all around returned to full glow and the awkwardness of the moment passed.

53

    Over the next couple of days the weather improved dramatically. The sun decided to grace us with it's presence, once again, and it turned the glistening white landscape into an enormous solar reflector. Jacob and I dressed in layers of warm clothing and left scout our perimeter, yet again. With no sunglasses to our credit, we had to squint our painful, watering eyes to keep from going blind. The intensity of the brightness was so severe that even closing my eyes all the way did very little to mute the ultra-white. I could see every vein that ran through my eyelids like a doctor could see bones while looking at an X-ray.

    I started to consider turning around and going back to the caboose. Too much exposure to reflected sunlight can cause a burning of the retinas, a condition commonly known as snow blindness, and something like that could prove to be fatal to us. Without being able to properly see, Jacob and I would be nothing more than targets.

    Almost out of sheer desperation, I pulled my stocking cap down over my face. The shade that the knit cap provided turned out to be just the ticket. Slowly adjusting to the newfound comfort of the thready protection, my thankful eyes began to slowly respond.

I told Jacob, who was holding both hands up to his face in an attempt to shield his eyes from the invading light, "Pull the edge of your stocking cap down over your eyes. It seems to be working for me. I can see through the threads without being blinded."

Tugging his cap down over tear-swollen eyes, he must have felt the same sense of relief that I had a few moments before. In typical Jacob style, he matter-of-factly said, "That is better. At least I can see, now."

Biased as I may be, I had always been extremely proud of Jacob. He was an exceptionally imaginative and creative child. A true beacon of joy in our household. But since the onslaught of this catastrophic craziness, my admiration for the young man had grown by leaps and bounds. He had become an indispensable partner in our family's quest to reach safety.

As we began the daily trek to check out our perimeter, I had a flash of inspiration. At once, I felt foolish and stupid. "Why hadn't I thought of this before?" I chided myself. It could have saved us so much time and energy.

Excited by the prospect, I spun around to look in the direction of the expansive main building.

A smile spread across my tear soaked face. I hadn't been imagining it, after all. Standing about two hundred yards away, tucked in next to the back of the main building, stood a massive metal tower. The triangular shaped structure extended far up into the clear, blue, winter's sky.

Jacob, who had nearly ran into me when I stopped and turned around, followed my gaze in the direction of the big building.

"Whatcha lookin' at?" he asked inquisitively.

"That tower, Jacob," I answered. "That beautiful tower."

As we made our way over to where the tall, pointed object stood, we noticed that the snow was getting easier to walk through. The combination of abundant sunshine and more seasonal temperatures had done a real number on the white stuff. Instead of the hard, crusted over coating that had dominated the landscape the previous couple of days, the snow had grown soft and our footing was much improved. Although the sun's warmth had helped to melt the snow's depth but a few inches, it made all the difference in the world. Not having to lift our heavy boots quite as high, on every one of a countless number of steps, added up to a big savings of energy in the end. We traversed the entire distance to the base of the structure without having to stop for a breather.

Standing next to the bottom of the tower, the true enormity of the spire became distressingly apparent.

Jacob looked up in the direction of the peak and incredulously asked, "You mean you're going to climb up there?"

When I nodded my head to the affirmative Jacob's eyes got even larger and his forehead more crinkled. "You're crazy," he said emphatically. "What if you fall?"

"I won't," I answered. "I'll hold on tight and be really careful." Inside though, when I tilted my head back and looked up at the top of the spire I could feel butterflies flutter around in the pit of my stomach.

I could only guess at what the tower had been used for. The building, itself, looked as though it had been there for quite some time. Possibly since the 1930's or 40's. The tower, however, didn't appear to be of the same age. Again, only guessing, I pegged the tower to have been erected about 1960, or so. The lack of paint and abundance of surface rust also told me that no upkeep had been done on the triangular monster for many years.

Scary visions of getting halfway up the tower and falling leapt into my imaginary movie projector and played over and over on a continuous loop for me to view.

"Oh well, here it goes," I muttered, and began to slowly climb the triangular titan.

"Be careful," Jacob yelled from behind me; absentmindedly adding, "Mom won't be very happy if you get hurt, ya know."

When I had been standing down on the ground the wind didn't seem to be blowing very hard. As I started to get higher up on the side of the lofty leviathan, though, that once mild breeze began to turn into a light gale. Intermittent blasts of frigid air rushed in beneath the waistband of my jacket and assaulted the sanctity of my warm inner core. I immediately began to feel the winter chill creep into my body.

All of the buildings and stacks of pallets had served as a nice windbreak down on the ground, but up there, I was at the total mercy of the wind. Forcing my eyes away from my tightly clinched hands, I chanced a look down at the ground. Jacob was gawking up into the light blue sky at my dark silhouette with one hand shielding his eyes from the glare of the intense sunlight. From my perspective he almost looked like he was saluting me, military style. From that height, even the roof of the main building looked like it was a long way down.

Slowly raising my face skyward, I followed the spire until it came to a point far up in the blue expanse. For a moment I had the sensation of flying along on the wind with no earthly restraints to encumber me.

A bird has to be the luckiest animal of them all, I thought. To be able to take off and soar through the sky at will has to be the greatest gift bestowed to any of Earth's enumerable creatures. No motor required. No fuel. Just spread your wings and take off to wherever it is that your heart desires.

"That would sure come in handy about right now," I mumbled.

Trying to judge the height of my perch nestled amid the triangular, iron jungle gym, I came up with an approximation of between thirty and forty feet off the ground.

Wondering how much of the surrounding area I could see, my eyes moved their focus out into the vast, open areas surrounding the pallet factory. Even at a relatively low altitude I could see a remarkable amount of the snow covered landscape. Maybe this would work, after all, I surmised.

Remembering the trail of unfamiliar footprints that I had hurriedly followed back to the pallet yard the other day, my eyes moved to the north of the factory. Scanning the area carefully, it didn't take me very long to pick out the tell-tale signs of our cross country jaunt. Small, black shadows, created by the low slant of the February sun, marked every footstep as they crossed the white terrain.

Two days of plentiful sunshine had finally started to obscure the signs of our recent passage, but from that high up everything was still easy to see.

My inquisitive gaze turned toward the St. Clair River, located at the bottom of a gentle slope, less than half a mile away. Small, white-tipped waves magically slid down the river as if they rested on an invisible escalator hidden beneath the water's surface.

Beyond the glittering whitecaps and the tall, razor wire fences, the promise land stretched out as far as the horizon for my lusting eyes to see. The sight of our long desired goal being so close, but yet hopelessly out of reach, made me feel both sad and angry.

Sad, because I knew how badly Kelli and the boys wanted to get back to some sort of a regular life. Angry, because after all of the misery that we had endured to get there, we were stopped cold at the border and I didn't have a clue how to get across the river.

Over on Canadian soil, scattered houses dotted the snow laden countryside. Aside from the military patrols and manned watchtowers, everything looked to be pretty much normal.

My brain started to race, once again. Maybe from up here I could see some sort of weak point in their defenses and we could try to cross there. But, search as I might, I saw nothing that gave me a burst of renewed hope. I thought about climbing even higher to get a better view, but then decided that it might be best not to expose myself any further. If I could see someone from up there, then chances were good that they, in turn, could also see me. Not wanting to draw any attention, I quickly scanned the area once more and then started to retreat down the side of the metal tower.

As I reached terra firma, Jacob asked, "Did you see anything?"

"No, unfortunately not," I said dejectedly.

The soft, mushy snow felt so good on the bottoms of my feet after climbing the thin, steel trusses that I had to sigh out loud in relief. I repeatedly slapped my frozen hands against my thighs to get some blood flowing back into them. Even though I had gloves on, the cold had found it's way in and penetrated deep into my flesh and bone from holding onto the metal of the tower so tightly.

Trying to sound a little more upbeat, I told Jacob, "I could see a lot more of Canada from up there, though." He smiled at that and I did the same. I slapped him lightly on the back of the shoulder and said, "Let's go back and get warm."

54

    Walter greeted us warmly when we got back to the caboose. Kelli was surprised to see us back so soon. With an inquisitive look on her face, she asked, "Is everything O.K.? Usually it takes a lot longer for you to walk the rounds." By the time that she had finished her sentence, a look of concern had taken over her features.
    Not wanting to alarm her, I smiled and calmly said, "Don't worry, everything's fine. Jacob and I found an easier way to scout around, that's all."
    Kelli looked really confused. "What do you mean you found an easier way?"
    Laying my coat down on the bench seat next to our woodpile, I said, "Tell them what we did, Jacob."
    Everyone in the train car turned toward Jacob with inquisitive expressions.
    Feeling the heat of many eyes upon him, Jacob's cheeks began to blush noticeably. He hated being in the spotlight. Dropping his chin, he spoke very softly while looking at the floor.
    "We just went over to that big tower and climbed it." Adding with a mumble, "Then we came back here."
    Now the ping pong ball bounced the other way. Everyone's eyes turned back to me.
    Trying to draw attention away from the overly shy Jacob, I told his audience, "I could see a lot of Canada from up there!"

55

    Dinner was a nice change of pace that evening. Jacob had spotted a rabbit just before sunset and dispatched it with a single shot from his .22 rifle. He was becoming quite a skilled marksman.

    I gutted and skinned the animal and Kelli roasted it over the fire, nice and slow. It wasn't much. One rabbit between six people isn't exactly a feast. After eating nothing but jerky for over a week, though, it tasted like filet mignon to us.

    After dinner the conversation once again turned to the tower.

    Everyone seemed to have a question to ask. "How far up did I go?" "How far could I see?" "Did I find any way to get across the river?" Etc. etc....

    I was glad to see that everyone was excited. We didn't get much to crow about, anymore, but after a few minutes of tower talk I began to grow bored. My mind had already moved on to other things.

    Turning to face Butch and Vickie, I began asking some

questions of my own. "When you two were in the city was there any food around?"

After a quick glance at each other, Vickie shook her head lightly while Butch told me, "None that we could see. Of course, we weren't there all that long."

"About two or three hours, total," Vickie added. "Long enough to meet those guys that we had a run in with and then climb out the window."

Continuing with my questions, I asked, "What did the houses and stores look like up there? Were they burnt down or all torn up?"

Once again the quick look toward each other. I could see them squint slightly and stare blankly into thin air for a second trying to think back. Both of them started to talk at the same time and quickly stopped in embarrassment as soon as they realized it.

After the giggling stopped, Butch smiled slyly and said, "Well, I did see a couple of buildings that were burned down but most everything else looked alright."

Vickie, who patiently waited for Butch to finish talking this time, now relayed her memories. "That's the same thing I saw," she agreed. "We were mostly just thinking about getting across the river. Then all that stuff happened with those guys and we just ran. We didn't really have time to look around very much."

Kaleb, who was now beginning to feel quite comfortable around our new friends, said with large, round eyes, "I don't blame you, I would have ran as fast as I could, too." As if to offer some sort of condolence, he reached out his with his right hand and softly patted Vickie's shoulder a couple of times.

Asking the last thing that I needed to know before making my decision, I said, "Did you see many people there or only the guys that you had the run in with?"

This time, surprisingly, Butch and Vickie didn't look at each other before answering. Shaking their heads in unison, they both said, "No, only those guys."

56

    Once again we chewed our jerky dinners slowly while daydreaming about other food.
    The boys had replenished the wood pile earlier in the afternoon. Starting to feel stronger and healthier again, Butch had even pitched in and carried a few loads.
    He told me afterward, "Well, I am a little winded, but it felt nice, anyway." Putting a big smile on his face, he joked, "I guess being a little sore is a whole lot better than the alternative."
    Kissing Kelli goodbye, I followed Jacob out the train's door. We were heading into town to check out the situation for ourselves and look for some food.
    A lot of the snow's depth had eroded in the mild weather of the last few days. In some spots there was still four or five inches covering the ground, but in others there was nothing more than a dusting.
    Hoping to avoid anybody else in the area, we stayed well away from the fast flowing river. Walking at a slow but steady pace, it took us about half an hour to reach the outskirts of town. We tried to stay in cover as much as we could but there were a

lot of open areas along the way. We hid out in a small barn behind the Tractor Supply Store and waited for darkness to achieve it's full effect before entering town.

We moved slowly and cautiously as we snaked our way through a bunch of new vehicles at an auto dealership. Trying hard not to be spotted, we made sure to be extra careful with every step.

All of the cars and trucks in the lot showed evidence of being unceremoniously mugged. Exposed gas tank caps dangled down the side of every worthless vehicle. Round and square fuel access panels pointed rudely outward in all imaginable directions. To me it looked like they were discussing which direction would be the best way to go and couldn't quite figure out who was right.

I could see the glare of bright electric lights on the other side of the river between obstacles as we crept forward and their brightness was comforting. Knowing that there actually was a place of civilization across the cold, flowing water, gave me inner strength.

Slowly sneaking forward, Jacob and I made it to the far side of the dealer's lot and slid underneath a four wheel drive pickup truck. Lying side by side on our bellies, we took a moment to catch our breath.

The hotel that Butch and Vickie had been taken to was directly across from us. A small, empty lot stood between the two businesses. There were people in the hotel, alright. That was easy enough to tell. There was a sentry posted outside the door on our side of the building.

Standing about halfway inside the little shelter provided by the doorway's facade, the guard was running in place in an obvious attempt to stay warm. Then, without missing a beat, the energetic lookout started to shadow-box. Ducking, weaving and enthusiastically jabbing, he blew out huge plumes of smoky, white breath as he swung.

Jacob and I both had to chuckle a little at this outburst. The things that people do when they think no one is looking at them, I thought.

The flicker of what had to be a candle or an oil lamp came from a couple of the windows on the ground floor. I don't know the exact length, but I lost track of time for a little while. My thoughts drifted away to what it must be like to be inside a warm, secure hotel room. What it must be like to have an actual bed to sleep on. How long had it been since I had slept on a bed, anyway? I asked myself.

My mind went back to our last night at home. Home. What did that even mean anymore? I'm glad that Jacob snapped me out of my funk because I didn't like where my thoughts were headed.

"So, what now?" he asked.

Looking back up at the hotel across the small, rubble strewn lot, I tried to pull my thoughts out of the shitter.

"Well," I answered, "if there's someone guarding this side of the building, chances are they're probably watching the other sides, as well."

Jacob looked at me out of the corner of his eye and asked, in a whisper, "We're not going in there, are we?"

"No." I said. "Not right now, anyway. I just wanted to eyeball the place that they were talking about, that's all."

Looking over at the hotel again, trying not to pay attention to the flickers of candlelight this time, I scoured the grounds surrounding the building for any sign of more sentries. Without knowing the size of the occupying force we had no way of guessing how far out their circle of defense might be. For all we knew, we could have already been inside of it. Then again, I remembered thinking, we hadn't seen anything suspicious, thus far. Maybe this group was small and could barely afford the few lookouts that they had posted. Trying to figure out which line of thinking proved to be correct would have to come later, though. When the time was right.

I scanned the property that the hotel sat on and noticed an object that piqued my interest. In the back, right hand corner of the building's parking lot sat a trash dumpster with both of it's lids open and tilted back. They looked like big, empty, black eyes gazing up at the night sky.

A wooden fence about six feet high enclosed the trash receptacle on three sides. The section at the front looked as though it had been torn down long ago. Possibly in an effort to rummage through the metal hulk in hopes of finding some discarded treasure.

Directly behind the dumpster housing that served the hotel sat another, almost identical one that belonged to the building back there.

Dropping my head a little closer to the asphalt beneath the truck, I could see a sign proclaiming that the business sitting directly behind the neighboring vacant lot was a KFC.

As I Looked further in that direction, I knew that I had found a weak spot in their perimeter. The road that fronted the KFC was the last paved piece of real estate before the land's slope gave way to the mighty St. Clair. On the other side of that street was what looked like a small office building of some kind, with about a hundred yards of gradually declining river bank behind it.

If a person could sneak up from down by the river and around the KFC to the dumpster, I thought, they might have a chance to get close to the sentry on this side of the building before he even realized that they were there. Especially if they waited for an opportune time, such as the guard taking a piss, before they pounced. But, once again, that was for later.

My main concern at the moment was that our jerky supply would only last a couple of more days. If we stretched it out, that was. Since the number of hungry bellies in our group had recently increased by two, we needed to find some more food, and fast.

Carefully working our way back out of the auto lot, Jacob and I headed toward the center of town in hopes of finding a building that looked promising. It didn't matter if it was only a convenience store or a gas station. If it looked like there might be some food inside, we were going to explore it. We didn't have any choice.

57

"Pay close attention to the snow cover, Jacob," I told him. "You'll be able to tell if anyone has been around here over the last few days."

Choosing the sidewalk on the west side of the street, we started moving in toward the center of Marine City.

During our trek we went through an area of town where the houses were larger and the yards more spacious and ornate. Perhaps it was like the same neighborhood that most typical small towns had. The one where the influential and well to do of the community lived. All of the doctors and lawyers living harmoniously alongside the owners of the successful local businesses. It was the neighborhood that you simply *must* live in if you had money. Sure, you could find more modern homes. Ones with better plumbing and electrical wiring. Better everything, for that matter. Probably even get one for a lower price, too. But that made no difference. These were the kinds of places that people lived in as some sort of a misplaced badge of nobility. It didn't matter if there wasn't a single stick of furniture on the inside of the house. As long as you had the address and other people knew that you lived there, that was good enough.

Keeping our eyes peeled, we carefully made our way through "Better Than Thouville". We could see no signs of human activity in the snow, whatsoever. The only tracks that we spotted during our search was one wandering set of what looked like either dog or coyote tracks, and literally hundreds of cat tracks.

"Seems like this situation isn't bothering the cats, at all," I said with a slight shake of my head. "They seem to be flourishing." I had thought about bringing Walter along with us before we left the caboose, but only briefly. While Walter may have been a great watch dog and protector of our family, he was by no means stealthy about anything that he did. He would have eagerly come with us, but there was no way that we could have moved around unseen with him along.

Walking down the streets of that empty town had a very eerie feeling to it. All of the houses were dark and there were no streetlights. It seemed as if a giant vacuum had come along and sucked everybody up. Everyone, that was, except the worthless trash down at the local hotel.

For a moment I considered trying to look through some of the larger homes that we were passing by, but after looking a little closer at all of the broken windows around I figured that we were probably way too late to find anything of use, anyway. The neighborhood probably had a bullseye on it after the attack. Everybody and their brother probably flooded into the area looking for whatever they could find. Medicine, jewelry, firearms and ammunition, along with anything else they could use to trade or buy more food with. Those houses had probably been ripped apart inside. Every wall stripped of plaster and each floorboard pulled up in an attempt to find every possible hiding place.

Trying to find a market in an unknown city while staying out of sight is much easier said than done. Neither one of us had a clue which way to go. One would think that in a town that small it shouldn't be too difficult. Sooner or later you would turn a corner and run right into one. But Jacob and I were having no such luck. Figures, I thought. The longer the madness went on the more hopeless our search for food became.

My mind thought back to the human forearm and hand on the skewer at the surplus store and a terrible thought struck me.

What if there was no more food in town? What if the place had been picked clean and humans were the only source of nutrition left? And what about those thugs over at the hotel? Were they going to use Butch and Vickie as food?

Shaking that thought from my mind, I looked around frantically to try and find someplace in the area that looked promising. We were starting to get pretty far away from the caboose and walking on unfamiliar streets so I didn't think that we should be making too many turns. Getting lost under the best of circumstances is no fun. These were definitely not the best of circumstances.

Stopping to take a breather, Jacob and I climbed up onto the porch of a partially burnt out house to get out of the cold winter wind. It was blowing straight out of the north and we were both freezing from walking directly into it most of the way. With tingly, half frozen noses and watery eyes, we could do little but look at each other dejectedly over our fruitless search. Our blood was still pumping fast and hot so it didn't take very long for us to begin to warm up. It didn't warm our spirits any, though.

"What are we gonna tell mom?" Jacob asked me in a soft, almost pleading voice.

Seeing him with that helpless look on his face made me hate the whole damn world all over again for what he was enduring.

Keeping my emotions in check the best that I could, I turned my head to keep him from seeing the same desolate look in my eyes.

Why? I asked myself again, for what seemed like about the 487th time. Why the hell did this shit have to happen? I thought of a quote that a friend of mine had once cited. He said, "This is the only democracy on the face of the earth that has ever lasted longer than two hundred years." Sad, but true. Are we humans really that stupid? I asked myself. How can an entire race not know when to leave well enough alone? Taking a good, long look at our surroundings was the only answer that I needed.

From the corner of my eye I noticed Jacob shrink back away from the front of the porch, and when I looked at him, his eyes were round with surprise. Raising his right hand a little, he pointed a finger at something further up the street, to the north.

Sticking the edge of my face around the front corner of

the porch, I could make out two figures in what appeared to be camouflage clothing about half a block down. They were in the middle of the street, moving in a circle and carefully scanning the area in every direction.

My half frozen brain rapidly lurched into gear. I wondered if we had we been spotted? It didn't really matter who they were. Whether they were part of the hotel clan or someone totally unrelated, the result would be just as ugly.

Before my thoughts got too far along on any course of action the ante was upped and the stakes were raised. What appeared to be a whole squad of similarly outfitted figures ran out into the street from the eastern side to join the first two.

I looked at Jacob and saw that he, too, had seen them. He appeared to be as shocked as I was. His face wore the look of a patient that had woke up in the hospital and had no clue as to how in the hell they got there.

The sound of their booted footfalls, sounding strangely enhanced in the silence, filled our ears. I forced my eyes from Jacob as my mind screamed out, "Please don't let them come this way."

I turned and peeked back up the street. The last two members of the mysterious group were just disappearing from view between two houses on the west side of the street.

A flood of relief swept over me. If not for our decision to stop for a minute to get out of the biting chill of the winter wind, Jacob and I may not have had to worry about what we were going to tell Kelli. If we had continued our exploratory stroll down the snow covered sidewalk, we would have walked right into them. Completely exposed on an empty street with a bright, snow white background behind us, it would have been a nice, pleasant round of target practice for the squad of camouflaged wearing marauders.

Swallowing the lump in my throat, I asked Jacob in a hoarse whisper, "Do you hear anything?"

His eyes were still round and large. He seemed not to hear me for a moment before recognition snapped back into his eyes. We both listened raptly while trying to hold our breaths in order to be as quiet as possible.

After about ten seconds he looked at me and shook his head back and forth a little.

"Me either," I said. I found myself having to take a few

deep breaths to catch up on air. Holding it so tightly while listening for the ominous sounds of those footfalls to return had left me short winded.

Filling my lungs to capacity again and trying hard to sound calm, I turned to Jacob and said. "So, what do you say we head back? We can try again. Maybe even tomorrow. But let's try a different neighborhood next time, OK?"

Without hesitation, Jacob said, "Sounds good to me. Let's go."

Carefully taking in our surroundings, we slowly left the relative safety of the little, half-burnt porch and headed back toward the caboose, longing for both its safety and the luxurious heat of the roaring fire.

58

As Jacob and I got close to the little path that led to our shelter we could see Kaleb and Walter through the gaps between the tall stacks of pallets. It looked like potty time again, with Kaleb holding the looped end of Walter's big, red leash. The dog couldn't smell us because the wind was still coming out of the north at a pretty good clip and we had come in from the east, alongside the river.

For some reason I got an urge to play around a little. Suddenly feeling like a school boy again, I leaned my rifle against a stack of pallets and stooped down to grab a handful of snow.

It took Jacob until about the middle of my second snowball to get the idea. When he did, a little grin spread across his face. The young man had been through so much turmoil lately, I was glad to see that he hadn't lost touch with his wonderful sense of humor.

He leaned his rifle against the pallet stack next to mine and began to feverishly manufacture his own little stack of granulated ammunition.

With about a dozen nicely packed snowballs finished and

Walter completing his business, we knew that the time had come. I grabbed one of the projectiles and flung it in a high arc toward the unwary targets. Hidden from their view, Jacob and I anxiously waited to see where the sphere would come back down.

A small, dark hole appeared in the snow about 6 feet behind Kaleb. The noiseless impact of the missile went completely unnoticed by the quick striding pair. They continued to move toward the train car, totally oblivious of our presence.

Jacob sent another projectile airborne and in quick succession, I let another one fly. The first snowball landed directly between the two marching forms and, once again, went undiscovered. Then a neat, little, round hole appeared in the snow just a few inches in front of Kaleb's planted right foot. There was no missing that one. He froze, mid stride, and then two things happened.

The first was the leash in his left hand snapping tight due to the continued momentum of the large dog's bulk, and the second was another snowball that I had lobbed exploding on his right thigh.

He let out a tiny, startled yelp and started to run for the caboose at full speed. Walter, who was obviously glad that Kaleb wasn't pulling back on his leash like he normally did, joyfully helped to propel him across the clearing by keeping the lead pulled taut. Jacob and I absolutely howled with laughter. Mean, I know, but we couldn't help ourselves.

Kaleb had just about made it to the back of the caboose when the look on his face changed and he stopped cold. Hearing us roaring with laughter, he knew that he'd been had.

"Very funny, you guys," Kaleb angrily yelled in our direction. He sounded annoyed and perhaps a little embarrassed, but his voice also housed an unmistakable touch of relief.

Grabbing our rifles and spewing raucous laughter, Jacob and I ran toward the back door of the caboose and all the comfort that our little shelter provided. Thankful to be back in one piece, we were ready to get some much needed rest and eat, eat, eat. Even if it was nothing but deer jerky, again.

59

    A bright, intrusive light striking my face brought me out of a slumber. Still half asleep and puzzled at what the piercing brightness could be, I opened my eyelids a little to have a peek. Although they were only open for a split second, the blistering sunbeam that attacked my eyes left searing orbs emblazoned on my corneas. Throwing a hand up to shield myself from the painful intrusion, I held back a flash of anger and waited for my blind, watering eyes to slowly recover.
    As my eyes slowly adjusted to the light blaring in through the train car's windows, I could see why it had been so bright. The sky was a beautiful, clear blue and looked to be absolutely cloudless.
    Kelli leaned out a little from where she sat at one of the booth seats and smiled at me. "Good morning, sleepy head," she said pleasantly. "Did you sleep well?"
    Nodding my head, I said, "Yes," through a dry, croaky throat.
    "We thought you two were gonna sleep all day." Kaleb playfully said from the other side of the enclosure. "Jacob's still sleeping."

A quick peek in his direction did indeed confirm that Jacob was still sleeping. It didn't surprise me, though. We had gotten back really late and were completely worn out from our exploratory jaunt.

Kaleb was the only person in the train car that was still awake when we arrived. He was taking his turn at watch and glad to have a little company, even if it only lasted for a few minutes. Jacob and I didn't tell him what we had seen in town, only that we hadn't been lucky enough to find any food.

Bathed in the brightness of the intense morning light, the previous night's episode seemed far, far away. Like a barely remembered bad dream or a scene from a horrible "B movie" that you only watched because some moronic friend told you, "No, really, it's good. Take it from me!"

A carousel of the obstacles that we faced began to swirl around inside my head like the perpetually spinning second hand on a clock. Each passing moment brought with it a new problem that would need to be solved in order to cross the border.

A loud rumbling in my mid-section shoved all those other thoughts to the back of the line. Food, it reminded me, had to be our number one priority. We barely had enough jerky to get us through another day. After that it was back to empty, gnawing bellies. Whatever decision we were going to make about our future course of action, our urgent need for food said that it had to be figured out soon. Real soon.

After downing a couple pieces of jerky for an unsatisfying lunch, I asked Jacob if he would be willing to climb the tower without my supervision and have a look around. In light of the comments that he had made the previous day while we were standing at the base of the tall spire, I was uncertain as to what his answer would be.

Trying to make the task sound less daunting, I added, "You don't have to go too far up. Just go high enough so that you can see around the area, then climb back down and let us know if you see anything out of place."

I watched his eyes search the wooden floor of the caboose as he thought the undertaking over. It was clear to those of us who knew him well that he was having an internal battle with the idea. Jacob had never been a big fan of high places and, as a general rule, was usually overly cautious about *everything.* On the other hand, the young man's confidence *had* grown by leaps and bounds during our recent trials. He would be far more likely to do attempt something like that at that time than he ever would have in the past. Plus, I knew that he didn't like to appear weak in front of anyone, especially his brother or strangers.

Finally raising his downcast eyes from the plank flooring, Jacob looked at me and said, "Sure, I can do that."

His arrival at that decision caught Kelli off guard. A look of obvious distaste fell over her features and she leered at me with that "you have got to be kidding me" look that I had previously seen on a countless number of occasions.

A wink from my right eye flew her way and the angry expression changed to one of mild bewilderment.

I wasn't done, yet. Transferring my gaze to Kaleb, I suggested to him, "Perhaps you could go along with your brother and keep an eye out for him while he climbs the tower."

Surprise and reluctance fought for the upper hand on his face. Good, old Kaleb. You could always count on him not wanting to take part in any sort of physical activity.

"I was kinda wanting to stay here and talk with you guys," he said as he pointed toward the little booth that all four of us adults were sitting in.

Kelli's "are you serious?" look intensified and she asked me, "Do you think that's a good idea? Sending the two of them out there without one of us going along?"

Trying to sound reassuring, I told her with a crinkled brow, "They'll be fine. They know the area well enough and it should only take them about ten or fifteen minutes. They'll be back before you know it."

60

After the boys had left to go survey the area, I told Butch, Vickie and Kelli about our nighttime reconnaissance trip into Marine City. I recounted our search for food, the fast moving squad of camouflaged wearing soldiers and the guards stationed outside the hotel.

Nodding in unison several times as I spoke, Butch and Vickie seemed to be re-living their own harrowing trip into the city.

Kelli just looked shocked. She was incredulous. "I can't believe this," she groaned. Leaning forward and placing her elbows on the surface of the booth's little table, she buried her face in her outstretched hands. In an attempt to steady her nerves she drew in a few, deep breaths and exhaled very slowly.

Finally, after an uneasy bout of protracted silence, I heard a small, muffled voice come from behind her concealing palms. "What are we gonna do now?" she wanted to know. I could tell from experience that she was close to tears because her voice kept rising in pitch until the sentence ended.

Unfortunately, I had no answer.

For the next minute, or so, all four of us spent time keenly studying our wringing hands and the train car's wooden floor. After our short wallow in a bout of self-pity, we finally summoned the courage to raise our heads and look into each other's disheartened, woeful eyes.

Wanting to break the somber mood that had enveloped the train car, I asked Butch and Vickie the first question that came to mind. "Did you two happen to see any groups of camouflage clad figures running around when you were in town?" Each of our new friend's faces turned my way, at once.

"Yeah," Butch said, as if coming to out of a dream. "We saw those guys a bunch of times when we were down by the river. They had a shootout with the guys that ended up grabbing us." Suddenly seeming awake and animated, he went on. Holding his right hand out in front of his body with his finger pointed out like the barrel of a pistol and his thumb cocked high, he said, "They were shootin' at each other and bullets were flying everywhere. One guy got shot and killed, right there."

"One of the military looking guys got shot in the arm, but he ran away from the rest of them toward the center of town right after that," Vickie softly said, while looking off into space remembering the brief, but violent exchange of gunfire between the two groups. "We had no idea who was who or what they were fighting about. After the shooting was over we were stupid enough to go and help the group that was closest to us. They got the worst end of the deal, that's for sure. Two of them were dead by the time we got over there and the other two didn't have a scratch on them. Weird. Anyhow, that's when the two remaining guys lied about being able to help get us across to Canada. Then they led us back to that hotel and held us hostage."

Another short bout of silence filled the caboose as we all got lost in thought. Realizing that there wasn't a lot of time left before the boys would return, I cleared my throat and began to lay out an ambitious plan. "We need to do something tonight."

61

Kaleb and Jacob returned to Walter's joyous jumping and slobbery hand licks and reported that they hadn't seen anything amiss or any unknown tracks in the nearby snow cover.

Kelli looked relieved when the boys came in through the caboose's door, almost like a heavy weight had been lifted from her chest allowing her to breathe freely again.

After they had gotten settled back in from their short trip, I steered the conversation back to what we were in the process of planning for later that evening.

"The answer is going to be inside that hotel," I told everybody. "Those guys are obviously in control around here. Whether it's from being here the longest or because they have superior firepower and numbers, we don't know. But we need to. We need to know exactly what's going on around here and the only way to do that is to get it straight from the horse's mouth."

Everyone's chin dropped and their mouth's gaped open when the next sentence out of my mouth had been completed.

"We need to kidnap one of the guards outside the hotel and make him talk."

For a moment there was nothing but utter silence. Then a vociferous chorus of astonished exclamations filled my ears. It almost sounded like I had just thrown a rock into a beehive from the continual buzzing. As the deluge of excited chatter finally started to die down, single voices began to stand out from the crowd.

"How the heck are we going to kidnap someone?" Kaleb wanted to know.

"What if we get shot?" asked Jacob.

"How are we going to make him talk?" Kelli wondered aloud.

A plethora of questions, one after another, came in quick succession. Not knowing how or even if I could answer all of those questions, and more, I decided to ignore them for the time being and started to lay out the details of my elaborate plan.

62

    Well rested from our afternoon naps, warmly dressed and heavily armed, we set out on our attempt to bag a bad guy.
    For some reason, this time the walk into town didn't seem to take as long. With all of the different thoughts going through my head, the scenery seemed to fly by.   I'm sure that it was the same for all of us. The main component of my plan, which I had emphasized repeatedly, was, - "please, nobody forget their part or one of us is likely to get hurt."
    We followed the river's path, staying about a hundred yards off it's shore until we saw the large KFC sign appear out of the darkness. Making our way up behind the small office building across the street from the Colonel's kitchen, we split into two separate groups.
    Kelli and Jacob continued heading north to take up their positions on the northwest corner of the hotel. From that vantage point they would be able to put the guards on those two

sides of the building in their rifle sights. If there was any trouble they were to down them both, without hesitation, and hightail it back to our rendezvous point on the river's bank.

Butch, Vickie, Kaleb and I cut across the darkened street to the KFC, careful to stay out of the line of sight of Hotel Hell's guards. Skirting the south side of the Colonel's building closely, I peeked around the back corner by the old drive-thru lane. As I had hoped, this was a blind spot for both the southern and eastern hotel entrances. We would be able to walk from that corner of the building to the dumpster and it's fence, sitting in the back corner of the lot, at a leisurely pace. Moving from that dumpster's wooden facade to the other would be just as easy. The hard part would come after that.

Kaleb would set up behind the cover of the nearest dumpster fence with his sights on the guy guarding the eastern entrance. He also knew that if something went down to take out his target and run like the wind.

Butch and Vickie had the most dangerous and uncomfortable job. They would act as decoys to get the southern-most guard's attention. It had to be them, I reasoned, because he was familiar with Butch and Vickie, having seen and captured them before. He wouldn't be very alarmed by their appearance and might even get over confident. If it would have been one of our family, I'm sure that the guard would have been much more cautious and on edge. Since we needed every little advantage that we could get, it had to be them.

They were supposed to calmly walk toward the man, looking as if they hadn't a care in the world. In fact, Butch and Vickie were going to act like they were deliriously happy. Smiling and waving like they were out for a raucous evening of cocktails with their friends. Telling the baffled guard that they needed to see the boss, and immediately. They had just found enough gold to buy their passage across the river. To make sure that they stood on his western side so that I could sneak up on him from behind the useless automobiles that sat around like dusty, old memories in the hotel's parking lot.

My job was to knock him unconscious, quickly and quietly. Then Butch and I were to carry his limp body back to the cover of the dumpster, first, and then down by the river.

Safely making it to the rear of the closest trash housing, our group sat and waited for a while to make sure that Kelli and

Jacob had time to get in position. We were only going to have one shot at this, I told myself. There wasn't enough time to try anything else. If it failed, we would be in dreadful shape.

After about fifteen minutes had elapsed we silently exchanged nods that said it was time to go.

"Good luck," Kaleb and I whispered to Butch and Vickie as they hugged one another.

Stooping down until they got behind a big, white Econoline van sitting about ten feet away from us, the two then stood erect and turned to look at us behind the dumpster fence again. Seeing that we were paying attention, they nodded again and started around the van, arm in arm.

63

    Kaleb and I hurried around to the other side of the small enclosure. He sat behind a stack of old garbage bags and rested the barrel of his rifle on top of them. Crawling on hands and knees, I moved forward behind the closest row of cars.
    Halfway to their location, the voice of the guard on this side of the hotel came to my ears. In a calm sounding, I-can't believe-this tone of voice, he uttered, "You two again?"
    Vickie's voice, loud enough for me to hear but not loud enough to carry halfway around the building to the other guards, answered. "That's right," she told him. "It's us. We want to talk to the boss. We just found a lot of gold and now we can pay for our passage across the river."
    A short pause as the armed sentry tried to decide if they were for real or not.
    By that time I had made it behind the protection of a large car and raised my head up to look through the tempered glass.
    "Let me see it, then," the guard said, doubtingly.
    "Not yet," Vickie countered, white circling ever slightly to the west and the guard turning with her.
    Seeing my chance, I hurried across the parking lot to the

safety of the next row of vehicles.

"Oh, no," Butch said, adding a small chuckle. "We want to talk to the boss. He said that we could buy our way across with enough gold, and by God, we've got plenty."

The guard was totally absorbed in Butch and Vickie and their large discovery of gold. As quietly as I could, I moved behind a big Dodge pickup truck parked in the handicap space next to the door.

"We're only going to deal with the boss," Vickie went on in that impossibly good, cheery tone of voice. "Who's to say that if we showed it to you, you wouldn't just take it for yourself?" she asked the goon guarding the hotel door.

I could see his head tilt slightly to one side and heard him say. "Well, maybe I would and maybe I wouldn't. But nobody gets to see the boss unless it's for a damned good reason. He doesn't like to be disturbed, ya know. He's a busy man."

Vickie shot right back. "He didn't seem to be too busy to see us the other day," she said scornfully. "In fact, he seemed to be very happy to see us the other day."

The demanding door guard didn't get the opportunity to respond to that statement. The butt end of my SKS smacked into the back of his unsuspecting head with the sound of a baseball hitting a bat. Blood flew and the sentry dropped. First to his knees, and then flat on his face on the hard surface of the asphalt parking lot. There was no question that he was out cold. If the shot to the back of the head hadn't done it, the blow to his face when he fell forward sure did.

Placing my rifle's sling over my left shoulder, I grabbed the goon under the armpits and lifted his upper body so that he was in a sitting position.

His face was in bad shape and all three of us couldn't help but wince when we got a decent look at the damage. The guy looked like his face had been used as a tackling dummy on a particularly tough day of football practice.

"Grab his legs, you guys," I quickly whispered.

Butch grabbed one leg and Vickie the other. Our odd little human caravan slowly made it's way back across the parking lot to the cover of the dumpster's housing. Collapsing in a heap when we reached the safety of a blind spot, we huffed and puffed heavily. A result, no doubt, of both carrying the mass of a large, limp body a good distance and the pure exhilaration of getting away with it. So far, at least.

In a panting whisper, I asked Kaleb, "Anything?"

He shook his head and quietly answered. "No."

"Do you think you can carry one of his legs?" I asked the wide-eyed boy.

Hesitantly, he said, "Sure, if you need me to." Classic Kaleb.

"At least until we get away from here," I told him.

"OK," he whispered back.

Butch moved over next to where I was and grabbed onto an arm. I grabbed the other one and with Vickie and Kaleb each holding a leg, we started out for the river. It was a totally surreal experience carrying around an unconscious, captive human body. It's still hard to believe that we actually pulled it off.

I had no idea how long it would be until the hotel bullies discovered that one of their lookouts was missing, but we didn't want to be anywhere around when they did.

Behind the shelter of the KFC we took a quick breather. Our prisoner's bleeding had slowed down as the fluids began to thicken and clot. Nobody said a word until we were ready to move on again. We just sat there blowing humid, white plumes of breath into the cold night air and frantically looking around.

Reluctantly, I shrugged my shoulders and asked, "Ready?"

Once again we hoisted our human cargo and lit out at the pace of a staggering, drunken sailor. Pushing ourselves to the max and maybe a little beyond, we managed to make it all the way to the back of the little office building across the street from the KFC in a single outburst of energy. On the way by the structure, I saw a sign in the front window. It read "Koffman's Insurance. Home. Life. Auto. Call Today." I'm guessing old Koffman wouldn't want to field all the phone calls that he would get from people trying to collect on their policies after a disaster like this. If, that was, he was lucky enough to survive the ordeal in the first place. Or unlucky enough. Sometimes it's was hard for me to decide which was which.

I could see the rippling reflection of the lights from the Canadian side on the surface of the dark, flowing water down in the river.

With a small grin on my face, I told the others, "At least

it'll be a little easier to carry him now that it's all downhill from here to the river." Nobody else seemed to find my joke very funny, though, and my little smile faded as I resumed sucking air with everyone else. The goon had to weigh close to two hundred pounds. Didn't he realize that there was a food shortage going on?

Feeling like we could afford a little longer rest that time, the four of us stayed behind the insurance building until our breathing was pretty much back to normal. Then, once again, we lifted our well-fed friend and slowly waddled down the gradual slope toward the river.

It only looked to be about a hundred yards from Koffman's back door to the water's edge, but it felt like four hundred.

When we got down to within fifteen feet of the water, the unconscious bulk that we were carrying was deposited in a small snowdrift. He lay there not seeming to care while we collapsed all around him, our lungs burning like white hot coals with every indrawn breath.

It was safe for us to talk normal then but no one did. None of us wanted to do anything but breathe.

64

After the lightheaded feeling of hyperventilation had passed, I untied my left boot and removed the lacing from it. I released the snap locks on each end of my rifle's sling and the leather strap fell downward to land in my lap. Emitting a grunt, I picked myself up and grabbed one of our guests limp arms and flipped him over onto his stomach. Pulling both of his arms behind his back, I bound them by tightly wrapping the leather sling around his wrists. I used the two foot length of strong nylon bootlace to secure the ends of the strap so that it wouldn't unwind, no matter how hard he pulled on it. Moving down to his feet, I untied the prisoner's boots and then retied them to each other with large, tangled knots. If he did manage to get on his feet and make a break for it, he wouldn't get very far.

    I removed Walter's big, red leash from my left coat pocket and his stainless steel choker chain from the right, and snapped them together with a small click. Sliding the chain down over the sleeping thug's head, I placed it around his neck and delivered a small tug to get it into position.

    When I looked up I saw Vickie wearing a huge, fiendish looking grin that stretched from one ear to the other. I froze for a moment. It looked so out of place at the time that I almost felt alarmed by it's presence. She looked like an insane serial killer that was thoroughly enjoyed every second of her gruesome work.

Perhaps it was the intense pressure that we were all under, I can't say for sure. For some odd reason, though, the longer that I stared at that hideous grin, the funnier it became. It looked so cartoonish that I couldn't help but smile, too, and before long, it had snowballed to the point that we were all laughing so hard that we were blowing snot out of our noses from trying not to make too much noise. Good, hearty, belly laughs. They took my breath away again, but this time in a good way. Once all of the knee-slappin', snot slingin' laughter was done, we all seemed to feel a lot better. Everyone looked to be a little more relaxed and at ease. At least, for a moment.

A gurgling moan escaped from our bound prisoner's mouth and his fingers started to twitch. I saw one swollen, bloody eyelid slide open and an unfocused eye try to take in it's surroundings. The scenery must not have been to the battered eye's liking, though, because as soon as a semblance of recognition flashed within the dilated pupil, the body that it belonged to began to thrash around violently like a fish caught on the end of a hook. His mouth set in a furious sneer, he tugged at the strap that bound his wrists together until grunts of exertion came from his tightly clenched jaws and the cords of his neck became obvious.

Feeling the last of a smile disappear from my lips, I knelt down on the middle of the squirming mass's back and pulled up sharply on Walter's leash. The bright chrome steel of the choker chain dug into the soft, vulnerable flesh of the marauder's neck. He struggled violently in an attempt to throw me off, but only for a few seconds. Finally finding the effort to be futile, he prudently gave up.

"Would you like to breathe again?" I asked the prone prisoner. There was no way in the world that he couldn't have heard what I said, yet there was no indication, whatsoever, that he did. From the look of it, neither of his ears appeared to be badly damaged. I began to wonder if he was still conscious. I was just about ready to ask again when the stubborn shyster began nodding his head. At first it was slow and almost imperceptible, but it grew to a jerking, panicky nod before I remembered to ease up on the leash a little.

Near even portions of gagging, coughing and harsh, rapid breathing emanated from his raspy throat. All of it coated in a heavy mist of spittle.

Not wanting him to get too comfortable, I leaned over and looked down into his badly battered face. Even though the damage around one of his eyes was awful, the discolored swelling had nearly closed it, I could still clearly see his searing rage when he glared at me.

Ignoring all of that, I told him in a steady, even voice, "If you try that again, you're gonna wake up in hell the next time." What I said clearly registered in his lone working eye, but it only lasted for a moment before the intensity of his glare returned to full force.

"If you want to play tough guy," I spoke down at him, "that's fine with me. You can be a dead, tough guy. You've caused your last bit of trouble around here, my friend."

His good eye was searching all around, trying to size up the situation. It was almost like I could read his mind and listen to the tumblers clicking in his brain, calculating all of his options and the odds associated with each one. I had no way of knowing if he would decide to press his luck, or not, so I tried to nip it in the bud.

Speaking calmly and quietly, I told the insolent hoodlum, "If you try to give me any more trouble, I'm going to drag you down to the river by your neck and see how well you can swim with your hands and feet tied."

His operating pupil swept down the riverbank and took in the icy flow of the St. Clair. A fleshy bubble ran up and down the length of his throat as a gulp fought it's way along against the restraint of the choker.

When he looked back up in my direction, the look in that bruised optic had softened, ever so slightly. Lying on the cold ground had obviously chilled his sedentary body. Small shivers began to shake his upper torso at almost regular intervals. It became abundantly clear that he wanted no part of the water. Perhaps it was because he couldn't swim, although we'll never know, for sure. Maybe he was just too cold already to be able to withstand a leisurely, moonlight dip in the world's largest glass of ice water. Whatever the reason, Cyclops decided to play nice and chilled out.

Kaleb's voice rang out, "There's Mom and Jacob!" Two shadowy figures were swiftly making their way down the gentle slope behind Koffman's Insurance building.

The lights from the Canadian side of the river reflected off the water's choppy surface, throwing small facets of white light up and across the river bank like thousands of mirrors on a revolving disco ball.

Kaleb stood facing the descending forms, waving his right arm slowly back and forth above his head. An answer wave, quick but certain, returned from one of the shadowy figures. Their pace quickened until it appeared as if the two were running at full speed. In long, loping strides, they covered the intervening distance in short time.

Smiles and hugs were exchanged among our joyous little group. The rush of adrenaline coursing through our veins seemed to make us downright giddy. Punch drunk, runner's high, whatever you want to call it - we had it. We had been successful, thus far, in carrying out a seemingly impossible task, and it felt great. The silly grins and feelings of sheer exhilaration just would not go away.

Breaking our temporary euphoria, Cyclops elevated his head from the snow covered ground and looked toward us with one insolent eye. "What do you people want with me?" he demanded to know.

Our smiles withered as we looked back at our captive and began to contemplate the daunting tasks that still lay ahead of us. In just a few seconds, those shit-eating grins were as gone as yesterday's time.

After all, only the first phase of our plan had been completed. The worst part was yet to come.

65

"You're gonna die, you know that, don't ya?" pinata-face said with as much of a sneer as he could muster through his mangled mug.

Butch and I had drug our prisoner over and sat him under the nearest pine tree, propping his back against the knotty trunk. Whirling around to face him, I was suddenly angry. Very angry.

I unslung my rifle and stuck the end of the barrel about three inches from Cyclops' nose. Horrific mental images of my family dying at the hands of that barbaric group were flashing through my mind. "If any one of us go, you're going, too," I growled at our prisoner.

One bloodshot eye belligerently peered out at me. I suddenly had the urge to shoot the man. I wanted to kill him, right then and right there. To hell with the rest of the plan, this joker needed to die.

As if he could read what I was thinking, the look on the battered fellow's face softened a bit. A slight smile appeared and grudgingly spread across his swollen features. "No need for all that, my friend," he cooed hoarsely. He tried to hide the panic in his voice but his shaky vocal chords betrayed him. Maybe this man *is* human, after all, I thought. At least what passes for it nowadays.

    My anger gradually subsided enough that I was able to think clearly again. I knew that I couldn't shoot the man. At least, not yet. There was way too much riding on the outcome. We needed to get some information out of him about what was going on around there. Without it, we didn't stand much of a chance of surviving.

    I took three steps to the left and stood on our prisoner's blind side. Silently motioning for Butch to give me the handle of Walter's leash, I placed it around one side of the trunk and pulled mightily.

    The bloodied, swollen mass that was this hoodlum's head hit the barked surface of the tree with an auditory thump. "Ow!" he sharply cried out. His body jumped as it tried to recoil away from the source of pain.

    Paying no attention to his discomfort, I wrapped the long leash the rest of the way around the tree and handed the end of it back to Butch.

    Vickie was smiling, once again, and whispering excitedly back and forth with Kelli.

    Kaleb and Jacob stood slightly apart from the girls and each other, silently watching the proceedings.

    I knelt down next to him, rifle butt at the ready.

    The hooting of an owl floated down from a nearby tree. For some reason the bird sounded happy, almost like it was cheering on the best entertainment that it had seen in a long time.

    "We'll start with something easy," I told the captive thug. "What's your name?"

    The man was silent for a moment, then he chuckled and mockingly said, "My name?" He sounded absolutely incredulous. "You want my name?" He laughed out loud.

    Between outbursts of insincere laughter he managed to find a little more courage and his voice turned arrogant and cocky, once again.

    "What? Do ya have a warrant for my arrest, or something?"

    My rifle butt slammed into the blind side of his tree strapped head. It jerked back and forth violently and a startled scream escaped from Cyclops' mouth. Dark fluid began to flow from the ear closest to me. It looked painful. A loud sucking sound followed the scream. It reminded me of the sound someone would make if they had just touched a red hot burner on a stove. He tried to turn his head to look at me, but the tightened leash wouldn't allow it.

"What the hell did you do that for?" he yelled in rage. He momentarily started to struggle against the leather strap that bound his wrists but must have thought better of it with his head lashed tightly to the pine tree. Easy pickings for me and the battering ram that was my rifle butt. This guy was dumb, but he wasn't stupid.

Exasperated, the goon asked in a pleading tone of voice, "What do you want from me?" Panic was back in his voice, and stronger than ever.

"I want answers," I told him, "and if I hear anything other than answers come out of your mouth again, I'm going to crack your skull. Then we'll drag you down to the riverbank and let you float away."

Cyclops didn't say anything, but he started to shiver, once again. His one good eye closed and stayed that way for a few seconds. He looked dead.

What are we doing? I suddenly chided myself. This guy looks like he's been in a bad car accident and we have him bound, hand and foot, and lashed to a tree. But deep inside I knew exactly what we were doing; surviving, and that's the only thing that mattered.

Regaining my composure, I spoke to the goon in an exaggeratedly cordial tone.

"Let's start over, shall we? What is your name?"

Only slight hesitation, this time.

"Charlie," he squeaked in a thin voice.

"That's better, Charlie," I said, half amazed. He sounded like a scolded child who was whiny and in need of a nap. "Tell me, Charlie," I smoothly went on, "what goes on in that hotel over there that you were guarding?"

Cyclops Charlie tried to turn his head in my direction and was, once again, denied by his bindings. "You can hit me if you want," he warned, "but I'm not saying anything about the hotel." It was plainly evident that this guy wasn't going to cooperate willingly. He would try as hard as possible not to reveal anything important to us.

"Charlie," I said, like I had been deeply hurt. "I don't

want to hit you. I have to hit you."

The rifle butt crashed into his head again with a heavy thud.

"Damn it," he roared. "What the hell? Look, I can't tell you anything or I'm a dead man."

Butch still stood behind the pine tree, holding the dog leash taut. The two ladies and Kaleb and Jacob had formed a rough, semi-circle around our prisoner. They stood looking down, fully engrossed in the ghoulish spectacle. Their eyes exhibited the glossed over look of someone who just witnessed a bad accident which had resulted in severe carnage.

Getting down on one knee, I spoke quietly to the mangled, bloody pulp that used to be an ear. "Charlie," I said, "Do you think we would tell on you? Not a chance, ol' boy. I promise you that if you tell us, no one else will ever have to know."

"You don't know what they're capable of," he blurted. "They...." he stopped mid-sentence, obviously terrified.

More curious than ever, now, I tried to coax it out of him. "They what, Charlie?"

He was trying to shake his head in spite of the chain around his neck.

"I can't tell you or they'll kill me."

Striding around Butch to keep from interfering with the leash, I moved to the other side of the tree and a fresh ear. Once again the rifle butt found it's mark. At first, I thought that I had hit him too hard. His head didn't rebound the way it had previously. It hung limply against the choker chain and seemed incapable to righting itself.

In a sudden state of panic I looked over at Butch and hissed, "Loosen it up or he'll choke."

He released the tension in the leash and the battered lump that was Charlie fell forward and to the left. Striking his forehead on the hard ground, he lay motionless in a fetal position with one wayward leg sprawling out to the side. His breathing was harsh and rapid like he had just finished running a long, grueling marathon. One blood encrusted eyelid flicked open but the pupil was unable to focus itself. It looked as if Charlie's lights were on, but he definitely wasn't home.

Motioning for everyone else to help, I pointed toward the river, "Let's drag him down there."

Kaleb looked absolutely mortified. His eyes grew large and round. They looked almost as bright as flashlights in the semi-darkness of the river bank. Nodding slightly in Charlie's direction, he asked in a reverent whisper, "Is he dead?"

Kelli shook her head and tried to assure him in a soothing voice, "No, Kaleb." she said. "He's not dead, he's just kind of unconscious."

Kaleb's eyes squinted and his brow furrowed as he tried to figure out what being "kind of unconscious" meant.

Charlie had begun to moan again and now that his head was free of the tree trunk, he shook it groggily. The lone working eye in the puss filled mass that used to be Charlie's face started to register it's surroundings, once again, but the swollen optic could do little more than watch us hoist it's bodily bulk down the riverbank to the water's edge.

As we laid Charlie down by the shoreline of the St. Clair, he began to mumble incoherently. His babbling reminded me of some of the drunks that I had witnessed at parties in the past. Collapsed in the room's corner and having to piss themselves because they couldn't stand up to get to the bathroom, they would begin mumbling and fussing at the world, blaming it for all of their short-comings. Then they would end up crying uncontrollably or puking all over their own shoes. Often, they would end up passing out and sleeping it off, right there, in their piss soaked clothing.

"Damn it," I cursed myself. "Why did I have to hit him so hard?"

"Don't blame yourself," Vickie said forcefully. "I might have done worse than that if I had gotten ahold of him. He deserves it," she went on. "He's one of the guys that roughed Butch up back at the hotel. And besides that, how many people has he done this to?"

I had no way to answer that question, but I got the point.

Vickie sure was a straight shooter. She knew how to get right to the bottom line.

"Thanks, Vickie," I sheepishly said. "You're right and I know it, but, still." I trailed off, not finishing my sentence, but Vickie was looking at me and nodding her head, just the same. She knew. I didn't have to say a word.

Charlie's slurred words broke the somber mood. "What the..?" he softly mumbled. A tongue flicked out and licked down a pair of demolished lips. Trying it, once again, this time he managed to get out, "What the hell?" all at one time.

Walking into his good eye's sight path, I greeted our friend warmly. "Well, hello Charlie," I said in an artificially cheery manner. "You seem to have fallen."

Reality began to register in the lone focusing pupil of Cyclops and it didn't take him long to become panicky again. Seeing the water's edge only a few feet away from where he lay, Charlie seemed to have a sudden change of heart.

"Wait a minute!" he desperately pleaded. "You can't throw me in there, I'll drown."

Startled by this sudden reversal of demeanor, our little group looked around at each other in bewilderment for a moment.

I looked back down and asked the prone prisoner in a mocking tone of voice, "What's the matter, Charlie, can't swim?"

"That water's freezing cold," he shot back. "I'll die in no time."

"Don't worry, Charlie," I sighed. "You'll drown long before you have a chance to freeze to death."

Once our new friend finally did start talking, it didn't take long to get all the information that we needed. He only tried to hold back once more. A quick soaking from the waist down in the icy river put an end to that. I believe that after that, Charlie would have told us anything.

By the time the divulgence of information had reached it's end, Charlie was a quivering mess. He appeared to be on the verge of hypothermia. After a short group consultation, we decided that the only humane thing to do would be to take him back to our shelter.

In danger of freezing to death and wrought with severe shaking, Charlie's bootlaces were untied so that he could walk better. Butch still kept a solid hold on the end of Walter's leash and I walked behind both of them with my finger on the trigger.

He never gave us any trouble, though.

66

    By the time the caboose appeared in our sights, Charlie looked like a solid block of ice from the waist down. His knees no longer bent with each step. He walked with a straight-legged gait, plowing his way through the snow in jerky, shuffling motions.
    Once inside the little train car, he was unashamed as strange hands stripped him of his frozen clothing. The cloth had become solidly encrusted in ice and it made the work very difficult. Charlie moaned and shivered violently, his teeth chattering away like the keys of an old typewriter. I had a feeling that Charlie wasn't gonna be himself for quite a while.
    After checking his wrist bindings, we wrapped him in a blanket and sat him in a booth seat, near the window. The choker chain was still attached to his neck. It ran down behind the back of the bench and was securely fastened to the seat's leg.
    Walter had taken an instant disliking to our guest. He laid about four feet away from Charlie, constantly staring and occasionally growling.
    Trying to clean up our prisoner's face and head was a daunting, messy task, but we all pitched in a little to help get it

done.

Outside the train car, snow had begun to fall from the winter sky again. Kaleb and Jacob took the time to replenish our wood supply to ensure that we would have plenty to burn if the weather turned ugly.

Not much conversation took place. We were all exhausted and content with just sitting quietly and resting.

We passed around what was left of the deer jerky. The six of us split the five remaining strips as evenly as we could. It wasn't much of a meal after all of the energy that we had exerted, but it was all that we had. No jerky was offered to Charlie and he asked for none. It was decided that he had been eating way better than we had lately, and could therefore afford to miss a meal. Walter received a small portion of everyone else's meager ration and then quickly returned to staring and occasionally growling at our quivering guest.

67

I awoke to a surprise the next morning. Since it had been my night off from our watch rotation, I slept soundly, throughout. While I did, about four or five inches of fresh, powdery snow had fallen and it appeared from looks of the low, gray clouds that more would follow.

Putting on my boots in a hurry, I grabbed my coat and headed for the door. Walter was usually bounding at my heels in the morning, eager to go outside and go to the bathroom, himself. Not this time, though. I turned and discovered that the big dog was still lying in the same spot that he had been before I went to sleep; about four feet away from Charlie. I called to him. His large, melon sized head turned my way and gave me a cursory glance, then it turned back and re-fixed itself on our houseguest.

"He only went out once last night," Kelli offered.

"Yeah," Jacob said. "When I was on watch, he went just outside the door, peed and then wanted right back in. All he does is stare at him," the boy said, pointing at Charlie.

For some reason, Walter clearly didn't like Cyclops. I had learned long ago to pay close attention to an animal's instincts about someone.

Charlie's head looked even worse in the light of day. The swelling had become extensive and the bruising was in full bloom. Different shades of black, purple, red and yellow covered nearly the entire surface of his head. He needed medical attention. Some sort of clear fluid ran at a continual, slow seep from his deeper wounds. Infection looked like it might be a problem where a large flap of his hairy scalp had been torn back. It was now curled under another portion of hair, upside down and stuck fast with a massive coating of coagulated blood. A doctor's arm would have felt like a limp noodle after putting in all of the stitches that old Charlie One Eye needed.

The only thing was, there *were* no doctors to be found. No working hospitals, either. And definitely no medicine. That had been one of the first things to disappear after the calamity. Drugstores and medicine cabinets from coast to coast were raided. Some people looking for drugs that would get them high, others looking for drugs that could possibly save a life.

Charlie sat in the window seat of the booth with downcast eyes, occasionally chancing a quick glance at us or out the window.

I began to suspect that something was seriously wrong with him. He hadn't said a single word since about the halfway point of our trip back to the shelter the previous evening and had not so much as asked to go to the bathroom in over twelve hours. He appeared dazed and lost. It must have hurt like hell to turn his head because every time he did so, it was at an excruciatingly slow pace.

We untied the leash from the bench seat's leg and helped Charlie slowly lower his head until it rested on the table's surface. He spent the rest of the afternoon that way, motionless and silent.

68

    Putting our worries about Charlie's health aside for a while, we started working on the next phase of our plan. With the information that he had provided, we felt like we had a real shot at pulling it off.
    The two water cans made their way around the train car's interior more frequently, now. We were trying to keep something in our bellies, even if it was just water.
    According to our now comatose friend, there were only eight members of their marauding mob left. Without Charlie, they would be down to seven.
    At one time, and not so long ago, he had told us, their band of bullies had numbered twenty-three. Over the last couple of months, their group had been battling it out with the remnants of a National Guard unit that was training around Grayling at the time of the disaster. Encamped in a large, thickly forested area to the west of Marine City, they made regular forages into town.
    My mind sprang back to the squad of camouflage

wearing, fast moving figures that Jacob and I had spotted. Charlie said that Hotel Hell's inhabitants were slowly and systematically being eliminated, with military precision. He said that it had gotten so bad that no one left in their ever shrinking mob had any desire to leave the safety of the hotel anymore.

The reason for all the fighting was simple enough: food.

The band of thugs that Charlie belonged to were all locals. Most of them born and raised right around Marine City. When the shit hit the fan, they knew where everything was and greedily helped themselves to it. Inside that hotel, he said, were rooms filled with food and drink. Case after case, stacked so high that they almost touched the ceiling.

They had raided every warehouse and storeroom around the city, snatching everything edible that wasn't nailed down. Insatiable in their quest, they grabbed every last cigarette, pack of gum and bag of beer nuts to be had. Every can of soda and every single bottle of beer and liquor that they found was carted off back to the hotel.

They had feasted mightily and drank wastefully, he said.

One corner room upstairs had been used as a cold storage locker for the meats, cheeses and other perishables. A cold winter's wind blew across the room, from one window to the other, and kept the room as cold as a giant walk-in cooler.

I think that room starred in all of our dreams that night.

Their leader, who went by the name of Steevo, was a local hoodlum with a long list of convictions and jail time. Charlie said that he was very charismatic and could talk just about anyone into doing just about anything. He was heavily armed with automatic weapons and even had possession of a few grenades that they had found while plundering through some nut's house.

We had taken all of the information that Charlie had supplied up to that point in stride. Everything that he divulged was almost expected. We could have guessed most of it before hand. The thing that made our heads instantly snap toward each other and our eyes widen in surprise was when Charlie calmly said,"Steevo has a contact on the other side of the river. He's a member of the Canadian Coast Guard. Stationed directly across the river from Marine City."

Acting as though he was confiding to us a deep secret, Charlie's voice had lowered to barely more than a whisper.

"The guy guards one of the huge drainage tunnels that run out into the river from the Canadian side. Steevo pays him in gold and jewels to smuggle people through the big pipe and into the sewage tunnels under Sambra."

So it wasn't just a ruse designed to ensnare unsuspecting victims, after all, I thought. There really *is* a way to get across the river. As we snuck sly glances around at each other, I could see embers of hope begin to glow in our desperate eyes.

Our new best friend didn't stop there, the beans continued to spill.

"He keeps in touch with the guy by using a Ham radio," Charlie drawled. "He has a few real nice ones that'll reach all over the world. We found them in an electronics store downtown. There must to be thousands of batteries for the thing. Seemed like every place that we hit had batteries." His voice turned whiny for a moment. "Those damn things get heavy," he groaned. "Always walking around with your pockets full of 'em. I bet you that for about the first month after this all started, I didn't spend a single day without having to haul a heavy load of batteries back to the hotel."

Poor Charlie, I thought facetiously. We had been living in twelve hours of darkness a day and scrounging for scraps of food and this well-fed bastard was complaining about heavy pockets full of batteries. Interrupting my ill-natured thoughts, our prisoner went on.

"You know," he said with what used to be an eyebrow slightly rising, "the Canadian government will let Americans stay there, if they can get there."

Once again all of the heads in our little group spun to look at each other. Could it be?

America had that policy with Cubans. It wasn't encouraged by our government, by any means. In fact, our Coast Guard was quite diligent in their efforts to keep out these so called Boat People. If, however, one was able to set foot on American soil, they would be afforded immunity and allowed to stay in the country.

Our new friend's droning voice snapped me back into focus. "Canoes are what they use," he explained. "Canoes are small and low to the water. They're hard to see at night because they have them painted the same color as the water." He sounded proud of his gang's shrewdness. Like a school kid that had outwitted a dim authority figure and went around bragging to all of his friends about it.

"Reggie usually leads them over in his canoe and then tows the empty one back," Charlie confided.

Pressed about Reggie, Cyclops had said, "Reg is second in command. He's an ex-con, too. A twisted individual. He likes to hurt people." Pausing for a second, he then added, "I guess he gets off on it, or something."

The story among his motley crew was that Steevo and Reggie had done time together and now were as tight as two peas in a pod. Sharing their visions of anarchy and chaos the same way that some folks talked excitedly about football or collecting stamps. Their two rooms on the ground floor of the hotel had connecting doors, Charlie told us. And, since their minions had been dropping dead at an alarming rate, neither man wanted to leave the sanctity of those rooms.

69

    In some ways, our planning was much simpler this time around. With the knowledge provided by Cyclops Charlie about the hotel and it's occupants, we were also more confident than ever before. Knowing that every food source left in town was stored inside the building didn't hurt, either. We were hungry.
    In other ways, though, the planning for this assault was far more meticulous and detailed. The last time we had only made contact with one member of their team, (good old Charlie) and had not tried to enter the hotel or get into a shootout over it's possession. Things would be quite different this time.
    After a lengthy discussion, we arrived at the end of our formulating phase and a deep silence took over the interior of the caboose. The six of us were lost in our own apprehensive thoughts about our upcoming excursion. Busy contemplating both the gleeful prospect of sweet success, and the gut-wrenching agony of failure. The possibility of having to take someone's else's life and the fear of death, itself. The only sound that filled our ears was the almost popcorn-like snapping

and popping of the pine slats burning in the fire. Between those intermittent pops it grew so quiet that each individual person's breathing and Walter's rapid, heavy panting all became clearly audible.

An alarm went off in the back of my mind telling me that something wasn't right. Reluctantly forcing myself from the depths of a now forgotten daydream, it took a few tension filled moments for me to figure out what the problem was. I had been registering and paying attention to the sounds that I was used to hearing all the time. The crackling of the wood burning in the fire and the howl of the wind outside. What gave me cause for concern, though, was something that I couldn't hear.

Turning from the fire to face our guest, I focused upon Charlie's upper torso. Panic shot through me like a bolt of electricity when I noticed that the blanket wrapped around his shoulders wasn't moving. It was no longer rising up, ever so slightly, and dropping back to it's original location in a steady rhythmic pattern. It wasn't moving in any pattern, at all. It was totally still. Charlie wasn't breathing.

I got up and promptly rushed to his side. Removing the blanket draped around his unmoving shoulders, I dropped it onto the floor behind the seat. I hesitated for a moment, suddenly wary of touching Charlie. My subconscious was screaming, "Be careful. This may be some sort of a trick." Deep down inside, though, I knew better. Charlie wasn't faking anything. He was dead.

Placing the first two fingers of my right hand against the side of his neck, I felt for the steady thump of flowing blood beneath the surface of Charlie's skin. Everyone in the train car fell completely silent. Even though they all had gathered around me and Charlie like a bunch of football players in a huddle, I couldn't so much as hear anyone breathe while they waited for an assessment. I kept hoping to feel a pulse, even if it was a faint one. But the longer that I tried, the more reality sank in. Charlie was gone.

I raised my eyes to meet Kelli's and gently shook my head back and forth.

We all seemed to be emotionally confused over Charlie's death. Although he wasn't a family member or even a part of our little group, his passing still struck us hard. Up until that point in our crazy adventure, death had always been something that happened to other people. People that we didn't know and had never talked to. But with the up-close and personal demise of Charlie, death had finally been brought home to our doorstep.

His head propped up on a little, fluffy hill of snow behind the caboose, Charlie looked more at peace than he ever had during our brief acquaintance. Anyway, it would have been sort of spooky sleeping inside the train car with him still there.

With darkness only about an hour away and our planning finished, we tried to relax and get a few hours of sleep. It looked like it was going to be one hell of a long night.

70

    We said our goodbyes to Cyclops Charlie on the way back to the hotel later that night. His stiff, rigor mortised body made him relatively easy to transport. Removing the choker chain from around Charlie's neck, Butch slid it up over his boots and secured it around his ankles. The big, red leash was long enough that it allowed three of us to pull on it at the same time and, considering it's bulk, Charlie's body slid along surprisingly well.
    When our caravan got down to the edge of the river, we removed the chain from around Charlie's ankles. Turning him around so that his battered head was in the water, we launched him into the icy cold liquid like we were christening a battleship. He only carried forward for about six feet before the powerful flow began to sweep him downstream. Bobbing and twisting like a wayward log, we stood on the river bank in silence and watched him go until the night's darkness covered his body.

71

We were fully expecting the guards stationed outside the hotel to be on high alert. From what Charlie had told us, Steevo and Reggie were the paranoid type. Already spooked enough to lock themselves inside their rooms, they weren't just going to let anyone waltz up on them unexpectedly.

The last time our plan had been one of stealth. This time it was one of cold, calculated murder. We were still outnumbered by the thugs, seven to six. Taking out all four of the guards at once would give us a two to one advantage.

It was decided that the four shooters were going to be myself, Butch, Jacob and Vickie. From what Butch said, Vickie was a crack shot. She had evidently been killing groundhogs out on their rural property for years, and a groundhog is only a fraction of the size that a man is.

Once again, we split into two groups behind the red brick building that used to house Koffman's Insurance Agency. Vickie, Kelli and I continued going north to take up our sniping positions on the northwest corner of the hotel. Butch, Kaleb and Jacob crossed the street there and used the KFC building as cover to slip into the dumpster housing behind the hotel.

Kaleb would move west through the parking lot from there, using the cars for cover. He was tasked with finding a spot where both teams of shooters could clearly see him, but the sentries couldn't. When he could make eye contact with both groups at once, he would give each squad a thumbs up. If everything was fine on our end, each crew would give Kaleb a thumbs up in return. If, and when, he received our return signals, Kaleb would slowly raise his arm into the air and then swiftly let it drop like a man with a flag starting a race. Each shooter would then silently count one thousand one, one thousand two, one thousand three and then shoot to kill. There could be no mercy shown if we, ourselves, wished to survive. If, for any reason, something wasn't right, any one of us could stop the whole thing with a simple wave of a hand.

It took a lot longer than we had expected for all of us to get into position, but after much jostling around everyone was finally set. Kaleb ended up having the most trouble. It was exceedingly difficult for him to find a spot where he could see all of us but not be seen by two different guards. He diligently kept trying location after location until he was finally successful.

Looking first toward Butch and Jacob and then our way, Kaleb gave both groups a thumbs up. His head moved back and forth between us and the guards a couple of more times before he hesitantly raised his right arm.

There are moments in your life that you never forget, and the look in Kaleb's eyes, even from a hundred feet away, was an image that will be burned into my mind forever.

His arm came down in a rapid, sweeping arc.

Sucking in a small breath and steadying myself to fire, I began my silent count to one thousand three. I never made it, though. The booming, nearby explosion that came from the .30-.30 in Vickie's hands made me jump. The movement caused me to lose my sight picture and I immediately feared that my bullet would stray from it's intended course and blow the whole operation. It could be that I had simply counted slower than she did and ended up falling behind. It's also quite possible that after what her and Butch had endured at their hands inside the hotel that Vickie was in a bit of a hurry to dispatch the jack booted thugs to hell. Perhaps it was a little of both. No matter, though. It all worked out well.

Vickie's target dropped like a stone in the spot where he

had been standing. Having also heard the thunderous report of the .30-.30, my victim actually turned his body toward us, making for an easier target. There was no time to thank him. The SKS in my hands roared and the guard outside the front entrance of the hotel wobbled slightly before dropping down on one knee. The jolt dislodged the weapon from his arms and it fell onto the concrete sidewalk with a rattly clang. Both hands clasping his upper chest, the startled sentry fell forward onto the hard, cold surface and didn't move any more.

After exchanging quick glances with each other, Kelli, Vickie and I sprung forward to carry out the next phase of our plan. Running over to the goon that Vickie had shot, we grabbed his limp corpse and placed it's mass up against the outward swinging door at that entrance. Quickly moving around to the front of the hotel, we did the same thing with that guard's body.

I could only assume that since there was no shouting going on and no additional gunfire, that the other squad had been successful, as well. The same thought must have went through Kelli's mind because she looked at me and asked, "I wonder how they're doing over there?" as she jerked her head in that direction. The concern clearly revealed in her eyes.

Without another word, we hustled around the corner of the building to meet up with the other team. Moving at a brisk walking pace with our guns pointed forward, we rounded the building and were greeted by absolutely nothing.

Butch, Kaleb and Jacob were nowhere to be seen. Neither were the guards. There was nothing there to greet us except empty space and an eerie, unnerving silence.

72

    The hair on the nape of my neck stood at attention and my throat suddenly grew dry. As we edged closer to the side entrance and the sidewalk which serviced it, a large, freshly deposited pool of blood appeared on the concrete surface.
    The contrast between the two substances was amazing. The concrete, new and well kept, was almost as white as the snow which skirted it's boundaries. The blood, so shiny and such a dark, rich red, that it almost looked black in the low light.
    We slowed way down and cautiously crept up to the doorway. Lying up against the bottom of the glass door was the body of a dead sentry, dressed in all black. The expression frozen on his face was that of an innocent child who had just opened a present on Christmas morning and found it to be so spectacular that it left them wide eyed and speechless.
    Once again, we exchanged unsure, nervous looks between the three of us. No words were needed. Kelli led the way and we followed her toward the back of the hotel.
    A little more than halfway between the bloody sidewalk

and the back corner of the building, a dark, solitary figure appeared out of the darkness like an apparition.

Kelli involuntarily let out a small, startled yelp.

"Sorry, Mom," Kaleb apologetically said. "I was just coming to get you guys."

Recovering surprisingly fast, Kelli told him, "That's OK, honey," and strongly embraced him with a racing heart.

"Where's Butch and Jacob?" Vickie asked, with more than a touch of concern in her voice.

"At the back door, waiting for us," the boy answered.

Jacob stood just inside the shadowy doorway and Butch held the glass door open for us. Vickie grabbed him around the neck in a vice-like hug and delivered a huge, slobbery kiss. Eagerly accepting it, Butch matched her intensity with his own strong embrace.

Jacob's eyes looked wide and alert as he turned in our direction and gave us a little nod from inside the darkened building.

From that point on, the level of danger to our little band of half-starved, adrenaline-pumping crusaders would increase exponentially. According to our old pal Charlie, there were seven members of the misfit mob left. Since we had just dispatched four of them in one fell swoop, that should leave three remaining occupants still inside the building. If, that is, there hadn't been any recruits in the previous twenty four hours.

We felt confident that when the shit went down, Steevo and Reggie would barricade themselves inside their rooms with their hand grenades and automatic weapons.

We knew exactly where their rooms were located, thanks to Charlie. On the southwest corner of the building's first floor. Our plan was to let Steevo and Reggie sit and stew inside their chambers while we went from room to room and floor to floor in a systematic and thorough search to find the third, and hopefully only other, resident of Hotel Hell.

73

    Dead sentries were now guarding three of the four entry doors for us. I hoped that they would serve the purpose until we could check out the rest of the hotel and get back to properly secure them. We didn't want to permanently close the exits off, just yet. If we did that, the remaining inhabitants of the hotel wouldn't be able to flee if they wanted to and we would be forced into fighting them in order to clear the premises. If Steevo, Reggie or whoever climbed out of a window and took off, that was fine with us, too. We would prefer not to have to deal with anyone, at all.
    Butch and Kaleb took up posts just inside the last doorway, hunkering down in the cover of the dark shadows. Anyone going in or coming out would have to pass within a few feet of their watchful eyes and nervous trigger fingers.
    Jacob, Kelli, Vickie and I hustled in to where the hotel's two hallways intersected and turned to the right. We scampered as fast as our malnutritioned bodies would allow to the end the long corridor. Opening the door that housed the stairway for that side of the building, we started to ascend the steel steps at a slow, cautious pace. The stairwell was eerily quiet and every little noise that we made appeared to be amplified. Every breath and every footfall seemed to sound abnormally loud. Even the swishing sound that our pants and jackets made as they rubbed together boomed throughout the tight little space. Each individual noise was also accompanied

by a healthy helping of echoing reverb for good effect.

We had decided that the third floor would be the best place to start, thinking that if anyone *was* left in the hotel, they would probably be housed on the first floor with Steevo and Reggie. After all, as the old saying goes, there's safety in numbers. By starting on the third floor and noisily making our presence known, we hoped that if there was anyone else in the building, they would scurry away from us like cockroaches do from light.

Once the third floor had been swept clear, we would go to the second story and repeat the same process, all over again. After that we would work our way through the bottom floor, moving from north to south. Unless we absolutely had to, we had no plans to bother the rooms that housed Steevo and Reggie. Some things were better left for daylight.

Arriving at the top of the stairs, I led our procession through the fire door and out into the darkened hallway. Standing at one end of the long, narrow corridor, we silently watched while Kelli slowly crept down to the other. She and Vickie were tasked with covering Jacob and me from opposite ends of the building while we went from door to door, searching every room.

When Kelli got to the other end of the hall, she turned and knelt down in the corner.

Gently nodding my head in his direction, I whispered, "You ready, Jacob?"

A short, breathy, "Yeah," was his only response.

The bottom of my boot smashed into the first door. It sprang open and jumped into the wall behind it with a shuddering crash that resonated down the entire length the hallway. The hinged slab of wood started to rebound to it's original position like it was a child's rubber ball thrown at a brick wall.

Quickly planting my foot in the middle of the door's intended path, I halted it's forward progress. I stared into the pitch black room and listened closely for a few seconds, but saw or heard nothing.

Taking a closer look at the strike plate and door jamb revealed why there had been no resistance when I kicked on the door. The inside section of the wall was a splintered mess where the door fastened to it. The damaged portion of the facing looked as though it had been blown outward by a small but powerful explosion. Someone had already kicked the door in.

Gun barrel leading the way, I cautiously stepped through the opening with Jacob close behind. It took a few seconds for our eyes to adjust to the darkened atmosphere inside the room, but when they did, it's features began to stand out more clearly.

Funny, I thought to myself. When all of this first happened, we hated to see the sun set and the onset of darkness. Electricity and light at the flick of a switch had been so easy to use and so ingrained in us that we felt helpless and at the mercy of the long winter nights. Over the course of time, though, our night vision had developed to the point that we no longer loathed the darkness, and in fact, could see reasonably well.

I stood to the right inside the doorway. Jacob was on the left, his gun held high in a firing position.

Two double beds, still neatly made, were sitting off to the left. Little lamps that magically extruded from the wall framed each of them. A small, boxy night table stood in between. A long, low chest of drawers sat against the wall to the right, with a very large, rectangular mirror mounted above it.

The bathroom door stood wide open, revealing the white tiled floor. It glowed in the near darkness with an effervescence usually reserved for a Hollywood star's porcelain veneers.

I was suddenly thankful that we weren't searching through someone's house or apartment. It would have been hell looking through piles of personal belongings, in addition to the obstacles that we were currently facing. The sparsely furnished hotel rooms actually made anyone's attempt to hide a foolish and futile effort.

Stepping lightly, I made my way across the room's floor while carefully scanning it's contents. From my vantage point next to the room's window, I could see nothing that looked suspicious.

The beds had no legs and laid atop dark colored, pedestal-like platforms. No way to hide under there. That left only the bathroom and the shower stall that it contained.

Trying to keep the horrific images that I had seen in the movie *Psycho* out of my head, I re-crossed the shadowy room. Stopping right outside the open bathroom door, I leaned forward and stuck my head inside.

A long, thin, white marble vanity stretched all the way from one wall to the other, on the left hand side. A huge, borderless mirror fastened to the wall hovered above it and also stretched the entire distance. The room seemed to be a little bit brighter than the main room. The mixture of the mirrored surfaces and white tiling combined to magnify all of the available light and send it cascading about inside the tight, little space.

The toilet was straight ahead, directly in line with the door opening. There was even a fresh roll of toilet paper in the dispenser. The shower stall was to the right, hidden behind closed sliding doors made of frosted glass.

A voice in the back of my head cried out, "If there *is* any place to hide in here, this is it."

Trying to block out my meddling conscience, I eased my way into the small, confined space of the hotel bathroom. Once again, the sound of my breathing seemed to be louder than normal as it bounced back at me off the sterile, white ceramic tiles.

Creeping across the room in four big steps, I turned and put my back against the wall between the toilet and shower. Reaching forward, I extended the barrel of my gun and placed it up against the handle of the sliding glass door. With a short, quick thrust, I pushed the shower door open. Stopping as it reached the end of it's track with a rattly *whack*, the frosted panel snugly nestled alongside it's lifelong companion.

From where I stood nothing was visible inside the shower. The front portion of it, anyway. I had to stick my head inside the stall to examine the back corner. Drawing in a deep breath, I nervously edged closer to the open shower.

The combination bathtub and shower unit, along with it's surrounding walls, were the same bright white as the rest of the bathroom. The only difference being that the tile lining the shower's interior was a lot smaller in size. I could see thousands of tiny, white tiles stare out at me while I stood there mustering the courage to invade their private space.

Acting as though I was a child playing hide and seek, I slowly peered around the shower door's edge with one searching eye. A huge, involuntary sigh of relief escaped my lungs.

The shower stall was empty.

74

    Jacob and I relentlessly made our way down the hallway, going from room to room and making as much noise as possible.
    Most of the rooms on the third floor were pretty much the same. The only difference between them being the size of the beds.
    Two rooms, however, were very different.
    One was a small supply room filled with mop buckets, housekeeping carts and sweepers. Along the right wall, three thin wooden shelves ran almost half the length of the space. Generously stacked on these shelves was box after box, case after case of toilet paper, shampoo and soap. I was almost shocked into paralysis by the sight of it all. Items that we had always taken for granted and never even thought twice about, now looked like a king's ransom in gold. Kelli and Vickie would be absolutely ecstatic, I thought to myself. Now if we could only find some laundry detergent and deodorant.
    The other room that differed from the rest was located on the northeast corner of the hotel. When Charlie had first told us about it, it sounded like a far-fetched fairytale. A figment of one's overactive imagination. Even as Jacob and I stood there looking at all of it, we still couldn't believe what our eyes were seeing.
    Just as Charlie had said, both windows of the corner room were wide open and it was freezing cold in there. And, just like Charlie had also said, there was stack after stack of boxes filled with meats and cheeses. There was bologna,

sliced ham, turkey, bacon, sausage and who knows what else. Boxes filled with cheddar, mozzarella, pepper jack and colby cheese. Piled neatly upon one of the beds was a good sized pyramid of whole hams. On the other, an even larger pile of turkeys. In the far, right hand corner was a massive mountain of Pepsi, Mountain Dew, Diet Coke and almost any other brand of soft drink that you could think of, all mixed together. Another large stack stood in the opposite corner. This one composed of nothing but beer, and seemed to include every nearly variety available. Bud, Miller, Pabst, Michelob. I even saw a twelve pack of Heineken poking it's green nose out of the alcoholic scrum.

There was so much merchandise stored in the room that we would have to wait until it grew light outside to know exactly what all was in there. All that we were worried about at the moment was making sure that no one was hiding in there.

"Oh, my God," a quiet voice whispered in awed reverence.

I glanced back and saw Kelli standing in the doorway, mouth open, chin hanging and eyes bulging as she scanned the horde of merchandise. The urge to stop what we were doing, tear into those provisions and gorge ourselves until we were bloated was exceedingly powerful. So powerful, in fact, that I almost succumbed to it's temptation and did just that. It had been a long time since we had even laid eyes on such a wealth of caloric riches, and we were all very, very hungry. Somehow I convinced myself that there would be time for that later.

We still had two more floors to search, minus Steevo and Reggie's room, of course. Once that was completed, we would be able to stuff ourselves silly at a leisurely pace. Just in case, though, I grabbed two packages of Oscar Meyer Thick sliced Bologna and two blocks of Colby cheese, and stuffed them into my coat pockets.

Exiting the walk-in cooler of a room, we pulled the door tightly shut behind us. It was time to move our operation to the second floor.

Jacob hustled to the other end of the hall to team up with Vickie, and in unison, we descended the stairs at each end of the building. Arriving in the second floor hallway at almost the exact same time, we set up again and started to repeat the same process all over again on that level.

75

    Everything went well until we got to a room near the center of the hotel. Kicking the door open and looking inside, I was so startled at first by what was there that I almost opened up with my SKS. It took a moment for me to fully realize what I was looking at, and when I did, I rushed Jacob out of the room. The boy had seen it, too, of that I had no doubt. I just didn't want him to have time to understand what he'd just had the misfortune to witness.

    In the hallway, still trying to regain my composure, I looked at Jacob and whispered, "Stay out here for a minute, O.K.?"

    His eyes were large and round, showing a sea of white around his tiny pupils. "Are they dead?" he asked, a slight quiver in his voice.

    I couldn't lie to him. I didn't know if he had taken in every detail that I had, but he had seen enough.

    "I think so," slipped from my mouth, even though there wasn't a doubt in either one of our minds that they were. "Why don't you stay here for a minute and let me check?" I tried to sound calm and sure of myself, but at the end of the question my voice wavered and cracked a little, betraying me and revealing my emotions.

    In the excitement of the moment I had completely forgotten about Kelli and Vickie. As Jacob and I stood talking in the carpeted hallway just outside the room's door, we heard a noise and nervously jerked our heads in that direction.

"What's going on?" Kelli excitedly hissed. She and Vickie had noticed our hasty retreat from the room and were looking our way attentively, weapons at the ready.

"Nothing," was the first answer that popped out of my mouth. Everyone was already wound-up enough, I thought to myself. There was no need to add to it. Knowing that my response was nowhere near sufficient enough to explain our sudden departure from the room, I added as a quick afterthought, "I don't know for sure, yet."

It was a lie, though. I had a fairly good idea of what was going on in there. At least what *had* gone in there, and it wasn't pretty.

Turning to Jacob again, I told him firmly, "Stay here, I'll be right back."

My heart was thumping so loudly when I re-entered the room that it sounded like a bass drum kicking out the heavy beat to a rock and roll song. I didn't really want to go back in there, but I knew that I had no choice. Having come this far in our eradication process, it would be stupid to leave, as they say, any stone unturned.

The scene inside the room was one of total madness, the stuff that the most horrific nightmares are made of. But from the look of things, it hadn't just been a dream. It had been a real, living, grotesquely huffing and puffing, sadistic and twisted nightmare.

Tied naked and spread eagle on each one of the beds was the body of a woman. Even in the near total darkness it was impossible not to notice that decomposition had begun to have it's way. The eyes of the one closest to the door were wide open and glaring up at the white, swirl-patterned ceiling. Her face was locked in an agonizing grimace, front teeth exposed like that of a snarling dog. Her body appeared bruised and broken. Discoloration from what looked like a severe beating covered almost the entire surface of her skin. Visible lacerations were scattered about on her extremities and blood stains dotted the bedspread's flowery surface like they had been raindrops from a brief spring shower.

The poor woman had been violated in every way imaginable. Her body, beaten and horrifically abused. Her mind, thrust into a painful and demoralizing situation, knowing deep down, despite repeated attempts at plausible denial, that no one would be coming to help. How she must have suffered. Charlie's voice and what he had told us about Reggie popped into my mind. 'He likes to hurt people,' he'd revealed. 'I guess he gets off on it, or something.' There had been a whole lot of hurt in that room, alright, and if that sort of thing got Reggie off, then there had also been a fair amount of that going on in there, as well.

    The victim on the other bed looked fresher, but still just as dead. She appeared to be older than the first woman and heavier set. The level of abuse her body had endured, however, was no different and perhaps even worse. Her face had been beaten so badly that, even if you had known the woman well, it would have been impossible to recognize her. Part of a cheekbone was showing through on the side of her head nearest the window. Her jaw had been knocked completely askew and was dangling from a small strip of tightly stretched flesh on the other side. A huge, gaping wound was visible on the right side of her lower abdomen. Her intestines had spilled out of the gash in a tangled mess to mingle with the roses printed on the bedspread.

    Looking at all of that carnage made me want to go barreling downstairs, burst into Reggie's room and snuff every last bit of demonic life out of him. He deserved to die a very painful death and I made a silent vow to those ladies that if I got the chance, I would see to it that he did. At the moment, though, we still had a lot of work to do and I didn't want to spend any more time in that room than I absolutely had to.

    After quickly scanning the remainder of the sparsely furnished space, I headed for the bathroom. The only horror that awaited me in there was a toilet overflowing with human excrement and piss. The floor, which used to be a bright, spotless white, was now a dingy yellow with misshapen pools of brown mixed in. When the plumbing stopped working, what could you do? I asked myself. Stop going to the bathroom? The stench burned my nose and mouth with every short, putrid breath that I sucked in.

    Rapidly sliding the shower doors in both directions revealed that the tiled enclosure was empty. I turned on my heels and wasted no time in leaving the room, pulling the door closed with a hearty tug.

76

Searching the remainder of the second floor produced nothing of interest. Just another string of nearly identical hotel rooms with very minor differences.

For some reason, they reminded me of a large condominium association in the town that we used to live in. Wide, gently curving streets with witty little names, lined with overpriced, cookie-cutter dwellings. Every one of them looked identical to the one next door and if you walked inside, each of them would have the same basic layout. Just like these rooms.

I sensed myself starting to get cranky. Probably a combination of being both mentally and physically tired and feeling hungrier than I had ever been in my life. The pain in my stomach had become intense, almost as though the organ had begun to feast upon itself. On top of that, we still had a lot of hotel to go through and I had a strong suspicion that the worst was yet to come. All along, our money had been on the first floor being the living quarters. It would be a lot easier for them to defend the building and their looted stores from down there. Besides, with the elevators not working, who wanted to climb those stairs all the time?

Wearily, we trudged down the stairways to tackle the last obstacle in our way before we could rest; the first floor. Once again, we entered the hallway from both ends at about the same time. It was clearly evident that we were beginning to drag a little. Our initial jolt of adrenaline had completely worn off.

An outbreak of repeated, big, open mouthed yawning struck our little group like the onset of a severe affliction. Closed fists and flat, open hands flew up to cover mouths as though yawning was a dangerous and infectious disease. First would come the high-pitched sucking sound of lungs filling up with air until they couldn't possibly hold even a tiny bit more. Then came the exhale. A massive volume of stored air being released at a steady, controlled rate, producing sounds that mimicked an air raid siren, only at a slightly lower pitch. We were in dire need of a break and some nourishment. All of us were extremely low on energy from being dreadfully hungry for so long. Despite the carnage taking place around us, I knew that we had to stop and eat something or we would never have enough energy to finish the job. Hoping to kill two birds with one stone and raise the morale of our search party, I had a moment of inspiration.

Digging into my coat pocket, I produced a packet of thick sliced bologna that I had procured from the walk-in cooler upstairs.

Kelli eagerly accepted it with a gleam in her eye. I hadn't seen that look since I gave her a pair of diamond earrings for Christmas a couple of years back. From my other pocket, I brought out a block of Colby cheese. Kelli started giggling as she grabbed for it.

"Gimme that!" she cheerfully whispered, as her hand closed around the block of cheese. In the time that it took for me to get my knife out, she had already torn open the cellophane wrapping with her teeth. The sight of the knife in my hand caused another round of nervous, excited giggles to escape her mouth.

We sat in two little groups at opposite ends of the main hallway, feasting on bologna and cheese while we took a short breather.

Jacob led Kaleb back to the third floor and they both stuffed their pockets full of soda cans. Waddling out of the stairwell's access door weighted down with a large variety of sweet, carbonated beverages, both boys wore huge, devilish grins. They passed out drinks to everyone else with one hand, while holding onto cans of open soda, that they had started chugging while on the way down, in the other.

How wonderfully delicious every precious bite tasted! It had been so long since we had eaten anything except jerky that bologna and cheese tasted as good to us as a three course, gourmet meal.

The soda was absolutely fantastic. I grabbed a can of Dr. Pepper, pulled the tab and took a long, deep drink. The tingly, tasty fluid ran down my throat with a slight burning sensation and the taste of sugar was very strong. Used to drinking nothing but water and the occasional juice from a scrounged can of fruit, it almost tasted too sweet!

I couldn't help but chuckle lightly to myself. Kelli noticed the smile on my face and the grin that was on her face widened even more.

"It tastes so good, doesn't it"? she said elatedly. My mouth once again stuffed full of bologna and cheese, all I could do was smile back at her and shake my head up and down repeatedly like an idiot.

77

  It didn't take long for my belly to feel full, no doubt a byproduct of a reduced diet and shrunken stomach. The break was such a nice reprieve from the madness that I loathed the thought of continuing our crusade. My mind began to wander and, despite all that was going on, I felt calmer than I had in days. I actually started to feel sleepy. Not just tired, but sleepy. I thought about going back upstairs and grabbing a big pile of blankets, carting them back down to where we were and going to sleep, right there. We could carry on with our plan in the morning, well rested and more alert. Besides, I reasoned, it would be light outside and we would be able to see better.

  I had almost talked myself into doing just that, when a wonderfully odd thing happened. Sitting with my back planted against the hallway wall, I suddenly started to feel more alert and alive. I could actually feel energy surge through my body's emaciated system like small jolts of electricity. In a very short span of time, I grew so jumpy that I could no longer stay seated. My toes began to tap and my fingers started to bounce as the caffeine from the soda deeply embedded itself into my nervous system. I felt like Popeye looked after he had consumed an always handy can of spinach in a last chance effort to stave off disaster. I felt as though I suddenly had the strength of ten Grinches, plus two. The transformation was startling and it was complete. Thinking back, I couldn't remember the drug ever having that profound of an effect on me before. The only conclusion that my racing mind could reach was, that in our past lives we had built up a healthy tolerance to caffeine. It was a common additive in many products. With our systems having since purged themselves of the stimulant, the effect it now produced was dramatic. Instead of being tired and downtrodden, Kelli's and Kaleb's faces were vivid and excited.

From the other end of the hall, rapidly talking voices whispered back and forth in a lively exchange. The effect appeared to be universal and it was exactly what we needed to make our final push. Pumped on artificial stimulants and ready to finish what we started, our little force once again took up it's positions.

While we searched the rooms on the ground floor, Kaleb would move forward to cover the front entrance and Butch would guard the rear, alone.

The hotel was entirely surrounded by a parking lot. Most of the guests would have used either the back or one of the two side entrances to gain access to their rooms. The front was used only by those checking in or checking out. The architect of the structure had seemingly taken this into account because there was only a handful of permanent parking spaces out front next to the covered entranceway.

There was only one door in the short rear hallway. A quick look as we passed by upon first entering the building revealed it to be the hotel's laundry room. Rows of white washers and silver dryers stood like sentries on duty waiting to clean soiled linens at your beck and call.

The front hall was very short and opened up abruptly to reveal the spacious lobby. The service desk was on the left, built in so that it became a part of the same continuous wall. To the right, a well-furnished seating area, complete with tall arrangements of fake potted plants.

78

On the night that we had kidnapped Charlie and eventually persuaded him to talk, we learned that Steevo's room was located on the southeast corner of the hotel's first floor. Jacob and I verified the information during a reconnaissance trip to the city when we witnessed the constant flicker of candlelight coming from behind the room's drawn curtains. We were also aware, once again thanks to Charlie, that Reggie's room was right next to Steevo's and the two spaces had a private, interconnecting door.

It was the one thing that we didn't know that bothered me the most. Charlie had also told us about a third member of the gang that was supposedly still hanging around somewhere inside the hotel. Before we could get any sleep we needed to find out if he was or not, and if so, where the hell he was hiding?

79

    With their filthy backs pushed up against the wall, Steevo and Reggie sat staring at the doorway of Steevo's hotel room. Reggie had grabbed everything that he thought might be of use to them in a rush of frenzied excitement when he heard the bevy of shots outside. The thunder of four simultaneous high-powered rifle reports had startled both of the nervous residents into a state of near panic. The two friends almost crashed headlong into each other when they unexpectedly converged in the doorway that divided their adjoining rooms. The faces of both men clearly showing the fear and strain that they felt.
    Deciding to make their stand in Steevo's corner room, the duo set about barricading both doorways. They wrestled Steevo's bed across the carpeted floor and deposited it's bulk up against the hallway door. The bed and it's pedestal were heavy, but these were two big men and they were too frightened to be bothered by such a trivial matter. Latching onto each end of a long chest of drawers, the two panicked souls picked up the piece of furniture and placed it across the doorway that connected their rooms.
    Taking cover behind a small writing table laid on it's edge and the nightstand from between the two beds, Steevo and Reggie cowered in uncertainty and fear. A small pile of hand grenades were stacked between them on the carpeted floor and the barrels of their automatic weapons poked over the top of their meager protection.

80

    Having once again taken up our positions, we began to search the first floor of the hotel. Knowing that Steevo and Reggie's rooms were situated at the south end of the structure, we started on the north.
    The first room that Jacob and I entered made us eager to see the rest. Boxes of tasty treats were stacked everywhere inside the room, nearly filling it to capacity. Cases of potato chips, King Dons, candy bars and just about any other kind of snack food that one could dream of was crammed into the tight space. The sight was visually overwhelming after having endured for so long on such meager rations. Swallowing a huge lump in my throat, I somehow managed to finish searching the room while keeping one eye trained on all of those goodies.
    Forcing ourselves to leave the room empty-handed, Jacob and I continued to push southward. About half of the rooms that we entered had obviously been used as sleeping quarters, the other half as storage for more warehoused groceries and supplies. The wonders never ceased as we explored the first floor of the building. One room would be filled with canned goods and jars of spaghetti sauce and the next one

piled to the ceiling with boxes of cereal and crackers of all imaginable variety.

Charlie hadn't been just "whistling Dixie" when he told us that they had looted every store around and that their efforts had taken them over a month.

Our emotions were continually being wrenched back and forth. In those rooms that contained large stashes of food or supplies we would experience wonderful, uplifting feelings of pure elation. Standing gape-jawed and glassy eyed, we were totally awed by the sheer volume of stored provisions. We ended up discovering more groceries on the ground floor of that hotel than our local Wal-Mart used to have in stock. I caught myself, time and time again, being nearly hypnotized by the power those provisions held.

In the rooms which had been used to house now defunct members of the ill-fated regiment of rejects, our emotions would plunge as rapidly as a roller coaster picking up speed going down the first big hill. The reality of the ever present danger would return and smother our moods like an enormous, all-encompassing, black blanket.

As Jacob and I relayed the news about all the new items that we had discovered inside the rooms on the first half of the floor, hoots and hollers rose to take the place of initial astonished gasps. Exchanging looks of unbridled joy and huge, clasping hugs, our weary little band celebrated, ever so briefly.

After Jacob and I finished sweeping through both the lobby and laundry room, we decided to take another quick break. Butch found a piece of galvanized pipe in the laundry room and ran it through the push bar on the inside of the door to securely wedge the exit shut. We sat down together in the middle of the last unsearched hallway in the hotel.

Kelli and Kaleb made a return trip to our new personal stash of soda and retrieved another round of sugary sweetness. Jacob had taken Butch back to the newly discovered room filled with snacks and selected some Nutty Bars, salted peanuts and a bag of BBQ potato chips for us to piece on.

Munching and crunching away, we rehashed our strategy to clear the final section of the hotel.

81

    Reggie was feeling brave so he decided to take the chance. Were his ears lying to him or were those really women that he heard talking and laughing out in the hallway? He just had to know. Crawling from behind the meager protection afforded by the overturned table and nightstand, Reggie crept across the carpeted floor and knelt down next to the thin hallway wall.
    Gingerly placing his right ear to the wallpapered surface, he listened intently while vacantly staring off into space. He could hear the sound of voices talking at a low volume through the barrier. Not quite well enough to hear exactly what was being said, but well enough to know that there were definitely women out there.
    With his insatiable appetite for females, Reggie was transfixed by the sound. One grubby paw reached up and began to absent-mindedly stroke his pointed chin. A part of him wanted very badly to move the bed from the door's path and forcefully introduce himself to those ladies.
    It had been almost a week since his last friend had died and he was feeling lonely. Doris had been her name, at least

that's what she had told him as he beat her to beat his boredom. He hadn't been attracted to the overweight, almost middle-aged woman, at all, but she had been better than nothing. A way for him to pass the time. After all, it was excruciatingly boring around there.

Reggie knew that he was a bit sadistic. He also knew that others looked down on him because of it, but he just couldn't seem to help himself. It had all started out as a perverted boyhood fetish at about the time he reached puberty. Before it was over, though, it had blossomed into a cold blooded, well publicized killing spree.

The first time that Reggie killed he was just a confused young man of eighteen. He did not know the girl, had never seen her before in his life. All of a sudden she was just there, walking along on the path next to the river.

The Maumee River ran through his hometown of Toledo, Ohio. On the hot, muggy, mid-western summer nights Reggie would go walking down by the river in the cool air. Sometimes he would run into a friend or two and smoke a joint or down a forty ounce bottle of beer to get a buzz on. But on that particular evening, no one else was around.

The poor girl had no knowledge of his presence. A pretty, little, dark haired thing of about sixteen. She was casually strolling along the earthen path next to the water, worn down by so many footsteps over so many years. Her head hung down limply as if she were sad or upset about something. Kicking one foot out in front of the other, she solemnly made her way along. Reggie saw her coming.

He was standing on the other side of a large oak tree next to the path, and she was approaching quickly. Crazy thoughts and ideas began to run through his twisted head. Sadistic impulses coursed through his ill-formed, adolescent mind, screaming out to a side of him that Reggie had not yet been introduced to. Without his rational mind being completely aware of what he was doing, the part of him that had now fully awakened reached down next to the tree's trunk and grasped a short, dense piece of a fallen branch.

Reggie peeked around the tree and saw that the girl had closed to within a few steps of his location, but she was still just as lost in her own universe of thought.

A break in the canopy above had allowed the glow of the

moon's light to filter through the leaves and onto the dirt path next to the tree that Reggie was standing behind. Tightly clutching a stout piece of branch in both hands, he stood with his arms raised menacingly above his head, waiting.

    Unaware of the impending doom and lost in her own deep thought, the pitiful creature was without defense. The heavy piece of solid oak crashed into the top of her skull with the sickening sound of an egg being cracked. Collapsing in a heap and lying motionless in the middle of the little, narrow path, the unconscious girl was totally helpless.

    Reggie, or whatever the part of Reggie's mind that now had control was called, stood over her limp body, club still in hand. His eyes slowly and cautiously searched the shadowy path in both directions with the glaring look of a vicious predator.

    He was not nervous. Now that that side of him had been awakened, he felt animalistic in his instincts and was certain that they were alone. Spying a thick patch of shrubbery about ten yards further inland from the path, Reggie reached down with one hand and clasped it around the wrist of the concussed girl. With a grunt and a mighty tug, the new Reggie began to drag his unlucky prey in the direction of the secluded spot. His right arm held the length of solid oak branch out in front of him like it was a torch lighting the way. The left was locked around the wrist of a small, unconscious high school sophomore that would never make it to another prom.

    Reggie had no ties of any kind to the girl, so when her battered and mutilated body washed up on the shore of Lake Erie a week later, the cops were completely baffled. Homicide kicked into high gear. They had some still intact DNA recovered from semen during the autopsy, but no other evidence. It was considered a miracle that there was anything left of the body, at all, after being in the brown, murky water of the lake for so long, being nibbled on daily by hungry fish and pincered creatures of the deep. Grateful to have that decisive, concrete evidence to go on, the boastful boys of Homicide pushed the angle hard.

    After two months of painstakingly comparing their evidence to sample after sample in the national DNA data bank, the cops were no closer to a suspect. Reggie kept a tab on the case and the dicks in Homicide by reading the paper his mother had delivered to their home every morning.

When the news first broke and the headlines screamed of murder, Reggie was terrified. He had watched TV shows like CSI and Criminal Minds and knew that modern forensics was a powerful weapon in the fight on crime. Seemingly impossible cases were cracked by using the latest in ultra-high tech, scientific gadgetry. The premise of these shows was that you could never commit a crime without leaving behind some sort of evidence. Even if it was the tiniest trace of matter, the modern forensic techniques would always reveal the guilty party, without fail.

Reggie grew panicky. For days on end he hardly slept, waiting for that knock on the door. On the rare occasions that exhaustion got the better of him and he did manage to temporarily fall asleep, vivid nightmares would torment his fantasizing mind. Ones of him being chased and shot at by the police as he raced along the same beaten dirt path that he had taken that poor child's life on.

Bullets whizzing by his head, heart pumping so hard that it felt like it would burst through his rib cage with each hurried step. He could see it up ahead. The same tree that he had stood behind while waiting for his innocent victim to draw close. It was approaching quickly because he was running at full speed and Reggie was not slow. His breath whistled in and out of his mouth and his legs pumped with all of their youth and stamina. As he pulls to within fifteen feet of the large tree, a form begins to appear from the opposite side. At the scorching speed that Reggie is moving in his desperate bid to outrun the long arm of the law, any attempt to stop or change the direction of his momentum would be futile. As the form moves out into the middle of the path blocking Reggie's way, his eyes focus on the apparition. There, standing in his route with a shit-eating grin and holding a pair of handcuffs out in front of him, is one of Toledo's finest. A scream escapes Reggie's mouth as the two viciously collide.

Fighting with his blankets and trying to push them off of him, Reggie would wake up screaming. His body would be bathed in the same deep lather of sweat that had coated him as he scrambled along the riverside in a panic. After having the same nightmare every night for over a week, Reggie thought that he might go insane. Then, one bright and sunny fall morning, the newspaper that landed on their front porch step changed everything. It revealed that the only evidence the police had to go on at that point in the unsolved murder case was a DNA sample.

As this news slowly soaked into Reggie's abnormal brain he felt an overwhelmingly unjustified release of pressure as the weight of those worries fell from his shoulders. If all the authorities had to go on was DNA, then Reggie was in the clear. He had never been in trouble with the law, had never been fingerprinted and was certainly not in the national DNA databank. A wicked smile spread across his face.

Reggie slept like a log that night.

For more than a year and a half after learning that bit of news Reggie managed to control his diabolical impulses. He lost control of them again on a cold, cloudy January morning near the very same river.

A twenty-seven year old woman, who had recently divorced and fallen on hard times financially, was beaten and abused underneath a large bridge embankment on the river's edge. A crew of engineers that were inspecting a nearby structure spotted Reggie in the act but were too far away for their shouts to do any good. Incapable of intervening, they watched helplessly as he sadistically brutalized the poor lady.

Frantic calls on their radios to the public works dispatcher prompted an emergency call to the police department. Reggie was surrounded by a throng of uniformed cops as they swarmed underneath the bridge from both sides, just as he was about to throw the body of his second victim into the water.

82

      Caught red handed, Reggie did hard time. His lawyers had initially tried to mount an insanity defense, but that fell flat. All of the court ordered psychiatric examinations came to the same conclusion. Reggie was certainly odd, there was no doubting that, but he was not certifiably crazy. He ended up taking a deal offered by the prosecutor and pled guilty to manslaughter.

      Reggie did seven years at the Marion County Corrections Center in central Ohio. His time there was not easy, sexual predators are frowned upon in prison society. They occupy the lowest rung on the ladder of respect. The brotherhood behind bars has it's own laws and code of ethics. Reggie learned that the hard way.

      In the shower stall one day, shampoo from his wet hair dripping into his eyes, he had been restrained by two very large individuals while a third mercilessly pummeled his face with his fists. He lost consciousness so his attackers stuck his head underneath the forceful flow of the shower to revive him. They weren't quite done with Reggie, yet. When his welcoming committee was sure that he was cognizant again, he was violently thrown, face first, into one of the tall, porcelain urinals partially recessed into the bathroom wall. Sliding down it's silky smooth surface, Reggie's head left a smeared, bloody trail.

On the edge of blacking out, yet again, his helpless body was thrown back in the shower like a rag doll and then draped over a stainless steel sink.

His torn and bleeding, motionless body was found by a guard a short time later.

After the doctors stitched Reggie back together he spent three weeks in the prison's infirmary. While further recovering from his wounds, he was placed in protective custody and housed in the solitary confinement wing at Marion. His face would forever be a reminder of that day. Every time that Reggie looked in the mirror, the physical damage clearly revealed itself.

Far worse, though, was the damage that couldn't be seen. Reggie had needed major surgery to save his life. He was bleeding profusely internally from a punctured and torn lower intestine. The doctors had to do emergency surgery and remove the last eight inches of his shredded digestive tract.

Withdrawing into a shell, Reggie did the rest of his time in the prison's segregated unit, and for the most part, it proved uneventful.

After his release, he went back home to his mother's house and lived a hermit like existence for almost two years until she had a massive stroke and was placed in an expensive permanent care facility. With the bills mounting up and Reggie having no income, the debtors forced the sale of his mother's assets, including their home. With no place else to go, he ended up at the local homeless shelter. While staying there, his downward spiral continued to pick up speed and he fell deeper and deeper into a bout of severe depression.

Reggie's luck changed one morning during his monthly visit to his assigned parole officer. He recognized a familiar face from his time behind bars waiting patiently in one of the three fold-up chairs in the small reception area.

A large, pot-bellied man that had spent eighteen months in the cell next to his when he had been housed in the isolation ward. The only inmate that Reggie ever felt comfortable having a cordial relationship with after the incident in the shower. A quiet spoken, slightly balding and always smiling man by the name of Steve Johnson.   Steevo to his friends.

Perhaps they got along so well because of Steevo's pleasant, polite way of speaking. Or, perhaps because he was always there to offer a word of encouragement when Reggie was feeling low, which was an increasingly frequent occurrence at that time. His mother had been the only one to ever offer the young man any kind of support or sympathy and he desperately needed and wanted a friend. Or, maybe they got along so well because birds of a feather... well you know.

83

      Steevo's sentence was for child molestation. He was older than Reggie and that was his second stint in the gray bar hotel. By that time Steevo knew exactly how the system worked and took full advantage of it. On his first day back in the big house, he savagely stabbed the man sitting next to him at the table in the mess hall with a dinner fork. The guards forcefully wrestled a writhing, cursing Steevo to the hard, vinyl tiled floor and secured the blood stained fork from his tightly clenched fist. He was written up and thrown in the hole for three months as punishment. During that time he experienced no human contact whatsoever, except for the hand of an unseen guard that slid the sloppy gruel they called food through a narrow opening in the bottom of the cell's heavily riveted steel door. Once his penance was paid, they released Steevo from his dark, windowless cell and sent him back to the prison's general population to resume serving his sentence.

      But Steevo knew what happened to child molesters in that God forsaken place. Having been punked and sodomized by his cellmate during his first term, Steevo wasn't about to let that happen again. The very first day back among his fellow inmates, he once again attacked an unsuspecting victim. This time he didn't even wait to sit down.

A lunch tray in his left hand and a fork protruding from his right, Steevo exited the end of the cafeteria's serving line and headed out among the rows of tables filled to capacity with hungry cons. His unlucky victim was easy enough to spot. Eating like a starving refugee, the unwary fellow was too busy sopping up a nasty, brown-green gravy coating the bottom of his scratched aluminum serving tray with a piece of half stale bread to notice Steevo as he approached.

With all the force that he could generate, Steevo rapidly plunged his fork down into the top of the famished felons shoulder. An earsplitting roar filled the air as the steel tines bore through the soft, parting flesh and buried itself deeply in the solid density of the bone beneath.

Steevo was given the same punishment as before, only this time it was twice as long. He spent six months in the hole for that transgression. A heavy price, but Steevo was certainly willing to pay it to keep himself safe from the mobs that would do to him what he had done to his own helpless, innocent victims.

Steevo was a coward. Always had been, always would be. He didn't care if he caused catastrophe and pain in other people's lives, so long as it didn't happen to him.

While on his second torturing tour in the hole, Steevo wrote rambling letters to every authority figure listed in the prison directory. In those dispatches were strongly worded, hate filled threats to injure, maim or kill another inmate every time he came close to one, if he were housed in general population. Having already made good on those very threats, twice, the prison's officials decided that it might be a good idea to seclude Steevo from his fellow prison mates. After all, if anyone else got hurt and the word got around about those threats, there could be a liability lawsuit, and that was the last thing that a prison constantly struggling to stay in the black needed.

Steevo was a dirty pedophile and a sniveling coward. But Steevo, if nothing else, had a lot going for himself upstairs. If not for his penchant of molesting stray neighborhood children, he could have made a decent go at life.

So, Steevo got his way and they locked him in the isolation wing, right next to Reggie.

84

When the two old pals saw each other again for the first time as free men, huge smiles appeared on both of their astonished faces. It was the first genuine smile that Reggie had worn in a very long time and it felt good to him.

Learning of Reggie's circumstance, Steevo invited his troubled friend to stay at his place until he could get back on his feet. The two ex-cons got along very well and over time became the best of friends, each totally involved in every aspect of the other's life.

The summer after Reggie moved in, both men were hired by GM when they added a new production line for the wildly popular SUVs that everyone just had to have. Getting the OK from the board of parole, the men moved north to Detroit and into a dingy, rat infested apartment unit that bustled after dark with the trade of drugs and the sound of thugs.

Steevo and Reggie were not happy there, at all. Both of them worked full time day jobs, and not being able to sleep at night grew to be an ever constant pain in the ass. Afraid to confront the gang members that controlled the apartment complex, the two roommates cowered in their filthy little abode to hide from the threatening glares and the vulgar, hurled insults. "Faggot" and "homo" were the two most commonly heard. Closely followed by "fairy" and "queer".

Steevo and Reggie had no idea on earth why anyone would think that they were gay. They never held hands or kissed, or did anything else that would imply such a thing. In fact, neither one of the men had any homosexual tendencies, whatsoever. Steevo liked pre-pubescent children and Reggie liked to violate and mutilate women. The two old prison mates did not care for each other in that way. They just enjoyed each other's company and felt comfortable around each other, knowing that neither would judge because they had both been down the same road.

Steevo and Reggie endured this humiliating treatment only because they had no choice. Being ex-cons with no credit, they were lucky to even have their jobs. There wasn't a landlord around that would rent a home to them.

A phone call that came one cold, rainy evening in late March changed all of that. Steevo's great Aunt Tilda had passed away and he was the only family member that lived anywhere near the old place, the rest having long since relocated all across the country with their careers and families.

An old, two story farmhouse, it sat right on the outskirts of Marine City, Michigan. It wasn't a fancy place, by any stretch of the imagination. Aunt Tilda had been 92 when she left her earthly boundaries behind and the place had fallen in severe disrepair.

Unbeknownst to Steevo, the place had a leaky roof, holes in the floorboards and crumbling plaster walls. There were more than a few windows gone and it stank wretchedly with the odor of the thirty half wild cats that had resided with the lonely, old woman.

The yard was cluttered with abandoned trash and overgrown with tangles of wild vines and tall brush. Unable to care for the property at her advanced age, Aunt Tilda finally gave up trying when she had suffered a mild heart attack at the age of eighty. For the next twelve years, nature and it's inevitable, relentless destruction ate away at the old structure until it became a local eyesore.

Steevo's mother had been short and to the point in one of her very rare phone calls to her son. She was openly embarrassed of him and tried to maintain as much distance as possible between the two. Steevo didn't mind. Even before his tendencies to molest minors had manifested itself, the two didn't get along. He thought that his mother was a manipulating, cold hearted, drunken bitch. A wretched, old hag that lit one cigarette after another and smelled like an industrial smokestack when she was around. She was only interested in one thing: money.

The property had belonged to her less fortunate, spinster aunt, and *her* parents before that. In accordance with the old woman's wishes to keep the house in the family, her will legally transferred the ownership of the property into Steevo's mother's name. Not wanting to take time out from a busy shopping and drinking schedule to fly in, cross country from California, she had enlisted the help of a local, fast talking real estate agent named Rick Stenko.

"Slick-Rick", as his sales associates called him, wore his black hair parted down the middle and sported a pencil thin mustache made popular by Clark Gable back in the 1930s. Fond of leisure suits, even though they had been out of style for a long time, Rick was hard to miss in a crowd. After driving his customized, metallic green AMC Pacer just outside the limits of Marine City to look the old place over, he reported his findings.

Mortified by what she saw in the pictures that Rick had e-mailed to her and what he relayed during their almost one- sided phone conversation, Steevo's mother got an idea on how to handle the situation. She would pass it on to her child-molesting son and let him deal with it. She wasn't about to soil her reputation by being connected to a hovel like that. There was no money to be made there, anyhow, she lamented. Why, the place was ready to be torn down and was unfit for human habitation. Why waste her time and energy to go across the country and preside over the sale of a rambled old shack? By the time her travel and hotel expenses had been accounted for, fees for the real estate agent and the back taxes on her departed aunt's property, Steevo's mother would have been lucky if she cleared more than two grand. Her precious time and, more importantly, her precious reputation, were worth far more to her than the paltry sum of two thousand dollars.

So, feeling relieved to have her latest crisis solved, she called Steevo and gave him the news. "Aunt Tilda has died," she told him abruptly, as though she were telling him his dinner was ready, (on the few occasions she had bothered to make it when he was a child.) Without missing a beat, his mother began to ramble in a monotone, nonstop voice for the next two minutes. She hadn't been to see her aunt in quite some time, so she had no idea what kind of shape the place was in, she lied. Aunt Tilda had always liked him a lot, she said with a slur, despite an obvious attempt to mask her drunkenness, and since she herself was too busy in her self-indulging lifestyle to oversee the necessary affairs, she was passing the family property down to Steevo. After all, she unconvincingly cooed, he deserved a break for once in his life. He wouldn't have to do a thing, she would make all of the necessary arrangements to have the property legally transferred into his name.

85

    Steevo couldn't quit smiling after he hung up the phone. Maybe his ship *had* finally come in. The old memories of his numerous visits to his great Aunt Tilda's place as a boy came rushing back through the thin veneer of time.
    The old, two story farmhouse was located on a good sized piece of ground, right outside of a quiet, little town called Marine City. The property had many large trees in it's big back yard. One of them, a huge maple with many thick branches, had once held a tree house that Steevo and a neighbor boy clumsily constructed. He dreamily wondered if any part of the fort would still be there after all these years.
    He fondly remembered the hot, lazy, summer afternoons he had spent on the front porch there, chugging Aunt Tilda's homemade, freshly squeezed lemonade and gobbling down her delicious peanut butter cookies, lightly sprinkled with walnuts, until it seemed like his insides would burst.
    Going out to collect enough slimy worms in the dewy, early morning grass to use as bait down at the fishing hole that day.
    Those summers that Steevo had spent with Aunt Tilda held some of the best memories in his otherwise ugly, tortured

life. The thought that he would now own the very piece of property that had brought him so much joy as a child filled him with such emotion that he felt like gleefully shouting, jumping up and down and merrily laughing out loud, all at the same time.

Smiling ear to ear in a grin that Reggie found almost frightening, Steevo told the good news to his amazed pal. In a lengthy, convoluted stroll down memory lane, Steevo relayed all the information that he could remember about the old place from his boyhood visits. With each passing sentence both men grew increasingly excited.

"That would be perfect," Reggie happily exclaimed. "We would only be about thirty-five miles from the plant. We could commute back and forth to work."

Visions of a peaceful existence in a small, friendly place like Marine City sounded like a dream come true to the pair. Vibrating with anticipation, they were barely able to sleep a wink that night. Right after work the next day, the fast friends hopped in their beat up, red Grand Am and flew out of the parking lot to go and explore their new castle.

It had been many long, arduous years since Steevo had been in the area of his aunt's house and much was changed, but he still managed to find and turn onto the correct road. It only took about a minute after that for the farmhouse to become visible, sitting on the left hand side about a mile further down the lonely blacktopped lane.

Steevo's heart leapt in his chest at the sight. It looked exactly as he remembered it from his childhood. Every last detail. Even the large, gently swaying trees that stood at the back of the property.

The sheer exhilaration that the two men felt was overwhelming, bubbling up inside them like lava that could no longer be contained inside a volcano. Cheers, hearty shoulder slaps and high fives were the order of the day.

"Goodbye, mangy apartment!" Reggie joyously cried.

Both men looked as though they had just won a large, multi-million dollar jackpot in the state lottery. Finally seeing the property for real with their own eyes, the two men let their minds believe what their aching hearts desired. They were quickly lost in wondrous daydreams about packing their belongings and moving out of the cockroach infested apartment that they lived in. Musing about the long summer ahead, the front porch, lemonade and peanut butter cookies lightly sprinkled with walnuts.

Steevo and Reggie were so transfixed on those idyllic mental images that the reality of what their eyes were seeing was slow in being transmitted to their preoccupied minds. The visual signals began reaching their brains at full speed about the time that they casually wheeled into the narrow stone driveway.

The front of the mailbox was open, it's lid hanging down like a tongue being stuck out in a rude, child-like gesture. Unfortunately, that wasn't the only rude thing that awaited the two dumbstruck friends. After surveying the damaged property in a slow, silent, funeral like procession, first downstairs, then up, neither man could bring himself to speak, even to try and comfort the other, for what seemed like a very long time.

After all, what was there to say? They were both on the same emotional roller coaster. Their hopes and dreams had been dashed in a horrifically cruel understanding of just how hopeless the situation was. This worn down, smelly, leaky, moldy, paint peeling place was not the one of Steevo's boyhood recollections. It didn't even look close enough to be a distant relative. All that the two downtrodden perspective property owners could do was look at each other with a vacant, withdrawn look in their eyes.

The ride back to their fleabag flophouse was silent. Neither man offered any empty words of encouragement.

The pain that Steevo and Reggie felt affected them so savagely that it became of a physical nature. They experienced a tightening of the chest, an increased pulse and shortened breathing. They even had a nauseating sickness in the pit of their stomachs. They felt much the same way that normal people do when they suffer their first broken heart. A quivering mass of human flesh lost in a haze of internal pain and suffering. The kind of pain that can only be fully understood with time. So, in a tormented and deeply depressed state, the two pals silently made their way back home and went to bed early.

86

For the first few days after their trip to Marine City, Steevo and Reggie felt really low. Neither one of them ate very much and it was as quiet around their little apartment as it was inside Grant's Tomb. Then the weekend rolled around again with it's usual assortment of loud parties, shouting and ritualistic, adolescent fist fights.

Aimlessly flipping through the channels on their little portable television to take their minds off the sounds of ignorance and the pain of poverty taking place outside, the two friends stumbled onto a home improvement broadcast called *This Old House.* The mesmerized duo became totally absorbed with the charismatic host Bob Vila and his cheery gang of can do contractors. The DIY marathon ran late into the night and Steevo and Reggie watched each episode with mounting enthusiasm.

While watching the show into the early morning hours of Sunday, the two suddenly rejuvenated do-it-yourselfers in the making hatched an ambitious new plan. With April only a week away and warmer weather right around the corner, they would move in to the house and do the work that needed to be done a little at a time. Both men were making decent money at the GM plant and both were willing to pitch in on the materials necessary to make the place habitable.

Steevo and Reggie would do most of it by themselves in the evening after work and on the weekends. There were, after all, plenty of do-it-yourself books to be had, and they covered everything. All they would have to do is drive right on down to the library and check them out, after they had applied for library cards, of course. When the pair did run into the inevitable problem that was too big for the both of them to handle, they would interview contractors and pay to have the work done.

The next week flew by as Steevo and Reggie prepared for their big move. That Friday after work, the two very happy new homeowners made the first of many overloaded, tightly packed trips in their little Grand Am. They managed to squeeze in two loads that evening, four on Saturday and the last partial load on Sunday. It was hard work. Tedious and boring, as moving always was, but it seemed to Steevo and Reggie that they had never been happier about anything else in their lives. When the last bit of their belongings were sat down inside their new house, the two men shared joyous, clasping bear hugs and did silly, little, odd looking dances with beaming grins breaking their faces and war cry like whoops of victory escaping their mouths.

Steevo and Reggie spent the next two and a half years constantly making improvements to their new dwelling. In fact, when the power outages first hit Marine City, they were upstairs hanging drywall in the half bathroom. They never did get to finish it.

87

    Those were definitely women's voices out there in the hallway, Reggie was sure of that. He would have really loved some company. It was always so boring and lonely around the hotel. But Reggie certainly wasn't about to go out the door and introduce himself. Oh, no. If it had *only* been women's voices that he had heard, then he most certainly would have. It was the sound of the other voices, the lower pitched ones, that kept Reggie right where he was. Crouched down next to the bed with his ear pinned tightly to the wall.
    The voices abruptly stopped and then Reggie heard the sound of someone's shoes scuffling toward him on the hallway's carpeted floor. He shrank away from the wall for a moment in fear as the footsteps passed by his location. Quickly regaining a bit of nerve, he placed his ear back up against the cool, smooth surface and listened as the footsteps continued toward the exit door, located about ten feet further down the corridor.
    Steevo, who had been looking at his old pal inquisitively from across the room, could bear his curiosity no longer.

"What do you hear?" he testily whispered across the room at Reggie.

Not moving his ear away from the wallpapered surface, Reggie threw up his left hand and flapped it dismissively at his partner in crime. Still hunkered down behind the overturned table and wooden nightstand, Steevo revealed nothing of himself but the crown of his filthy head and large, staring eyes.

Reggie heard the muffled footfalls stop. It sounded like whoever was producing them had halted in front of the southward facing exit door. Then he heard a deeper voice than either he or Steevo possessed ask whoever else was out there with him if they were ready.

Ready for what? Reggie had barely enough time to ask himself.

A heavy, booming crash from out in the hallway broke through the tenuous dam that had been barely holding Reggie's touchy nerves back. The resulting flood surged through him like a tidal wave. In four quick, very nimble leaps, Reggie completely re-crossed the corner hotel room.

Diving behind the small, overturned table, Reggie desperately grabbed for his 12 gauge shotgun. Resting the front of it's barrel on the top edge of the little, square table, he waited along with the wide eyed Steevo for all hell to break loose.

88

Once everyone had taken their positions for our run down the last half of the ground floor's hallway, I kicked open the first door and waited for a response.

For the last leg of our sightseeing tour through the funhouse maze some of us had shifted around a bit. Kelli and Vickie both stood guard by the south exit door. Each woman tried hard not to think about what lay just on the other side of the glass. Butch and Kaleb, no longer having to cover the front and rear exits, stood a short distance behind me and Jacob as we began to assault the wooden doors separating each room from the hallway. It was a very reassuring feeling to know that we were all so close together.

Our biggest worry was that, according to Charlie, there was at least one other person still inside the hotel, and we had no idea where he could be hiding. The first eight rooms we scoured, four on the east, four on the west side of the hallway, were empty. No food, no supplies. They looked as though they were used by the now deceased defenders of the hotel as sleeping quarters. Darkened, grimy looking sheets lay half hidden under tussled, flower infested bedspreads.

It did appear as if they had cared about one thing. In many of the rooms plastic, five gallon buckets sat dutifully next to the white porcelain toilets, some still nearly full of water. As it dawned on me what I was looking at, I just had to smile. "That's very resourceful," I thought to myself with a slight nod of the head. Maybe some of those hoodlums weren't so dumb, after all. They had figured out that the toilets would still work and flush properly as long as you manually refilled the tanks after every use. Perhaps they made excursions down to the river to fill up their large, wire-handled buckets. Maybe they had set them outside during a heavy rainstorm or placed them under one of the hotel's many downspouts. However it had been accomplished, though, it was a pretty neat trick.

The next room that Jacob and I entered was a gun lover's sweetest dream come true. Rifles, shotguns and handguns of all make and manufacturer filled the space. In the corner farthest from the door stood a hastily constructed pile of compound, recurve and crossbows. I had never seen that many weapons in one place before, except at a large gun show. Carefully searching throughout the room for hidden surprises, I saw nothing suspicious. The bathroom was also empty. The shower doors stood wide open.

Certain that no one was hiding in the room, I took a moment to briefly look over the cache of weapons. There were several very nice firearms in there. I had to fight the urge to thoroughly check out each and every gun, one by one. But, once again, the fun stuff had to wait until later.

In the room directly across the hall we discovered huge, carefully stacked mountains of ammunition. Other than the completely overwhelming supply of food that the hotel contained, this finding made me the happiest. Not that anyone in our little group was running dangerously low on ammo, but you could never seem to have enough of the stuff.

Butch whispered to Jacob and me as we exited the hotel's fully stocked ammo dump. "We're halfway, now," he said. "Ten down, ten to go." A quick door count in both directions from where were stood proved him to be correct. There were forty rooms on that floor of the hotel and we had already searched thirty of them. Steevo and Reggie occupied two of the remaining ten, so that left us with eight more nerve-wracking, door busting entries into the unknown.

I could feel the effects of the soda's caffeine slowly fading in intensity and it didn't take a genius to figure out that others also did. Kaleb's open mouth was stretched to the breaking point in a long, moaning yawn. I remembered thinking to myself that we needed to get those last eight rooms done, and fast, before we all ended up falling asleep.

Taking in a deep breath, I picked my leg up and booted the next door open. Crashing into the wall behind it at high speed, the panel produced a flat sounding hum as it shook and vibrated from the impact.

More wonders awaited us inside that room. Camping and hiking supplies littered the entire surface of the floor and the two twin beds. Sleeping bags, tents, backpacks, tons of hiking boots and a plethora of other outdoor necessities lay in jumbled, messy piles, not at all like the other, neatly stacked storage rooms. Picking my footing carefully, I made my way through the tangled masses of items covering most of the room's barely visible floor. Knives of all sizes and varieties. Coats, gloves, hats, long johns, you name it, it was there. Wow, I thought, once again amazed at the quantity of resources at our disposal, wouldn't this stuff have come in handy about a month ago?

That feeling of being totally overwhelmed arose in me again, much as it must have when young Charlie Weatherby visited Willie Wonka's Chocolate Factory. It was nearly impossible to walk through the cluttered room without stepping on something or other, but I didn't want to take a chance on overlooking any potential hiding spots. Clearing what came to be known by us as the Cabela Room, our cohesive little caravan moved on.

The next three rooms that Jacob and I entered held nothing special. Just more spaces used as housing for additional, currently missing and presumably dead, Marine City marauders.

My mind wandered back to our old pal Charlie as the next door, in what had been a seemingly endless string of doors, noisily flew against the wall behind it. His voice was crystal clear inside my head. 'I don't think a single day went by during the first month that all of us didn't have our pockets bulging with heavy batteries. Seemed like every damn place we hit had tons of them.' Once again, old Cyclops was right on the money.

"Holy crap," Jacob breathed as he brushed past me.

Silently sliding halfway down the length of the wall on the left side, he covered me as I searched the room.

Holy crap was right. It looked as though an eighteen wheeler had backed up and unloaded it's full parcel of batteries into that little, square hotel room. There must be enough stored power in here to run a small third world country for about a month, I thought, as I shook my head in wonder, yet again. Thinking about all of the different things that we could use those wonderful batteries for, I slipped away for a second. Jacob seemed to momentarily lose himself, as well. A trance like gaze covered his features as he stood staring at the colossal volume of batteries. To Jacob, or anyone close to Jacob's age, batteries were a way of life. A lot of their toys ran on them. Hand held video games, cell phones and remote controls also did. These items were staples in their lives, not luxuries. Having been without the aid of these wondrous little power devices for an extended period of time, Jacob appeared to be lost in memories of a happier, simpler time.

"What do you think, Jake?" I asked the dreamy eyed boy.

Quickly turning his head in my direction and snapping back to reality, he answered, "Huh?"

Getting a small bit of pleasure from the surprised look frozen on his face, I had to smile. Seeing my spreading grin only deepened the inquisitive look already in Jacob's eyes and he asked, "What?"

Not wanting to make him the butt of a silly joke, I attempted to remove the smile from my face and asked, as serious as ever, "Did you see anything?"

That glassy eyed look made itself scarce and Jacob diligently scanned over the space. By the time, "No," had haltingly exited his mouth, I was already making my way to the other side of the room. The power room, as we called it, ended up being totally empty except for the ton, or so, of batteries stuffed inside it.

Good thing this room is on the ground floor, I thought to myself. All of this weight would be break right through one of the upper floors.

Directly across the hallway from the Power Room, laying on top of the twin hotel beds as though they were tourists soundly asleep in the middle of the night, we found the two fabled canoes that Charlie had told us about. I was beginning to think that perhaps old Chuck wasn't such a bad guy, after all.

Painted a dark, grayish-black color, it was easy to understand why the sleek watercraft were so difficult to see at night. Only about fifteen inches high, they would easily blend in with the dark, choppy waves of the St. Clair. If someone was smart enough to bend over and paddle slowly so that they didn't produce any splashes or waves, it would be virtually impossible to spot them.

Standing there looking at our possible ticket across the river stopped me dead in my tracks. Butch's voice coming through the doorway behind me snapped my muscles back into motion.

"So there they are," he excitedly whispered. The elation was plainly evident in his voice, much like Carter's must have been when he first discovered Tutankhamen's lavishly adorned tomb. I couldn't have agreed more.

Along with the two canoes, nestled snuggly in their soft, comfy beds, was a row of wooden and plastic paddles neatly standing in a line along one wall.

The canoes appeared to be well cared for and were in excellent condition. After what Charlie had told us, I wouldn't have expected anything else. Those canoes were Steevo and Reggie's golden goose. Charlie said that the two men had it all figured out. They would gather and hoard all of the supplies that they would need to survive on, then sit back and wait for the inevitable reversal of fortune to re-stabilize the country.

In the meantime, the duo would stockpile large quantities of gold, silver and precious stones by demanding outrageous ransoms to transport starving and desperate people to safety across the river.

89

    Before all of the misery began, Steevo used to drive over the bridge separating the two nations and have a few cold beers at a lively little place called Rita's. He became a regular customer there, so it was only natural for him to end up talking with a lot of the other patrons. That's how he met and became friends with Rene Lafontaine, a member of the Canadian Coast Guard.

    Rene was an avid outdoor enthusiast and amateur ham radio operator. Many lengthy conversations took place between the two about this last, universal hobby. Steevo eventually become very interested in pursuing the pastime and started to buy some entry level equipment. Rene gave him a business sized card with his radio's call numbers and frequency printed on it and the two began communicating over the airwaves.

    Luckily, one of the many items that Reggie purchased for his new found hobby was an AC/DC converter so that his radio would work on battery power, if needed. After the initial shock of the assault had worn off, the first thing that Steevo did was hook the device up to a car battery to see if it worked.

Able to successfully transmit and receive on his ham radio, Steevo picked up news reports from around the world. He was also able to talk to his friend, Rene. The two kept the lines of communication open and Rene would occasionally relay important news and weather reports across the river.

Hearing just how dire the situation actually was and how long it would be before normal conditions would be restored, Steevo hatched a devious plan that would enable him to ride out the catastrophe in a comfortable manner.

After he and his gathered band of thugs had looted everything around and holed up in the town's hotel, a bored Steevo came up with yet another way to take advantage of the situation. He would charge half starved, desperate people a small fortune to ferry them across the river to the safety of Canada. Rene's help would be required to pull it off, so he got in touch with his old pal. It just so happened that Rene wasn't adverse to making a few extra bucks on the side, either, provided it was done his way. After all, it was his neck on the chopping block if they got caught.

So, a very lucrative exchange began to take place across the fast flowing St. Clair River. Traffic was heavy at first because there were still a lot of people alive at the time and more jewels to be had. But as the weeks wore on, the number of daring nighttime crossings slowed to a mere trickle. Most of the remaining population had vanished, by then. Either dying a slow, painful death from starvation or being killed off as a food source to keep someone else from starving. There were no other options left. Every other resource had been plundered and picked as clean as a snow white bone lying in the hot sand of an expansive desert.

90

  Amassed in the middle of the building's first floor hallway, our weary band was left with four unexplored rooms. The two located on the left side belonged to Steevo and Reggie. The two on the right, well, we were about to find out.
  Kicking yet another door open, I wobbled and nearly fell backward because my legs had grown so tired. Inside the room there were two double beds pushed against the wall on the right hand side and one of the windows was open, the freezing, night air pouring in unchecked.
  As Jacob slowly sidestepped into the room along the wall to the left, I started to go around the beds to close the open window. Turning my head to the left, I glanced through the bathroom door while rounding the foot of the first bed. I heard a rustle of commotion behind me and turned just in time to catch a flash of movement.
  When I saw that there was another person in the room with us a quick jolt of adrenaline ran through me. Lucky for us, he was running in the opposite direction. I then watched in amazement as this fast moving, human form fully extended itself and dove headlong for the open window.

Swinging my gun barrel in that direction, I clicked the safety forward, into the off position. The leaping form had somehow misjudged the athletic ability that it takes to propel a human body through a space as small as a hotel window. The unlucky, and certainly not of Olympic caliber diver, caught his upper thighs at about groin level on the marble window ledge protruding from the hotel's wallpapered surface.

Two piercing sounds rang out, although the second was much louder than the first. Mr. Greg Louganis-not shrieked unintelligibly in pain from the severe, head-on collision to his bagged boys.

A split second after that, I heard the boom of Jacob's Mini 14. It broke through the sound created by the Olympic reject like it had never even existed. A huge wash of bright red appeared on the wall beneath the marble window ledge.

Twitching violently about like he had just touched a high voltage electric wire, the screaming human mass fell to the room's floor with a thud and didn't know whether to latch onto his crotch or grab his gunshot ass. A very panicked and painful look in his eye, the prone, heavily panting figure looked up to see me and Jacob looking down our rifle barrels at him and a charging Butch rushing in through the hallway door at full speed.

Thinking that the only chance he had to live was to play on our mercy, the bleeding, ball busted bandit gingerly raised his open hands into the air in front of him. With sturdy rope procured from the Cabela room, we secured our new captive and put a thick dressing on his wounds to stop the heavy bleeding.

There had been no one else in the room.

91

    Through his grimacing, pain clenched jaws he reluctantly answered the few questions asked of him. His name was Carlos Encarnacion, a plumber by trade. He had first met Steevo and Reggie while helping them fix the antiquated, leaky sewage system beneath the old, inherited farmhouse. After the consequences of the EMP attack took full effect, Carlos had been aimlessly milling around the center of town with a small group of his friends when he ran into Steevo and Reggie again. They were highly motivated. For the first time in their lives these men were hungry. Not just the "gee, what are we having for dinner tonight?" hungry, but real hunger. The kind that says "I don't care what the hell we're having for dinner tonight, as long as we're eating." Exceedingly desperate and very scared, they had no idea where their next meal was coming from or what the next day would bring.

    Trying to assemble enough manpower to enable their get rich quick scheme, Steevo and Reggie put out a sweetly baited hook for Carlos and his pals. The situation being what it was, no major arm twisting was necessary to lure the men on board, anyway. Afraid of starving and without any other options, what choice did they really have? Carlos and his friends reached out and grabbed onto the only hope that was being offered and held on for dear life.

Steevo and Reggie enticed many young, desperate souls into their hodgepodge unit. The assembled group must have looked something like the Bad News Bears of bandits. According to Charlie, though, whatever this untrained, out of shape unit lacked in one area, it more than made up for in others.

Carlos told us that there wasn't anyone else in the hotel other than Steevo and Reggie. I believed him, but we checked the last remaining room, anyway. Just to be sure.

The hotel finally secure, except for Steevo and Reggie's rooms, a collective sigh of relief went through all of us. It had been a long, nerve wracking night and we were all exhausted. Too bad we couldn't rest, yet. Walter was still waiting for us back at the caboose, along with all of our packs and gear. Also, while the hotel's four entrances were temporarily blocked, they would need to be properly secured before we could go to sleep.

Kelli, Vickie and Jacob volunteered to walk back to the caboose and get Walter and two of our backpacks. The other two packs would have to stay there until we could make another trip. Stuffing snacks and sodas into their pockets for the hike, the three exited the back door located next to the laundry room and quietly slipped away into the night.

While Kaleb stood watch in the hallway outside of Steevo and Reggie's doors, Butch and I prepared the hotel for our visit. Going back to the laundry room, we located some more pieces of steel pipe and a sturdy looking handcart. For the next hour, or so, Butch and I ferried large, heavy washing machines down the hallways to place in front of all the exits and securely barred the doors off. We did the back door last and left the handcart underneath the washer so that it could be moved in a hurry. We also left the steel bar's right side short of the door jamb, so that it could be pushed open just far enough for someone to yell through if we weren't around.

Making a return trip to the third floor, Butch and I stuffed our pockets until they were bulging with ham, cheese and salami. Butch then grabbed onto two cases of soda and I did likewise.

Heavily laden with a load of goodies, we went back

downstairs and piled it on the floor of the hallway a few doors down from Steevo and Reggie's rooms. Next, the two of us wrestled three king size mattresses out of some ground floor rooms and laid them down in the passageway. Then we split up and stacked the soda and food between them.

Another return trip to the laundry room produced two huge armloads of clean sheets, pillowcases and blankets. It had been such a long time since I made up a bed, but I didn't mind it, at all. To sleep on a mattress again would be pure, unadulterated ecstasy, and I was looking forward to it very much.

92

    Kaleb had barely stretched out beneath his blankets when we heard a noise at the back door. The metallic clang of the galvanized pipe hitting the aluminum doorframe rang through the empty halls like an echo bouncing through a canyon. Automatically jumping in a nervous twitch, I instinctively reached for my rifle. Before my hand had time to fully close around the weapon's stock, I heard a very familiar and calming sound. An eager, high pitched whine that was immediately followed by a sharp, impatient bark.

    Butch and I moved the heavy washer back and unbarred the glass door to Walter's joyous leaps and energetic tail wags. Smiles, hugs, and, in the case of Walter, head rubs made their way around our circle.

    Kaleb appeared around the corner of the hallway and saw Walter. He called to the big dog and Walter darted in his direction with a clear look of canine joy on his face.

    After re-securing the back door, we returned to the hallway housing Steevo and Reggie's rooms.

    As they rounded the corner that connected the two hallways, Kelli and Vickie started to laugh out loud. For some reason they found the made up mattresses lying on the hallway floor funny. Well, not just funny. Hilarious would be more like it. They could barely contain themselves during the sudden fit of delirium. Their faces turned red and their eyes teared up as the two became entangled in a hysterical laughing fit. All that Butch and I could do was look at them with raised eyebrows and share short, worried glances back and forth. Slowly regaining their composure, the two giggle happy ladies managed to stagger their way down the hallway and plop down on a nice, thick, wonderful slice of heaven, otherwise known as a mattress.

Kaleb and Jacob would sleep together on the middle of the three mattresses and Butch, Vickie, Kelli and I would sleep on the outer two.

No watch was needed that night. The hotel doors were secure and Steevo and Reggie weren't about to come out of their rooms. Carlos was badly injured and bedridden. It would be quite a while before he was much of a threat. Besides, Walter was in the hallway with us. If we did happen to miss something, he would certainly catch it.

Oooh's and aaah's filled the hallway as we climbed beneath our heavily layered blankets and the feeling of softness cradled our tired, aching bodies. It felt so wonderful. I don't know about anyone else, but as for myself, I was fast asleep in less than five minutes.

93

    Steevo and Reggie sat behind their meager cover and peered out with frightened eyes like mice hiding inside their tiny hole from a cat. The sound of the intruders grew steadily closer and they knew that it would only be a matter of time before they tried to enter their room. Steevo and Reggie weren't going to go down without a fight, though. They were scared of the consequences of being in a shootout and might even end up pissing their pants when it happened, but the two men were not going to just lay down and give up.

    They had been the ones in charge the day before, barking out orders to the last five members of their putrid posse and roaming the hotel at will. Now they were clamoring for safety like desperate rats on a drowning ship. It was possible that they could end up dying. In fact, they both knew that they probably would, in the end. But the pile of hand grenades stacked between them on the hotel's floor and the automatic weapons resting quietly in their hands said that the game wasn't over, yet.

    The militia had been after their food supply for quite a while. Steevo and Reggie even knew where they were camped out. The two men had briefly considered conducting a guerilla style raid on their camp in retaliation for the continued harassment of the hotel.

But that had been more than a month ago, when their manpower was still at it's peak. Since that time, the hellions of the hotel had experienced a dramatic loss in membership and didn't range very far from the hotel, if at all. They had even resorted to waiting until after dark and grouping together to go on their bucket brigades down to the river's edge for water.

After the round of gunshots that they had heard earlier that evening, Steevo thought he and Reggie may have to go to the river and get their own water from now on. If they lived that long.

The two nervous and frightened men heard sounds of heavy things being moved about out in the hallway through the paper thin walls. They also heard many, unmistakable, click hiss sounds of beverage cans being opened by tugs on pull tabs. Even high-pitched, jovial laughter came from these intruders. They had obviously found the large stash of beer upstairs and were now half sloshed on the conquered alcohol.

The two men had even heard, of all things, a dog. There had been no dogs around for quite a while. The last one had been eaten over a month ago. It was so hard to get fresh meat anymore that you did what you had to do.

Of all the different puzzling sounds that Steevo and Reggie heard coming through the hallway that night, the one that they heard next filled their hearts with the most fear.

Silence.

The two men tensed, waiting for the door to Steevo's room to catapult open and chunks of hot lead to fill the air. They stayed like that all night, halfway between sleep and wake, getting more confused by the minute.

94

    Sleeping on a nice, plump mattress again was simply fantastic. Sleeping in late on a soft, feathery mattress again went far beyond words. I had to literally force myself out of the warm, comfortable pocket of heaven.
    Shuffling my aching, tired legs, I slowly waddled into the closest bathroom to relieve myself. It felt so strange to be using a toilet again. For some reason it almost seemed unnatural.
    Butch and Kaleb had both been up for a while by that time and had already taken Walter outside to do his thing and have a brief look around the building.
    "They're still in there," Butch told me, with a slight glance and a quick nod at Steevo and Reggie's doors. "No tracks outside their windows and no new tracks anywhere around the building." Butch swung his extended first finger in a small, arcing semi-circle to accentuate his point. So much for that silly wish, I thought dejectedly.
    Our breakfast tasted especially wonderful that morning. After a quick check on our prisoner, I made a trip to the snack room to grab some more Ho Hos. That was when I came across something that I hadn't noticed in the harried rush of the night before. At the bottom of a small, neatly stacked pyramid of many other snack filled boxes, was a full case of Double-Stuff Oreos.

"Oreos!" excitedly escaped my mouth, although there was no one there to hear me.

Carefully un-stacking and setting aside the boxes residing above that particular case, I gained full access to the chocolate and cream filled treasure. Easily slicing through the packing tape at each end of the carton, I quickly drew back the cardboard flaps. The sight was truly amazing to an Oreo lover. Shiny, cellophane wrappers printed with bright blue ink stared up at me. Scooping up three of the beautiful, crinkly packages, I walked back down the hallway as fast as my sore, door kicking legs would allow.

As I drew closer and everyone saw what I was cradling, smiles appeared on their sleep lined faces.

"Oreos!" Kaleb elatedly yelled. He threw his hands up like a quarterback celebrating a clutch touchdown.

Passing one of the packages to the boys and handing another to Butch and Vickie, Kelli and I opened the third one and began to greedily gobble the tasty cookies.

Through cookie crumb filled mouths, we reluctantly discussed the pressing business of the day. First off, there were still two of our packs in the caboose and someone would have to traipse back and get them. Secondly, Steevo and Reggie were still holed up inside their rooms and it appeared like they weren't ready to budge, yet. And last, but not least, we had a badly wounded prisoner on our hands that needed immediate medical attention.

For some reason, just the thought of dealing with those issues made me want to crawl under the warm blankets piled on top of my mattress again and go back to sleep. As Winnie the Pooh would say in a situation like this, "Oh, bother."

Butch, Jacob and Walter volunteered to make the final trip to the caboose and retrieve the rest of our personal belongings. Kaleb would continue his vigilant watch over Steevo and Reggie's doors in case one of the men should happen to get too brave or overly curious. Vickie and Kelli would see to our prisoner's wounds and care for him.

"So," I asked with raised eyebrows and a sly grin dressing my face. "Does that mean I can go back to sleep?" Nobody else seemed to find my joke funny. I got a couple of sympathetic smiles, a couple of "are you serious?" looks and a pillow planted firmly upside my head by Kelli.

95

    Standing back a bit, I watched as Kelli and Vickie re-dressed Carlos' wounds. Jacob's bullet had passed completely through the man's upper left thigh, right about the point where his leg turned into ass. From the location of the entrance and exit wounds, if the bullet hadn't actually hit any bone, it had damn sure come close. Carlos was in severe pain and even the slightest movement of the wounded area caused him to draw in rapid, whistling breaths of anguish.

    Seeing this man lying on a hotel room bed, helpless and in agony, suddenly made me feel very sorry for him. After all, he hadn't tried to hurt us; just the opposite, in fact. The man had hid from us, and when he knew that there was no other option, he tried to run.

    Moving forward slightly to attract his attention, I spoke in a quiet, reverent tone. "Carlos," I told the prone prisoner, "I'm going to untie your hands and feet. I don't think you're going to try anything stupid, but just in case, only one of these ladies will be close to you at a time. If you *do* try something, the other one is going to shoot you, again."

    His tired, pain filled eyes felt like they were burning right through me, but he said nothing.

    "Do you understand?"

    Carlos slowly nodded his head up and down twice.

96

    I decided to roam the halls for a while. Everyone else was busy doing something constructive and I felt a tad bit guilty. I didn't know where I was going or exactly what I was looking for, but it was better than just sitting around doing nothing.

    As I strolled along my thoughts returned to the case of Oreo cookies in the snack room and how, in our rush to clear the space, the cookies had been overlooked. Yes, it had been dark and we were looking for people, not objects, but if we could overlook a case of Oreos, what else might we have missed?

    I wandered down the hallway to the junk food filled room. In the light of day the full magnitude of the mountains of munchies was staggering. The volume was so overwhelming that, just by looking at it and taking it all in, I almost became sick to my stomach. Having all of those quick, energy producing calories was certainly nice, but we needed some real food.

    I remembered that somewhere near the snack filled fantasy room we had also found a room containing stacks of canned and boxed goods. I couldn't recall exactly which room it was, but with all of the doors standing wide open, I didn't think that obstacle would pose too much of a problem.

Strolling away from the south end of the hotel where we were camped and swiveling my head back and forth as I walked, I began to look into each room as I passed by. I found it about four doors down from the snack room and on the opposite side of the wainscoted hallway. I remembered seeing some soup and crackers in it during our initial search, along with a lot of other provisions. Right now, though, we had no clean water to cook with, so anything but soup would have to wait.

There was tomato, chicken noodle and minestrone. Split pea with ham, celery and vegetable. It was like a Campbell's Soup warehouse in there. After searching the printing on the outside of the first few rows of highly stacked boxes, I found what I was looking for. Tons of Chunky Soup. That stuff was exactly what our bodies needed. Two of the cases had already been opened and a lot of those cans were missing. From what the evidence told me, someone around there had liked clam chowder and steak and potato soup.

Going with the flow, I stuffed my pockets full with cans of both kinds and headed back out the door. Strutting down the hallway heavily laden with precious proteins and vitamin enriched nutrients, I passed by the open door of the Cabela room. A sudden flash of inspiration ran through me.

From being inside the room briefly and trying to negotiate our way through the tangled masses, we knew that it was well stocked. Perhaps, I thought to myself, there might be a small backpacking or military style cooking stove in there. We would need fuel as well, but maybe that would also be in there. The way that the merchandise was piled up, it certainly wouldn't be beyond the realm of possibility.

Unloading all of my pockets onto the mattress that Kelli and I had slept on, I gained a newfound appreciation for something that I had taken for granted, up to that point. Chunky Soup came with pull top lids, so no can opener was needed. Allowing myself only a brief moment to ponder the marvels of modern technology, I turned on my heels and set a course for the messy and cluttered Cabela room.

Upon entering, I was struck by the same puzzling question of the night before. Why were all of the other rooms of pilfered belongings so neatly stacked and put away and this room, alone, was as messy as a pig sty? The place was such a wreck that I didn't have a clue where to begin looking.

Visually examining the tangled contents closer, I recognized that perhaps there was some slight separation between the different types of objects. The tents were, for the most part, in one corner and the sleeping bags were strewn along the west wall. Boots, outer clothing and heavy jackets filled the entire length of the east wall. Just to the right side of the bathroom door I spotted what appeared to be a large, jumbled pile of miscellaneous items. I could make out hatchets and knives. Rope and tent stakes. Even a few fish nets were poking their heads out of the pile like they had wanted a better view of their disheveled surroundings.

Looking toward the bathroom, I noticed that the clutter trail continued on unimpeded and had taken over that small space, as well.

With nothing to lose but a few minutes of time, I carefully crept through the tangled tonnage of outdoor clothing and camping gear. I made it to the white tiled bathroom safely and curiously peered inside. Sitting on the long, white sink to the left were hundreds of containers of mosquito repellant. Every brand and delivery system that I had ever heard of was duly accounted for among their numbers.

My eyes carefully scanned every bit of the room's content. Among the cluttered mass of merchandise to the right of the porcelain throne, my eyes hit on a promising target.

Feeling kind of like Tiny Tim tip toeing through the tulips, I eased across the small, claustrophobic space. Poking the tip of my gun barrel into a hastily piled volcano of thick winter gloves, I gently swung it to the right. Part of a box that was hidden beneath the pile came into view. The graphic printed on the surface of the cardboard stopped me cold.

For a long moment I could do no more than mutely stare at the picture. My breathing became fast and shallow and I was almost overcome with giddiness by the sight of it. I had to make sure that what I was seeing was indeed real and not just a wishful figment of my imagination.

Kneeling down on one knee, my rifle in my left hand and my knife in my right, I slipped the tip of the sharp blade between the lid and the end of the box and cut the wide strapping tape. Gently, like I was a bomb disposal expert working on a tricky explosive device, I gently pulled the brown flaps up.

My lips grew thin and pressed together as my cheeks

tightened into a grin of massive proportions. My chest quickly began to heave and fall in a violent, shaking manner. At first, my laughter was silent, shared only between my brain and the body that it controlled. After a few seconds, though, my body became unable to contain the overwhelming joy of the discovery inside its fleshy bounds any longer and trumpeted the good news to the rest of the world. My ears exploded as the sound of mad, cackling giggles bounced back at me off the tiled walls of the little bathroom. I was at a complete loss to control my soaring emotions.

Standing back up, I looked into the huge, flat mirror mounted above the sink and caught a revealing glimpse of myself. I hardly recognized the creature that I saw there. He of the hideous, twisted grin, the long hair and the shaggy, unkempt beard. The bright blue eyes were the same, but they looked like they had been commandeered and transplanted into a wild man's face. One who was now cackling like a raving lunatic under my watchful gaze. How different I looked! For that matter, how different we all looked. Being around each other all day long, each and every day, we couldn't see the big picture. The changes were so subtle and so slow, and we were so busy surviving day to day, that they, for the most part, went unnoticed. Standing there looking at someone that I didn't recognize brought the length of time and the hardships that we had endured home.

I looked older, more tired and dirtier than I could ever remember. Abruptly, the mad laughter stopped. The wild man in the mirror also stopped laughing.

He stared back at me inquisitively, his eyes boring deeply into mine.

After a moment, the weight of that stare proved to be overpowering and I sheepishly turned my head away and back to the business at hand.

Digging a half dozen cans of jelled cooking fuel, commonly called Sterno, out of the box, I stuffed three of them into each oversized jacket pocket. One down, one to go, I told myself. Now that we had cooking fuel, we just needed to find a stove to burn it in.

Rooting around underneath the pile of thickly insulated winter gloves, my right hand struck something with a cold, hard, metallic feel. Retracting my hand, I began to rapidly brush the perfectly paired gloves aside and out of the way. After several enthusiastic sweeps back and forth with my outstretched hand and forearm, the unwanted debris was finally cleared.

A very short but powerfully breathy, "Yes!" exited my mouth when I spotted the stoves. There were only two of them, but that was two more than we had at the moment. A dull black in color, both of them were neatly folded into little, flat squares, absolutely perfect for backpacking.

I snatched both of them up and hurried from the small, enclosed space without so much as a glance toward the large surface of the reflective mirror. I didn't feel like sharing my happiness with the stranger again, so I held it in until I made the safety of the hallway.

97

    My first thought was to exuberantly run back down the hallway at full speed and share my discovery with Kaleb, Vickie and Kelli. The only thing that stopped me from doing exactly that was an even better idea, which came a split second later.

    Instead, I would play it nice and cool and casually stroll back down the hallway like I was out on a Sunday afternoon nature walk. Once I reached the mattress where Kaleb sat vigilantly guarding Steevo and Reggie's closed doors, I would, without a word, set the stoves up and begin heating some soup.

    Kaleb must have heard me sauntering toward him. His eyes left the last two doors of the hallway and refocused on me. I lazily threw up my right hand and nodded in his direction. That always present smile lit up his face and he returned the wave with a little nod.

    "Hi," he cheerfully exclaimed. "Did you find anything?"

    I pointed toward the cans of Chunky Soup that were lying on the mattress as if they were vacationing in Mexico and it was siesta time.

    Kaleb nodded once more and, with widening eyes, offered his expert opinion. "That stuff's gonna be good," he emphatically stated.

"Mmhhmm," I agreed in return.

To the casual observer watching from a distance, Kaleb and I probably looked like two of those bobble headed dogs in the rear window of a sedan as it moved along a particularly bumpy stretch of road.

Looking at the boy's excited face, I decided to let him in on the rest of my fabulous find. Revealing the two flattened backpacking stoves in my left hand, I held them up high like a prized trophy fish on a stringer. Kaleb studied the small stack of stamped metal squares very closely for a few seconds. His brow furrowed and he turned his inquisitive, bright eyes to mine and softly asked, "What's that?"

Bringing a finger up to lay across my closed lips in a shushing gesture, I tilted my head slightly in the direction of the open door where Vickie and Kelli were. Understanding dawned on him and was instantly transferred to his facial features.

"A surprise?" he asked, his voice an octave higher than it had been a moment earlier.

Once again, I did my impression of the little dog in the sedan's rear window. A smile blossomed on his young, pleasant face, but it was short lived. Almost immediately it was completely replaced by the same questioning look of a few moments ago.

"But, what is it?" he repeated, his eyes darting between the object and mine.

Whispering quietly so that Kelli and Vickie couldn't overhear, I answered him. "It's a stove."

His look of curiosity quickly changed to one of scorn and disbelief. He looked at me like he wanted for all the world to believe what I was telling him, but just couldn't get his mind to stretch that far. Having never seen such a miniature cooking device, he couldn't decide if I was tugging his leg or not.

"Watch," I told him.

Turning to the right, I knelt down on carpeted hallway floor and unfolded one of the small, black metal stoves. In three quick flips of the lightly hinged flaps, a little, square box with an oven-like space in the middle of it miraculously appeared in my hands. Kaleb's eyes grew round and large as though I had just executed a wondrous, awe-inspiring magic trick.

Setting the little, metal box on the floor about six inches

away from the surface of the wall, I dug into my coat pocket and fished out a shiny, round canister of Sterno. I leaned my rifle against the wainscoted surface and made a beeline for our backpacks, which were resting on the floor of the Canoe room.

With Kaleb watching inquisitively through the open doorway, I dug into the left side, outer compartment of my pack and located the Bic lighter we had taken from the pocket of the dead cannibal that had kidnapped Kaleb.

With a frenzied feeling of anticipation, I brushed past Kaleb and hurriedly returned to the little stove's side. Making the sound of a cork leaving a bottle's lips, the lid on the can of Sterno gently lifted off and flew up into the air. It crashed back down onto the padded floor, almost soundlessly. After it had completed it's wobbly settling, the lid stared up at the hallway's white ceiling like it was totally ecstatic to see something other than the inside of that can, for a change. No time to mourn the loss of it's occupation, I thumbed the wheel on the bright blue Bic and touched the lighter to the side of the opening in the top of the aluminum can. A dark blue flame appeared on the surface of the gel when it first ignited. After a couple of seconds, though, the flicker became nearly transparent. Sliding the burning can into the opening at the front of the miniature oven, I closed the door with a gentle shove.

Rousting a can of clam chowder from it's resting place atop the spongy mattress, I stripped away the colorful paper label. Grasping the pull top's ring with my finger, I carefully eased the lid back a crack to allow pressure to escape while it heated up. Something our whole Cub Scout troop learned the hard way when I was about ten or eleven years old. Timmy Johnson probably still had nightmares about it.

98

    We were sitting around the roaring campfire bragging and lying, as most boys that age do to get on each other's nerves. Roasting bags of marshmallows, eating hot dogs and s'mores and drinking gallons of soda pop.
    Timmy decided that he wanted a can of soup. Getting up from the huge log that we were sitting on, he grabbed a can of tomato soup out of his tent and carried it over by the fire. To warm it up, he set it next to the dancing yellow flames on top of a large limestone chunk that we were using as part of our fire ring. It was a trick that Timmy had seen many other people, including his father, use numerous times. Feeling self-satisfied in his knowledge of primitive cooking techniques, he re-crossed the clearing to take part in more ritualistic boyhood banter.
    About a half an hour later, in the middle of all of our good natured ribbing and silly story stretching, Joe Baxter called out to Timmy.
    "Hey, Timmy," Baxter yelled out above the fray. "I think there's something wrong with your soup." Having done his neighborly duty, Baxter grabbed his blackened hot dog from the end of a whittled stick and rejoined our little group next to the

huge fallen log.

Timmy Johnson's face grew strangely contorted at the interruption. He was getting his butt kicked in a verbal battle, once again, and decided to use Baxter's distraction as an excuse to showcase some of his building irritation. Sporting a theatrically enhanced look of displeasure on his face, he rose with a disgusted huff to go check on the cooking can of soup. After crossing the clearing in an exaggerated, straight legged manner, Timmy leaned over the big limestone fire ring to assess his meals progress. A sharp, cracking, pop rang out, stopping all of the yarn spinning and bragadocious battles that were being waged in an instant.

Timmy squealed in surprise as his can of tomato soup rocketed up from the chunk of limestone and headed straight for his helplessly exposed face.

I'm sure that Johnson thought he was a goner. He threw his hands up to shield his face with inhuman speed and fell over backwards in an effort to escape certain annihilation.

He had always been blessed with great luck, though, and this occurrence proved to be no different. The only damage that he incurred was a few minor facial burns from the hot, spurting soup and some badly stained clothing. The can, only launching itself a couple of feet into the night air, never even came close to contacting Timmy. It fell back down to earth with a boing and sprayed even more hot tomato soup, far and wide.

I don't think anyone in our Cub Scout pack ever forgot that lesson, especially Timmy, and I certainly had no desire to repeat it.

99

  I slid the can onto the top of the little cooking stove.
  "Oh, wow," Kaleb breathed from behind me. "That's awesome."
  "Yes, it is," I agreed. "We'll be eating some warm meals today."
  Kaleb's right hand bounced lightly on my shoulder in anticipation as I repeated the process with the remaining stove. Once the other tin of Sterno was lit and safely inside the second steel enclosure, I lowered a can of steak and potato soup onto it's flat upper surface.
  Rubbing a brilliantly beaming Kaleb on top of the head, I asked, "Will you watch those for a minute while I go check on the ladies and Carlos?"
  Kaleb didn't say a word. He just nodded his head up and down while looking at me with that big smile on his face.
  Upon entering the prisoner's room, I saw that Carlos was lying on his right side, propped up and held in place by what looked to be about twenty pillows. He appeared to be sleeping soundly while Vickie and Kelli sat together on the other twin bed.
  "Hi," a smiling Kelli said when she saw me walk in.

"Hi," I quietly returned. Nodding a greeting in Vickie's direction and then looking toward Carlos, I asked "How is he?"

Both of their faces instantly turned grim and somber and their downcast eyes told me the prognosis before their vocal chords had the chance.

"He's lost a lot of blood," Vickie began, "and he's severely dehydrated."

Kelli's shiny brown eyes met mine. "He's really weak," she said. Then, with a barely noticeable shrug of her shoulders, she added, "We'll just have to wait and see."

Something in their subconscious body language and vacant, lost in the twilight zone gaze told me exactly what they really thought. They believed that Carlos had reached the end of his yellow brick road.

"We cleaned him up and finally got the bleeding to stop," Vickie confided, "but every time that he moves it seems like it starts all over again."

The concern was clearly evident on her strained face. I suddenly wondered why she cared so much about the health and well-being of Carlos when she had been indifferent and even downright hostile towards Charlie. My racing mind could come up with only two possibilities. Either Carlos hadn't been present when Butch was being worked over, like Charlie was, or she sensed that he was no longer a threat to us and would probably end up dying, anyway. I almost asked Vickie if she and Butch had seen this man when they were being held captive in the hotel, but wisely convinced myself that asking her some other time might be more prudent. I bid a farewell to the two concerned nurses and headed for the door.

As I re-entered the hallway, my nose picked up the faint scent of something cooking. I couldn't tell for sure if it was the steak and potato soup or the clam chowder, but I knew that it smelled really good.

Kaleb was still sitting on the mattress closest to Steevo and Reggie's doors, his rifle pointed their way. I wondered what those two were doing holed up in their rooms, or perhaps room. After all, Charlie did tell us that the two rooms they were staying in had connecting doors. We had seen many such doors in the hotel as we searched it, so I had no reason to doubt what he said. Up to that point, everything that Charlie told us had been spot on. That thought made me feel kind of sorry for old Cyclops, all over again.

With the soup cooking and everyone else keeping themselves constructively busy, I decided to look around the hotel a little bit more.

Wandering down the building's hallway at a slow, leisurely pace, I ended up turning to the right and heading toward the barricaded back door and the laundry room. Something was tingling in the back of my mind about the last time we were in there. That had been when Butch and I got the industrial sized handcart that we used to move those massive, white washing machines with.

Upon entering the room, it only took me a moment of searching to spot it. On the far side of the wash basin, mounted into the wall, was a solid steel door. A shiny, light gray in color, it was encased in a steel housing that was imbedded directly into the block outer wall of the hotel. There was a common, push button type lock on the shiny metal handle and a large diameter sliding bolt about two thirds of the way up.

In our sleepy rush the previous evening to finish securing the hotel's exit doors, we had neglected to give that one any attention. The steel slab was equipped with a tiny, fisheye peephole, right at about chin level. Nestling my forehead up against the flat, cold surface of the door, I looked out into the winter afternoon's gloomy gray.

"This must've been the delivery entrance," I whispered to no one.

A maze of diagonally striped yellow lines marked off the area directly in front of the door. Painted in the middle of the cordoned off area, in the same neon bright yellow, was the warning, NO PARKING, LOADING ZONE. Two things occurred to me. The first was, once again, if we had wearily glossed over a huge steel door in our initial search, what else might we have missed? The thought gave me real pause and the hint of a chill trickled down my spine. A crashing wave of self-doubt swept over me like black clouds from a sudden, unexpected thunderstorm. *Had* there been anything else that we had missed in our hurried quest for some much needed rest?

My mind began racing over the blurred, incomplete images of an almost endless string of very boring, aesthetically sterile hotel rooms. Fighting to regain control over my thoughts and restore my confidence, I reminded myself that this was, after all, just a door.

A solid, flat object mounted smoothly within the structure's wall and not a person. The door posed no threat, whatsoever. We were all looking for holdovers or hideouts and intently searching for human forms. Not much attention was paid to anything else. We were in fear of running into one of Hotel Hell's patrons and having to shoot it out. There wasn't much time to take in the peripheral scenery.

Having temporarily restored my faith in the thoroughness of our grueling midnight search through the hotel's premises, I turned to the happier portion of my double headed thought.

It would be much easier for us to use the steel door to enter and exit through than the main glass door. It would also be quicker and a whole lot safer. We could permanently block off the door that we were using, as we had the others, and make the hotel more secure.

I jumped involuntarily as heavy pounding besieged the barricaded back door in the nearby hallway. Taking a moment to catch my breath and recompose myself, I peered out of the small, glass peephole in the steel door.

To the left, on the very extreme edge of my vision's range, stood Jacob. Wearing his big blue backpack, he waited patiently at the entrance while Walter bounced around energetically scooping up bits of snow in his long, open jaws.

Thumbing the sliding deadbolt's protruding knob out and dragging it to the left, I released the door's upper lock. A quick twist of the shiny, steel handle and the slab swung inward, admitting a cold, gusty, winter breeze into the laundry room's interior.

100

    Bellies bulging with hot Chunky Soup, we sat around on our billowy mattresses burping and inadvertently nodding off. It felt so good to have a belly full of warm food that it produced a hypnotically powerful calming effect. Eyelids began to droop noticeably, speech became less frequent and pronunciation more lazy. Exchanges gradually shortened to one word and then stopped altogether. The soft, inviting space of the cushiony mattresses became our best friends. I'm sure that none of us meant for it to happen, but in only a few short minutes of time, we would look like the remnants of an overly inebriated, wild frat house party. For the next two blissful hours, we slept the sleep of dead men.

101

    A tap on the shoulder and soft spoken words that seemed very far away. A gentle knee into the fleshy part of my behind. Finally, I returned to a fuzzy, confused consciousness. It was Kelli calling my name in a quiet, gentle whisper accented with repeated, bird like peckings on the back of my right shoulder.
    At first, I couldn't tell if my eyes were open or not, so I repeated the process several times, just to be sure. Yep, my eyes were open, alright, but someone had turned out all the lights. To get Kelli to quit bruising my shoulder blade, I answered her. "What?" I said. I sounded like a croaking bullfrog with my throat not yet fully awake.
    Her answer was short, simple and to the point, "It's dark."
    My initial response was 'No shit, Sherlock,' but I didn't vocalize it. One learns over the many years of a relationship that's it's best to filter your thoughts, if possible, before relaying them aloud.
    "I see that," was my filtered response. Sitting up, I swiveled my groggy head around and squinted my sleepy eyes in all directions. Gradually, my night vision began to work well enough to allow the surroundings to once again reveal themselves.
    A tiny sliver of white light appeared to the left of the

mammoth industrial washing machine blocking the south entrance. It rose and fell in intensity as some unseen Canadian soldier ran his searchlight back and forth through it's full range of motion.

No one else appeared to be awake. Putting a fisted hand up to my mouth to help stifle a growing growl of a yawn, I tilted my head back and stretched my mouth beyond wide. Blinking the dewy teardrops of the deep, heavy gape away, I quickly scrambled to get all of my brain's circuit boards up and running again. As my onboard computer booted up to full speed, one word kept flashing over and over like a neon sign in the forefront of my mind.   Light.

Slipping my jacket on, I began stepping back down the carpeted hallway in the dark and re-entered the Cabela room. I had seen a small, haphazard looking pile of flashlights on the floor earlier that day and was going to retrieve a few for our use.

Once more picking my way carefully across the clutter strewn floor of the messy room, I fished out three worthy looking models and safely deposited them inside my jacket's large, outer pockets.

Grateful to make the open, un-littered ground of the hallway once again, I eagerly rushed toward our overflowing stash of batteries. Two "D" cells later, I pressed the rubber coated button on the flashlight's side down and a beam of clear, white light invaded the darkness of the little room.

"What a wonderful invention," I breathed to myself.

Holding onto a working flashlight again gave me a curiously powerful feeling. I almost felt like a heroic "Luke Skywalker" wielding his deadly light sabre. Just for grins, I swung the flashlight in quick, slashing motions about the room. Light flew around freely in all different directions, even rebounding off the dresser's large, oval mirror in a temporarily blinding flash. Blinking the bright, white dots emblazoned on my corneas away, I grabbed two more packages of batteries.

Triumphantly turning around, I returned to the side of my sleepy-eyed comrades with a beautiful, brightly lit path in front of me.

The next couple of days were, without a doubt, the most stress free and relaxing that any of us had spent since the whole disaster began. We occupied our time by eating, sleeping and further exploring the hotel's many rooms.   Then we ate and slept some more.

Boiling water in some small mess kit pans enabled us to finally clean ourselves properly. Making liberal use of the large supply of fragrant shampoo and soap, we were all soon smelling like a very large bouquet of fresh cut flowers. Brushing my teeth for the first time in over a month was a wonderful blessing. My gums felt especially tender and when I spat, there was some blood mixed in with the saliva and toothpaste. Kissing Kelli with a fresh, clean mouth made it all worth it, though.

Over the last month I had made a mercifully conscious effort to not let her smell my ever worsening breath. It had grown to be so rancid that, I myself, could not stand the rotten, putrid stench my own mouth emitted.

Vickie and Kelli took turns washing our soil caked clothes in the laundry room's big, utility wash basin. There must have been close to two hundred pounds of laundry detergent on hand and close to that in fabric softener, and the ladies weren't shy about using either.

Butch, Jacob and I kept ourselves busy by repeatedly hauling heavy buckets of water back from the river's edge. Five gallon buckets get heavy fast when they're full and you have to carry them for over two hundred long, agonizing yards, again and again. By the end of that second day, all three of us suffered from arms that felt as though they would break cleanly off at the shoulder and drop to the ground if we so much as attempted to raise them.

In the end, it was all well worth the trouble. We smelled like human beings again instead of livestock and I could kiss Kelli once again without feeling self-conscious.

A lot of our stuff was beyond cleaning, so during brief lulls we "went shopping" in the Cabela room and picked out new boots, packs and warm, sturdy outdoor clothing.

The beaming, new found smiles displayed on everyone's faces, mixed with that "stiff as cardboard" new clothes feel, made me think back to past holiday seasons and the wonderful collection of memories that they contained. A slideshow of happy images began to cascade through my mind's eye like a Saturday afternoon matinee. For a brief moment in time, I could see everyone inspecting their new outdoor gear and watch as their mouths moved but couldn't hear a word that they were saying. It reminded me of watching a scene from a movie with the mute on. In place of the noise emanating from my celebratory friends, a soundtrack featuring bubbly, childish laughter and high pitched squeals of joy from Christmases past played at full, stereophonic volume inside my head.

If not for Kelli casually tossing another can of Sterno my way, I might possibly have stayed in that wonderful place a while longer. Instead, my body automatically reacted and gently cradled the small aluminum can between my tired arms and chest. In an instant, that serene, luxurious feeling of being happy, healthy and safe vanished.

Replacing that elated, top of the world sensation, was the hard, cold truth that no matter how much food and clothing we had, our situation was still basically the same. Stuck in a lawless land where hostility toward your fellow man was the rule, not the exception, I desperately wanted to get my family across the river to freedom. The only thing keeping me from doing that, was figuring out exactly how to accomplish such a lofty goal. Newly determined to succeed, I resided myself to bringing up the subject at our evening meal. After all, we finally had the time to donate our energy to solving a problem other than worrying about where our next meal was coming from.

Every day that we stayed in the hotel, I knew that we would become better rested and stronger. And, each day that Steevo and Reggie stayed hunkered down in their rooms, they would become increasingly more nervous, tired and ultimately weaker. Time was on our side, alright, when it came to Steevo and Reggie. But it was our enemy, as far as I was concerned, in finding a way to get across the cold, deep St. Clair.

"Is mom talking to herself?" Jacob asked, to no one in particular. A puzzled expression on his face, he rapidly turned his head toward the open doorway through which Kelli was watching over Carlos. His mostly finished bowl of Ramen noodles still sending up steamy smoke signals, he turned his questioning eyes to mine as if I, alone, could answer this burning question.

Before I had a chance to even open my mouth, the mystery solved itself. Kelli appeared in the doorway, almost as if on cue. Clutching our stainless steel Ruger nine millimeter in her right hand, she anxiously motioned for Vickie with her left.

"He's awake," she hissed excitedly. "And he's hungry."

102

Clearly elated by this fortunate turn of events, Vickie scrambled to her feet and bolted through the open doorway.

Being just nosy enough to go check out the situation for myself, I grabbed my open can of Dr. Pepper and trailed after the two of them.

Carlos was indeed awake and looking remarkably better. A little color had returned to his ashen face and his eyes looked alert and clear. He stared at me defiantly, like a wounded animal caught in a trap. Half sitting, half laying on his back atop a generous, wedge shaped stack of pillows, he was totally helpless and no doubt felt very scared.

Vickie was understandably excited and appeared to be very relieved at her patient's promising progress. Her radiant, motherly smile never left her face as she scurried around to the other side of the bed and lifted a glass of water to Carlos' parched lips.

Drinking greedily in large, noisy gulps, the small, plastic hotel cup ran dry in just a few seconds. Vickie smiled at this like a young mother might over a toddler that just went poo in his training toilet for the first time.

Carlos' features softened noticeably when he looked at

Vickie's caring, smiling face.

"Would you like some more water or are you ready to eat?" she asked in her most nurse-like tone.

After a long moment's pause, he quietly answered. "I'm hungry."

Vickie's smile widened even more at this news and she reached into the nightstand and retrieved a Hunt's Snack pack of creamy chocolate pudding. Using a disposable, white plastic spoon, she began to shovel the contents of one delicious Snack pack after another into her famished patient's mouth.

Moving to occupy the twin bed next to him, I gently sat down. Our captives eyes relentlessly darted back and forth between the three of us as he emptied spoonful after spoonful of creamy, brown pudding.

He appeared to be carefully gauging each one of us and our intentions. The world being what it those days, he was no doubt wondering why he was still alive and being so well cared for.

To cut through the tension and break the silence, I said, "Hello, Carlos," to our prone, pudding eating prisoner.

His gaze turned to meet mine but he said nothing. Then, after a few, very long, uncomfortable moments, he minutely nodded his head in my direction.

Suddenly finding what she was doing to be a waste of her valuable time, Vickie shoved the pudding and spoon into her patients own two good hands and started to check on his bandages.

With as much bedside manner that I could muster, I asked him, "How do you feel, Carlos?"

A red hot glare instantly emanated from his eyes as if it were an insult to ask him such a stupid question. A sneer enveloped his face and he angrily spat out, "I feel like a man who's been shot in the *ass*." His jaws immediately clenched as a bolt of pain shot through his wounded body from the added emphasis that he placed on the word ass.

Gritting through his teeth in obvious, excruciating pain, he picked up the plastic spoon that he held a little higher into the air and pointed it in my general direction. A sneer on his face, he hissed at me through tightly drawn lips, "Why don't you just go ahead and kill me instead of playing games?"

I was taken aback for a moment by the sheer ferocity in

this man's gaze. It was obvious that he didn't like the situation he found himself in.

"Carlos," I said gently. "We don't want to kill you. In fact, I feel really bad about you getting shot, at all."

"Yeah, right," he shot back. "That's why you blasted me in my *ass*." Again, with the emphasis on the word ass, he grimaced as another spasm of pain wracked his wounded body.

With her patient's best interest in mind, Vickie tried hard to soothe our angry captive. "Carlos, none of us want to hurt you," she told him evenly. "We're all good people and we're really sorry about shooting you." Looking at him steadily, she went on. "That boy out there in the hallway has spent the last two days worrying himself sick, since he shot you."

Her patient squinted in reaction to Vickie's last sentence like a man with a teeming migraine headache. In a flash, his facial expression did a complete one eighty and a small, disbelieving smirk appeared on his once pained face. Spreading to reveal a genuine, large, toothy smile, Carlos incredulously asked, "Boy?" He blinked his eyes repeatedly like his eyes couldn't believe what his mind was seeing. "A boy shot me?"

He looked from person to person like he was waiting for one of us to break a smile and let him in on the gag. After anxiously looking at each of our faces at least a couple of times, he still had trouble believing.

"A kid shot me?" he asked, turning his plastic spoon around so that it pointed back at himself.

In perfect unison, as though we had been rehearsing for this very moment for many long years, Vickie, Kelli and I all nodded simultaneously.

What happened next was one of those indescribable moments where everything seems to magically fall into place like tumblers in the cylinder of a lock. Raucous, loud, pent up laughter filled the room, as not only did the ice break, but the whole dam melted and rushed downstream in a surging torrent.

Although he was trying his best not to, Carlos couldn't help himself. Bellowing hearty laughter as his long built up tension eroded, he pushed the palm of his non-spoon hand flatly against his hip down close to the exit wound in an attempt to lessen his body's piston like shaking.

Poor Vickie was laughing so hard that her cheeks turned

bright red in color, but both of her hands still stayed drawn up to her chin out of concern for Carlos' wound.

Kelli covered her mouth and bent over as she laughed to try and lessen her impact on the punch drunk situation.

Slowly but surely, our uncontrollable laughing fits became less numerous and shorter in duration. They eventually diminished to sporadic outbursts of mass giggling, then finally withered away to the occasional, intensely felt chuckle.

Vickie rushed to tend to Carlos' now seeping wounds and the hostility that had been present just a few moments before disappeared as quickly as morning dew in bright sunshine.

103

  Steevo and Reggie were starting to go stark raving, cabin fever mad in their barricaded bunker of a hotel room. For three long days the invading National Guard unit had been occupying the building, but in all of that time had not once tried to breech their pitiful defenses.
  Their heavy, drooping eyelids hung down like half drawn window shades over red, sleep deprived eyes.
  Having grown sick and tired of being in such close proximity to each other for so long, the two men had slowly slid apart and now resided in their own, separate corners.
  Steevo had become increasingly resentful of having Reggie in his room. The stench in the tiny space was virtually unbearable, and that was saying something for these two. Unable to make it to the river and refill their toilet's supply tank, the men had used what little clean water they had on the first full day of the siege. Since then, the toilet had become so clogged with excrement that a full bowl of frothy piss wouldn't flush it. The odor had become so pervasive that even closing the bathroom door did little to alleviate the awful, burning ammonia and sulpher smell.

On top of the ever present nasal nuisance, Steevo also had to deal with Reggie's stomach and it's voracious appetite. Being used to moving about the hotel to gather his food and drink at will, Steevo did not keep much of it in his room. A few assorted snacks or maybe a six pack of Coke every now and then. The duo had eaten sparingly in an attempt to ration what meager provisions were on hand. They had consumed everything in the room over the last few days except a couple of oatmeal cookies and half a bag of sour cream and onion potato chips. The Coke was long gone.

With each passing hour Steevo grew increasingly more angry and frustrated, both at the ridiculous predicament that he found himself in, and at the ever present, human thorn in his side, named Reggie. He wondered which heat source would make him boil over first.

104

Carlos was busy stuffing himself full of peanut butter and jelly on saltine crackers as we all sat around and talked. There had been no bread around for quite a while and he had stumbled upon this combination one day out of sheer luck. Since then, Carlos informed us, it had become one of his favorite snacks. Being unable to resist trying these crunchy, little, gooey squares ourselves, we all became hopelessly addicted to them, as well. Kelli said that she preferred hers without jelly, but overall the nutritious little treats were a smash hit.

Our conversation drifted about from one topic to another as easily as a warm summer breeze. Carlos was chatting away with us like we had always been the best of friends.

"When I found out that a kid shot me," he told us, "I knew that you weren't local. Why, all the kids around here have been dead for quite a while, now. Survival of the fittest and all, you know."

He finished with a small tilt of his head, as if that small movement could inexorably explain away all of the atrocities that had taken place. But really, what could anyone say about the unfortunate chain of events that had driven us all to this agitated, confused and dangerous state of mind? Willing to kill each other over food and sometimes *as* food, there was nowhere and nothing that was safe.

The pain of Carlos' own personal journey was clearly etched on his features as he relayed to us how he came to be there in the hotel with Steevo and Reggie. Telling us that he should have left a long time ago but didn't because it was much safer to stay there, he then brought up the food. If Carlos had left, he too would have been desperate to find nutrition and there was no food to be had anywhere around Marine City. Steevo and Reggie had made sure of that. If he had decided to leave, he would have only two choices for dinner, either get lucky enough to harvest one of the last few remaining wild creatures in this area, or resort to cannibalism, himself. He reluctantly chose to remain in the hotel and take his chances with the rest of his ever shrinking band of brothers.

Carlos told us that the local militia unit had been very active lately, thinning the population of the hotel dramatically over the past month, or so. With a disgusted shake of his head, he said, "Every time Steevo sent a group of us out, somebody always got killed. Sometimes two or three of us at a time."

Vickie broke in, "This Steevo sounds like a real nice guy." The facetiousness in her voice was not lost on Carlos' ears.

Looking at Vickie with his head nodding in agreement, he said with clear disdain, "He's an ass. A *big* ass."

Carlos went on to tell us that he had grown to strongly dislike Steevo and Reggie and, as the days passed, had started keeping more and more to himself. He confessed to us that he had pretended to be very ill in order to escape having to go outside the hotel for water or to stand guard duty.

"I told them that I had been diagnosed with bone cancer a few months earlier and if I moved around too much the pain would become unbearable. I kind of became a persona non grata to them after that because they thought that I couldn't carry heavy buckets of water up from the river or stand watch for hours at a time outside the hotel's doors. After a while they just kind of left me alone, but I don't think Steevo was too happy about me not doing my part." With a small quiver in his voice and unblinking eyes, he then told us, "I think that he was looking for any excuse to kill me."

We stayed up late that evening and talked long into the night, sharing stories of our childhoods and our past lives. The more we talked, the more Carlos revealed to us. About the hotel, Steevo and Reggie and the business of ferrying folks across the river with the help of their Canadian Coast Guard friend. By the time that we had started yawning heavily and were ready to turn in for the night, we had come up with some excellent ideas on how to deal with the two crooked culprits in the corner room.

105

    Somewhere between asleep and awake in the early morning hours, my mind churned restlessly. As I lay in our fluffy, ground level bed with Kelli's deep, rhythmic breathing serenading me, it kept returning, again and again, to the things that Carlos had said earlier in the evening.

    I couldn't help but wonder how much he knew about the specifics of the river crossing operation. The thought had first occurred to me during our animated chat session when he had readily offered up so much other useful information. At the time, though, I felt as if it would have been unwise to push our new friend too much on any particular subject, so I made a mental note of it and moved along. But as I lay there, just this side of dreamland, the endless possibilities began to swirl around and around inside my sleepy head. I finally had to assure my nagging, questioning mind that I would find out more from Carlos as soon as possible before it would stop grinding.

    If he *did* know everything about getting across the river, it would completely change the way that we ultimately dealt with Steevo and Reggie. A small smile played on my sleepy lips at that thought, and I fell asleep and dreamed of happier times.

106

Hunkered down in their respective corners to face another long and miserable night, Steevo and Reggie were beginning to lose touch with reality. They had eaten the last of their snacks and there had been nothing to drink for almost two days. The parts of their minds that were still cognizant wondered how much more they could take.

Steevo had already thought about killing Reggie many times. His infuriated, deranged side wanted to slice open his throat and drink the warm blood as it spurted from his neck like a stone cherub pissing into a goldfish pond.

Reggie wanted out. He didn't care how, he just wanted out of that room. Reggie had begged Steevo, repeatedly, to allow him to open one of the room's windows and scoop up some fresh snow. He told him that he could fill up all of the empty cups and bowls in the room and, once it melted, they would at least have a little water to drink.

But Steevo had squashed that idea as flat as a flyswatter does a fly. "Are you stupid?" he inquired of Reggie. A look of utter contempt lining his face, he spat, "As soon as you open that window and stick your head out, somebody's going to blow it off. Not that that would be such a bad thing. At least, then I wouldn't have to put up with your incessant whining."

Reggie could tell by the crazed gleam emanating from Steevo's eyes that he meant just that. He wouldn't mind watching Reggie buy the farm, one bit. With little else to do, Reggie slunk back into his designated corner and shut his mouth. He had already made up his mind, though. When Steevo went to sleep later on, he was going to try to reach out and scoop up some snow. Reggie had never been so thirsty in his entire life. His throat felt as if it was hopelessly clogged by thick, dust encrusted cobwebs. Steevo might try to stop him when he tried. Hell, he might even shoot him. But to Reggie, dying any other way than dehydration almost sounded acceptable at the moment.

Meanwhile, at the same time in the opposing corner, Steevo was busy making a few plans of his own. He was thirsty, too, and feeling the same overwhelming sense of urgency that Reggie did. He knew, though, that they wouldn't stand a chance if they confronted the hotel's invaders. Their only option was to try and outlast the looting horde and hope that they didn't attempt to enter their corner room. Once they had left and if was safe again, he would contact Rene and escape across the river, himself. He had more than enough ransomed valuables to pay for his passage and start a new life. And about Reggie, Steevo couldn't care less. He had served his purpose and that was all that mattered. Steevo sure wasn't about to fork over any gold for that sorry shit's passage. If it came right down to it, he didn't have any problem with shooting Reggie, himself.

As he daydreamed about doing just that, Steevo sat blankly staring at Reggie with a bright, shiny light dancing in his eyes. Mixing with the twisted smile residing below, it made for the most horrific looking combination that Reggie had ever witnessed.

107

    I awoke feeling more refreshed and better than I had in a long time. That mattress was fantastic. Much better than the caboose's wooden floor and way better than the cold, damp ground. My body was reacting very favorably to the pampering that it was receiving. All of my aches and pains were slowly diminishing and my knotted, aching muscles finally got the chance to fully relax.

    I remembered being struck by a brief tinge of sadness. Depending on the outcome of my impending conversation with Carlos about his knowledge on the details of the river crossing, our stay at the hotel could be coming to a premature close. In fact, for all I knew, that may well have been the last time that the luxuriously padded bed would support my body's mass.

    We were all extremely thankful to have spent the last couple of days inside the hotel and have access to it's many stored provisions. However, I could feel a change in the air that morning and a shift in everyone's general mood. The initial euphoria of our occupation had worn off and we had come to the painful realization that we couldn't stay in the heavily stocked building much longer. Sooner or later, the militia or some other band of armed marauders would attempt to invade the hotel, especially with the welcoming sight of rotting corpses laying by the exit doors. Having all that food to eat was nice, but it wasn't worth our deaths.

Planning to keep the promise that I had made to my endlessly inquisitive brain the previous night, I grabbed an open box of Honeycomb and went to find out exactly what Carlos did know about the river crossing. Walter at my side, I began to pop handfuls of sugary cereal into my mouth as I slowly walked toward his room.

As I was passing by, I looked through an open doorway and saw the pair of canoes snugly nestled in their twin beds, silently awaiting their call to duty. If only we knew how to get in touch with this Rene and exactly where to cross the river, I thought while looking at them dreamily, we could put those beauties to use.

Once again, I was surprised to see how much Carlos' condition had improved overnight. He was smiling and talking to Vickie and Kaleb while he ate some brown sugar and cinnamon Pop Tarts for breakfast.

The massive, wedge shaped stack of pillows that had been under his back the previous day was gone. In their place were but three overstuffed pillows, perfectly arranged by Vickie to support Carlos' head and shoulders. If I had not seen the severity of the man's wounds for myself, just a couple of short days ago, I would not have believed that there was a wounded person lying underneath those blankets.

"Good morning, Carlos," I said to our new found friend.

108

It had been a slow paced, relaxing day and I had done no strenuous physical activity. Yet, no matter how hard I tried, I could not get my mind to slow down long enough for me to fall asleep. As prepared as we felt for our sunrise assault on the last two unsearched rooms, there was always the chance that something could go wrong. Hardly anything ever went as planned, either here or back in what we now called "the real world." Especially when it involved hand grenades and paper thin hotel walls.

"Hand grenades?" I had asked with my mouth hanging open far enough to catch flies. I probably looked like a backwoods, country bumpkin who just gotten his first good look at New York City.

Nodding his head, Carlos had replied, "Yeah. He found them in some crazy dude's house in town. That place was filled with all kinds of weird stuff. Guy must have been a real nut bag."

As I lay there in the darkness feeling the oppressive weight of this devastating catastrophe, I thought that maybe the guy with the hand grenades wasn't the nut bag, after all. Maybe it was the rest of us who were nutty. All of us that went around mindlessly paying attention to our own little, sheltered worlds and paying no attention, at all, to the big picture. Perhaps we *all* should have been a little more prepared.

With only a few hours left until "go time", I forcefully herded my thoughts back to our previous life and to the simpler, happier times. That always seemed to do the trick.

109

Kelli and Kaleb each had a fire extinguisher at the ready, just in case things started to get out of hand. All of the windows on the hotel's first floor were wide open to permit the cold, winter air to flow through the building unimpeded. The heavily varnished doors were going to let off a lot of toxic fumes when we torched them, and none of us wanted to breathe in too much of that crap.

Jacob and I were stationed on the second floor, in the corner room directly above Steevo's. If one of the smoke choked scoundrels tried to flee by jumping out of their window, we would have a very nice view of them.

Butch and Vickie would stand guard a short distance away from Reggie and Steevo's doors, in case the two had no fear of fire and chose their burning entryway as an avenue of escape.

Walter would stay with Carlos, in his room. We pulled the door closed as we left to discourage him from trying to follow us.

Once again, our main objective was for none of us to get hurt. Our second objective was to extricate the dangerous duo from their respective rooms without doing too much damage to the sensitive electronic equipment that Carlos said Steevo's room contained. If we were to let the fire get out of hand and end up doing that, it would make it virtually impossible for us to ever see the other side of the river.

Jacob and I stood and silently watched the sky began to lighten in the east. It was the first sunrise that I had seen since we started sleeping on the hotel's thick, luxurious mattresses. I sure was going to miss those things if we ended up burning down the hotel.

It was a breezy day. The leafless tree limbs were swaying to and fro restlessly and the few pine trees that I could see shimmied and shook with the forceful gusts like a dog exiting a farmer's pond.

"Perfect," I whispered to Jacob, as I pointed out the window. "That wind will keep the smoke from building up inside."

Jacob nodded his head in agreement multiple times but never said a word. He just continued to absently stare off into the distance.

From our vantage point, we could see no sign of an attempted exit from either man's window. In fact, there were no new tracks anywhere to be seen, except the ones that we ourselves had left on our repeated excursions to retrieve water from the flowing St. Clair.

As the first hint of the orange glow marking sunrise came into view, I turned to Jacob and whispered, "It's time."

Slowly easing back across the room's carpeted floor with feather light steps, Jacob went downstairs to give Kelli the signal to light the first door. After he left, I silently coaxed both of our windows open along their well lubricated tracks.

110

    Kelli thumbed the wheel on the blue Bic lighter and held it close to the bottom of Reggie's Sterno caked door. She had spread the squishy, clingy, jelly like substance all over the lower portion of the exposed hallway side of the door as soon as everyone else began to take up their assigned positions.
    The little, yellow flame atop the Bic made contact with the flammable substance and modern chemistry did the rest. In a matter of seconds, the entire lower portion of the door was aglow in multi-colored flames that were greedily lapping their way up the door's shiny, varnished exterior. Nasty, noxious tendrils of grayish smoke raced away ahead of the advancing flames like terrified peasants fleeing before an invading army. If not for the steady breeze blowing through the building, everyone in the vicinity of the door would have been overcome by the volatile vapors.
    None of us knew for sure what would happen on the other side of the flaming door, but with the room's windows closed, the toxic fumes had no way to dissipate and should only swirl about and intensify.
    By the time that the ravenous flames had claimed three

fourths of the door's outer surface, Kelli, now holding one of the hotel's red fire extinguishers, edged forward with her cone shaped, black nozzle pointed toward the thin strip of wall above Reggie's door. Her job was to try and keep the fire contained solely upon the surface of the glossy wooden slab. When it started to overrun those boundaries, she was to stop it's progress with well placed, oxygen depleting blasts.

The sound of the fire's hissing and rumbling grew louder by the second as it hungrily devoured the thin, chemical soaked wood. Even with the added assistance of the stiff breeze, the smoke began to back up and accumulate heavily in the hallway's upper reaches.

Intermittently blasting away with the fire extinguisher, Kelli did the best she could at keeping the nearby wall and ceiling from continually burning. Each time that the flames tried to lay claim to a new patch of territory, she drove them back with an uncanny, natural firefighting grace.

The inner core of the thin, cheaply made hotel door began to show through it's skin like the skeleton of a bony model walking the runway. The roaring, crackling sound of the wooden fuel being consumed became loud enough to make any kind of vocal communication difficult. Perhaps it was a good thing that everyone else just stared at the growing fire instead of talking. There wasn't much to say, anyway. It was merely time for us to do what needed to be done.

The searing effect of the heat became so intense that it drove Kelli back out of the effective working range of her extinguisher. Taking just a moment to draw in a sweet breath of cool, fresh air, she rushed forward again and heroically rejoined the fray. Despite the overwhelming ferocity of the rapidly growing inferno, she battled the endlessly tenacious flames back with accurately placed discharges from the business end of the nozzle.

Blazing pieces of the fully engulfed door showered onto the carpeted floor below, instantaneously setting it ablaze. Suddenly appearing and standing slightly to his mother's right, Kaleb let loose with his own concentrated barrage of lethal firefighting force.

The synthetic fibers in the burning carpet began to put off an odor much stronger than that coming from the blazing door. A thick, black smoke that smelled like a mixture of burning styrofoam and plastic curled up from the floor and instantly permeated every open orifice on both Kelli and Kaleb. Their heavy, labored breathing openly welcomed the noxious fumes deep inside the core of their bodies. A severe burning sensation accompanied the putrid smoke's ingestion. The effect of the airborne toxins was no less lethal in it's assault on their eyes. In an attempt to keep out as much of the blinding smoke as possible, the duo squinted their eyelids shut until they were looking through slits that were paper thin.

But their efforts proved woefully futile. Their eyes dripping water like an old, leaky faucet, neither was able to clearly see any of their chaotic surroundings. They began to violently erupt in spittle throwing coughs as their bodies tried to forcefully clear their smoke clogged lungs. Besieged by gut wrenching, fluid expelling coughs and blurred, prismatic like vision through tear filled eyes, the two brave souls were fighting a losing battle.

Between the gargled, phlegmy sounding coughs and the wheezing, whistling intakes of polluted air, Kelli began to emit a high pitched wail of desperation and horror. Unable to effectively battle the rapidly expanding fire any longer because of the blinding smoke and body crippling fumes, her and Kaleb's previously accurate dioxide discharges started to go hopelessly astray.

Taking full advantage of it's foe's lapse in accuracy, the fire quickly expanded. Flames began to appear on the wall and ceiling near the burning door and in a matter of seconds, a large portion of both were fully engulfed in bright, orangish yellow flames.

No longer able to see at all, Kelli began spraying out blindly with the extinguisher in a desperate attempt to control the ravenous, raging beast. Unable to withstand the extreme intensity of the heat's skin melting radiance, Kaleb made a hasty retreat. As he turned to make a quick exit, he took two steps and blindly ran into the wall on the opposite side of the hallway. The force of the bone shaking collision buckled his knees and, with the weight of the fire extinguisher leading the way, he started to plummet toward the carpeted surface of the hallway's floor.

In the middle of his free fall, Kaleb encountered an object that offered firm resistance, yet in a surprisingly soft way. His first thought was that he had fallen and accidentally hit his mother, but when his body began to reverse it's course and right itself again, the sound of the voice calmly speaking into his right ear stopped that thought cold.

"Slide your hand along the wall and just keep walking," Butch firmly commanded. He relieved Kaleb of his fire extinguisher and wasted no time in putting the device to it's intended use.

A sobbing, choking Kelli felt a tender hand on her left shoulder and Vickie's voice coming from the blackness. "Here, honey. Let me do that until you can see again."

Amid the scorching heat of the quickly growing fire, Kelli passed her extinguisher to Vickie. Bending over and walking with a slight stoop, Butch and Vickie managed to stay below the worst of the endlessly billowing smoke and harmful vapors.

Working in unison like a well-oiled machine, the two hit back hard at the raging fire. While Butch was busy extinguishing the floor and the blazing wall to the right side of Reggie's door, Vickie steadfastly concentrated her efforts on the ceiling and the left side of the doorway. Valiantly throwing every ounce of will and courage into the showdown with their fiery foe, they battled in desperation to save the endangered hotel.

The fire proved itself a worthy adversary, in it's own right. Seeming to sense the added ferocity that was directed it's way, the blaze in the hallway suddenly kicked itself into a devilishly higher gear. All of the wallpaper in the general vicinity of the flaming door finally ignited from the prolonged exposure to the extremely high temperatures. Erupting into flames so quickly that it looked like it might have been flash paper thrown from a magician's hand. The effect that it produced was both visually startling and terrifyingly destructive.

The temperature in the hallway rose to a dangerous, oven-like level and the smell of singed hair joined the other unpleasant smells that circulated in the hot, heavy air. With it's aggressive outburst, the fire had gained the upper hand and was now spiraling toward the point of total uncontrollability.

Appearing as suddenly and as on time as the charging cavalry in a western movie, Kelli and Kaleb rejoined the harrowing fight with two more fully charged fire extinguishers. The firefighting foursome stood tall in the face of the fiery threat and blasted away at the white hot home wrecker, non-stop.

A see-saw battle of give and take ensued as the two contestants bitterly fought each other for the upper hand. Just like in all wars, there were both gains and losses. And, just like in all wars, there was always a pivotal turning point that caused victory to fall to one side or the other. In this war, it turned out to be the collapse of Reggie's totally consumed, charcoal colored door.

With the flaming inferno's support base removed, the fire seemed to lose it's stomach for the fight. The thick, fire rated drywall that lined the hallway's surfaces left little for the fire to consume, except the fancy, floral wallpaper. Caught between the constant onslaught of the discharging fire extinguisher nozzles and the lack of readily available fuel, the fire died a slow, merciless death.

111

    Fully awake after yet another gruelingly long, semi-conscious night, Steevo and Reggie split their time between staring at the room's barricaded entry door and each other. In the soft glow of the early morning's light, their large, white eyes stood out remarkably well against their darkly shadowed features.

    The first unmistakable smell of something burning had begun to circulate through the frighteningly odiferous corner room. Steevo started to become mildly concerned about the severity of the situation. He wasn't ready to bolt just yet, or, for that matter, to let Reggie. Oh, no. Steevo had decided that if worse came to worse, he would send Reggie out the hotel room's window first. If no one ended up splattering his guts all over or blowing his brains out after the first few steps, Steevo surmised, it would probably be safe for him to exit, as well. Until then, he would merely continue to do the only thing that he could do, wait.

    That is, unless the idiot National Guardsmen succeeded in accidentally burning the damn place down. Just like a bunch of stupid, drunk kids, he thought disgustedly. Give 'em a little bit of alcohol and they lose every bit of sense they ever had.

Steevo had smelled the mouth-watering aroma of bubbly warm clam chowder in the air just a short time before he smelled the smoke. One of the clumsy, drunken oafs must have accidentally knocked over the cooking stove, he soundly reasoned, and now the polluted piss ants were out there in the hallway with loudly hissing fire extinguishers taking on the resulting fire.

"Dumbasses," he mumbled, though lips that barely moved.

Steevo began to pick up an occasional panicked or pain induced scream coming from beyond his barricaded, bed wedged door, and could tell that the situation was getting worse. But the fire was none of his concern, at least not yet. If the bozos in the hall couldn't put it out, what the heck was he going to do about it? He didn't have a fire truck parked out back. If they couldn't put it out he would..... trailing off in mid thought, Steevo never reached the end of his sentence.

A terrifying, nightmarish reality suddenly dawned upon his sluggish, sleep deprived mind. If those stupid guardsmen couldn't put out the fire, he would lose whatever advantage he might have had because of his little pile of neatly stacked grenades. After all, it wasn't like he could hope to stay hidden in his room and magically extinguish the fire with grenade blasts. If those drunken, bumbling fools failed to put out the blaze, Steevo would have no choice but to vacate the relative safety of his corner room and flee for his life. Once outside in the open air, he would become instantly vulnerable. Bullets flew far faster and much further than any hand grenade that Steevo knew of. He would undoubtedly be cut down in a hail of gunfire the moment he cleared the window's opening. It wouldn't matter if Reggie jumped out first or last, they would both be just as dead.

Sitting in his partially shadowed corner, Steevo was busily contemplating the consequences of this new disheartening scenario. He was so lost in thought about the harrowing predicament that he found himself in, that at first he didn't notice the sharp decline in the noise level outside his door. In fact, not until Reggie had repeatedly tried to get his attention did he notice anything at all.

Pssst-ing much louder than he had in his previous

attempts, Reggie finally brought Steevo firmly back to this world. Jabbing his filthy thumb a couple of times toward the barricaded door, Reggie excitedly whispered, "I think they put it out."

Shifting his focus away from Reggie's ugly mug, Steevo turned and listened intently in the direction of the hallway. A few blessedly silent seconds later, he believed that his designated human shield had proven himself to be remarkably correct.

There were no more loud hissing sounds from discharging fire extinguishers. No more popping, crackling sounds of materials being consumed by ravenous, constantly spreading flames. There was no sound to be heard, at all. Silence had broken out and completely taken over the spaces where only a few short moments ago, there had been nothing but the sounds of utter panic and chaos.

The silence sounded good to Steevo's troubled ears. Oh, yes, the silence sounded just fine. A small, creepy looking smile began to develop in the place where his tense, flattened lips had been a moment earlier and a look of relief washed over his previously tightened face. Maybe the jig wasn't up, just yet, he thought gleefully. Maybe Steevo and his little pile of pineapple shaped pals still had the upper hand, after all. His gruesomely cruel smile slowly getting wider, Steevo nestled back into the crook of the two walls and let out a deep, joyful sigh of relief.

112

    The fire was completely out. Bluish-gray smoke lazily drifted up from the portions of the wooden door which had not been completely reduced to ashes. The once bright, colorful wallpaper had been turned into a black, sooty mess. The carpet on the hallway floor was in total ruins. The flames had even advanced far enough down the corridor to take out a corner of the closest mattress. Wispy clouds of smoke still clung closely to the ceiling and moved along slowly like dense, early morning fog.
    If not for the added safety features built in to the recently constructed hotel, the results would surely have been devastating. Losing the structure would have meant a return to the provision-less, tiny, clutter bound caboose. No more cushiony mattresses to sleep on and no more rooms full of food stacked to the ceiling. No more lovely canoes and no chance in hell to make it across the river.
    The firefighting foursome of Butch, Vickie, Kelli and Kaleb observed the damage through red, watery, smoke irritated eyes. Fire extinguishers limply dangled from the end of their tired, aching arms.

The door that had previously enclosed Reggie's room was almost entirely gone. Most of it had turned into a powdery, white ash and lay scattered on the surface of the floor amid the blackened, charred clumps of lightly smoldering synthetic carpeting. Through the recently vacated opening spilled the soft, pastel orange glow of sunrise. For a few tranquil moments, the four of them stared at the invading ray of sunshine like they had been mesmerized by a swinging pendant into a state of hypnosis.

The trance like spell was finally broken when Vickie blurted out, "Oh, shit." Remembering who was behind the missing door, she headed back down the hallway at a brisk pace and quickly retrieved her waiting rifle.

Under her watchful cover, the rest of the former firefighters followed suit and quickly re-armed themselves, as well. Gathering just outside the crisply charred opening of Reggie's door, the foursome readied themselves for a mass entry.

Gun barrels pointing off in all different directions, the unit barreled into the room at full speed.

113

    Jacob and I had started to become very concerned about the tremendous volume of black smoke exiting the south end of the building. The smell of all the different building materials mixing together as they burned was exceedingly strong. Occasionally it came in through the room's open windows in big, rolling waves and we fought hard to silence and muffle the deep, body shuddering coughs that came from breathing in the noxious fumes. If Jacob and I had given away our location, our little surprise would have been ruined. Besides that, if the corner room crustaceans were so inclined, they could have started shooting up through the ceiling and killed both of us. It was in our best interest to stay as quiet as possible.
    Jacob was facing out the south window, the same direction that the rebounding smoke was coming from. I asked him if he wanted to trade positions with me but he stubbornly refused. The gesture made me both proud and sad at the same time.
    Looking to the east from the room's other window, I could clearly see the wide, choppy St. Clair River. Finding myself getting lost, time and time again, in the rhythmic pulsing of the

white capped waves, I daydreamed about what it would feel like to joyously scoot along the top of the cold water to freedom in one of those fancy canoes.

Both of us would periodically lean out of the windows as far as we safely could to look below. All of the windows belonging to the last two rooms on the first floor were tightly closed, and Jacob and I wanted to know the moment one slid open.

We had barely noticed the smoke beginning to diminish when Kaleb's whispering voice floated to us across the silence. Turning to face him, I could tell that the boy was shaken and very exhausted. He was covered in dark, smeared splotches of grime and his wet hair was thin and flat and stuck to the sides of his head. He casually loped halfway across the second story room to quietly confer with Jacob and me.

Speaking in a tone normally reserved for misbehaving in church on a Sunday morning, Kaleb informed us, "We got through the door into Reggie's room." Then after pausing for a couple of seconds added, with a finger pointing at me, "And mom wants to talk to you."

Leaving Kaleb and Jacob to watch the windows, I scurried downstairs and met up with Butch, Vickie and Kelli, just outside of what used to be Reggie's doorway. My incredulous, wandering eyes must have given away the fact that I was surprised by the amount of collateral damage.

"It kind of got out of hand," Kelli said in a sheepish, almost apologetic nature.

"I see that," I returned, while not taking my eyes from surveying the surprising amount of destruction. "No wonder there was so much smoke."

"It was touch and go for a couple of minutes, there," Vickie said emphatically. "All four of us had to go at it pretty hard to put it out." Kelli nodded her head vigorously in agreement with Vickie's assessment.

Butch was standing with one foot planted slightly inside Reggie's room, looking as if he had just gone a few grueling rounds with Mike Tyson. Underneath his feet lay an almost bare patch of concrete. Once covered by thickly padded carpeting, it had been stripped nearly bare by the voracious flames.

Thumbing like a hitchhiker toward the space inside the

burned out doorway, Butch said dryly, "He's not in there."

From the look of Reggie's room, it was clear that he hadn't been in it for days. Both of the beds were meticulous, looking like they were made by someone who was a real neat freak. The oversized, floral bedspreads dangled evenly over each edge of the twin beds with haunting perfectness. At the head of each one, the pillows had been neatly tucked into little pockets of bedspread and all of the wrinkles had been painstakingly removed. Even the more personal items that cohabitated on the tops of the nightstand and dressers had been placed and spaced, just so. Every single article, from his pocket comb to a well-thumbed copy of True Detective magazine, had been positioned so that it was perfectly aligned with the outer edges of that particular surface.

Reggie was a neat freak, alright. He was also a sadistic weirdo who had tortured and killed at least two people that we knew of, and by the way Carlos talked, there had undoubtedly been more. It seemed as if Reggie might just be the world's neatest serial killer. He was a no good, ruthless torturer and a vicious, cold blooded killer, but he was a neat one.

I marveled at the oxymoron that was Reggie. On one hand he was such a good housekeeper and, my guess was, probably a smart, snappy dresser, as well. But he could also be responsible for the kind of mind bending carnage that we had regrettably witnessed for ourselves, upstairs.

Whatever Reggie was or wasn't didn't matter, though. The only thing that really mattered was where the hell he was hiding, and of that, none of us had the first clue.

My mind began it's incessant second guessing process again. Was Reggie still in the hotel? Was anybody at all in the hotel, for that matter? Was he over in Steevo's room hiding out with him? Had they somehow silently snuck away, sight unseen? Unfortunately, we weren't going to be able to answer any of those nagging questions by standing around.

Motioning to the others with an arm swinging "follow me" gesture, I silently led the small procession of weary, soot blackened firefighters back out into the ravaged hallway. Leisurely ambling a few doors to the north of Reggie's old room, we had a squat on the hallway floor where the carpeting was still bright, colorful and clean.

Rehashing our plan, yet again, we all agreed on two

things. The first was, to a person, we fully believed that Reggie and Steevo were still inside the hotel, and the simple process of elimination told us that there was only one place they could be. The second thing we all agreed on was that we weren't about to stop. Despite the danger from the fire, the bullets and the hand grenades that we knew Steevo had, we had our minds set on extricating those two urchins, come hell or high water.

Scavenging from both the second and third floors, we came up with a total of six fully charged fire extinguishers. The partially discharged ones that had served so valiantly in the first apocalyptic struggle were kept for backups, as well. Having to get back to them was the last thing on earth that we wanted to do, but at least they were there if we needed them.

Our plan of attack was essentially the same as before, save one huge exception. This time when the Sterno encrusted door was lit, it would only be allowed to burn long enough to create the much desired smoke and toxic fumes, but not long enough to get venturesome and out of control. If repeated applications were required to get the job done, then so be it. We had come a long way in the process of eradicating the hotel. On the brink of finally being able to complete the task, we couldn't let anything stand in our way.

114

    Touching the flame from the blue Bic to Steevo's Sterno coated door for the first of many times that morning, Kelli watched as the flames greedily wicked up the highly varnished wooden surface.
    When the fire started to approach the point of uncontrollability, she and Kaleb would completely douse the burning door while Butch and Vickie stood guard nearby.
    Repeating this process numerous times, our hope was to create enough black, lung killing smoke inside Steevo's unventilated room to drive the duo outside in a desperate bid for fresh air.
    The dark, rolling clouds that left the south end of the hotel this time were less ominous looking, and nowhere near the consistency that they were before. Jacob and I watched them being swept away by the strong, gusting winds as we gazed from our second story windows.
    A long and boring twenty minutes later, there had still been no change in the situation. Despite our constantly looking down upon the windows to Steevo's corner room, the glass panels remained tightly closed. Every time I glanced down, I

thought, this will be it. The window will slide open this time and Reggie and Steevo will come bopping out and take off, high tailing it toward the river. But every time that I checked, I saw nothing. Once again, I began to doubt that anyone else was still inside the hotel with us. How could they be? The room down there had to be full of some of the nastiest, foulest smelling, putrid smoke that anyone could ever imagine, and there still there weren't any signs of life. No one could stay in that toxic mess for that long, unless, of course, they were dead.

    That happy thought opened up a whole new line of penetrating questions for my endlessly nosy brain to seize upon. Did Steevo and Reggie commit suicide? Were they nothing more than bloated corpses waiting to be discovered? Did they kill each other in some sort of testosterone fueled struggle? I thankfully remembered that it was time to look back down at Steevo's window again and slowly leaned out as my always inquisitive mind began asking another in it's line of seemingly nonstop questions.

    The asking stopped in mid-sentence, because all of those questions and more were answered by what I saw. The glass panel in the easterly facing window of Steevo's first floor hotel room began to leisurely slide open.

115

    The smoke that was rapidly filling Steevo's room was so thick and black that neither man could see the white, swirl patterned, plaster ceiling anymore. Both of them were laying outstretched on their bellies while facing the room's barricaded door.
    The duo had been forced to continually sink lower and lower in order to stay within the shrinking pocket of breathable, good air. Up to that point in time the simple little maneuver had worked well enough, but at the rate the smoke was dropping, it wouldn't continue to do so for much longer.
    "Damn it," Steevo cursed. He was very angry with himself for carelessly falling back to sleep after the first round of excitement had ended. But he felt so relieved after the bumbling guardsmen had somehow managed to put out the earlier fire that he relaxed and lowered his guard. After all, why wouldn't he? As long as the hotel wasn't burning down and he still had his little pile of green grenades, he was the one in charge. Wasn't he? So, unshaken, Steevo had let himself drift back to sleep wrapped up tightly in one of the hotel's large, flowery bedspreads.

Awaking to a mumbling, panicking Reggie and a room already half full of foul, stinky smelling smoke, Steevo's mind froze up like the surface of a pond in the winter. Muddled, incoherent thoughts collided headlong into each other within Steevo's groggy, somnolent brain. Should I throw a grenade? What good would that do? Should I start shooting toward the door? How would I know where anyone was and how is shooting toward the door going to stop a fire?

The confusion enveloping his waking mind delayed any possible redeeming course of action until it was far too late to make any difference. As the ever encroaching smoke started to take over the remaining space inside the snug little room, Steevo's desperate bid to steadfastly remain in the hotel had reached it's bitter conclusion. There were only two choices left for Steevo and Reggie. Leave the room, or die. No more holding on and no more holding out. If they didn't get their asses out of that room within the next couple of minutes, they would both spend eternity there.

A raging anger began to build inside Steevo. How dare they? he belligerently thought. How dare those thick headed National Guardsmen come in here and take over my hotel? But the realization quickly dawned on Steevo that all of the complaining in the world wasn't going to change the here and now.

Looking into the desperate, pleading eyes of a terrified, shaking Reggie, Steevo commanded him through gritted teeth, "Open the damn window."

While stuffing as many of the grenades as possible into his big overcoat pockets, Steevo's fury grew by the second. "I'll give those bastards something to remember me by," he rankled as he pulled the safety pins from two of the grenades.

116

I had to say, "Jacob, get ready" twice, because the first time I tried, the huge lump in my throat made my words come out sounding all garbled.

As the sliding window reached the end of it's track, thick, black smoke tumbled from the new opening. Drawing back just a pinch to make sure that I was out of view, I aimed my SKS sharply downward. Looking through the sights on the barrel of my rifle, I waited for the smoked scum to surface.

Without warning, a thunderous, ear-splitting eruption shook the entire foundation of the hotel. Caught off guard, I was violently thrown forward and hit my head on the right side of the window jamb, producing an oddly hollow sounding thump.

A second explosion, this one of pain, tore through my head and it felt like my right eyebrow had been completely scraped off.

With barely enough time to recover from the first painful blast, a second detonation ripped through the air of the cold, winter morning.

Bits of whitish, orange dust floated on the air, featherlike, and ragged, misshapen holes littered the carpeted floor. The damage didn't stop there, either. Glancing up at the ceiling, I noticed a few irregular shaped, black gashes nicely contrasting with the stark whiteness that resided there.

Jacob looked totally stunned. He was still standing next to his window, but the look in his eyes said that he was really a million miles away. His large, staring eyeballs had followed my upward gaze and he stood looking at the ceiling in a dreamy, trance-like state. He appeared to be fine, physically, and I felt a momentous rush of relief surge through me.

The two explosions had obviously been Steevo carelessly playing with his recently found hand grenades. If any of those rocketing fragments had hit Jacob, I could never have forgiven myself for putting him in harm's way. Then I thought about Kelli, Kaleb, Butch and Vickie downstairs and my blood ran cold.

I hoped with every fiber of my being that they were alright. I badly wanted to run across the hole strewn floor, rip open the door and fly downstairs to find out, and almost did. If not for the dark, streaking blur that I picked up in my peripheral vision, I would have.

My head involuntarily turned so that both eyes could focus upon the moving object. "Shit," I breathed. In all of the excitement I had completely forgotten about Steevo's open window.

About fifty yards away from the smoking hotel, a lone figure loped off in the direction of the river.

Promptly stepping back up to the screen-less opening, I made to draw a bead on the distant, moving form. Just about to squeeze the trigger, I watched as my target awkwardly tripped and crashed, face first, into the frozen surface of the parking lot. The gawky, gangly stride and the supremely uncoordinated face plant made me want to laugh out loud, in spite of our situation. The crooks around here, I humorously thought to myself, are some of the most un-athletic people I have ever seen.

With 'Mister Ungainly" taking a moment to relocate his feet, I exhaled and went to suck in another breath. As I did, I also opened my left eye to give it a momentary break from all of it's incessant squinting. When I did, a second figure appeared in the bottom of my field of vision.

Stepping backward away from the building was a lone gunman swinging an M-16 rapidly from side to side with one arm. In his opposite hand, I saw a familiar looking green oval shape and immediately knew who I was looking at.

Not wanting to waste a precious second, I put my rifle sights directly in the middle of the receding man's face. Steevo was so busy scanning for danger down at ground level that he never looked up until the last second. He reminded me of a guy that I knew back in high school, so long ago. Scraggly, unkempt, long hair and a stringy, moth-eaten beard surrounding a round, boyish face. He looked like a long forgotten cast member from an old 1960's hippie movie.

Our eyes momentarily locked and I saw fear plainly register on his upturned face. Steevo started to bring his M-16 up in my direction but he didn't make it.

The top of his head lifted off in a stunted, but graceful launch. A large circle of snow around him turned a bright pink in color. Like it had no clue as to what it was supposed to do, now, the rest of Steevo's body stood motionless for a moment before plopping down in a tangled heap.

As what was left of Steevo harmlessly fell to the ground, the hand that was tightly clutching the hand grenade popped open as it came in contact with the man's meaty thigh. Bouncing once off his right toe, the spherical explosive buried most of itself in a wind crusted snowdrift about two feet away.

Realizing what was about to happen, I hit the deck and yelled for Jacob to do the same. About a second later, a massive, low pitched, rumbling explosion shook the floor that we were laying on and turbulently rattled the windows in their frames. Uncovering my head, I picked up my rifle and looked back out the window.

Steevo was a mutilated mess. The remainder of his body lay about twenty feet from the hotel's outer wall. His reign of relentless looting and unmitigated terror was finally over.

I looked around downrange for Reggie but never caught another glimpse of our fumble footed friend. I hoped like hell that he wouldn't try to come back.

117

Jacob and I successfully dodged the scattered holes in the room's floor and promptly rushed downstairs to check on everyone else. We almost ran over Kaleb on the stairs as he was making his way up.

Jacob beat me to it and assertively quizzed his older brother. "Is mom alright?"

Kaleb's upturned face nodded in an unhurried manner a few times and then, in a breathy voice, he answered, "Yeah, she's fine. Everybody is. That one time, though, stuff from that bomb, or whatever, just missed us because we were up by the door, but we're okay."

Very relieved to hear the great news, I pulled him close and gave him a big, clenching bear hug and then headed downstairs to survey the damage.

118

Collapsing like bags of rags all over the floor and extra bed in Carlos' room, we kicked back to relax and catch our breath. It had been one hell of a long morning. After our triumphant reunion in the blackened hallway of the first floor, the feeling of *what next*? had already started to make the rounds.

Steevo and Reggie were now gone and out of our way. Steevo permanently and Reggie, at least for the time being. Kelli thought that we should go after Reggie. Track him down and finish him off to make sure that he wouldn't try to come back to the hotel. Nobody raised their hand to volunteer, though. We were far too drained to try anything that physical.

Butch and I wearily made the rounds and closed all of the windows that we had opened earlier for ventilation. Kaleb and Jacob busied themselves transporting a variety of soda downstairs while Vickie and Kelli searched for something creative to throw together for lunch.

The macaroni and cheese embedded with chunks of tuna was delicious and disappeared far too fast. Even Walter agreed. Happily licking the remnants of his portion off of his big, droopy chops, he made sure not to miss a single speck.

Our bellies full of good, warm food and feeling much safer than we previously had, all of us unwound and enjoyed each other's company in Carlos' room. Laughter flowed freely as we sat around talking and wise cracking, everyone telling and re-telling their part in the earlier fray.

It was nice to let our guards down for a while. How much I had missed the sound of the boys' merry, full throated laughter. It was like listening to an old song on the radio that would always hold a special place in your heart.

Once again, I found myself catapulted back in time through a collage of vivid memories that were so breathtakingly beautiful, but yet horribly bittersweet at the same time. Beautiful, because those carefree memories were now the most valuable treasure that I owned, and bittersweet, because they so clearly reminded me of the woeful state that we were existing in.

As much as I wanted to fully engage everyone else in the joyous, verbal banter, my thoughts were hopelessly preoccupied with other things. For a moment I found myself daydreaming about the items that we would find waiting inside Steevo's room. Then I contemplated the euphoric feeling of firmly setting foot on Canadian soil.

I found myself beginning to feel very impatient. I didn't want to sit around and make small talk anymore, I only wanted to talk about getting across the river. Not aspiring to be too much of a buzz kill, I tried to think of a way of subtly slipping business into a pleasant conversation.

Kelli must have read my face, just like always, because she turned to me with her sparkling brown eyes and generously asked, "What are you thinking about?" With the door I was longing for now open a crack, I stuck my foot in and kept steadily pushing.

119

If not for the exceptionally good fortune of finding Carlos, the morning's blitzkrieg would have been far more difficult and frightfully more dangerous. His ability to heal miraculously fast, coupled with his complete and intimate knowledge of the river crossing, made both Steevo and Reggie expendable.

Standing in the hallway next to the charred remains of Steevo's door it became immediately clear why the two men had been so anxious to escape the room. The burning of the entry door had also ignited the foam rubber mattress that had been pushed against it as an added barrier from intrusion. Even though the fire had been out for well over an hour, the bitter, acrid smell of the melting foam still lingered heavily in the air.

Much of the wooden door remained intact, despite the intense torture it had endured.

Almost the entire top half, although totally black and crispy, still looked solid. The door handle was even still in place, held along the left side of the opening by a thin strip of cracked, charcoal colored wood.

Placing the bottom of my boot against the soot encrusted doorknob, I pushed. The top part of the vandalized door reluctantly broke free of the charred jamb and swung inward. It noisily collided against the room's blackened wall before crashing down in a dust smearing heap upon the white bed sheet below.

A good deal of smoke was still floating about inside the room and it's smell was brutally strong. The generic hotel furnishings were rudely scattered around within the meager space and the eastern facing window stood wide open. Aside from the pitch black ceiling and upper walls, the room thankfully appeared to be in pretty good shape.

Without any sort of fanfare, Jacob abruptly stepped up on top of the debris filled bed that was blocking the doorway and entered Hotel Hell's headquarters.

The complete and total opposite of Reggie's neat, well organized living area, Steevo's room was as filthy as a pig sty. Trash and dirty clothing lay in scattered piles all over the messy floor. Soda cans and beer bottles littered the barely visible carpet like discarded confetti after a boisterous and bawdy New Year's Eve celebration.

Every item, in every part of the dumpy, disheveled looking room was an utter mess, except for the long, low chest of drawers on the right hand side of the room. Sitting on top of this sleek, shiny dresser was exactly what we'd all hoped to find there.

Carlos had correctly revealed, "That's where he keeps his short wave radio and he won't let anyone else near it."

The gleaming wooden surface on which the radio sat looked completely out of place inside the otherwise trash infested room. Clutter free and spotless, the area was undoubtedly a place of great importance to Steevo.

The radio appeared to be fine physically, outside of a light coating of what looked to be coal dust.

Our group exchanged excited, smiling glances as we took in the amazing electronic shrine. Finally being able to see the radio for ourselves left us hopelessly mesmerized.

"It doesn't look as big as I thought it would be," Kelli said as she eyed the dialed dandy.

"Me neither," I threw in. "The last one of these that I saw was a lot bigger." And indeed it had been, but with the continued miniaturization of everything these days, it was only natural to assume that short wave radios would follow suit, as well.

An almost surreal feeling encapsulated me as the absurdity of the scene firmly sank in. Here we were, six desperate survivors of a horrific, modern day holocaust, standing in a crude semi-circle completely entranced by a small electronic device. The expressions on our faces said that we wouldn't have been surprised a bit if the radio had suddenly grown legs, hopped up and started kicking out the Charleston.

The reverence with which we looked at this object reminded me of a documentary that I had seen on the hordes of Jewish faith during their annual pilgrimage to the venerated Wailing Wall. These rapt souls would march for hours and hours, sometimes days, all the while rubbing their Tallit Beads and wearing a look of insufferable ecstasy on their faces. I sort of believe that we all felt something similar to that as we gazed in wonder at this small piece of electronic gadgetry that could save our harrowed hides.

"I wonder if it still works?" Butch asked inquisitively, his brow deeply furrowed.

"I hope so," Jacob immediately replied, a touch of desperation clearly evident in his young voice.

Needing badly to know the answer to that question for myself, I leaned in closer to the radio and searched for the power switch. On the top of the radio, a black, plastic slide was embedded into a short groove marked "off " at one end and "on" at the other. With our futures hanging in the balance, I hesitantly pushed the switch to the "on" position.

120

An auditory pop could be heard that I instantly recognized as a speaker abruptly coming to life. Immediately after the beautiful popping sound came an even more breathtaking noise. Bright, crunchy static filled the air as the shortwave radio crackled out it's existence for the world to hear.

An impromptu cheer spontaneously erupted and easily drowned out the scratchy static coming from the small radio. Huge, clasping hugs of joy, fist pumping and even a vicious air guitar punctuated the momentous occasion.

A huge wave of relief washed over me. After all the time spent thinking and dreaming about getting across the river, we were now one *major* step closer to attaining the goal.

Once the initial wave of excitement had subsided, we returned to the business at hand, newly energized. It didn't take us long to ransack the messy corner room. Six people, each with two very happy hands, can go through a place of that size very quickly.

Steevo, it turned out, was a stasher. In every nook, cranny, door and drawer were items that he must have thought either vital to his smuggling operation or extremely valuable.

In one of the long dresser drawers beneath the radio was what looked to be at least a thousand "D" batteries. It took a lot of effort to get the thin drawer to slide out, due to the enormous weight of the big batteries.

"Geez," exclaimed Butch from behind my left shoulder. "I guess he didn't want to take a chance on running out, huh?"

"Evidently not," Vickie answered with a little chuckle. She had slid open the upper drawer next to mine and had found even more packaged batteries.

"Wow," Jacob's excited voice cut in from across the room.

Turning our heads in almost perfect harmony, Butch, Vickie and I found Kelli and Jacob kneeling next to a small night stand in the far corner. Laying on the floor between them was a small avalanche of bright green paper money. Stacks and stacks of cool cash, tightly bound with rubber bands and sporting pictures of dead presidents had cascaded freely from the opened door. They lay heaped on the trashy floor of the smoky, corner hotel room, looking out at us smugly from the safety of their green dotted presidential portraits.

"Oh, my God," involuntarily escaped Vickie's parted lips as she stared wide eyed at the gorgeous little landslide of loot.

Jacob adoringly ran his hands through the pricey pile like a pirate might through an overflowing chest of stolen treasure. He looked up in astonishment, first at Kelli, then across the room at Butch, Vickie and me. He was hopelessly lost in mind numbing wonderment at the sight of this little mountain of money.

Kelli found that she couldn't resist the temptation, either, and lovingly ran her delicate hands amongst Steevo's old stacks of stashed cash. Before she could help herself or even knew what she was about to do, she jubilantly launched a handful of the banded bills skyward while emitting an excited, high pitched scream of unbridled ecstasy.

Riotous, hearty laughter broke out at what happened next and it took a few minutes for us all to catch our breath again, let alone return to what we had been doing. As the stacks of cash began their natural plummet back down to earth, Jacob reached up, almost absent mindedly, and deftly snagged one out of mid-air.

Seeing her son perform this wonderful little athletic feat at close range, an obviously proud Kelli started to raise her hands to clap for him. As she did, another of the descending bundles landed flatly on the crown of her head with a sound very similar to that of a thick book being slammed shut.

A few minutes later, after we had all caught our breath and wiped our tear watered eyes, our search through the corner room light heartedly resumed. Kaleb called out from the bathroom, where he had wandered during the tail end of our laughing fit.

"Hey you guys, come and look at this," he yelled.

After exchanging a quick, assessing glance between themselves, Butch and Vickie started toward the bathroom to witness our latest wonderful discovery.

With the two bottom drawers of the dresser on which the radio sat still unsearched, I decided to have a quick go at them before making my way into the little, white bathroom. Placing my fingers inside the long, deeply routed handle of the one on the right hand side, I eagerly yanked the drawer outward. I could tell that the compartment was filled with much heavier items than the top two drawers, because it took an inordinate amount of energy to sustain it's outward movement.

When the chamber finally opened far enough for me to clearly see it's hidden contents, I was so dumbstruck that for at least a minute, without exaggeration, all I was capable of doing was gawking, open mouthed, at the frighteningly fantastic, awe inspiring sight. Brilliantly bright and endlessly shiny, catching and throwing off every available facet of light, a king's ransom in gold, silver and jewels radiantly winked up at my stunned, thunderstruck face.

Not only could I not speak, for a couple of completely horrifying seconds, I couldn't even breathe. But not surprisingly, more than anything else, the thing that I couldn't do no matter how hard I tried, was avert my eyes from the fever inducing stash of ill-gotten goodies.

Kelli and Jacob magically appeared to my left and were also taken under the treasure's magical spell. By that time my body would once again willfully respond to my commands and I had successfully managed to pull the other bottom drawer out about the same distance as the first. Butch, Vickie and Kaleb had also joined us by then and we all took in the mind boggling sight.

Unable to say anything, at all, our awestruck party spent the next five minutes waging an unwinnable staring contest against the brilliant booty. No matter how much we stared, we never seemed to tire of it.

There were watches, necklaces, rings, pendants, bracelets, earrings and every other imaginable form of jewelry tightly packed into the two bottom drawers.

As the stupefying effects of the fantasy-like fortune began to wane ever so slightly, my mind was able to refocus on the business at hand. We now had a working radio and enough gold and jewelry to easily pay for everyone's safe passage. The only other thing that we needed in order to succeed, besides that, was for Carlos to show us how to get in contact with Rene on the other side of the river.

121

"Dino Ciccarelli?" I thought I had heard Carlos correctly but wanted to be absolutely sure, since it was of the utmost importance.

"Yes, he said. "He was a pro hockey player, really popular around here."

I knew who Dino Ciccarelli was. Not being an avid hockey fan, I didn't know a whole lot about him, only what I saw during the hockey highlights shown on ESPN's Sports Center. I remembered that he had played for the Red Wings in the mid-nineties when Detroit made the Stanley Cup Finals.

Revealing none of this to Carlos, I merely nodded my head while keeping solid eye contact with him.

"He was born just up the river in Sarnia, about twenty miles from here," Carlos went on. It was clear from the smile on his face that he was indeed very proud of his local hero. He spoke in a quiet, reverent tone like Dino, himself, was the second coming.

I supposed he probably was a pretty big deal around there. A small town, local boy who made it all the way to the big stage. What wasn't there to be proud of? Folks sure have crowed a lot louder about a whole lot less.

"You know, he almost never made it to the pros," Carlos confided. "He broke his leg really bad during his second year of junior hockey over in Ontario. The doctors said he would never play hockey again." Carlos' facial features underwent a sudden, sweeping change. "I guess he showed them, didn't he?" he said, with a sneering grin adorning a face that a moment ago had looked as saintly as old Mother Theresa's.

Continuing his testimony on the character of his boyhood idol, Carlos went on. "He worked hard for a year and a half to get back on the ice, worked his butt off. Dino wasn't even drafted because of that injury, but he still only spent half a season in the minors. He was such a standout and scored so many points that someone had to give him a shot. Minnesota picked him up and the rest is history."

Leaning slightly forward in his bed like he was about to reveal a closely guarded secret, Carlos informed us, "Do you know that when he retired, he was just two goals behind the great Bobby Hull?"

Kelli and Vickie looked at each other like Carlos was speaking in some unintelligible, foreign language. He might as well have asked them if they knew the model number for the new Craftsmen heavy duty air compressor.

Not quite done extolling Dino's prowess with a curved stick, Carlos emphatically stated, "He should be in the Hall of Fame."

I was really happy for Carlos and the success of his local hero, but we were getting a little off track. Not needing to know Dino's shoe size or what type of toilet paper he used, I tried to steer the conversation back to business.

"So they decided to use his name as the signal?" I asked, more than ready to move on.

"Yeah, it started out as a little joke between them but the more they thought about it, the more they liked it," Carlos answered. "It's worked well, so far."

Glad to finally be off the subject of Dino, I then inquired, "How will we know when to contact Rene?"

"That's easy," he quickly answered. "Every Monday at 10:00 p.m. Steevo calls Rene. If there's a paying customer, the fare goes across the next night, at midnight."

We all exchanged puzzled glances.

"Monday?" Butch asked. "When the hell is Monday?"

122

Huddled around a calendar as though it were calling out our next play, we all took a stab at trying to figure out exactly what day it was. Carlos pointed at the month marked February.

"Steevo always used to put an "X" on the calendar every day, in order to keep track."

Sure enough, in the first six squares marking the first six days of the month, a little black "X" appeared in the upper, right hand corner.

Jacob had volunteered to run back across the hall and retrieve the document. We had all seen it lying next to the shortwave radio, but at the time, compared to all the other exciting things that we had found in Steevo's old room, this numbered piece of paper seemed inconsequential. Now all of us stood around the calendar looking down upon the ancient timekeeping knowledge like we had just unearthed the mythical Holy Grail.

The very last "X" was in the corner of box number 6, a Wednesday. All that we needed to do then was figure out exactly when Steevo had last marked his calendar and we were home free.

Vickie let her thoughts on the subject be known. "I think he marked it every day, regardless," she said. "It was more important to him than anything else, he wouldn't have forgotten."

"I agree," Butch jumped in. "If he missed a day it would throw his whole operation out of whack."

"He *was* very meticulous about it," Carlos assertively concurred. "He wouldn't let anybody touch any of his stuff. He would just have us stand around behind him so he could show off."

The animosity in Carlos' voice registered loud and clear. If there had been any doubt left for any of us about the real depth of his disdain for Steevo, the hate filled leer that escaped his scowling face put them to rest for good.

"What if he didn't mark it today?" I threw in, playing the part of devil's advocate.

"Then, that would actually make this Thursday," Kelli responded.

We looked around at each other in confusion, trying to decide one way or the other. Did Steevo mark his calendar that morning, despite all of the chaos and confusion surrounding him? Or did he forego his usual ritual due to the ever increasing severity of the situation? We tossed around the pros and cons of each line of thinking for a while. In the end, we came to the conclusion that Steevo probably hadn't marked his calendar that day because our assault had begun so early.

"So that gives us four days," I surmised.

"Four days?" echoed Jacob. "What are we supposed to do for four more days?"

Nobody had an answer for that.

123

    Over the next few days, all we did was eat, sleep and stare out the hotel's third floor windows at Canada. The view across the St. Clair River reminded me of that old saying; so close, but yet, so far away.
    Bright, glowing, electric lights illuminated the far shore like it was the middle of the afternoon on a cloudless, sunny day. They almost looked close enough that we could lean out the windows and touch them.
    It was a great, satisfying feeling to know that we had come that far and were closer than ever to realizing our goal. But it was also a heartbreaking sight, as well. Like a tangled group of unruly vines, the questions and doubts started to slowly creep their way back into my thoughts. "What if this" and "What if that?" began to make cameo appearances inside my head as I stood dreamily staring across the river.
    Frequently passing the binoculars between us that evening, we took turns looking at the large, concrete waste water tube that poked out from the opposite shoreline. Carlos

had told us exactly where it would be located.

"Look for the gray block building to the right of the closest guard tower, then look down." And down it was. Partially submerged in the cold, flowing water was a massive tube that must have been at least ten feet in diameter. Chalky white in color with a pitch black opening at the business end, the pipe extended far out into the St. Clair. If you looked closely at the pipe's nearest end, you could just barely make out a grid work of iron bars inside the darkly shadowed circle. Momentary flashes of reflected light from the surface of the choppy water aided just enough to advance it to the edge of our visibility.

"So that's where it happens, huh?" I said to no one in particular as I glanced at the opening for about the tenth time.

"Yep," Butch answered. "Carlos said Rene would have one of his men unlock that gate and we could paddle the canoes right on in."

"I can't wait," Jacob fired off with typical teenage angst. "It's so boring here."

"Oh, Jacob," Kelli softly admonished.

"He's right, ya know. It *is* boring here," Kaleb chimed in.

Usually the boys took different sides of every issue, sometimes just for spite, but on this subject they both concurred wholeheartedly. I guess I couldn't blame them. Being teenagers, they had never known anything other than twenty-four hour cable television, cell phones, internet access and non-stop video gaming. All of their favorite pastimes, oddly enough, required electricity, and that was something we just didn't have.

Trying to soothe, as usual, Kelli tried to distract the boys while the rest of us looked out of the lofty windows and longed to be where our eyes were focused.

Three more long days, I thought to myself, then we'll know. If we were able to make contact with Rene, and if he was willing to do business with us now that Steevo was gone, things could still turn out in our favor. But, if for some reason we couldn't make contact with him, say, because we miscalculated what day it was or because Rene wouldn't recognize the sound of the calling voice, then we were in big trouble.

I hadn't told anyone else because I didn't want to cause undue panic, but yesterday I saw three camouflage wearing

National Guardsmen at the north end of the parking lot. Walter and I had been killing time by casually walking around the upper floor and checking out the view from each side of the building. As I gazed out to the north, a movement down below caught my attention. Zeroing in on the source, I saw a heavily camoed figure raise his binoculars and thoroughly glass the first floor of the hotel. To his right I could barely make out the shadowy forms of two more individuals through the swaying pine tree boughs. I watched them closely and stayed at the window until they slipped away about five minutes later.

    My guess was that sooner, rather than later, we were going to have to defend the hotel. Hoping that it wouldn't happen for at least three more days, I returned my gaze to the other side of the river and daydreamed about our long desired destination.

124

Hoping that this would be our very last trip down to the river for water, Butch, Jacob and I each grabbed two of the plastic, five gallon buckets and headed out the laundry room's steel door.

It was finally *the* night. The previous three days had dragged on as slowly as a month full of Sunday sermons. There had simply been too much idle time to deal with. We tried to keep ourselves busy, but there wasn't a whole heck of a lot for us to do.

Butch and I had thoroughly inspected the canoes, at least three times. Vickie and Kelli took turns seeing to Carlos' needs and coming up with exciting new recipes out of our limited option of ingredients. The boys mostly wandered around the halls horse playing or simply sleeping. Carlos continued his remarkable recovery and was already starting to move around and go to the bathroom by himself.

All of us, even Carlos, were sure that the bullet had completely missed his bones and passed through nothing but thick, meaty flesh. With any sort of luck, at all, he'd be good as new in no time.

I was beginning to think like Kaleb and Jacob, it *was* boring around here. So, happy for the time killing diversion, we grabbed our buckets and started out for the rock strewn shore of the St. Clair.

It was a nice morning for early February. The sky was a brilliant, cobalt blue dotted with puffy, round cloud formations. A light, southerly breeze had brought the temperature up above freezing for the first time in a couple of days and a minor thaw had begun to take place. The snow felt squishy soft and easily gave way underfoot as we tirelessly marched along.

Enjoying being outside, even if it was for only a short while, my spirits seemed to be lifted. By the time we had made it halfway to the river, a little smile had attached itself to my face. I've always had the habit of looking around a lot when I'm outside. Most of the time I wouldn't see anything special, just the trees, the ground and the sky. Occasionally, I would get lucky and see one of the many mid-western woodland creatures as they frolicked about or searched for dinner.

For some reason, unbeknownst even to me, birds had become my sentimental favorite. Back in the real world, Kelli and I used to have a full color bird identification guide with a handy checklist of all the different species inside. At last count, before the attacks, we were up to forty-four or forty-five different entries, just in our yard alone. It was a nice hobby because it gave us something that we could do together and it was always fun to learn about new birds. One of those wonderful, rare activities with the power to bring people closer together.

I had long known that bird watching was considered beneficial to one's health. It had a pleasant, calming effect that could ease your mind and lower your blood pressure. It could soothe frayed nerves and heal hurt feelings. Yet, of all the wonderful benefits of bird watching that I already knew of, on this trip I learned another one: It could also save your life.

As we started strolling down the gradual incline leading to the river's edge, my eye wandered to a small grove of pine trees about fifty yards over to our left. I was hoping to catch sight of a few birds and maybe enjoy their playful antics for a moment. Searching within the tightly packed branches for a little color or some movement, I found none. However, there *was* something there.

Slightly squinting in the bright morning sunlight, I tried to focus on the virtually invisible shape. It felt like the temperature of my coursing blood dropped twenty degrees, in an instant, when I finally recognized the object that I was looking at. Mostly hidden within the thick, lower branches of a large pine tree, was the unmistakable outline of a human head and shoulders. We had company.

The hairs on the back of my neck rose and rigidly stood at attention. Alarm bells rang inside my head. Knowing that where there was one, there were bound to be more, I immediately started scanning all the possible areas of concealment close by. Without breaking stride or stopping my visual search, I told Butch and Jacob what was going on.

Speaking at a low volume so that we couldn't be overheard, I tried to sound calm. "Guys?" I said, to get their attention. "Don't stop walking or start looking around everywhere, but we're being watched."

I saw Butch's shoulders tense up and his head raise just a bit as he kept pace directly in front of me, but he kept on moving. Jacob, on the other hand, came to an abrupt, panicked stop, mid stride.

"Huh?" he uttered, as if emerging from a daydream. His head began jerking around wildly, trying to look everywhere at once. "Where?" he asked, suddenly sounding fully awake and seriously alarmed.

Due to Jacob's hasty, unexpected halt, Butch ran headlong into his stationary body as it nervously surveyed the surrounding landscape. The empty, five gallon buckets that the two of them were carrying banged into each other with a huge, percussive crash. A symphony of hollow sounding bongs and thuds rang out like timbales in a Latin orchestra's rhythm section. In the cold, clear atmosphere of a quiet winter's morning, the sound seemed incredibly loud.

I wanted desperately to say, "Jacob, keep going," but it was too late for that. He stood there frantically searching about for the culprit and I knew the jig was up. Out in the open, with who knows how many guns trained on us, we were in a bad fix.

With a clearly heard urgency in my voice, I spoke forcefully, but remained quiet enough so that no one else could hear. "On the count of three, drop your buckets and run like hell back to the hotel."

Jacob's head immediately quit searching the landscape

and turned toward me. His eyes were almost comically large and round. "What?" he said again, like he didn't understand English, or something. Then, I watched as my spoken words slowly dawned on his reeling mind and his face crinkled into a new expression.

"Run?" he wanted to know.

"Yes," I emphatically answered.

Already having wasted enough time standing there like tackling dummies, I counted in snappy, quick succession. "One, two, three." Dropping the buckets that I was holding to the ground with a clatter, I turned and started for the waiting safety of the hotel.

Not even a full step into my hasty retreat, I heard a flurry of other buckets quickly hitting the ground. That sound was replaced a second later by a lot of rapidly pounding footfalls. I felt a surge of adrenaline kick in as I increased my pace and reached a respectable fleeing speed. As long as I could hear those lumbering footsteps behind me, my plan was to keep on truckin'. Having no idea how badly we were outnumbered, my number one priority was to get us out of the immediate area as fast as possible.

The better part of the main slope had been crested and we were within fifty yards of Koffman's red, brick insurance building when the first shot rang out. Something with a sound resembling that of a pissed off bumblebee passed less than six inches in front of my charging face. My horrified feet alertly picked up the speed and my lungs began to feel that first light burn start to creep in.

I felt it's contact at almost exactly the same time that I heard the next shot's booming report. The blow from the bullet's impact felt like someone had just smacked my left shoulder really hard with an open hand.

My mind silently screamed out, "I've been shot! I've been shot!" I half expected to keel over right there on the spot, but miraculously, my churning feet and pumping legs continued to carry me closer to the brick building standing at the top of the hill.

More shots were ringing out, and they definitely came from multiple guns. I heard the frighteningly solid impact of a round make contact with something behind me and I heard Butch utter, "Oh, shit!"

My brain screamed, "Stop. Stop. You've got to go back and help him!" But my feet said, "We're within a hundred yards of the damn building, why stop now?" A compromise was worked out between my two disagreeing body parts and I was allowed to turn my upper body around to have a look, as long as I still made forward progress. To my joyous surprise, Butch was still consistently ambling forward, wearing a look of total amazement.

He saw me looking back at him and through his coarse, raspy breathing, Butch managed to incredulously spit out, "They shot the rifle right out of my hands."

A quick step later and I was behind the comforting cover of Koffman's sturdy structure. Butch and Jacob entered the safe zone a couple of seconds later, running nearly side by side.

Bullets whined and ricocheted off the bricks of the life-saving building, sounding eerily like the special effects in old western movies. Butch and Jacob advanced to within a couple of steps of me as I slowed my stride.

Trying to talk through my rapid, overly excited breathing, I urged them both, "Don't stop running. No matter how much it hurts, don't stop. Our only chance is to make it to the hotel before they can get around that building." The panic in my voice came through loud and clear, to both my ears and theirs.

We flew as fast as our burning legs and lungs would allow as we tore across the once busy street that fronted the insurance business. As hard as I tried not to, and as much as I admonished myself that looking back would only slow me down, I was powerless to control the urges to do so.

We had sort of bunched up next to each other coming across the street so, between ragged breaths, I told both Butch and Jacob. "Spread out some, so that we don't make such an easy target."

Heeding my advice, the duo branched off ever so slightly, but retained their fast jogging gait. Those few words may have been some of the best advice that I have ever given, because as soon as we reached the outer edge of the hotel's parking lot, the sound of erupting gunfire once again filled the air.

The side view mirror on a sporty, little, foreign car violently exploded as I passed next to the useless hulk. Shards of brilliant, reflective glass flew outward in a spectacularly bright, oval display of destructiveness. Bullets whizzed and whined as they blindly flew by on their deadly courses. The metallic clink of automobiles being struck with hot, molten lead and the crash of glass shattering explosively became the only thing that we could hear as we dodged and weaved between the now useless cars and trucks.

As we neared the end of the parking lot and rapidly closed on the building, a dreadfully frightening thought occurred to me. Were we going to make it all the way to the hotel only to find the entrance locked and be shot down while we stood there frantically banging on the outside of the door? My haunting fears were put to rest, though, as we passed the last line of cars in our path to the building.

The gray slab of steel swung outward and Vickie's beautiful face appeared around the hinged side of the door. Feeling a smile part my lips in spite of the danger, I high stepped my way through the opening with a jubilantly triumphant feeling. Right behind me, I heard the sound of more rushing boots clacking on the concrete floor of the laundry room and then the big, steel door slammed shut.

125

    Butch, Jacob and I had to skid to a quick halt on the concrete floor as we flew into the room to keep from hitting the bank of clothes dryers lining the far wall.

    Beastly tired from our brisk morning jaunt, our legs felt as quivery as a bowl of freshly shaken Jello. But with the lifesaving adrenaline still being steadily pumped into our systems, none of us felt like sitting. Collapsing against the cool, white steel of the dryers, we greedily sucked in air by the lung full like it might all disappear forever at any moment.

    Every eye in the room was busy searching for any sign of physical damage. Vickie and Kelli were looking us over and we, in turn, were checking each other out.

    There was fresh blood slowly trickling down the right hand side of Jacob's face. The damage didn't appear to be major, probably just scrapes and cuts from flying glass or other debris. He had felt no pain, at all, and had no idea that he was even bleeding. He looked genuinely surprised when Kelli told him. She kicked into her mothering, nurse mode and started pawing his sweat soaked face with her delicate, assessing hands.

Butch had some nasty scrapes and a few large, deeply embedded splinters in the back of his right hand. Apparently, the sickening, smacking sound that I had heard behind me while running had been a bullet slamming into the wooden stock of the rifle that Butch was carrying. He appeared to be unfazed by his scattered injuries and began absent mindedly plucking on the exposed ends of the wooden slivers.

As for myself, I knew that I had been hit and a sharp, stinging pain began to burn brightly within my left shoulder. Reaching around tentatively with my right hand, I gingerly explored the area with my fingertips to try and gauge the damage. No luck. With both a sweatshirt and a heavy coat on, all that I could feel was padding and an increased burning sensation from my finger's presence.

I pulled my hand back to strip my coat and shirt off and that's when things got a little scary. My fingers were coated in a bright, scarlet red and drops of blood fell from the tips.

Looking up from my hand, I found Kelli's face. The alarm that was registered there hurt more than the pain I was feeling in my shoulder. Her mouth had turned into a perfect O shape and her eyes ballooned out so large that they looked in danger of exploding. A high pitched, squeaky cry exited her throat. Her mouth and tongue never made the slightest attempt to shape the noise into words, they just stood aside and let it roll on out.

"I'm okay," I quickly blurted out, trying to relieve the worst of her fears. Unfortunately, that's what I always said in situations like this, and today, Kelli wasn't buying.

"Okay? Does that look okay to you?" she inquired while pointing at my red stained hand.

The blood continued to drip from it's dangling digits and I had to admit, if only to myself, that I was a little concerned about the seriousness of the wound. With each passing second the burning sensation that I had been feeling was quickly growing into a full blown, three alarm blaze. Making a conscious effort to keep a painful grimace from making an appearance on my face, I smiled a false smile that felt foreign and fooled no one.

"We're gonna have to get his coat off," Vickie said. "We can't see a thing like this."

After carefully assisting me in the removal of my coat, Vickie and Kelli began to pull the sweatshirt up and over my head so that my shoulders were fully exposed. After a very brief examination period, the two doctors voiced their professional opinions.

"It looks like it just grazed you," Doctor Vickie said, authoritatively.

"Yeah," Doctor Kelli added. "It's about six inches long and kind of deep in the middle, but it's just a scrape."

"It doesn't feel like any scrape I've ever had," I protested. And it didn't. My left shoulder felt like it was growing a multitude of new nerve endings every second and each one of them came into existence screaming out in pain.

Doctor Vickie then judiciously gave out her marching orders. "Come on," she directed. "Let's all go down to Carlos' room where the first aid supplies are and get you guys all patched up."

126

At a quarter after six it was already pitch dark outside and we were chomping at the bit for ten o'clock to come. Vickie and Kelli had carefully cleaned and dressed our wounds, coddled over us for a little while, and then made a big, delicious supper.

All any of us could think about was making radio contact with Rene over in Canada and getting the hell out of that cursed hotel. With a few hours to kill, we took turns dozing off on little catnaps and daydreaming about finally being able to get across the river.

Kelli and I walked down the hall to Steevo's old corner room and changed the batteries in the short wave radio. She thought that it might be a good idea because we had no idea how long the old ones had been in the radio, and it was certainly no time for taking chances. Being unable to agree more, we had set out to tackle the task together.

As we sat in Carlos' room watching the minutes on his wristwatch tick by so slowly that it was painful, we could only wait and ponder the fate of our futures. Everything would be decided in a short while, one way or the other.

127

    The last twenty minutes took forever. We were all in place around the radio by twenty minutes to ten and every single second after that seemed to stretch on for hours. Carlos had carefully eased and waddled his way to the corner room and now sat comfortably in a thickly padded desk chair that Butch had commandeered from the hotel's main office. The rest of us had gathered straight backed, wooden chairs from nearby rooms and placed them in a graceful, curving arc behind the large, black chair that Carlos rested in.
    It grew so quiet in Steevo's old room that I could hear my heartbeat as it nervously pitter pattered inside my chest. Kelli sat to my left, squeezing my hand and trying her best to remain composed.
    Butch and Vickie sat next to each other on the right end of our little seating area. They both seemed to suddenly find a great deal of interest in the dirty, rubble strewn carpet and the sooty, smoke blackened ceiling.
    Kaleb and Jacob were just bored, as usual. They sat on the bed farthest from the door with Walter laying at their feet and a "Wow, isn't this fun?" look on their faces. They were feeling a

bit upset because I wouldn't let them open the curtains to look outside. We had thoroughly discussed the subject earlier while sparingly picking over our evening meal. Our decision had been no more open curtains on the first floor. It was simply too risky since the situation had escalated into our attempted murders. Only curtains on the second and third floors could now be opened, and even then, we wouldn't get any closer than three feet to the window.

Each person's separate and distinct breathing could clearly be heard in the silence as the time slowly ticked away. Each passing minute seemed to take longer than the previous one did. When there were only five left, the second hand on Carlos' Timex watch slowed to an impossibly lethargic crawl.

"Can we go somewhere else?" Kaleb whined.

Kelli and I looked closely at each other and, without words, the decision was made. "Yes," Kelli answered. "But stay away from the windows."

Maybe they heard her and maybe they didn't. By the time the word windows was out of her mouth, the boys were already outside the door with Walter eagerly racing alongside. Their fading footsteps could be heard for a few moments and then silence reclaimed the room.

At two minutes 'til ten, Carlos turned on the shortwave radio and tuned the softly glowing dial to Rene's designated broadcast frequency. At the sound of the scratchy static, I was suddenly filled with an almost uncontrollable burst of energy. I wanted to dance. I wanted to sing. I wanted to walk across the ceiling, upside down. In the end, I settled for sitting quietly in the chair next to Kelli while waiting for Carlos to make contact with the man who had the power to either grant us our long sought after salvation, or condemn us to an almost certain death in hotel purgatory.

At one minute 'til we were finally able to look around at each other with closely guarded enthusiasm. The anticipation was almost suffocating. All of our hopes and dreams rested on a small radio and the ability of two people to communicate with each other over a heavily guarded, international border.

When at last the hour of reckoning was upon us, Carlos keyed the little microphone and broadcast his voice for what was left of the world to hear.

"Hello, Hello. This is Dino Ciccarelli, can anyone out

there hear me?"

I felt myself tense up a bit as I eagerly awaited a response. After thirty seconds of attentively listening, though, nothing came out of the radio except the same crackling, popping static that had been there all along.

Nervously glancing back toward us, Carlos said, "Don't worry, I'll try again."

Pressing the little, red button on the side of the microphone, Carlos repeated the call sign once more. "Hello, Hello. This is Dino Ciccarelli, can anyone out there hear me?"

Once again I tensed, hoping so hard for a reply that I actually expected to hear one. We were bound to, right? I mean, isn't this the way those sorts of things work? You keep persevering and never give up and, in the end, all of your hard work and determination pays off with sweet success.

Carlos persistently tried, over and over, every couple of minutes to reach Rene. At a quarter after ten Butch and Vickie had endured the heartache long enough and solemnly strolled from the smoke damaged room. At twenty after ten, Carlos once again looked back at me and Kelli and said with genuine sincerity, "I'm sorry. I tried."

I felt a small pang of sympathy for Carlos. All of us had been so wrapped up in our own little selfish wants and dreams that we hadn't thought about his future, at all. From the emotion emanating out of every pore of his wounded body, it was clear that he wanted to get across the river as badly as we did. Before either Kelli or I had the chance to help him, Carlos had risen to his feet and began to slowly shuffle toward the burned out doorway.

We sat silently looking at each other while the short wave radio popped and hissed at us from the nearby dresser. Our eyes had always conveyed so much more than our words could ever hope to, and right now, I was scared of what I saw when I looked there.

128

    The static coming from the little radio had started to become annoying. It sounded too much like hope for me to handle, right then. Kelli and I sat motionless like marble statues, unable to bring ourselves to move. Small pearls of moisture intermittently seeped from the corners of her eyes. She was devastated by our inability to make contact with Rene.

    "Why?" she moaned. "Why wouldn't he answer us?" A helpless, pleading element had taken over her features as she looked at me.

    All I could do was softly shake my head back and forth and say, "I don't know, Kelli."

    "Is it because he didn't recognize the voice?" The look in her eyes said that she wanted something so simple to be the reason, at least then it would be something that she would be able to understand.

    I felt terribly bad for all of us, but particularly for Kelli. The only thing that she wanted in the whole world was to get her babies across the river and safely into Canada.

    Having had enough of the scratchy static sound, I broke the glue like bond between the chair and myself and rose to go turn it off.

"Could he have put it on the wrong station?" Kelli asked my backside as I stepped toward the dresser.

"I don't know," was once again the only answer that I had.

"Maybe we could try some other channel. Maybe we could find someone else to help us."

Unbridled desperation came through loud and clear in her voice and the sound of it broke my heart. To hear that tone coming from the woman I love was pure agony. I found myself impractically wishing for the thousandth time that the whole mess had never happened. That I could just close my eyes and when I opened them again, the hotel would be gone. I would be back home sitting on our couch with my feet kicked up, watching television. Kelli would be sitting close by and the sound of the boys' playful laughter would be floating through the house.

The thought was so enticing that as I stood in front of the dresser on which the radio sat, I gave it a try. Tightly squeezing my eyes shut, I waited for the magic to happen. But, unfortunately, when I peeked a few seconds later, I could still see vertical stripes of blackened wallpaper staring back at me. Disgusted, I looked down at the little radio and began to reach for the power switch. Kelli's shrill, pleading voice cut right through the static.

"Can't we at least try?"

Dropping my arm back down to my side, I turned in her direction. "Try what?" I asked, unsure if I even wanted to know the answer.

"A different channel," she said, looking at me as if she could mean nothing else.

I was about to tell her that the chances of us building an airplane from scratch and flying across the river was more likely than finding anyone else that would help us over the shortwave radio. Wanted to, but couldn't. The despondent, woeful look radiating from her tear soaked brown eyes made me change my mind.

Softly, and with a slight nod, I said, "Alright."

Placing my fingers on the chrome plated tuning knob, I watched as the lighted dial on the radio slowly changed frequencies. With each incremental movement of the dial, the crackling static differed in pitch. One moment it would be humming and popping in a deep rumble and the next it would be squealing wildly in an ear splitting, high pitched, whistling whine. I found the natural electronic interference somewhat interesting, but it was still only noise.

Turning my head to gauge Kelli's reaction to this latest setback, I barely had time to register her shattered, forlorn gaze. As soon as my eyes met hers, the sound of fast paced, lively music burst forth from the little speaker in the radio.

It sounded something like the Glenn Miller Band or maybe Count Basie and his Orchestra. The horns were blaring brightly and the drums pounded away at a frenzied pace.

Jerking my head back around, I stared in disbelief at the little electronic gadget before me. Unable to speak, Kelli and I took turns looking back and forth between the radio and each other. After listening to the music for a few moments, we were both sure that it wasn't just a wishful figment of our imaginations and smiles began to sprout on our surprised faces. The music was actually pretty good and I found myself being absorbed in it's rhythmic onslaught.

I had heard this type of music before, mostly in movies or on the radio as I searched through the different stations, but never like this. Maybe it was because we hadn't heard any music, at all, for months and I was starved for any kind of harmonious entertainment. Or, it could be that these guys were really good and I had overlooked an entire genre of fantastic music simply because it didn't contain an electric guitar.

The end of the song died away and the sound of a human voice filled the room. Easily identifiable as French, the language rolled from the radio in beautiful, poetic syllables that neither Kelli or I could understand. But, at least it was a voice.

A jolt ran through me as I remembered Carlos telling us that he spoke a little French. "'Around here, it's only natural,'" he had said, with a huge shrug of his shoulders. "'Everyone knows people across the river or does business there.'" Perhaps, I hoped, Carlos could make contact with this man or, at the very least, understand what he was saying.

Outstretching my arm in Kelli's direction, I excitedly notified her of my plan. "Stay here, I'm going to get Carlos." With a feeling of pure exhilaration, I turned and raced from the smoke blackened hotel room.

129

    I hadn't even made it to Carlos' door when he appeared from the opening. He was looking in the direction of the music, which had once again started, with wide, unbelieving eyes.
    Turning his wondering gaze to me, Carlos asked, "Is that music coming from the radio?"
    Through an uncontrollable grin, I said, "Yes, it is."
    Baby stepping down the hallway without stopping or even slowing his pace, Carlos started toward the corner hotel room's open door.
    "That's Rene's channel?" he asked, still unable to shake his look of amazement.
    Turning to amble along beside our hobbled friend, I filled him in on what happened after he left the room. The part involving the radio, anyway.
    As we entered Steevo's old, corner hotel room, the volume of the music jumped dramatically. Moving quickly, I made a beeline for the booming radio and twisted the knob to the left so that we could talk. With that little task completed, I resumed our ongoing conversation.
    "We were hoping that you could at least understand what

he was saying," I told Carlos. "Maybe it would help us in some way."

He looked in Kelli's direction but she sat with her head bowed to keep Carlos from seeing the tell-tale signs of her tears. She hated the way her eyes looked when they were all puffy. When his eyes turned back to meet mine, they were softer and full of emotion, themselves. Palms facing upward, Carlos shrugged slightly and in a tone barely above a whisper said, "Sure, I'll listen. Maybe I will be able to understand some of it, I don't know."

I nodded my head at what Carlos said, but I was looking at Kelli.

"I'm not fluent, you understand." A touch of alarm had edged it's way into his voice.

As I looked back at him, it was also evident on his face.

"That's okay," I gushed. "You know a lot more than we do."

Seeming to take this into consideration, Carlos tilted his head in a "well, you got me there," gesture and nodded perceptively a couple of times.

The clarinet dominated number emanating from the little radio came to a halt and I barely had time to find the volume knob before the disc jockey began talking again.

The smooth, cultured sound of this man's voice was almost as melodic as the music itself. It rolled from the speaker as smooth as greased glass. French is one of the world's most beautiful languages and this unknown broadcaster was certainly doing it justice.

From the corner of my eye, I saw Carlos flinch as if he had been physically struck. Our eyes met each other at the same time and I saw a look on his face that I couldn't read.

Even though I was afraid, I asked, "What is it? What did he say?"

Gulping down a big, oversized lump in his throat, Carlos turned to me and Kelli. The smile on his face broadening by the second, he revealed what he had heard. "He said it's the Sunday night Big Band hour. This is Sunday."

130

"Go ahead and go to sleep, honey. We can talk more about it in the morning," Kelli told Kaleb.

The boy looked exhausted. It had been a very trying day for everyone and a good night's sleep was just what we needed. The welcome news had returned all of us to better spirits and our feeling of hope had been temporarily restored. Our sleep would once again be filled with wonderful dreams of river crossings and peaceful, happy futures on the other side of the border.

Kaleb answered back, eyes already shut for the night, "Okay, mom, I love you."

"'Love you, too, sweet boy."

Vickie had been asleep for a little while and Butch lay on his back, hands laced together behind his head, staring up at the ceiling. Seemingly lost in quiet thought, he hadn't spoken a word since Vickie had dozed off.

Jacob sat on his mattress wrapped up in blankets, with his back leaning against the wall. He looked to be wide awake but extremely bored. Having turned into our party's resident night owl, he often stayed up for hours after the rest of us were deep in dreamland. He seemed to enjoy his time alone and the only side effect seemed to be sleeping half of the next day away. In other words, he was a typical teenager. Sometimes I felt so sorry for him that it made my heart hurt. Instead of running through the malls and chasing pretty girls, Jacob had somehow gotten caught in the middle of World War III.

Kelli was so elated about the turn of events that a glowing twinkle adorned her eyes for the rest of the evening. She had picked up one of the hundreds of phonebooks that were lying around inside the hotel and laid next to me reading about the surprisingly significant history of Marine City and the St. Clair River.

Kelli had always been an avid reader and longed for any sort of printed material. If the only thing available to read was a matchbook cover, you could bet that she would hungrily devour it.

Snugly laying there with all of the day's activities fresh in my mind, I couldn't wait to see what tomorrow would bring. A smile on my lips and thinking only happy thoughts, I was softly serenaded to sleep by the soothing sound of Kelli's beating heart.

131

    A thunderous, jarring explosion tore me from the deep, peaceful sleep that I had been so thoroughly enjoying. The concussion from the blast felt like someone had raised the hotel about a foot off of the ground and then let it abruptly drop. Rumbling echoes ran down the length of darkened hallway. The clinking and tinkling sound of flying glass striking objects and falling to the floor reminded me of someone repeatedly banging on the really high notes of a piano.
    "What the hell?" I heard Jacob mumble. We had started our watch rotation again as a precaution, and it was his turn. A split second later I heard him click the button on the flashlight that he was holding.
    The white beam cut a neat swatch of light down the hallway just in time to catch a ball of rolling, billowing smoke before it washed over us. The blast wave was soupy thick and imbedded with small, fragmentary crystals that burned like hell as soon as they entered our throats. My best guess was that the particles were either microscopic bits of glass dust or slivers of fiberglass insulation. Regardless of what they were, it was clear that our bodies didn't approve of the ingestion. Fits of

severe coughing broke out, doubling us over in deep, saliva dripping, stomach clenching spasms.

"Down," I tried to yell, but before I could even get the first letter to come out, I realized that trying to say anything was completely out of the question.

Another bout of spittle throwing, eye watering hacking befell me, and I was helpless to do anything except lay prone on the cushiony soft mattress and cough my lungs out.

Raising my head to look back down the hallway, I saw that the beam of Jacob's flashlight had been joined by Butch's. The two searching cylinders of light verified what I had been thinking. At the place where the hallways intersected each other on the first floor, piles of multi-colored debris littered the carpeting. Pieces of metal and shards of reflecting glass menacingly protruded from the drywall on the right hand side of the hallway. Bits of fine, shiny dust still hung suspended in mid-air. There was only one place in the hotel that contained that much glass. The lobby.

Most of the airborne particulates had thankfully settled by then and the fitful bouts of coughing began to subside.

"Turn off the lights," I loudly croaked through a scratchy, dust clogged throat. "They'll ruin our night vision and give away our location."

I had no idea if we were about to be stormed by troops or whether the blast was just an act of deliberate terrorism. Either way, I wasn't about to take the chance. The lights clicked off and cold, fresh air began to pool around us.

"If you see any dark shapes moving, shoot them," I yelled out. "Ask questions later."

132

"Butch, do you want to go with me?" I asked about five minutes later. There had been no squad of bloodthirsty stormtroopers rush into the building. In fact, there had been no movement at all. For five long minutes we hadn't seen or heard anything, unless you counted the persistent ringing in our ears.

He moved up to where I was kneeling in the darkness and we started toward the lobby together, moving slow and low.

The odor from the devastating explosion was still very strong. It smelled like a mixture of gunpowder, molten steel and badly singed hair.

Staying right up against the left surface of the hallway, we moved forward in a hunched over, crouching stoop. I could feel the cold night air rushing past me every time I put my hand down on the floor to steady myself. Even with no heat source in the building, it was still much warmer inside than it was outside on a frigid, mid-winter's night in Michigan.

Having safely made it to where the four hallways intersected, I cautiously peered around the corner toward the hotel's lobby. The epicenter of the blast appeared to be on the right hand side of the two sets of double entry doors. The wall of windows fronting the lobby's swanky seating area had been totally trashed. The only parts of the massive glass barrier that remained intact were a couple of separated panes across the top of the opening and one smaller one, still stubbornly clinging to the far side.

The furniture that had been unlucky enough to be in the immediate area was mangled and shredded. Bits of cotton batting poked out from the jagged gashes and broken frames of the pulverized pieces. One of the big, overstuffed armchairs that had set very close to the wall of windows was laying halfway down the short hallway to where Butch and I were.

The damage to the other three walls and ceiling appeared to be largely superficial. Different sized holes peppered almost every foot of the drywall, but there were no obvious signs of structural damage.

Ever so cautiously, the two of us inched forward, once again staying on the left hand side of the short hallway.

I stopped when we reached the near end of the check-in counter. From that spot we could both see the entire lobby and carefully check over it's scattered contents to make sure that no one had come inside. Once I was satisfied that we didn't have any visitors in the lobby, I turned my attention to the outside of the hotel.

"Do you see anything?" I asked Butch.

"No," he whispered back. "Not a thing."

"How about outside?" I inquired. This time it took a little longer for him to answer. I could feel his eyes scan the area in front of the building over my right shoulder.

"Ah, no, I sure don't," he said. "It's dark out there, though, and there are a lot of things to hide behind."

I nodded my head up and down. "Uh-huh," I agreed.

We both looked outside a little bit more, but it was almost impossible to tell one thing from another in the pitch black darkness.

"Crap," I said softly. There was no way that we could leave a hole like that go unguarded. We would have to watch the massive opening around the clock, and that meant more guard duty. What welcomed news that would be, I thought. But, until we either crossed the river in two nights or decided to abandon the hotel for our safety, we would have to guard the hole.

"Kaleb and I will take the first watch," I regrettably told Butch. "Could you send him up here with some blankets and a flashlight, please?"

"Sure," he replied. "Vickie and I'll take the second one," he graciously volunteered. "So, just wake us up when you're ready."

"Okay, thanks Butch."

He turned and quietly left to retrieve Kaleb and I settled in for a long, boring, cold evening of watching a massive hole in the hotel's wall stare back at me.

133

As daylight began to steadily creep over the snow covered landscape, I sent Kaleb back to wake up Butch and Vickie. In a few minutes they appeared around the corner looking like they, too, were in need of a good, strong cup of coffee. Too tired to say much of anything, I grunted my thanks as they sat down against the wall next to me.

With heavy, drooping eyelids and a very sore back, I slowly dawdled back to Kelli's and my mattress. Dropping down on my side of the padded paradise, I pulled the soft, thick blankets up over my drained derriere and, in mere seconds, left reality far behind.

134

When I awoke the sun was in the western half of the sky and Butch and Vickie were sound asleep. There was a snoring lump lying beneath Kaleb's pile of blankets that made them swell and deflate at a slow, steady rate. That meant Kelli and Jacob were enjoying their turn at watch down by the lobby.

Lowering my sleep fogged head back down on the soft, warm pillow, I decided to do absolutely nothing for a few minutes. It felt so good to just lay there all stretched out, completely comfortable and toasty warm under those wonderful blankets, that I was in no hurry, whatsoever, to get up.

Oh, how I sorely missed our old waterbed! It was always so delightfully warm to crawl into when it was cold outside. The heat helped me to relax and I slept like a baby every night.

I started to daydream about getting another waterbed if we got across to Canada. About another car, another house, and before long my daydream turned into a real dream. I fell back to sleep and had a vivid dream about our fabulous new existence across the border. Our new jobs. Our new friends. Even our new neighbors. Everyone seemed so nice in Canada and we were all so thankful and happy to have safely made it.

Jacob had a new French girlfriend named Brigitte Chevalier and he was head over heels for her. I had never seen him smitten by anyone like that before. Everything was going along fantastically well, until I had to pee. The nagging urge to relieve myself tore me from the beautiful, serene settings of picturesque Canada and thrust me right smack dab in the middle of a cold, smoke blackened hallway in the middle of Hotel Hell.

"Crap," I muttered, as I reluctantly crawled form the comfort of my warm bed and clumsily made my way to the closest bathroom.

135

"Do you think they'll come back, tonight?" Carlos asked. There was genuine concern, both in his voice and on his face.

"I don't know," I told him. I suddenly became unable to make eye contact with anyone because that was a lie. I *did* know, and my guess was that tonight, there would be a large number of heavily armed, camouflaged wearing invaders come rushing through that massive opening in the front of the hotel. But I didn't say that. There was no need to scare everyone needlessly. Between now and then there was a whole lot of work to do, and not much time to do it in.

"Butch," I began, "will you take Kaleb and Jacob up to the third floor with you? Take your backpacks and fill them with as much soda as each of you can carry, and then take them and Walter back to the caboose."

"The caboose?" Kelli asked, clearly surprised. I turned and met her startled gaze.

"Yes, the caboose," I calmly said.

She started to ask me a question but it came out as a series of garbled, false starts. "Why the, What are we, Today?"

"Yes," I repeated. "It's just in case. I don't want anyone to get hurt so we're moving back to the caboose for tonight."

"For *tonight*?" This time it was Vickie's turn to question.

"Well, yeah." I tried to sound collected and confident. "Tomorrow night we'll be sleeping in Canada, won't we?"

A softer look took over her features and she tilted her head ever so slightly to the right.

"Well," Vickie hesitantly began. "That's *if* we make contact with Rene, right?"

"Why wouldn't we make contact?" I challenged.

Butch, Vickie, Kelli and Carlos exchanged questioning, wide eyed glances, but no one said anything. Maybe they thought I was crazy. Or, maybe I wasn't doing as good of a job as I had hoped I would in selling the idea.

Kaleb and Jacob were guarding the big, inviting opening in the front of the building. Jacob didn't think we should stay in the hotel any longer and Kaleb hated the idea of going back to the caboose. Since we had some really important things to discuss, we let the boys stand watch together to keep them busy. There was little chance of anyone attacking right then, anyway. They would wait until late at night, when it was dark and they thought that most of us would be asleep, then they would try to use the age old element of surprise to it's fullest advantage.

"After your trip with the sodas and Walter; Vickie, Kelli and I will make a trip carrying as much food as we can while you guys rest and guard the hole."

Everyone was looking at me now like I was definitely loco, for sure. Never letting that be a deterrent to me in the past, I wasn't about to start then.

I boldly continued, "After that, we're all leaving and taking the canoes and the radio with us."

The looks that went back and forth among my four fellow compatriots was one of mild amusement. It was almost as if I had just told them a joke that turned out to be more odd than funny. Really more a look of bemusement than anything else.

"We're going to carry those two canoes all the way back to the caboose?" Kelli skeptically asked.

"What about Carlos?" Vickie chimed in. "He can't walk that far."

"Carlos will only walk about half way," I said reassuringly, "then we'll contact Rene and let him rest for a while. It will be fine because we'll be away from the hotel and in a place where no one will be looking for us."

There was a very long moment of silence while everyone mulled over this ambitious, labor intensive plan.

Finally breaking the uneasy silence, Vickie, now sounding resigned to the fact that my plan might be the best and only way to safely reach Canada, said, "Well, at least we'll be safer, I guess."

"What if they follow us?" Kelli protested. "We'll be leaving a lot of tracks, won't they just follow us?"

I seemed to take this into consideration for a moment, when in fact, I had already spent a good deal of time mulling the dilemma over.

"I don't think so," I said softly. "I think that those people will be so happy to have us out of here that they won't care where we went, as long as we're gone." Still seeing a touch of doubt in Kelli's concerned and questioning eyes, I quickly added. "We'll have to keep an eye on our back trail, of course, just in case, but then again, we always do, don't we?"

She thought it over for a couple of seconds, and when she looked back up at me, the look of concern on her face had softened measurably and those worry lines were gone.

Having been totally silent thus far in our discussion, I was a little surprised when I heard Butch's voice.

"Should we leave Walter at the caboose or bring him back with us?"

136

    I took over watching the big hole in the wall while Butch, Kaleb and Jacob made their trip back to the caboose and Kelli and Vickie stuffed our three backpacks full of food.
    Looking through the massive opening on the western side of the building, my practiced eye told me that we had about two and a half hours of daylight left. I figured a round trip to the caboose with a heavy load should take a little over an hour. The return trip, of course, being the faster leg.
    If everything went smoothly we could be out of the hotel for good by dark, and that suited me just fine. Every minute after that, the risk factor would go up exponentially. There was no doubt in my mind that as soon as it was dark enough the first lookouts would take their places around the hotel. If one of them should happen to spot us as we were leaving, it could spell disaster for our little group. They could decide to tail us, which would be bad. Or, they could open fire on us, which would be worse.
    Interrupting my thoughts, Kelli and Vickie appeared around the corner of the short hallway. They wearily sat down on the side of an overturned arm chair that had been tossed

across the glass strewn lobby by the thunderous, hole making explosion.

"Okay," Kelli huffed. "We're all loaded."

"Yeah," agreed Vickie, "and they're awfully heavy, too."

Hardly able to contain her spreading grin, Kelli playfully told me, "We made sure yours was the heaviest." At this poignant revelation both ladies simultaneously burst into laughter.

I couldn't help but laugh along as I witnessed their bubbly joy, but I also knew Kelli well enough to know that she was telling me the truth. My pack would be heavier, but after all, wasn't this my crazy idea?

"Great," I said, playing along. "Maybe I'll break my leg on the way there and you can just shoot me like I was a horse. Then I wouldn't have to worry about any of this, anymore." I accented my words with a sweeping swing of my right arm.

A serious look came over Vickie's face and she menacingly waggled her outstretched finger back and forth. "Oh, no, you're not getting off *that* easy," she informed me before busting out laughing again.

I was beginning to wonder if maybe the ladies hadn't taken a nip or two while they were stuffing our backpacks full of food. The exuberant smiles and playful laughter quickly turned into flat lines and looks of dread when I next spoke.

"Can I ask you two to do me one more thing for me?"

137

Vickie, Kelli and I pushed ourselves hard on the return trip from the caboose and arrived back at the hotel just before dusk.

We had passed Carlos and Kaleb on the way back. They were resting down by the river on a large, gnarled trunk of faded driftwood. Carlos was in good spirits and seemed to be doing fine. Aside from being a little cold, he had no complaints. Kaleb was all smiles, as usual, but Kelli and I could tell that he was a little nervous about being out in the open like that with little protection.

Their destination was a thick, brushy area about a half mile down the icy shoreline of the St. Clair. Once they were there, Carlos and Kaleb would wait for us to catch up with them and we would all hunker down together until it was time to contact Rene.

Butch and Jacob opened the laundry room's big, steel door for us and we drug our tired carcasses in through the opening. They already had the windows in the canoe room open and were anxious to go.

"Can anyone think of anything else that we should grab

before we leave?" I breathily asked our little group.

A series of unsure looks passed from person to person before everyone finally agreed; four shaking heads accompanied by four "no's," was their final answer. Two minutes later, Kelli and Butch were passing the heavily laden canoes out of the hotel room's open window to Vickie, Jacob and me.

Kelli and Vickie had taken all of the money and jewelry in Steevo's stash and lined the bottoms of both canoes with the glittering booty. On top of the load of loot, the ladies had piled a dozen thick blankets and an abundance of soft, fluffy pillows.

Once the canoes were safely outside the building, Butch and Kelli scampered out through the laundry room's open door and quickly joined the rest of us.

The setting sun that evening was a large, orange sphere that dominated the western horizon. As the bottom part of the glowing orb touched down on the landscape, our weary, canoe toting procession was already making it's way toward the sloping bank of the river's edge.

We got to the pebble strewn shore with less than half the sun still visible. To catch our breath, we momentarily rested on the same sun bleached log that Carlos and Kaleb had used, earlier. From where we were sitting, the hotel was no longer visible and I was extremely glad to be rid of it.

The closer that it got to sunset, the more sure I became that we were doing the right thing.

Butch must have been able to read my thoughts because he said, "I think this is best," with a slight nod and a sincere look on his face. "Who knows what would have happened if we had stayed there longer?"

"It certainly wasn't worth one of us getting hurt over," Vickie added. "I don't know if I could have handled that."

Jacob broke in and asked, "Is that where we're going?" as he peered down the river's edge, to the south. The rest of us automatically turned our heads to look in that direction. The tangled, overgrown patch of wild shrubbery clearly stood out against it's snowy white surroundings.

"Yep," I answered. "That's it, Jacob." With the sun rapidly disappearing from view, we reluctantly lifted the weighty canoes and started for the distant patch of dense vegetation.

The sun had completely disappeared and the onset of full

darkness had just begun by the time that we finally reached the tangled mass of brush and vine. We left the canoes just inside the entrance of a small trail and, following the sound of Kaleb's voice, carefully wove our way between the clasping arms of thorns and dense tangles of briars.

Carlos and Kaleb had found a nice, little opening in the seemingly impenetrable puncture palace. About eight feet in diameter and an almost perfect circle, it was a great place for us to hide out until we could make radio contact.

Totally spent from having carried the overloaded canoes for almost a mile, we all dropped like stones in the clearing, sweating profusely and feeling so warm inside that it almost felt like we were on fire. Carlos and Kaleb, on the other hand, were absolutely miserable.

"It's freezing out here," Kaleb complained, his arms tucked tightly about his chest.

Carlos, who had only been out of his bed for short periods of time over the last week, echoed Kaleb's assessment. His body's sporadic shaking was plainly visible, despite the limited light.

Kaleb and Jacob returned to the overflowing canoes and brought back more than enough blankets to keep everyone warm.

The towers full of lights on the other side of the St. Clair became brighter as the darkness became more pronounced. Even more than a mile away, the lights were still intense enough to cast ghostly shadows.

We wrapped ourselves up in warm blankets and began the nearly four hour wait that we would have to endure until it was time to contact Rene.

138

      The small light inside the radio's dial cast a soft, warm glow on all the faces huddled around it, elongating and distorting our features until each of us appeared to be strange and foreign.
      It had thankfully been a long, boring wait and so far there had been no noticeable attempt to follow our trail that ran back along the water's edge. We had taken turns standing up at about five or ten minute intervals to look back down the snow covered river bank for any sign of trouble.
      Kelli had once again put fresh batteries in the shortwave radio, unwilling to take a chance that something so minor could ruin our only chance at salvation.
      A feeling of nervous anticipation hung in the air as we eagerly awaited the pivotal moment. If we were able to contact Rene and convince him to do business with us, our emotions would undoubtedly soar skyward. But if we failed to connect with Steevo's old business partner or he refused to help us, we would be plunged downward to the deepest, darkest depths of despair.
      Carlos picked up the small, triangular shaped microphone with slightly shaking hands. Holding the face of his watch in

close to the radio's glow, as if to verify to all that it was indeed finally ten o'clock, Carlos turned up the volume knob and the familiar crackle and hiss of atmospheric interference exited from the glowing box.

His eyes became clearly visible when he leaned forward and closer to the radio. As he slowly glanced around the clearing at all of us, I could see that there had been a drastic change in Carlo's demeanor. He seemed to be distant and preoccupied, totally unsure of what he was doing. Knowing that time was of the essence, I began to feel a touch of impatience start to creep in.

"Are you alright, Carlos?" I asked the stationary figure in front of me. His eyes rose to meet mine and I could see distrust in them. "Carlos," I said. "What's wrong?"

His eyes started to look brighter in the low light and for a moment I thought that it must have been some bizarre optical illusion. Then a shining pearl of moisture fell from the corner of his right eye. It quickly rolled down his cheek and slipped out of sight into the waiting darkness. It was soon joined by another one from the left eye as the features on Carlos' face changed and revealed his true, inner anguish. His jaw jutted outward sharply as he fought to maintain his swirling emotions. The two glossy, opalescent streaks running down his cheeks became shinier and more pronounced as his tears started to flow freely. His chest quickly rose and fell in time with his distressed, sorrowful sobbing.

Totally caught off guard by this puzzling display of emotion, I could only look around helplessly at the rest of our little group. Vickie picked up on my cue.

She leaned in next to Carlos and gently placed a gloved hand upon his heaving shoulder. "What's wrong, honey?" she asked in her sweetest motherly voice. "You can tell us, we're all in this together."

My mind was suddenly besieged by a flurry of disastrous scenarios. What if the reason Carlos was crying was out of shame? What if he had purposely sabotaged the radio so that we would never be able to make use of it? What if he had been bluffing all along about knowing all the particulars of the river crossing, including Rene's correct contact frequency? My heart began to sink in my chest as the weight of the possible consequences of such an action came crashing down upon me with earth shattering force.

But I was wrong.

Aiming his tear soaked eyes directly at me, he revealed what was bothering him.

"Are you really going to take me with you?"

I involuntarily pulled my head back as if I had been slapped. The first time that I tried to answer him, I opened my mouth but couldn't get anything to come out. Swallowing hard to force some lubrication down my suddenly parched windpipe, I tried once again.

"Of course we are, Carlos," I told him. Curious as to why he would ask such a thing, I crinkled my forehead and asked.

Looking at me like a child who is full of hope but still expecting the worst, he said, "There are only two canoes and there are seven of us." Then it was Carlos' turn to swallow a huge lump in his throat in order to carry on the conversation. Regaining the use of his tear choked voice, he looked directly into my eyes and said. "I believe that you're going to shoot me after I make contact with Rene because there isn't enough room in the canoes for all of us."

139

    A vocal chorus of rebellion spontaneously arose within our little circle. Each individual adamantly protested Carlos' barbaric thoughts and assured him that he was one of our group and would go wherever we went, including across the river.

    Desperately searching each of our faces for the slightest evidence of betrayal, Carlos peered around the circle through water filled eyes.

    Kaleb rose from where he had been sitting and walked around to the other side of the small clearing. Approaching the crying man, he put his arm around the Carlo's shaking shoulders and slowly tilted his head inward until both of their forehead's made contact.

    Softly, like the feathery light coo of a dove, Kaleb spoke. "We're not gonna shoot you, buddy. You're part of our family, now."

    Through his tear drenched eyes, Carlos beheld a bevy of smiling faces and nodding heads. His mouth widened into a huge, earsplitting grin but the tears still continued to fall. A result of both the overwhelming relief that he was feeling and the sheer joy of finding someone to share his future across the river with. They were still falling when he placed the microphone to his lips and pressed the little red button located on it's side.

Part III

Deal with the Devil

140

"Hello, hello," Carlos' voice filled the space within our briar patch clearing. "This is Dino Ciccarelli, can anyone out there hear me?" Depressing the red button, he and the rest of us waited for a reply through the dense wall of noisy static.

We didn't have to wait long. A male voice with a decidedly French accent, speaking English in a cultured and sophisticated manner, returned our call.

"Who is this speaking, please?" It demanded to know.

The richly colored, red hue that had been prevalent throughout Carlos' face a moment ago instantly drained away, leaving him looking pale and waxen. He appeared to be completely flustered.

I knew that he must have gone over this moment in his mind at least a thousand times, mentally preparing himself for every possible scenario. Betting that it was nothing more than a simple case of nerves, I calmly encouraged him.

"Go ahead, Carlos," I said. "Tell the man who you are."

His eyes slowly began to refocus and register their surroundings. After a couple of long, drawn out blinks, he looked at me and the faintest trace of a smile pushed up both ends of his lips.

"I sure will," he said. Keying the microphone, Carlos once again repeated the smuggler's signal. "Hello, hello. This is Dino Ciccarelli, can anyone out there hear me?"

Almost immediately, the smooth, gentlemanly voice was back on the air. "This is most definitely *not* Dino Ciccarelli, for I know his voice well. I shall give you one more chance, my unknown friend. Who is this?"

Now we all looked lost and bewildered. Eyes wide as if we'd all just been soundly goosed in the rear end, we looked around at each other desperately searching for an answer.

"What are we going to do?" Jacob asked, sounding alarmed to a near panic.

Feeling totally helpless, all any of us could do was blankly stare at each other like a deer caught in the headlights of an oncoming vehicle. I could feel everything that we had worked for beginning to slowly slip away. All of the hardships and hostilities that we had endured to reach this point seemed meaningless in the face of this unsolvable riddle.

What do we say? "Um, sorry there, Rene, but we've killed off your old buddy Steevo and took all of his valuables. Would you be kind enough to trade us our freedom in return for some of his loot?"

But none of us were forced to say anything. Carlos did it all. Taking control of the situation, he now perfectly replayed one of the many possible scenarios that he foresaw in his vivid imagination.

"Rene?" he ventured. "Rene, it's me, Carlos. I know Steevo has mentioned me before."

The sound of scratchy static returned to our ears and stayed far too long for comfort.

The cultured voice finally returned, and when it did, this time there was a harder edge to its words. "The plumber?" it asked, sounding incredulous at the fact that he was communicating with such a menial, blue collar professional. One who actually made his living covering himself in his customer's shit, no less.

Composing himself, Carlos answered. "Yes, the plumber," and without releasing the red button, continued on, just like he had rehearsed. "There's been an accident, Rene."

Carlos had thrown the perfect lead and smiled

handsomely when the voice returned.

Rene sounded inquisitive and perhaps even a little concerned about the news. Whether that concern was about the health of his old pal Steevo or merely over losing his continued supply of pirated plunder was anyone's guess.

"What kind of accident?" the voice hesitantly inquired.

Without missing a beat, Carlos replied exactly as he had imagined doing so many times before. "Someone attacked the hotel, Rene. They shot through a window and hit Steevo." Pausing ever so slightly to create the right effect, Carlos somberly continued. "He died instantly. Never felt a thing."

The wait for a response took far longer this time and each static filled moment seemed to stretch on for an eternity. Rene's voice, now sounding cold and analytical broke the scrunching static.

"I am sorry to hear about that, Carlos, however, I can't see any of that as being the reason you contacted me. What do you want?"

Momentarily, but only momentarily, Carlos appeared rattled. Quickly collecting his thoughts, he continued the transmission with the same cool competence as before.

"I would like to continue the existing business agreement, on Steevo's behalf." Carlos released the red button and a sea of squalling static filled the little clearing.

All that we could do was wait. Our cards had been laid on the table and now we would find out if we had a winning hand or not. The static abruptly ended and Rene's smooth, sophisticated voice returned.

"Terribly sorry, Carlos, but I'm not interested."

In one little sentence, he had neatly severed all of our hopes as if they were nothing more than a thread in the path of a samurai sword. The looks of devastation were so bitter and severe that none of us could mask our feelings. We were absolutely thunderstruck. Eyes began to cloud over and faces to droop. The news was simply more than we could take.

My heart felt as heavy as a blacksmith's big, cast iron anvil sagging weightily in the middle of my chest. I had to make myself breathe because my body didn't seem to want to do it on it's own. Frozen into inaction by our own self-pity, the seconds ticked by.

Once again, Carlos' surprising mettle came through.

Being unable to take no for an answer, he defiantly thumbed the red button on the microphone. "I have seven paying customers ready to go, Rene."

Back after the shortest intermission since the conversation had begun, the reserved, richly accented voice sounded shocked and perhaps even a touch excited. "Seven?" it asked, in a pitch noticeably higher than it's normal, dry, blue blooded sneer.

"That's right, seven," replied Carlos, starting to sound more confident.

Once more, we were treated to a lengthy, starlit symphony of static, and like a tree that grows new leaves each spring, our hopes began to sprout anew.

"Surely he'll take the gold from seven fares, won't he?" Kelli whispered

"I don't know," Vickie doubtfully replied.

"I would," offered Kaleb. "That's a lot of gold."

As soon as the sentence had cleared his lips, a puzzled look crinkled his brow and he turned toward Kelli. "How much gold is that, anyway?" Kaleb's query went unanswered because Rene's voice exited the radio's speaker and brought our budding aspirations to a grinding halt.

"A very tempting offer, my plumbing friend, but I am afraid that I must still decline."

Without a moment's hesitation, Carlos upped the ante in dramatic fashion.

"They are willing to pay you double the normal rate, Rene."

The voice that came back across the airwaves this time didn't sound refined, cultured or elegant. It sounded completely flabbergasted.

"What?" the disbelieving voice stammered. *"Double?"*

"That's right, Rene," Carlos coolly answered. "Double."

The harsh, grating sound of the now familiar static replaced our cross river conversation and we sat around anxiously waiting as the seconds slipped away. Nervously fidgeting about, we passed the time by doing false tasks like picking the lint out of our pocket linings and mapping the inside of our teeth with our tongues.

Rene's voice parted the squalling static. This time his tone was almost accusatory.

"What's the catch?"

Answering quickly, Carlos attempted to ease his mind. "There is no catch, Rene. The same deal as always, for twice the pay."

The static only lasted a few seconds this time.

"Who are these people?" Rene asked, in a tone reminiscent of someone asking a question that they're not really sure they want to know the answer to.

Looking around the circle at our small huddled group, a smile began to appear on Carlos' face. It's proportions grew alarmingly until it had completely enveloped his features. When he keyed the microphone again, it was clear that Carlos was speaking from the heart.

"Good people, Rene. Good people."

A brief, static filled pause later, the smooth, cultured voice that had first greeted us returned.

"Do these good people have the resources necessary to pay double fare?" it cordially inquired.

"Yes, they do," Carlos replied.

Rene, sounding all business once again, delivered his final message of the transmission.

"I hope they do, Carlos. Because if not, they will all be shot."

141

    Waking up inside the caboose again gave me a jolt to start the new day. My sleepy mind couldn't quite grasp why I was back there again, at first. Then the memory of our conversation with Rene came flooding back and I could feel my sleep lined cheeks rise with joy.

    Sitting upright on the wooden floor in our hastily made blanket bed, I stretched mightily and took in the dry heat of the fire. It was so nice and warm in there, totally unlike the cold, damp, masonry structure of the hotel. We had taken full advantage of being able to build a fire again and it felt absolutely luxuriant.

    I turned and looked behind me, towards the sound of the crackling wood, and was greeted by a trio of smiling faces. Butch, Vickie and Kaleb were sitting at one of the booths on the western side of the train car looking my way. Seeing the identical, enormous, silly looking grin on each of their faces was a comical sight and I couldn't help but chuckle. With my own smile growing by the second, I crawled out of my warm bed with an angrily growling stomach.

    Walter seemed eager to accompany me as I did my

morning business, so out the door we both went to answer nature's call.

There was but the faintest touch of a breeze and the sky was a brilliant, rich blue. It would be a radiantly beautiful day after it warmed up a little. A perfect day for boating, I thought wryly, and then beamed with pleasure at my own little joke.

The good news had exhilarated and energized all of us. As what Rene had said began to soak in and we realized that we would indeed be crossing the river, our emotions had bubbled up and overflowed. In spite of the danger, there was some shouting and shrill cries of happiness in celebration. The relief that we felt was monumental. In the path down our own yellow brick road, we had nearly reached Oz. Just think, I marveled, a short twenty-four hours from now and I'll be waking up and peeing in Canada. The silly thought brought forth a new bout of hysterical giggling and I shuddered with the excitement of it all.

The trip back to the caboose was a mere blur in my memory. Even though we had carried the heavy canoes along with us, my elation was such that I can't recall my feet ever touching the ground.

About halfway back, Vickie and Kaleb broke away from our main group. Hurrying ahead of us, they came back early to get a fire going and let Walter out to relieve himself. By the time the rest of our party made it to the caboose and concealed the canoes, that fire was roaring. We sat around and talked for a while as we basked in the lavish warmth of the heated space. I had almost forgotten how wonderful it felt to be warm. Robust laughter filled our discussions, as we all felt worry free for the first time in a very long time. It was already late, though, and the joyous chatter began to wane after a short time.

It had been an exhausting day for everyone. I felt as if I had ridden an emotional roller coaster and suffered from a severe case of negotiation whiplash. But everything had finally worked out and now all we needed to do was paddle our happy asses across the river to freedom.

We settled on a rotation for guard duty before the conversation totally petered out and I was lucky enough to be excluded. Kelli had spread out a few blankets in the corner by the caboose's door, so I made my way back there and laid my weary carcass down. Even though I felt totally drained, the sheer exhilaration of the good news and the upcoming river crossing fought sleep every step of the way. It seemed as if every time I was on the cusp of dozing off, the memory of our transaction with Rene would come rushing back to the forefront of my mind and the excitement would suspend the onset of sleep, yet a while longer. Somehow, though, I must have managed, because I awoke feeling very refreshed and raring to go.

My business finished, Walter and I went back inside the toasty warm train car. Today is going to be a long day, I thought to myself. With so many hours to wait and so little to do, the time is really going to drag.

Once the loot was weighed and split up to pay for our passage, there would be nothing else to do. There was no need to pack. Four people in one canoe and three, plus a hundred pound dog in the other, left little room for luggage. The overloaded vessels would ride dangerously low and if the water was choppy, we might have to continually bail out the boats in order to stay afloat.

Carlos said that the normal crossing rate was a pound of 24 karat gold or twelve carats worth of high quality gems, per person. Half of that went to Steevo for arranging the passage and the other half to Rene for allowing it. There was no doubt in my mind that we had way more plunder than we needed. The rest we would use to start our new lives once we made it across.

All of the rifles and shotguns would stay. We would take the pistols, which were easily concealable, and a small amount of extra ammunition. Everything else would be left behind.

Grabbing a pack of brown sugar and cinnamon pop tarts for breakfast, I laid them close to the fire to warm up. Sitting down next to Kaleb on one of the wooden bench seats, I readied myself for the long, agonizingly slow day that was to come.

142

At nine o'clock that evening we began our long awaited trek to the St. Clair River. Carrying empty canoes this time around, our trip went much faster. We made it back to the tangled briar patch in less than twenty minutes, flat. Taking little more than a perfunctory break next to the dense puncture palace, we eagerly moved on. Lost in deep thought and pleasant daydreams, we marched alongside the flowing water.

All of us kept looking eastward at the beautiful, bright lights that were burning across the river with unmasked desire. After such a long and arduous journey, who could blame us? We had all grown so damned tired of the mess. The only thing that we wanted was to have a normal life again. A job. A house. Hell, even bills, as odd as that may sound. Someplace that Kelli and I could finish raising the boys without them getting shot at and lay our heads down at night without worrying about getting blown up. A drab, dull, ordinary existence in a quiet, safe community would be a dream come true.

We made it to the spot where our crossing would begin at five minutes after ten. A jutting, little spit of land about a quarter mile north of the hotel, it stuck out into the flowing water like a two hundred foot long finger that curved slightly southward at the tip.

"Just over a mile wide, huh?" I asked Carlos, as Butch and I gently sat down the canoe that we had been toting. It sure looked a lot wider than that. In fact, from where we stood, the river looked impossibly wide.

"Yes, just a little more than a mile," he answered. "The waves are small tonight, too. Should be an easy crossing."

Although we all wanted nothing more than to cross the last obstacle in our path to freedom, now that the task was close at hand I could see evidence of apprehension butting heads with eagerness.

The countless number of ice chunks floating along in the current stood as silent testament to the water's lethality.

"And the water temperature is just slightly above freezing?" I asked, without removing my eyes from the ice choked proof.

"Yes," Carlos returned. "If not for the motion of the river, the water would freeze solid."

"And if we fall in the water or capsize?"

Carlos turned and looked directly into my eyes. Speaking with genuine sincerity, he softly said. "If we go in the water, we will die. Even if we fall in and get right back out, we will still freeze to death. Our bodies would simply not be able to produce enough heat to dry our clothes and keep us warm at the same time in these temperatures. We would end up floating down the river like those ice chunks, and being just as frozen."

Overhearing what Carlos had been saying, Kaleb turned as white as a ghost. His eyes grew alarmingly large and round and his mouth turned itself into a perfect circle.

"Oh, my God," he said. "Nobody told me that."

And he was right, nobody *had* told him that. In order to keep from scaring the boys half to death, the only thing that Kelli and I had told them was that the water was very cold and it would be dangerous if we fell in.

For some reason, unbeknownst to me, both boys were worriers. Even in the best of circumstances they would fret and sweat over the most trivial of matters. Something this dangerous, however, could cause both boys to become so overly concerned that they would be frozen into inaction. If that happened, things could go from bad to worse in a hurry.

"You're going to be fine, Kaleb," I told him. "We won't tip over." Shooting a sideways glance at Carlos, he caught my drift and slowly turned away.

Kaleb was looking at me with an expression that seemed to say, how do you know that? How can you be sure? And, I couldn't. But there *was* no other choice. It was either get in the canoes and paddle across the river or stay there and die. That was it. One or the other.

A fleeting image ran through my head of me tying Kaleb up and laying him in the bottom of one of the canoes. Shaking the vision away, I spoke with a harder edge to my voice.

"Do you want to stay here, Kaleb? Do you want to keep on freezing and starving and being miserable?" As I spoke he actually seemed to be weighing the options and trying to figure out which one was the safest.

"Of course he's going with us," Kelli said, as she stepped over and put her arm around his shoulders. "He's just scared, is all, aren't you honey?"

"He's always scared," Jacob said in his normal brotherly fashion.

"Jacob, enough," snapped Kelli.

"Well, he is," countered Jacob.

"Alright, alright," I said testily. "Let's get these canoes tied together so we can get out of here."

143

The canoes rode dangerously low in the icy water. There was clearly way too much weight in them, but we weren't about to turn back. This was our long awaited chance to get across the river and we were determined to make it work. If the waves decided to pick up, we would more than likely become swamped with the frigid water and end up sinking. All of us would end up floating down the waterway like frozen logs amongst the millions of ice chunks that were slowly moving southward to their eventual demise. Luckily though, as Carlos had said, the waves were small that evening and we paddled cautiously, trying not to jerk around too much.

The average time for one of these crossings was said to be about forty to forty five minutes, so we disembarked from the finger's end at 11:15, sharp. Butch, Vickie, Carlos and Walter rode in one canoe, and Kelli, Kaleb, Jacob and I rode in the other. Kelli wouldn't stand for being separated from the boys. If something bad *were* to happen, it wasn't like she would be able to offer much in the way of assistance, anyway, but that's the way she wanted it and I wasn't about to argue with her. Not that it would have done any good.

Walter looked ahead at us from the second canoe with such heartbreaking sadness in his big, brown eyes that I wanted to reel in the ten feet of rope tethering the two craft together and pet the dog's big, melon-sized head. Unfortunately, I had both hands wrapped around a paddle.

The river's current tried it's best to push us to the south and we kept paddling hard trying to go east. For a few terrifying minutes it looked like we weren't making any headway, at all, and were in danger of being swept downstream. The river was so massively wide that if you could have seen us from up above, we would have looked like a bunch of ants trying to march across the blacktopped expanse of a four lane highway. The opposite shore was so distant that the only way to check and see if we were making any progress at first, was to periodically look back at the receding shoreline.

Kaleb had one hand on each side of the canoe, clenching the top edges so hard that his hands turned a ghostly white. He sat in the middle of the lead canoe, unmoving, with his head facing straight forward. I couldn't tell if his eyes were open or not and, in the end, I guess it didn't really matter.

"Kaleb, where are your gloves?" I breathed between paddles.

He gave no answer. There was no sign of acknowledgement, whatsoever. His body held as rigid as a statue.

Jacob turned and looked, first at his brother and then back at me. His eyes drifted out to Kaleb's right hand and I saw understanding dawn on his face.

"Kaleb," he said, sounding slightly alarmed. "Where are your gloves?"

I could hear no response and there must have been none offered because Jacob, now sounding annoyed, tried louder.

"Kaleb," he yelled. "Where are your gloves?"

I noticed Kaleb's head begin to move as he raised his eyes to meet his brother's.

"Leave me alone," he shrilly shot back.

Jacob crinkled up his face and was about to continue his brotherly beration when our canoe hit what must have been a large chunk of submerged ice. A terrifying crunching sound accompanied the collision and all four of us were thrown forward in the boat as though we were no more substantial than a few rag dolls.

I landed against Kaleb with a thud, jarring both of his hands free of their icy grip. He, in turn, fell forward against Jacob, who no doubt had fallen forward against his mother. After all of our weight had shifted forward in a giant pile up, I ended up in perfect position to see our next disaster in the making.

Water began to pour in over the left side of the canoe like a little waterfall. Unable to move because of the awkward position I was in, I watched in horror as the frigid liquid started to fill the bottom of the boat. Kelli cried out in surprise as it began to pool around her legs.

144

"Back!" I shouted, feeling nearly hysterical. "Everyone move back to where you were."

Finally finding something to grab onto, I pushed myself away from Kaleb's back. Quickly reaching out with my right hand, I grabbed the collar of his jacket and started to haul him backwards. When my behind struck the end of the canoe, I stopped pulling and shot a quick glance toward the front.

The ice cold water had ceased to cascade into the canoe, but now there was a new problem. The added weight of the frigid water meant that the sides of the boat were only a few inches above the water line. Every fourth or fifth ripple of a wave would send another small splash of icy water in over the side.

Remembering the two empty soup cans that we had brought along with us for just such an emergency, I feverishly implored the boys.

"Bail! Bail!" I yelled. "Use the soup cans and start bailing! Fast!"

Both boys immediately snapped into action. Kaleb seemed to have suddenly come back to life. Whether it was because of the seriousness of the situation or the freezing water soaking through to his legs and feet, it didn't matter, as long as he bailed.

Starting to slowly re-gather some of my wits, I checked our position and noticed that we were almost to the middle of the river. The current was stronger there than it was out on the edges, and our inactivity was starting to make us flow along in time with the icy St. Clair. Kelli had regained her balance by then and was looking over her right shoulder at the boys as they scooped the frigid water out of the boat.

"We have to paddle, Kelli, we're starting to drift," I told her.

Shooting just the briefest glance in my direction, she nodded her head and then turned forward and dipped the blade of her paddle into the river. By that time, the unencumbered second canoe in our caravan had started to edge ahead of the first one and the line tethering the two watercraft began to pull taut. I barely had time to yell, "Hold on!" before the piece of nylon rope snapped tight and stretched itself into a straight, rigid line.

Being that the momentum of the second canoe was still heading almost dead east and ours was now pointing southeast, the resulting jerk on the rear of our canoe was almost as violent as the collision with the submerged iceberg had been. Our bodies were unapologetically tossed to the right side of the boat by the force of the resulting tug. Luckily, the small amount of forward progress that Kelli and I had begun to build saved us from capsizing.

My right elbow came down and hit the top edge of the canoe with a very solid sounding crack and I felt my forearm and hand instantly go numb. Biting back a pain filled scream, I forced my unfeeling hand onto the wooden paddle and began thrusting the blade deep into the water trying to power the craft forward.

Kelli and I paddled like we were possessed. Long after our canoe had regained it's lead and the connecting rope had been drawn firm, we still continued to paddle. We made it through the strongest portion of the river's current before exhaustion finally began to catch up with us. Our panicked thrusts started to become more intermittent and the plumes of our exhaled breath looked like mighty smokestacks. We were well on the Canadian side of the river, by then, and starting to make great progress toward the foreign shore.

The boys had been bailing tirelessly to rid the boat of the bone chilling water and, considering what they had started with, had done a miraculous job. They were down to laying the cans on their sides at the bottom of the canoe and catching the last of the water as the boat's rocking motion drove it back and forth.

I took in a large breath of relief. Everything finally seemed to be going in our favor and it was a wonderful feeling. I allowed myself a little smile. We were past the worst part of the crossing and all we had to do was hold on for a little while longer.

Then, in a fraction of a second, the world lit up in a brilliant, dazzling whiteness so bright that it blinded us and burned it's glaring image onto our unsuspecting retinas. Throwing up our hands to shield our wounded eyes did no good. The light so permeated our darkened surroundings that it seemed to bore right through my outstretched appendages.

Squinting fiercely, I turned my head away from the source of optic pain and franticly looked about. A large, bedazzling circle of light about twenty feet in diameter had engulfed both of the canoes. Carefully following the beam of light back to it's origin, I immediately felt ill. A watchman in one of the security towers had spotted us and illuminated the river like it was New Year's Eve in Times Square. We were under surveillance of the Canadian Coast Guard.

145

    Being bathed in the ultra-white glow of the Canadian Coast Guard's spotlight did a number on my emotions.
    At first I felt sad, knowing that there was no possible way that we could get out of such a mess. We were still a third of a mile, or so, from the Canadian shore and floating in ice cold water. It wasn't like we could swim for it. It made me feel like a failure because I couldn't get my family across the border like so many had before. I felt grossly inadequate as a leader and ashamed of myself for having gotten us nowhere.
    Then, in the blink of an eye, my thinking changed and I felt instant rage. We had obviously been double crossed by Rene, I reasoned. Why else would that glaring spotlight be shining on us?
    "You bastard," I mumbled under my breath. "You dirty bastard."
    Enraged by the thought of Rene being somewhere, perhaps even watching, with a laughing sneer on his insensitive face made me almost incapable of rational thought. I wanted to grab the sophisticated sounding snob around his cultured throat and squeeze the ever loving life right out of his double crossing

body.

I made a crazy vow to myself, right then and there, that if I ever got the chance, I would do just that. But, somewhere deep down inside I knew that it was not only irrational, it was highly unlikely. From seemingly far away my sanity screamed out that none of those useless emotions mattered at the moment. What mattered was fighting to the end and not giving up until there was no other option.

The only idea that I could come up with was to try and "out paddle" the spotlight. It sounded crazy as I rolled it over in my mind but I couldn't think of anything else. It was the only thing that we *could* try to do. There was nothing else. I thought about what Carlos had said about attaining our freedom by setting foot on Canadian soil and that made up my mind.

Turning around to the canoe behind us, I yelled, "Come on, you guys. Paddle! Let's get out of this river!" Not waiting for a response, I turned and quickly began digging my paddle deep into the chilly flow.

The canoe lunged forward with a start and the icy water began to gently glide along the outside of the sleek craft. Kelli joined me in paddling, again, and we went at it full bore. I could tell that she felt the same urgency I did. It was our only hope at freedom and we both knew it.

Turning around to check behind us, I saw that Butch and Vickie were also paddling at a frenzied pace. Perhaps they had also remembered what Carlos had said, or maybe he had reminded them.

The tandem of canoes began to pick up speed very fast. All four of us pushed as hard as we could with our adrenaline filled muscles, and it didn't take very long to get the sleek watercraft humming. The water actually appeared to be parting for us as our caravan bolted forward. The spotlight, though, following along with our ever quickening pace, never seemed to falter in it's suffocating presence.

Those hi-tech canoes must have been built for speed because they were effortlessly skimming through the rippling water. I had been in my share of the vessels over the years, but I had never experienced another capable of that kind of speed. The innate pleasure of piloting such a finely made craft temporarily took my mind from our plight. For a few blissful strokes I completely forgot everything else and concentrated on nothing but raising the paddle and reaching forward to plunge the blade home again.

It was then that I noticed the first change in the spotlight. The water around our canoes started to grow darker by the second. It reminded me of a black storm cloud moving across the sky and blocking out the sun's rays on a humid summer afternoon. We continued racing toward the Canadian shore with the spotlight as our escort, but the intensity of the beam steadily weakened as we progressed. I wondered why something like that would be happening? Why would the light be getting dimmer if we were indeed being surveilled by the Canadian forces?

The ferocity of the beam abated enough so that I could look up at it's source. No longer paddling, I watched in pleasant surprise as the formerly glaring light gradually faded to a dirty brown color, and then finally blinked out, altogether.

The sound of ice filled water making contact with the hull of our coasting canoe was the only sound that I could hear. We glided forward through the welcome darkness, now less than two hundred yards from the waiting shoreline.

Then I heard warning sirens begin to wail and saw searchlights spring to life all up and down the approaching coastline.

146

My spirits sank when the coastline lit up. Even though every other spotlight in the area seemed to be working just fine, the one that had shone upon us remained dark.

Brightly illuminated, the contour of the Canadian shoreline was exposed in a showy display of rugged beauty. From our location out on the icy river, the scene was absolutely breathtaking.

I noticed that I had already started to paddle again, and when Kelli noticed my renewed effort, she quickly joined in.

The siren's screaming howl grew more pronounced as we got closer to the water's edge. A sharp flash of light from the approaching shoreline caught my eye. Since it came from near the water instead of higher up on the steep riverbank, it stole my attention. To my amazement, I discovered that the flashing light was coming from inside the darkened end of the same large, concrete drainage tube that had been our destination.

The huge cylinder projected out into the rapidly flowing

water, less than a hundred yards ahead our advancing caravan. A small, bright light was moving back and forth inside the tunnel's darkness. It looked as though someone was within the tube briskly waving a flashlight back and forth.

I looked back up the sharply rising shoreline to the elevated plateau that resided above. Shimmering blobs of multi-colored lights reflected from the surfaces of the buildings and towers standing there as emergency response military vehicles rushed to our coordinates.

The third story windows of the hotel had provided the perfect opportunity to study the opposing coastline. I clearly recalled looking through binoculars at the uncurbed, two lane blacktop road that snaked along atop the undulating embankment. It wouldn't take long for the entire area to be swarming with armed soldiers, thanks to that road.

Our canoes were swiftly closing the distance to the shore, but I knew that we were incapable of matching the speed of the approaching vehicles. It would be a miracle if we arrived at the water's edge before the repelling forces did.

As we closed in on the end of the massive drainage tube, I could see a large, iron grid work sealing off the opening. Another light clicked on inside the darkened cylinder. This one was positioned further back from the opening than the first, and proved to be much more revealing.

Two elongated, shadowy silhouettes were outlined against the artificial brightness. They appeared to be doing something to the massive, checkerboard patterned gate that closed off the end of the tube.

I began to hear the high pitched scream of sirens from the approaching vehicles mix in with the now familiar, ear splitting ring of the blaring air raid sirens. Despite the vigorous exertion of paddling a canoe, chills started to run through my body from having wet legs and feet. Both boys sat with their arms tightly wrapped around themselves in the middle of the canoe, shivering excessively. Regardless of whatever else happened, we needed to get out of the water and dry off or else we were in serious trouble. The only question was, could we make it to the shore before the approaching troops did?

Then, as if on cue, a remarkable thing happened. The huge, iron gate at the end of the drainage tube swung outward and I could hear a loud voice beckon. The complete opposite of Rene's smooth, cultured tone, this voice was rough and very low in pitch. Sounding almost as desperate as we felt, the frantic shouts easily crossed the distance.

"Hurry up!" It feverishly implored. "There isn't much time! The soldiers will be here soon!"

It only took a little glance to the top of the hill directly above us to know that the warning was accurate. The area above the steeply rising riverbank was alight with the glow of approaching vehicles. Before long, troops would swarm down the slope like an avalanche of rushing snow.

The man with the deep voice was standing at the end of the concrete tube with one hand gripping the open gate and the other frantically motioning for us to get a move on.

"Hurry up," he warned, "or I'll close the gate."

Still twenty yards away from the large, circular opening, the screaming military vehicles began to arrive on the scene. Trying to maintain a proper balance between paddling and steering, I carefully lined the canoe up with the waiting cavity. The opening almost looked like a small subterranean cave as we drew close. Metal walkways, elevated just above water level, lined both sides of the tunnel. The man with the deep voice stood on the left hand side of the tube holding the large access grid open against the rushing current.

"Don't slow down," he yelled. "There's plenty of room."

Heeding his advice, we powered our way forward and raced into the dark recesses of Canada's underground drainage system. The heavy gate swung shut behind us with a huge, clanging boom. The resulting echo continued down the length of the concrete tube until it disappeared far into the unlit depths.

147

    Bright lights bore into our unsuspecting eyes, rendering us virtually blind. Walter let out a quick, startled bark in surprise and then fell silent, once again. New voices, hidden behind the punishingly bright lights, ordered us to stop. A man's arm cut through the suffocating whiteness and took the paddle from my hands.
    "Don't move," the voice that belonged to the arm said.
    "A dog?" another voice asked incredulously. "A freaking dog?"
    Our canoe was pulled tight against the left walkway with a quick tug.
    "Put your hands up," a loud voice commanded. "Put 'em up and keep 'em up."
    A few seconds later most of the blinding flashlights were turned off and I could see that we were flanked on both sides by armed soldiers.
    I closed my eyes and hung my head when I saw the unwelcome sight. It seemed like we couldn't catch a break. I cursed myself soundly for steering us into the drainage tube. We could have reached the shore, I told myself. We could have

reached the shore and all of us would have had time to set foot upon the rocky coast.

"Should we shoot the dog?" One of the servicemen on the other side of the tunnel asked.

In unison, all four members of our canoe emphatically shouted, "NO!" Our loud response echoed back and forth inside the concrete chamber for a second and then rolled away like the sound of thunder across an open field.

I thought about the pistol tucked in the waistband of my pants, but knew that if I were to reach down we would all die.

Before the situation had a chance to escalate any further, a familiar voice spoke.

"Everybody relax," Rene said in his smooth, scholarly speaking voice. He took a step forward on the left hand walkway and jerked his thumb toward the darkness behind him. "Get them around the corner and out of sight. The patrol boats will be here any minute."

Strong arms grabbed the sides of our canoe and propelled it forward. Approximately fifteen feet further on, our boat was quickly turned to the left and hauled into the safety of a large connecting tube. We sat motionless, our hands still up in the air while being jockeyed about.

Speaking in his normal, calm and collected manner, Rene quickly got down to business. "I trust you have the required fare, my friends. We don't have a lot of time."

"We have it," I replied. "But it's kind of hard to reach into a pocket with our hands in the air."

Smiling slightly, Rene conceded the point. "That is very true, my American friend, but it can also prevent a tragic accident from happening."

Pointing at Walter, Rene said, "That is a nice German Shepherd. Full-blooded, no doubt?"

"Yes," I replied. "That's our dog."

Rolling his eyes up to the top of the concrete tunnel, Rene reminisced. "When I was a boy, my family had a dog like that. His name was Star. He was a very good dog. We used to have such good times together." With a dismissive shake of the head, he lowered his harsh gaze to meet us. "Nevertheless," he gravely said, "I cannot allow you to take the animal through."

Momentarily stunned to silence, I sat mutely staring at

the man in who's hands our fate rested.

Jacob didn't like that response, at all. He had always considered Walter to be his dog. The two had been like Batman and Robin since Walter had first come home as a furry little pup.

"Why not?" the boy wanted to know.

Although I could not see his face, I was sure that Jacob was giving Rene the same sad, "Oh, come on," look that Kelli and I were so used to. Usually very persuasive when he tried, this time his boyish charm proved ineffective against the highly seasoned criminal.

"So sorry, young man," Rene replied evenly. "This is a business. We can't allow anyone free passage, or," he said, gesturing towards Walter, "in the case of this animal, anything."

I heard myself speak up and was surprised at the volume of my voice and the way that it echoed back from the curved concrete surfaces.

"We'll pay," I said. "We have a little extra gold and we'll pay for him."

Rene's head snapped back to me. His eyes studied my face intently for a couple of seconds and then he curled the ends of his mouth upward into a devilishly sly smile.

"You have extra gold?" A devious, disheartening laugh escaped his throat. In the limited light of the underground drainage tile, Rene looked for all the world like the perfect fit for a Hollywood movie about the devil. The diffused light form the flashlights highlighted his forehead and cheeks, and as he laughed his evil laugh, he looked and sounded absolutely demonic.

A shiver ran down my spine. I knew that I was wet and very cold, but I thought the shiver wasn't entirely due to those things. This man grinning in front of us was nothing like the mental image I had formed of the smooth talking smuggler. I had expected a suave, debonair business man in an expensive three piece suit. Instead, he ended up being a balding, middle aged man who was overweight and as ugly as sin.

"We brought a little extra so that we could make a fresh start," I said, sounding far more forceful than I had intended.

The smile on Rene's face vanished. I saw his darkly shadowed eyes momentarily blaze in fury.

"If you wish to have any chance at a fresh start, my

insolent American friend, perhaps you should mind your manners." All of the silkiness was gone from his voice and his jaw had firmly set.

Speaking softly and hoping to sound humble, I attempted to diffuse the situation. "Look, Rene," I said. "All I want to do is get my family out of here safely. We made a deal with you, in fact a very generous deal. Plus, we'll pay you for the dog."

Looking momentarily placated, Rene's features softened a bit. He stood on the thin walkway of the tunnel without moving and staring off into space. After a few tense moments, he drew in a deep breath and placed his hands upon his hips.

"This must be your lucky day," he said, as he looked back and forth at all of us obediently sitting in the floating canoes.

We calmly waited for Rene to continue while our arms grew heavy and numb. When he started to speak again, it was with the smooth, confident voice that we had heard on the shortwave radio.

"One at a time, beginning at the rear, you will stand up and be searched. Do not be alarmed, it is in the best interest of us all. We do not wish to be shot in the back and you do not want to try. If that happens, you will all die."

Displaying the same devilish looking grin that he had worn a few minutes earlier, Rene began directing traffic. Pointing at Butch, he told him, "We'll start with you. Stand up slowly and keep your hands in the air."

One by one, we were searched and relieved of all of our possessions. They took away our pistols and found every last piece of our stashed gold and jewelry and every neatly bundled stack of cash. The thieves even felt around Walter's collar looking for hidden jewels. I guess I shouldn't have expected anything less. Those guys had obviously been through the drill numerous times and they were very good at what they did.

Feeling picked as clean as a Thanksgiving Day turkey, we were quickly herded down a series of narrow walkways, single file. Rushed three blocks further inland to a large, circular shaft that ascended to the surface, we were ordered to climb the tiny steel ladder attached to it's side. I took off my jacket and tied the end of it's arms in a knot around Walter's chest and through a combination of Butch pushing up on the dog's rear end and me lifting, we managed to get the massive beast up to the surface.

Rene must have been in contact with his men by walkie talkie because by the time that we had climbed halfway up the hand numbing, frozen, steel ladder, the manhole cover noisily slid to the side and revealed a clear, starlit winter sky. As each of us emerged out of the hole, the waiting accomplice would point toward the rear of the closest building and tell us to run.

Carlos was the last of us to make it into the relative safety of the deep shadows. His leg was healing well, but it would still be quite a while before he could walk without a limp.

Huddled in the darkness behind a two story, corner building, we watched as the man who had replaced the heavy manhole cover ran away in the opposite direction. He jumped into a car that was waiting halfway down the block and quickly sped away out of sight. Left to ourselves in the late night chill, we cautiously surveyed our surroundings from the dark recesses of the building's shadow.

After spending a few tense minutes waiting to be discovered and arrested, we began to relax and a feeling of true elation overtook us. Large smiles and rib crushing hugs made the rounds as we quietly celebrated our freedom.

Butch spotted a park nearby with thick evergreen shrubbery where we could hide out until daybreak. Being extremely careful, our weary group slowly worked it's way over to the cover of the dense bushes.

It was freezing cold and sunrise wasn't for about another five or six hours. We had lost all of our treasure and all of our cash. The only possessions that we had in the whole world were the clothes on our backs, but yet, we were all smiling. We had each other and we were all alive, and after what we had been through, that was more than enough for me.

Afterword

The first couple of weeks were definitely the hardest. Of course, the Canadian authorities ended up catching us. I guess we kind of stood out from the crowd with our dirty clothes and faces. They separated us from each other and did a lot of yelling and cursing, it actually turned out to be quite a traumatic experience. The interrogators threatened to jail us as spies and then send us back across the river. And why not? If that would have been their desire, we were certainly in no position to stop them.

We readily gave up all that we knew about Rene and his smuggling operation. After all, there was no love lost between our group and the thieving pirate, and besides, it wasn't like he would be getting any more customers, anyway.

After much aggravation and harassment, the authorities finally set us free. At first they kept us on a very short leash, it seemed like we were always under surveillance. Slowly, though, as we got jobs and acclimated ourselves into the native population, the intrusions into our daily life became fewer and fewer.

Kelli was the first to gain employment. She began waitressing at a diner close by and we lived solely on her tips for the first two weeks. We enrolled the boys in public school and, over time, all of us found work. The seven of us had to share the same fleabag hotel room for the first three weeks. As we gained our footing, though, we slowly spread out. First to two, and finally, to three separate rooms.

The first couple of times that we tried to rent a house, we were turned down flat. There was a lot of uncertainty about the wave of American refugees at that time, some of it still lingers to this day.

Our fortunes changed for the better late that first summer. Carlos had been hired by one of the largest plumbing companies in the area, and one day he went on a very lucky service call.

An old house, about four miles outside of town, had a leaking pipe in the basement and Carlos was dispatched to repair it. Upon arriving at the house, he was greeted by a very kind, unassuming, middle-aged woman, who lived only a short distance down the road. Her parents had been the owners of the old house and they were both now deceased.

During the course of repairing the old plumbing, Carlos learned of the house being unoccupied and inquired about the possibility of renting the property.

At first, the landlady was hesitant, but by the time that the old plumbing had been replaced, the two had developed an unlikely bond and she gave in.

Although there were only three bedrooms in the house, to us it felt as big as a castle after living in those tiny hotel rooms.

Carlos still lives in that house. He is a highly respected employee of the plumbing company and he and his wife are now expecting their first child.

Butch and Vickie have a nice little house on the edge of town. An experienced truck driver, Butch got a job delivering building materials for a local lumber supply yard. He says he loves it because, unlike his old job as a long haul driver, he has regular working hours and gets to sleep in his own bed every night. Vickie is the manager of a major retail store located out by the mall. She puts in a lot of hours and shoulders a ton of responsibility, but still somehow always finds time for friends.

We all visit each other often and have wonderful cookouts during the summer months.

Our family moved into an old farmhouse out in the picturesque Canadian countryside.

I work for a local construction company building houses and thoroughly enjoy every minute of it. Kelli eventually got a job as a librarian at the county library. It had always been somewhat of a dream for her to work in a library. I have never seen her so content in her work.

Kaleb finished up high school here in Canada and is now employed at a local manufacturing facility. He is doing very well for himself and enjoys spending a lot of time with his friends and playing video games.

Jacob is now a senior in high school. He can't wait to graduate and get a full time job. He seems to be doing so much better in school here than he did back in the States. Kelli and I are both very proud of him and we're sure that whatever Jacob decides to do, he'll be successful at it.

Walter loves living out in the country. He's a little older now and has a touch of gray in his muzzle. Since our harrowing ordeal he's grown a little more protective but, other than that, he's still the same great dog he always was.

We rarely discuss what happened anymore. We're content to concentrate on the future, though sometimes the memories make it difficult. At first, I wasn't certain whether or not to record what happened to us. If not for the constant encouragement from Kelli, I don't think that I would have. I'm not even certain why I felt so driven to write it all down. Maybe I thought that it would help me to make sense of the meaningless destruction and unspeakable carnage that we witnessed. Or, maybe I just wanted to bear witness to how selfish and short sighted the human race can be. Whatever the reason, I feel a lot better now that it's been purged from my system.

If someone else should ever happen to take the time to read this account, take it as a testament to our family and friends. We stuck together, no matter what the odds, and overcame every obstacle that was placed in front of us. The indomitable human spirit residing within each of us proved to be exceedingly strong. Perhaps there is a glimmer of hope for our self-destructive culture, after all. At least, I would like to think so. Then again, maybe I'm just a dreamer and being unrealistic. I guess none of us really know for sure. Only time will tell.

FIN

The list of those that I would like to thank is long, so if you find that kind of thing boring don't read the rest of this.

For those of you that are still reading, I would like to thank, first and foremost, Kelli. Without her undying support and wonderful typing and editing skills, this book may *never* have been finished. I would like to thank Kaleb and Jacob for their inspiration and love, my life would never have been as rich without them. I would like to thank my mother for being such a great example and instilling the same tireless work ethic in her children that she possesses. I would like to thank Uncle Butch and Aunt Vickie. I worked on this story for over two years and neither one knew they were involved until I was finished. What a surprise, huh? Vickie contributed to the editing and troubleshooting process on the book and for that I am eternally grateful. I would like to thank Professor Amy Withrow for being so generous with her valuable time and expert guidance. It was a great stroke of luck on my part to bump into a Literary Professor of such caliber in the course of everyday activity. And, last but not least, I would like to thank my family and friends because they are the ones who have shaped my life and made it as interesting and diverse as it is.

Thank you to anyone who took the time to read my story. You have no idea how much that means to me.

Archie Borders
September 16, 2013